DEATH

IN THE

AIR

DEATH

IN THE

AIR

A Novel

Ram Murali

HARPER

An Imprint of HarperCollinsPublishers

HarperCollins books may be purchased for educational, business, or sales promotional use. For information, please email the Special Markets Department at SPsales@harpercollins.com.

This Orient
Words and Music by James Andrew Smith, Edwin Thomas Congreave, Yannis Barnabus Emanuel Philippakis, Walter Gervers and Jack William Bevan.
© 2010 Transgressive Publishing LTD (PRS) (NS)
All rights administered by WC Music Corp.
All Rights Reserved.
Used by Permission of Alfred Music.

Punkrocker
Words and Music by Klas Frans Ahlund, Joakim Frans Ahlund, Patrik Knut Arve and James Newell Osterberg Jr.
Copyright © 2000 Madhouse Music AB and BMG Bumblebee
All Rights for Madhouse Music AB Administered by Universal Music - MGB Songs.
All Rights for BMG Bumblebee Administered by BMG Rights Management (US) LLC.
All Rights Reserved. Used by Permission.
Reprinted by Permission of Hal Leonard LLC.

FIRST US EDITION

Designed by Kyle O'Brien

Library of Congress Cataloging-in-Publication Data has been applied for.

ISBN 978-0-06-331930-1

24 25 26 27 28 LBC 5 4 3 2 1

For Vedavalli Krishna Iyengar (1926–2020)

For Buenaventura Durruti (1896–1936)

For Hector Hugh Munro (1870–1916)

For Christopher Coker (1953–2023)

For Nilanjan Banerjee (1978–2004)

For Maureen Buletti (1978–2008)

For Phatiwe Cohen (1977–2005)

For Thomas Mann (1875–1955)

For Jan Palach (1948–1969)

For Rollo (c. 860–c. 930)

For the United Kingdom

For the United States

For Dartmouth

For France

For India

Reginald closed his eyes with the elaborate weariness of one who has rather nice eyelashes and thinks it useless to conceal the fact.

"One of these days," he said, "I shall write a really great drama. No one will understand the drift of it, but every one will go back to their homes with a vague feeling of dissatisfaction with their surroundings. Then they will put up new wall-papers and forget."

Saki
Reginald's Drama

"Because the murderer is always the most interesting character in the book. So you've got to make me the murderer, Agatha—do you understand?"

"I understand that you *want* to be the murderer," I said, choosing my words carefully. In the end, in a moment of weakness, I promised that he *should* be the murderer.

Agatha Christie
An Autobiography

Table of Contents

BERMUDA

R o Krishna crouched on a white wooden dock and peered into the rapidly darkening Harrington Sound. Then he straightened his back and looked up at the fading sky. He didn't have much time. He slipped noiselessly into the water. He'd dive another day.

The water was the same temperature as the air, like in a sensory deprivation tank. He backstroked toward a large raft anchored a short distance away. Clambering on, he flopped onto his back and crossed one leg over the other at the knee. He placed his hands behind his head and lay on his back with his eyes open, studiously turning his mind blank. Ro had once read that soldiers managed to get through war by turning their minds blank. He was now uncommonly good at this, as he had been at war for some time now.

He lingered on the raft, looking at the first stars of the evening, deliberately cutting it close.

Finally, he lowered himself into the now-inky water and swam back to the dock. Pulling on his "Surf Leucadia" T-shirt, he padded barefoot up the hill. As the large Colonial-style house came into view, he saw that preparations for the party had advanced significantly while he was in the water. At least two bars were now set up on the lawn. A peculiarly international selection of food trucks had formed a queasy circle. Several people were struggling to set up a bouncy castle that was clearly too large for the space it was meant to occupy.

Ro continued up the path and entered the house via an inconspicuous side door. Walking into his room, he picked up the watch on the bedside table and saw he still had thirty minutes to get ready. He would be all right.

A shower first. He took off his T-shirt and his navy blue swim trunks. As he walked toward the bathroom, his eyes fell upon his phone, lying on the bed. He picked it up to give it a cursory glance, and then he froze. There were an unusual number of notifications, in an unusual number of ways: texts, emails, several missed calls. Other messaging apps. He decided to begin with his emails and scrolled down to the earliest unread message.

And then time stopped. Ro stared into space, his eyes vacant, his mouth hanging open. His phone dangled from his hand.

* * *

Post-shower, still toweling his hair, Ro stood in front of the closet and evaluated his options. A 40th birthday party in Bermuda in the shoulder season was a minefield in terms of attire and, whether innocently or mischievously, Rollo had not given a dress code. Every event had a theme, Ro mused. Sometimes overt, sometimes covert. He would have to figure out tonight's theme by himself.

Fortunately, he now had all the time in the world.

The shirt he eventually chose was plain white cotton except for its collar, onto which rocket ships, rainbows, and snakes were embroidered whimsically, ostensibly justifying the shirt's equally whimsical price. But the lower half of his body remained a problem. None of his jeans or trousers seemed right. Then his eyes fell upon a pair of sky-blue Bermuda shorts tossed over a chair.

When in Rome.

Ro added a grey-blue woven leather belt and grass-green suede moccasins. Buckling on his father's old gold-and-steel Cartier Panthère watch, Ro looked in the mirror and nodded. With regards to the theme, he was fairly sure he'd nailed it.

Leaving the room, he turned to the left, walked two feet, then knocked on the next door.

"Come in," a familiar voice said.

Connie was Ro's best friend from college. She sat at a table looking into a mirror, applying makeup, her hair up in a loose chignon. She wore an emerald green dress made of pleated silk faille. The room was chaotic. Connie's shoes were splayed gorily all over the floor of the closet. "Will you grab the gold ones?" Connie asked, applying mascara. "No, not those. The strappy ones." Ro silently handed them over.

She placed them on the floor. Once she was done with her eyes, Connie stood up, turning her back to him. She picked up a bottle of perfume, spritzed some—Samsara, by Guerlain, although Ro didn't know that—into the empty air in front of her, and walked into the cloud. Then she sat down on the bed and began to fasten her shoes.

"Can you hand that over?" she said, pointing to a fabric pouch Ro had bought for her in Bhutan. Opening it, she pulled out what seemed to be yards of gold and began to arrange them around her neck. The necklace was an improbably long Van Cleef & Arpels Alhambra chain made of gold, mother-of-pearl, malachite, and onyx. Connie saw Ro's admiring look in the mirror. "My mother's. It's from the 70s. Can you help?" Ro fastened it for her.

"Oh, I almost forgot." Connie unpinned the chignon, shook out her long, dark, lustrous hair, and stood up. She took a shopping bag out of the closet. "Rollo's present. Want to see?" Carefully untying the brown ribbon, she opened the orange box to reveal a large green travel wallet. "Dartmouth green," she said, satisfied.

Ro just smiled.

"Let's go," Connie said, picking up her bag. She caught Ro's eye in the mirror and sighed. "Ugh. You have the best hair."

Ro smiled again, shrugging.

It was true.

He did have great hair.

* * *

Connie and Ro walked onto the lawn through the side door. It had gotten dark, more or less.

"Joss isn't coming, right?"

Ro shook his head.

"He works too much. Although Bermuda's a massive schlep from LA, I'll give him that. Oh, there's Masha." She waved at a slender girl wearing a fuchsia dress, her pale blond hair scraped back into a ballerina bun.

Masha waved back frantically. "I need you guys!" she yelled.

They walked over to her. The bouncy castle waved uncertainly against the night sky. Masha gazed up at it. "I messed up. It's way too big. Where do you think we should put it?"

"Ooh, I'm not sure." Connie took off her shoes and started running around the lawn. "Oh, I see. You don't want to block the view. Wait." She ran another few feet and paused. "Maybe here?" Ro made a slashing motion with his hand. "Diagonally?" Connie added, grinning at him.

Masha came over and jumped, clapping her hands. "I think that might work!" The workers came over and huddled with her for a moment, then began to drag the castle into place. Ro grinned as he watched Masha squeal and clap her hands again, her eyes sparkling. "It does!"

She turned to Connie. "I think we deserve a Dark and Stormy." They began moving toward the bar, chatting with each other animatedly. Ro followed them, smiling to himself. He hadn't yet spoken the first word of his postwar life. He wondered how much longer he could go.

* * *

As it happens, he could go quite a long time. And it was delightful.

Ro bobbed around, nodded, smiled and waved, smiled and shook hands, gave and received kisses on both cheeks, shook hands without smiling, gave meaningful looks, shook his head, pointed, raised his eyebrows, sipped, chewed, made noises of appreciation, made grunts of disapprobation, sauntered, shrugged, hugged, gave a thumbs up, and gave two high fives. He was pretty sure nobody had clocked what he was up to.

He stood discreetly at the back of the lawn near one of the bars while Rollo, who was wearing a smoking jacket, a bow tie, and a kilt, gave a speech thanking his guests and welcoming them to Bermuda.

To much applause and laughter, Rollo announced the start of a limbo competition. Ro turned and walked toward the lawn's edge. He stopped in front of the ha-ha and looked down at the sound. The now-black water lapped gently at itself.

"Ahem."

He turned and saw someone he didn't think he knew, a somewhat puzzled look on her face. She was maybe a few years younger, early thirties or late twenties. Her short dress was covered in gold sequins. Her blondish hair was in a ponytail. She wore large gold hoop earrings. A Swatch was on her left wrist. The only makeup Ro could see was a carelessly applied smudge of red-orange lipstick.

"Hello," she said shyly.

Ro was charmed. He smiled and tilted his head toward her.

The woman smiled back at him, hesitant, visibly debating whether to say something.

Finally, she did. "Are you not speaking on purpose?"

Ro laughed, delighted. "Thank you. I was wondering when someone would notice."

"Oh!" She sighed, relieved. "We noticed a while ago." She waved toward a smiling man a few steps behind her, perhaps around Ro's age, sandy-haired, stocky. "But we were having so much fun watching."

"I'm glad I could be of service," Ro said, mock-bowing.

The woman hesitated again, looking down and chewing her lip. "But it wasn't just that," she said. "Your aura is amazing right now. It's remarkable." She paused. "Apologies, I don't mean to be a hippie. But it's energy. Something new."

"Don't worry," Ro said. "You know, it's weird, but you're right. My life did actually change today." He gave her a warm smile. "I'm Ro, by the way."

He leaned in to kiss her on both cheeks.

"Bronya. What's Ro short for?"

"Rohan. I literally never use it, though," Ro replied. "Is Bronya short for Bronisława?"

"Yes!" she squealed, jumping up and down. "I'm impressed. What does Rohan mean?"

"Ascending," Ro responded, a little surprised. He usually asked that question first. "What does Bronisława mean?"

Bronya thought for a moment, then laughed. "I don't know, actually!" She turned to the man behind her. "This is my boyfriend, Alex."

The man approached them with a friendly grin. "Hello, Ascending. I'm Alex. Short for Alexander, which means 'defender of men.' And this is Novi," he added, indicating the Pomeranian in the grey Goyard tote bag he carried. Alex was more or less the same height as Ro, a shade or two under six feet, but looked more solid, with broad shoulders. His light blue button-down shirt was tucked into pale yellow trousers. The sleeves of his shirt were rolled up, revealing tanned forearms.

"Hi, Alex. And hi, Novi." Ro leaned in and gently scratched Novi on the top of her head. "Novi, that's a cute name."

"It's short for Novichok," Bronya said. "So, how did your life change today?" she continued, looking at Ro. "If you don't mind my asking, of course."

Ro paused. Words were fluttering on his lips, but he didn't quite know what to say.

"I'm sorry," Bronya said, retreating a little. "I don't mean to intrude."

"No." Ro shook his head. "Please, don't worry. Really. It's just that I haven't talked about what happened yet." Except to lawyers, he added to himself. Lots and lots and lots of lawyers.

"You haven't talked about it? Not even to your girlfriend?" Bronya saw Ro's puzzlement. "The girl in the green dress."

"Oh, Connie. No. Connie's my best friend, by the way," Ro added. "More my twin sister than anything else."

"And you haven't even told her?" Alex asked, interested.

Ro shook his head.

A burst of applause came from farther down the lawn. "Are you planning to do the limbo?" Alex asked.

"No," Ro said. "I'm Indian. It wouldn't be fair to the others."

Alex laughed. "Let's go for a swim. Everyone will be down there soon anyway." He looked at Ro. "You're staying in the house, yes? Why don't you go change? Meet us at the dock."

How did he know that, Ro wondered. "Sure."

* * *

It was a full moon, or almost one, anyway.

Alex dived effortlessly into the water. "The water's so warm," he said as he surfaced. He swam toward Bronya, who was already on the raft.

Ro peeled off his T-shirt. "I love your swimsuit," Bronya cooed at him. "Is that Dsquared2?"

"No," Ro laughed. "H&M." He thought about diving, then had another idea. Walking a few steps back, he turned around and ran off the dock, jumping into the air and rolling into a ball. "Cannonball!" he heard Bronya shriek delightedly as he smashed into the water.

"What's Leucadia?" Alex asked as Ro climbed onto the raft.

"Huh?" Ro said, settling onto his back.

"Your T-shirt."

"Oh. It's a town near San Diego. Just up the coast from where I'm from."

"Oh, so it's a place?"

"Yes. Leucadia means 'place of refuge.'" Ro paused, suspicious. "What did you think it was?"

"I don't know. It's the sort of word that could be anything." Alex giggled a little. "An illness. A state of mind."

"Are you high?" Ro asked.

"No," Alex said.

"Oh." Ro settled back down. "Neither am I."

They lay there for a while, listening to the sounds from the party. Music and faint laughter.

"You're from San Diego?" Bronya asked.

"Sure am. I live in London now though. What about you guys?"

"I'm from Moravia," Bronya said.

"And I'm from Prague," Alex added.

"Oh." That was a surprise.

He hesitated.

"Oh," Ro repeated, this time meaningfully. "That's weird."

He flipped onto his stomach, resting his chin on his hands.

"Don't tell me it's about Prague," Alex said, raising himself slightly. "Your life-changing news, that is."

"It's about Prague."

Alex sat up. He looked at Ro expectantly, his arms around his knees.

Bronya sat up too.

"I don't know where to start. I wasn't joking. I haven't told anyone about this. About any of it, really."

The three of them sat in silence for a moment. Ro closed his eyes.

"You know, it feels like you need to release it." Alex's tone was unexpectedly gentle. "But it's entirely up to you. If you want to talk about it, just say whatever pops into your mind. The story will come together somehow."

Ro reflected on that.

"Also, tell me about the tattoos on your back," Bronya added. "They're sick."

"Oh," Ro said, surprised. "I always forget about them because I never actually see them myself."

"What are they?" Alex asked, looking at Ro's back.

"They're Thai. They were all done at different monasteries in Thailand. Over the span of about ten years, I'd say. By monks with bamboo needles."

"What do they mean?" Bronya asked.

"They're supposed to give you magical protection."

Alex smiled. "And did they work?"

Ro thought about it. "You know what? I think they did, actually." He flopped onto his back and looked at the sky. "I'm going to try to talk about this," he said to the stars. "Let's start with this. It looks like I'm leaving the workforce."

"Wow!" Bronya said. "Congratulations! How does it feel?"

Ro thought about it. How did it feel? "Like a surprise remission from cancer," he decided.

They all processed that for a minute.

"You know," Alex began cautiously, "maybe we should just ask you questions. And you can decide if you want to answer."

Ro slowly nodded. "OK."

"But if you don't answer the question, you have to tell us a joke," Bronya added.

"Truth or joke." Ro laughed. "All right. It's a deal."

"Did you get a payout?" Alex asked.

"I will."

"Why?" Bronya asked.

"Bad manager."

"Was it because of discrimination?" she asked delicately.

"Joke." Ro thought for a moment. "What's Helen Keller's favorite color?"

"What?" Bronya asked.

"Corduroy."

Everyone was silent.

"Is he or she white? How old?" Alex asked.

"A couple years older than me. She. Yes." Ro considered for a moment. "White trash," he clarified.

"Can you describe her in five words or fewer?" Bronya asked.

"A latrine with a face," Ro responded, counting on his fingers.

"Did she get fired?" Alex asked.

"I'm not sure," Ro said, considering it for the first time. "Probably not, given that they're paying me off."

Bronya slipped back into the water. "Not to be indiscreet, but will you ever have to work again?"

"Um," Ro said. "Not for a while. Maybe never, if I move to Honduras."

"Ugh," Bronya said, pouting. "I'm so jelly. I wish someone would try to discriminate against me."

Alex laughed. "I think you'd need to get a job first." He turned back to Ro. "So what's the but? I feel like there's a but here."

"There's a but."

They were silent for a moment.

Ro slipped back into the water, then dived deep, feeling the increasing pressure all over his body. He eventually resurfaced, floating on his back.

"I was in charge of a huge project," Ro continued, still looking at the stars. "A cultural center. Financed by a tech company."

There was a long pause. Alex and Bronya waited for him to proceed.

"I was responsible for every detail. Every last one. From beginning to end. And now, all of a sudden, I've been offered this payout." Ro thought about how to formulate his next words. "And I'm just realizing it. If I take it, it'll be like I never existed. And awful people will get the credit for everything I did."

"Such as the latrine," Alex said quietly.

"Yes," Ro said. "And she did nothing, by the way. The person who hired me quit, then the project got reassigned to her. She's in corporate marketing."

"I thought this was a cultural center," Bronya said.

"The money came out of the marketing budget. Because it's feel-good. She's a bean counter."

"What did she do to you?" Alex asked quietly.

Ro felt the rage boiling inside him. Stay calm, he told himself.

"You know, I thought everything was going well. She left me alone. Turns out she was sabotaging me internally the whole time. Spreading all kinds of lies about me to her bosses."

He sighed.

"So that she could take all the credit for my work. I realize that now."

"Wait," Bronya said. "So it's about credit? Not about race?"

"Of course it's about race," Ro replied. "She could never have done it if I were white."

"Got it," Bronya said. "My bad."

Alex slipped into the water as well. Ro could feel him choosing his next words with care. "You said this was about Prague. Are you talking about the Radetzky Center?"

"Yes," Ro replied, as light as possible.

"It's opening soon," Alex said.

"Yep. Right before Christmas. It's funny," he continued, floating on his back. "When I think about Prague, I always think about one person. Jan Palach."

The air went still.

"Who's that?" Bronya asked.

"Bronya!" Alex sounded reproachful. "You should know this."

"He was a student in Prague," Ro continued, serene. "Political economy. This all happened right around the Soviet invasion. And just after. Early 1969. January, I think." He looked up at the sky. "Anyway, Jan Palach sacrificed himself as an act of protest."

"How do you mean?" Bronya asked.

Suddenly, Ro found himself unable to speak. He continued to float in the dark.

"He lit himself on fire," Alex finally said.

"He was only twenty," Ro said, sending Jan Palach a silent prayer. Then, closing his eyes, he let himself sink, gradually allowing the cool water to envelop his body.

"My God," Bronya said. "I can't imagine a more horrible way to die."

"I agree," Ro said, coming back to the surface. "Almost nobody would deserve that. Anyway." He climbed back onto the raft.

Alex and Bronya looked at each other, then Bronya nodded.

Alex turned to Ro. "Do you want to do something about all this?"

"I don't know what you mean by that. Like what?"

"Well, you could sabotage the building," Alex replied, his tone light. "Have it flood right before the opening. Something like that, maybe. Easy as pie."

"No." Ro shook his head. "No, that feels wrong. It isn't the building's fault. I love the building."

"Well then, whose fault is it?" Bronya asked.

Ro considered the question. "There were systemic problems, of course, but in the end, it really was the fault of one awful person."

Bronya climbed onto the raft, flopping down next to Ro. "So why don't you target that person?"

"There are plenty of options," Alex agreed. "Maybe revenge would make you feel better."

"No." Ro thought about it. "No," he repeated, a little reluctant. "Revenge is basically the worst thing you can do for your karma."

"But what if it's justice?" Bronya asked. "Justice is good for your karma, isn't it?"

"Interesting," Ro said, thoughtful. "I'll chew on that." He listened to the sounds coming from the party. "Let's go back."

The three of them began to swim toward the dock.

"Have you come across any other latrines?" Alex asked unexpectedly as they were drying themselves. "With faces, I mean."

"One or two," Ro replied. "One was a Rhodes Scholar. That was a surprise." Alex chuckled. "Wait, actually," Ro continued, pulling on his T-shirt. "I feel bad. I shouldn't have denigrated latrines. They do a thankless job. They should get more respect."

"This is going to be a lot to process," Bronya said. "Do you have a therapist?"

"Not really," Ro replied, regretful. "I keep firing them for insolence. But you're right. I should probably try again."

"At the least, you really should get away for a while. Take a break." Bronya looked at Alex, who nodded. "You know, there's a great place," she continued. "A spa. Samsara."

"Samsara?" The name rang a bell somehow. "I think I've heard of it. Where is it?"

"In India." Bronya saw the look on Ro's face. "That's not why I suggested it," she added hastily. "It's in the Himalayas, near Rishikesh."

"Rishikesh?"

"You don't know Rishikesh?" Bronya sounded surprised. "The Ganges runs through it. Like Varanasi." She looked at Alex.

"The Beatles studied meditation there, actually," Alex added.

Ro thought about it. "Good idea. Also, I haven't been to India in a while."

They began to walk up the hill toward the party.

"What's one-sixteenth, by the way?" Alex asked.

"In decimals, you mean?" Ro replied, surprised. "0.0625. Why?"

"Never mind. Long story. You really didn't confide in anyone while all this was going on? Anyone at all?"

"Nope."

"Why not?"

"It would have just made it worse."

"Yes." Alex nodded briefly. A sharp jerk. "But you must learn to recognize when help has actually arrived. Which it does, sometimes."

"No, it doesn't," Ro said.

"I promise you, it does." Alex looked at Ro. "I know we've just met, but I want to help make this better. Justice can come in many different forms."

"And at a variety of price points," Bronya interjected.

Alex elbowed her. "I'm in London next month," he continued.

"Great," Ro replied, only half-listening. "You should come round for a drink."

"I will," Alex said.

* * *

After a quick shower to rinse off the salt, Ro came back outside. Connie was with Rollo.

"Happy birthday," Ro said, giving Rollo a hug. "I haven't seen you all night."

"Where were you?" Connie asked, her eyes narrowing.

"I just went for a swim. With your friends Bronya and Alex," Ro replied, turning to Rollo.

"Oh! Nice one. They're Masha's friends, actually."

"What do they do for a living, out of curiosity?"

"I'm not sure." Rollo considered. "He's a zillionaire. His father owns all the taxis in Eastern Europe or something. Or all the buses. Not sure about Bronya. She keeps a pretty low profile. Something with her family, maybe." Ro thought Bronya was probably very rich. Only very rich people wore Swatches. "What about you?" Rollo turned to Ro. "Are you going to quit your job? You were thinking about it, yes?"

"Yeah," Ro said casually. "You know, it might actually happen pretty soon. Let's go do shots."

"Shots?" Rollo said, surprised.

"Just one," Ro clarified. "I don't want to get naked wasted."

Rollo thought about it, then shrugged. "Fine. Live it up before you die it up, that's what I always say."

They walked over to the open bar. "Three Jägers, please." Ro turned to Rollo. "I'm buying."

"Thanks," Rollo laughed. They downed the shots. Then, suddenly, Rollo began to gurgle, his eyes opening wide. He coughed, alarmed, his hands reaching to clasp his throat. "Poison," he choked, gasping for breath. Finally, after two or three grand spasms, he fell to the ground, still.

Ro looked at Connie. "Quick. To the safe room. Right now, before anyone notices. I know the combo."

Lying on his back, Rollo opened his eyes, worried. "Do you really?"

"Of course not," Ro reassured him. He was pretty sure he did, though.

"I'm going to change it anyway," Rollo declared, standing up and dusting himself off.

"You should," Ro agreed. Rollo drifted off.

"What should we do for our 40th?" Connie asked. Their birthdays were relatively close together.

"I don't know. It's not for another two years," Ro replied. "Just not Mykonos."

Connie shuddered at the shared memory. "Big time yikes."

"I could totally kill some galbi right now," Ro continued, looking over at the food trucks.

"Me too," Connie said. "And oysters."

"Yum."

* * *

The next hours floated by. Ro wandered, had a drink, sat on the grass, sat on a chair, saw friends from Dartmouth, saw friends from Bermuda, played dominos, ran into a friend from Paris, helped a very drunk girl get into a taxi, spoke to the driver on the phone after he'd dropped her off, waved at a friend from Harvard of a friend from Oxford whom he cordially detested, said no to a cigarette, said yes to two cold French fries, drank an espresso that someone unexpectedly put in his hands, played a few songs at the DJ booth, informed someone that there was in fact a nonstop flight from Munich to Los Angeles, tried on a pair of sunglasses that he already knew would be too small for his face, helped Masha find her shoes, sang "La Bicicleta" in the karaoke room with Connie, who was tone deaf, ate some foie gras slathered onto a warm baguette, and refused to go back to Portugal.

He ended up in the bouncy castle with some giggling friends of Rollo's younger sister Theresa's as the sky slowly started to turn pink. Dawn always made Ro anxious. He forced himself to take deep, slow breaths in rhythm with the movements of the castle. After all, he said to himself, it was Sunday, and he didn't have to go to work. Bounce. And tomorrow was Monday. He didn't have to go to work then either. Bounce, bounce. Nor the day after that, which was Tuesday. Bounce. Nor the day after that. Nor the day after that. Bounce. Nor the day after that. Nor the day after that. He began to calm down. He would soon be mixed up in five murders, maybe more.

LONDON

Ro and Alex sat in the living room of Ro's apartment in London a month or so later. It was Ro's birthday, as it happens.

"It all boils down to one thing," Alex said. "What outcome would make you feel the best?"

"This isn't about my feeling good," Ro reminded Alex, his tone reproachful. "This is about justice."

"The sweet spot's where justice and feeling good intersect. Take a look at this."

Alex handed Ro a manila folder.

Ro opened it and began to read. It took him some time. He became emotional on several occasions and, once or twice, had to stop to collect himself. When he reached the end, he stood up and began pacing around the room.

"So she's done this before."

"Her whole career. Doing whatever she can to sabotage her coworkers, almost always minorities. Spreading lies to damage their credibility." Alex took the folder from Ro, searching for a specific page, then nodded. "I think she gets pleasure from it."

"She loves to lie. And she's so good at it. It's actually terrifying." Ro paused. "How many people have gotten paid off?"

"I've found five so far," Alex replied. "At five different companies."

"And none of the people who were paid off has been able to do anything about it." Ro flopped into his chair, closing his eyes. "Because everyone was gagged."

"Exactly," Alex said. "Everyone got settlements. With strict NDAs."

Alex stood up and walked toward the window, peering outside.

"Then the latrine would change jobs—a promotion, every time—and nobody at the new job would know about what had happened before. So she'd do it all over again. And get away with it again." Alex paused. "You know, I never did like marketing people."

There was a long silence.

A strange energy began to fill Ro's body. An unfamiliar feeling mixed with a familiar one. He recognized the familiar one as rage. But what was the other one?

He couldn't put a name to it.

And then he knew.

It was powerlessness.

This would be the first and last time he felt it, he decided.

He opened his eyes. "You asked what I wanted? To start with, I'd really like her to get fired."

Alex smiled. "Well, I think we have a few options to make that happen. At a few different price points."

* * *

Ro lived at the unfashionable end of Chelsea in a vast apartment upon which he lavished an affection that had few other outlets at present. He had just settled back into his custom periwinkle leather Eames chair with *Les Bien-veillantes* when his phone rang. "Oh, bother," he said.

He looked at his watch. It was 6:00 p.m. on the dot. Which meant 10:00 a.m. in Del Mar. He picked up the phone without looking at it. "Hello, Father."

There was a startled silence.

"Ro. I didn't think I would catch you." His father sounded uncertain. "I just wanted to wish you a happy birthday."

"Thanks," Ro replied. He closed his eyes and sank back into his chair, pinching the bridge of his nose.

"Where are you? Doing anything to celebrate?"

"London, actually. Nothing special. Just dinner with some friends."

"That sounds nice."

There was a long pause.

"Let me buy dinner," his father said unexpectedly. "You still have our credit card, don't you?"

"Thank you, Father," Ro said. "That's very generous. Very generous indeed."

Ro was about to wrap it up when his father cleared his throat.

"Are you coming home for Christmas?"

"No," Ro replied, surprised. Then he mentally kicked himself. "Oh. I guess I haven't told you yet. I'm going to India, actually. This Ayurvedic thing."

"Oh?" his father asked, sounding mildly curious. "Where?"

"Someplace called Samsara."

"Samsara?" Suddenly, his father's tone was totally different. Sharp.

Ro sat up. "Yes. Why?"

"Samsara's my friend Vijay's place. You remember Vijay? You met him at lunch, oh, several years ago now. At the Inn. In Rancho."

Ro only vaguely remembered lunch with Vijay but was surprised nonetheless. "Your friend owns Samsara? The Samsara near Rishikesh?"

"Yes. Apparently it's excellent."

"What a funny coincidence," Ro said, shaking his head. "I'll be sure to look him up."

"Rishikesh is a very holy place, you know. It's where the Beatles went to study meditation," his father replied, nonchalant. "I'll send Vijay a message today. Have fun tonight. Don't forget, it's on me."

Ro heard his father's chair creak as he stood up.

"Oh. Your mother says happy birthday, by the way. Her Pilates instructor is here, but she'll try you later."

* * *

Tonight was Ro's birthday, and therefore he got to choose the theme. He looked in the mirror, satisfied with his choices.

He was wearing a slim-cut navy suit that he had bought in Paris a few years prior. The wrists of his white-and-pale-blue striped shirt were fastened with cuff links bearing the shield of the Oxford college where he had done his graduate studies. His tie was of woven navy silk and his shoes were black brogues. He was just about to call a taxi when his phone rang.

"Hola," Joss said. "And happy birthday. I ended up having to go to Pinewood today, so I can actually pick you up on the way to dinner, if you want. In like ten minutes?"

"Oh! Sure. That sounds great." Ro paused. "You know it's jacket and tie, right?"

Joss sighed. "Ro, I'm an agent. I'm always in a suit anyway."

* * *

The taxi made its way sedately down the Fulham Road toward Knightsbridge.

Ro looked at Joss. Joss was wearing a sober grey suit with a white shirt, a blue Hermès tie, and a flashy watch, exactly like the talent agent he was. His dark red hair was freshly cut and precisely combed. He smiled at Ro. "Who's coming tonight?"

"We're just seven," Ro replied. "Connie. My cousin Parvati. Then my friend Eliza from high school. You've met her before, right?" Joss nodded. "Then Rollo's friend Alex. And a friend of his whom I haven't met."

"How was Rollo's birthday? I was super bummed to miss it."

"It was great. Connie thinks you work too much, by the way."

Joss snorted. "She's one to talk. She literally does nothing but work." Connie was an investment banker. "So, who's this Alex? Is he a prospect for me?"

"I don't think so." Ro considered the question. "He has a girlfriend. He and I might do some work together, I think."

"What kind of work?"

Ro squirmed slightly. "This and that."

"Why'd you quit so close to the opening?" Joss peered at Ro. "What happened?"

"I can't really talk about it." Ro kept his tone light. "Legally."

Joss looked Ro directly in the eyes. "Ro. Are you all right?"

"I'm fine, Joss. Really." It sounded mechanical, even to his own ears. "But anyway, I don't want to talk about it. It's my birthday."

"You've changed so much over the last year." Joss shook his head. "You're so much more withdrawn than you used to be. Is it because of all this?"

Ro sighed. "Look, what happened wasn't great. But it looks like justice will be served."

After the park, the taxi turned off onto an unpretentious street, then turned left and right once or twice.

"Anyway, enough about me. What's going on with you?"

"Well, actually," Joss replied, flushing, "I do have big news."

Ro grinned. Joss always flushed when he had something to spill. "Well, go on, then." Joss looked at the driver suspiciously. Ro laughed. "He's not listening. Spit it out."

Joss looked at the driver again, then turned back to Ro, leaning in and lowering his voice by two octaves. "Chris wants me to quit the agency. To be his producing partner."

"That's amazing!" Ro beamed. Chris Forrester was Joss's biggest client, a legitimately huge movie star. "It's about time!"

"Thanks," Joss said, blushing. "It's a really cool opportunity. You know, it's an interesting time for him. He still has the franchises, but he knows he's not getting younger. So he wants to branch out, try some new things."

"Like?"

Joss looked at the driver again, suspicious. Ro grinned. "Joss, he can't hear us."

"Fine." Joss leaned in even closer, his voice dropping another octave. "There's this spy novel he's always loved. It took years, but we finally got the rights. And now it looks like it's going to happen. Super fast. Means tons of travel, but whatever, it's not like I'm leaving anything behind." Joss shrugged. "First stop is India, in like a month."

"What?" Ro exclaimed sharply. "This is crazy. Joss, I'm spending Christmas in India. I just booked it. Where are you guys going?"

"For real? That's amazing," Joss said, surprised. "We don't know exactly where yet. We just need to find a place where Chris can train."

"I'm going to this Ayurvedic spa. It sounds epic." Ro paused, thinking. "Maybe he could train there. I bet he could."

The taxi came to a smooth halt. Joss paid and thanked the driver.

They stood for a moment and looked up as the taxi drove off. The club, which was unmarked, looked precisely as Ro imagined it would have looked a hundred years ago: dignified, unostentatious, and quietly expensive.

The uniformed doorman stood to attention. "Good evening, Mr. Krishna," he said, opening the door for them.

"Thank you," Ro replied, smiling. He and Joss walked in.

* * *

"We'll start off with three dozen oysters, please," Ro said to the hovering server.

He looked at the reflection of the bustling room in the antique mirror above their table. The room's comfortable, well-padded banquettes were upholstered in various jewel-toned velvets. Amethyst. Ruby. Sapphire. The odd flash of topaz or aquamarine. Although the room was large, it remained intimate, perhaps because of the columns that impeded lines of sight and made every table feel cozy and private. The dress code at Reginald's was "smart," and everyone there had made an effort to look nice. Perhaps counterintuitively, this formality did not lead to stuffiness. Dressing up to go to Reginald's made every meal there feel like a special occasion.

"Well, this is certainly the Nice Department," Connie commented, surveying the room with a practiced eye. She wore a sapphire-blue silk dress with cap sleeves, her wavy dark hair bouncing down her back. Black-pearl-and-diamond earrings glinted from her ears. Eliza wore a simple but extremely well-cut black dress. Parvati was in a printed silk jumpsuit that she had possibly made herself, her long hair piled on top of her head. Many admiring glances were being directed at Parvati, Ro observed, although she herself did not seem to notice the attention. The three women were on the emerald banquette, an empty place at one end. The men, all in dark suits, sat on ormolu chairs facing them.

"The Nice Department?" Alex inquired.

"Ro's elder sister is notoriously difficult," Joss explained. "She occasionally walks into a store and asks someone where their nice department is."

Connie snorted. "That's nothing. One time, I was at dinner with Ro and his sister and the service was slow. She flagged down a waiter and asked him about the order she'd placed with his ancestors."

Alex whistled. "Color me impressed."

Connie looked at Alex and scowled. She turned back to Ro. "Who's the last person?" she asked, chomping on a parmesan breadstick.

"I don't know." Ro looked at Alex. "It's a surprise. I've never met her."

"It's a friend of mine," Alex admitted.

"You invited someone you've never even met to your birthday dinner? Ugh." Connie broke the breadstick in half. "You're such an extrovert. It's exhausting." She turned to Parvati, who was rummaging through an electric-green python clutch. "Was he always like this?"

"I can only vouch for him from birth, but yes." Parvati put her clutch back on the table.

Alex turned to Ro. "You're an extrovert?" He sounded surprised.

"He used to be one, anyway," Joss said. "Who's your friend?"

"She's a friend from high school."

"From Prague?" Ro asked. The sommelier arrived, offering him an iPad. "That's fine," Ro said, smiling. "We'll start with the Chassagne-Montrachet. Two. The Drouhin."

"That T is silent?" Joss asked.

"No," Alex said. "Switzerland, actually."

"You're Swiss?" Eliza said. Connie snorted again.

"French is vicious," Ro responded. "Allow me to remind you about Moët."

"No," Alex said.

"Cute," Parvati mused. "The Chalet School."

"Not exactly." Alex smiled. "And there she is."

He stood up. Ro turned his head.

A woman had come through the velvet curtains. Her long, wavy dark brown hair merged almost uncannily with the well-cut dark brown fur coat loosely belted at her hips. She looked around, charmingly at sea, until she saw Alex making his way toward her and smiled warmly. Lovely, Ro thought.

Alex hugged her and quickly helped her remove her coat, revealing a primrose yellow silk dress that fell to her knees, then handed the coat to someone behind the desk. They exchanged a few private words, then turned and walked toward the table.

"Everyone, this is Amrita Dey," Alex said.

"I'm so sorry I'm late," Amrita said with a dazzling smile. "I hate being late."

Joss looked at his flashy watch. "Only seven minutes."

"Even so."

Ro stood up to greet her. "How do you do," he said, kissing her on both cheeks. She took him warmly by the shoulders. "Happy birthday." She looked into his eyes, and Ro had a shock. Her eyes were of a blindingly clear blue-green . . . He couldn't find the word for their color. Ro had seen others of South Asian descent with green eyes, but hers were truly remarkable. As he pulled back from the embrace, he noticed her dangling Alhambra earrings, of diamonds and turquoise. Turquoise. That was it. That was the color of her eyes.

Facing her, he saw that she nonchalantly carried a string of diamonds around her neck that was probably worth the Earth. She wore a vintage gold Cartier Panthère with a diamond bezel on her right wrist. "Oh," Ro said, looking down. "We're watch twins. Sort of."

"Oh!" She took Ro's left hand in hers to examine his watch more closely. Ro caught a whiff of her perfume. Jasmine. "It's vintage. 1980s?"

"Yes. It's my father's, actually," he admitted. "I sort of borrowed it, then never gave it back." He looked down at hers. "Yours is beautiful too."

"Thank you," Amrita said. "And such a coincidence. This was my mother's."

"So you two went to high school together," Ro continued as the three of them sat down. "Eliza and I did too." Eliza waved hello. "Do you still have a lot of high school friends?"

"A few," Amrita replied. "I even married one once, but that didn't work out too well."

"I'm sorry," Ro said reflexively.

"Don't be," Amrita responded, at ease. "It's fine. We've both moved on with our lives."

"And you live in London?"

"Most of the time. I also have a flat in Zürich."

"Why's it called Reginald's?" Connie asked, turning over the menu.

"After the character in Saki," Ro said. "Although Saki did write that to have reached thirty was to have failed in life. And now I'm thirty-eight."

"You look great for your age," Alex said.

Ro considered the oyster in his hand. "I think that's because I'm asleep most of the time. Being awake is very aging, I find." He slurped it down.

"Where in India is your family from?" Amrita asked.

"Tamil Nadu. What about yours?"

"Bengal. But my family was from what's now Bangladesh. They had to leave. Partition."

"I'm sorry." Ro winced. "I'm afraid I don't know all that much about Partition beyond the basics." He looked at Parvati. "It didn't really affect our family. Since we're from the South."

Parvati saw the look on Connie's face. She leaned over, putting her hand on Connie's forearm. "I'm sure you know this, but when the British left India, they divided it into Pakistan and India. Between Hindus and Muslims, essentially, but it's more complicated than that. Anyway, the division's now referred to as Partition." She paused. "It did not go well."

"It was a terrible time," Amrita said. "But no need to discuss it during your birthday dinner." She looked at Parvati. "The two of you are related?"

"First cousins, once removed," Parvati replied. She winked at Ro.

"The Tamil Tigers are Sri Lankan, right?" Connie asked. "Not Indian?"

"Correct," Ro confirmed. "I do have a great Tamil Tigers story, though. It involves my uncle, a kidnapping, and an amputation." He paused, remembering. "And a fruit basket, actually. But let's leave that for another time." He turned back to Amrita. "Were you born and raised in Bengal?"

"No. Belgium," she replied, smiling.

"Diamonds?" Ro asked, looking at her necklace again. It was funny. If you separated the stones and put them in a pile, it would be obscene. But together, somehow, they felt discreet.

"How'd you guess?" Amrita said with a half-smile.

"ESP," Ro responded. Connie chortled.

"Do you guys have Indian passports?" Joss asked.

"No," Parvati said. "India doesn't recognize dual citizenship. So I'm an 'Overseas Citizen of India,'" she continued, making quote marks with her fingers. "OCI, for short. Sort of like a Green Card, actually."

Alex leaned forward. "Would India extradite someone if they had one of those?"

"Good question." Ro considered. "Ultimately, I'd roll the dice. If someone tried to extradite me from India, I'd bet they'd get a final decision in the year 2355." He saw Alex's look. "Yes. I have an OCI too."

An elegant elderly man on his way out of the restaurant saw Amrita and stopped in his tracks, surprised and delighted. "My dear," he said, extending his arms.

"Eugène!" Amrita stood up. "So lovely to see you." The elderly man and Amrita chatted for a moment in low tones, then she sat back down. He and his group moved away.

"Who was that?" Connie asked, taking another breadstick.

"The Duke of Scaw."

"Fancy," Connie muttered. Ro shot her an amused glance. Connie was allergic to Eurotrash.

"Trust me," Amrita said, earnest, "that's not the sort of person I normally hang around. But he's lovely." She paused. "For the most part, being in a family like that is really more of a curse than anything else."

"How so?" Eliza asked, interested.

"Well, let's see," Amrita replied, thinking. "First of all, the eldest son usually inherits everything, including the title. So if there are any other sons, they're generally praying for the eldest one to die. Or, at least, not to have any sons of his own."

"Also, that eldest son's probably constantly praying for his father to die so that he can accede to the title. Thank you," Ro added, to the waiter delivering his main course. Ro gazed at it, slightly dismayed at how large it was. "Dear Cassoulet," he murmured, "you may well end up too much for me."

"And as soon as you get the title, your own son starts praying for you to die," Connie added, giggling.

"Plus they're never encouraged to do anything in life," Amrita continued serenely. "It's as if you're taxidermized right at birth. Like something in a horrid secret room at Deyrolle. Imagine going through life knowing the only surprises you'll ever have will be nasty ones." She turned to Eliza. "Have we met before?"

"I think so," Eliza said. "Were you at Tabitha's birthday?"

"Yes," Amrita said, satisfied. "That's it."

"Oh. How was it?" Connie asked them.

Amrita considered. "It was a great party, if you'd never been to a party before."

"Oh, good," Ro said. He saw Amrita's surprise. "I hate her," he explained. "It was on Halloween, right? I hate dressing up."

"Me too," Joss said, shuddering.

"Joss wore the same Halloween costume for at least ten years," Connie said to Alex. "A tuxedo and a vial of insulin. Claus von Bülow."

Joss looked at Ro. "Ro dressed up as Malala once."

Alex choked on his wine.

"What's India like in the winter?" Joss asked Amrita.

"Well, India's a big place," she responded, laughing. "But it's not extreme. It can get chilly, but you'd never need more than a fleece or a light jacket." She turned to Alex. "And you? Are you hibernating again this year?"

"What do you mean?" Joss asked.

"I do a meditation retreat over Christmas and New Year's every year," Alex explained. "A silent one."

"He's making it sound normal," Amrita said, "but it's hard-core. They go completely off the grid. No contact."

"Where is it?" Parvati asked.

Alex smirked.

Connie scowled. "Oh, even that's a secret?" She sounded skeptical. "It's probably in Lamu. Or, like, Newark."

"God is everywhere." Alex sat back in his chair. "All around us."

"I beg to differ," Connie replied, terse. She looked at Ro. "Do you remember that birthday party you threw for that girl in Paris? The one where you yelled at the birthday girl because her friends were ugly?" Connie smirked back at Alex, satisfied. "God definitely wasn't at that party."

"Tabitha's moving to London, right?" Eliza asked Amrita.

"Yes," Amrita said. "I think she's going to Lower Sloane Street."

"She certainly will," Ro agreed. "If she's moving there, anyway."

Parvati smiled, but she was the only one who'd understood.

Joss had been surreptitiously checking his phone under the table. "Wait, Ro, what's that spa you're going to in India?"

"Samsara," Ro said.

Amrita put down her fork, startled. "Samsara? I go there every December."

"Really? Joss and I were . . ." Ro trailed off, remembering that Joss's news about Chris Forrester was still top secret. "I'm going this Christmas. Will you be there?"

"Yes!" Amrita exclaimed. "That's wonderful news!"

"What's it like?" Joss asked.

"Marvelous." She thought for a moment. "Perhaps not what you'd expect. Mostly very well-to-do Indian people. It's not at all exotic. No spices and scents and hot pink. It feels more like Switzerland. Don't go there if you're looking for something Bollywood."

"Ugh." Parvati shuddered. "I'm so sick of everyone talking about India in terms of colors and smells and noises. In the end, it's so patronizing." Amrita nodded. "If I ever wrote a book about India, I'd make sure that India was on top. The entire time."

"How's the spa?" Joss asked. "Is there a fitness center?"

Amrita nodded again. "Yes, and it's world class. Great trainers. And probably the best yoga and meditation programs in the world." She paused. "They would never put it this way, because it would be very ghastly, but it's sort of 'Ten Days to a New You.'"

"What's the vibe like?" Ro asked, leaning in. "Is it quite austere?"

"Not at all," Amrita laughed. "I'd say it's quiet but very, very comfortable. Discreet. A bit like here," she said, looking around the room. "There are no rules. But because there are no rules, everyone pretty much puts away their cell phones. It's a real break." She giggled. "My favorite part is the note cards."

"Note cards?" Eliza leaned in.

"It's like an Agatha Christie novel," Amrita continued. "You communicate at Samsara through notes. The staff delivers them to everyone. A couple of weeks before you go, they send you a form and you order these cards with your name on them. You choose the color and the font."

"Ah," Ro said. "I get it. So that you can socialize with everyone without fear that they're going to text you in four weeks looking for an internship for their sister's nephew."

"Precisely," Amrita said, turning and beaming at him. "It's all rather brilliant."

Ro excused himself and walked to the front of the room. "I'd like to pay the bill for my table, please."

"Of course," the man behind the desk said. "With a credit card?"

"Yes." Ro pulled out his wallet and looked at his parents' credit card.

The man waited, discreet.

"Actually, on second thought, could you please put it on my account?"

Ro put his wallet back into his pocket. He could splurge. It was his birthday.

He wandered back to the table.

"Should we take a photo of everyone?" Eliza asked.

"Pass," Ro replied. He thought photographs were nothing more than the murder of moments in time.

They stood up.

"Where are we going?" Connie asked.

"Groucho, maybe?" Ro said. "I may only stay for one." As far as he was concerned, it was never too early to leave a party.

They left Reginald's and headed toward the taxis waiting outside.

"You're obsessed with your apartment," Connie said. "It's not healthy."

"Thought I was an extrovert," Ro said lightly.

"In all fairness, Connie," Alex said, "it is a great apartment."

"How would you know that?" Connie replied, suspicious.

PARIS

Like nobody ever, Ro was flying from London to Paris. This just felt wrong, like Opposite Day. But Air France had had cheap business class fares from London to India via CDG, so why not.

Also, time was running out. The grand opening of the Radetzky Center was the following day. Ro took a deep breath, surveying his disheveled bedroom. Then a secure messaging app on his phone rang. Ro picked it up. "The Vatican."

"I think you're literally the weirdest person I've ever met," Alex responded.

"Grazie," Ro said absently, checking that he had his passports.

"Getting ready for the trip?"

"Yeah. I should be packing, but what I'm actually doing is watching the music video for 'Vienna Calling.'"

"You're flying nonstop?"

"Actually, I'm stopping in Paris tonight," Ro replied. "To see my cousin Parvati, whom you met. Then flying out from there tomorrow."

"What exact time do you take off and land?"

"Hold on." Ro consulted his itinerary. "I leave CDG at 9:00 p.m. on the 22nd and land in Delhi at 9:30 a.m. on the 23rd."

"That's perfect," Alex said. "So you're at Charles de Gaulle during the gala. Not alone."

"Yep."

"And you'll land in India before anyone wakes up the following morning." Ro heard some papers rustling in the background. "All of them are staying at the Four Seasons, by the way."

"I know," Ro sighed. "I chose it."

There was a long pause.

"Ro, once again, I'm not going to get in touch unless something's wrong," Alex said, his tone unexpectedly soft. "And what happens isn't going to be a big enough deal to make the world news. So if you don't hear from me, it means everything worked out fine. Just fine. So relax. Take a Xanax."

Ro laughed. "Thank you. And you're totally unreachable?"

"Totally. Until January 2nd." Alex hesitated. "I always think one should discuss difficult subjects," he continued abruptly. "If you avoid things, you still store them in your body. Back pain. So I just want to say I'm really sorry you won't be celebrated at the opening tomorrow."

"It's for the best."

"I'm very proud of you," Alex continued. "I want to make sure you know that. You're getting justice for a lot of people." After reading Alex's report, Ro'd hired his own investigator, who'd verified Alex's report and also found several other cases of latrine misconduct.

"I know." Ro paused. "It's still hard, though."

"Is it?"

"Not really," Ro admitted.

They were silent for a moment.

"Anyway," Alex continued, "in a couple of days, you won't have to think about any of this ever again. Ever. The Radetzky Center will have opened. People will have been born. People will have died. The world will have kept turning." He paused. "And you will have spent the day traveling to India. And it will be another day."

"Indeed," Ro said. "Is Bronya around? Give her my love."

He heard Alex turn and murmur something.

"Hi, Ro!" Bronya called in the background.

Ro smiled. "Hi, Bronya!" he called back.

"Smell ya later," Alex said.

They both hung up.

* * *

Flying to Paris might have felt unnatural, but it certainly beat navigating the squalor of the Gare du Nord. Ro landed at CDG mid-afternoon and got into a taxi. The driver sped off toward Paris, going against traffic. In what seemed like no time at all, they had arrived at Ro's destination, a quiet street near Etienne Marcel.

Ro buzzed at the gate. "Come on up!" a disembodied voice said.

He walked through the courtyard, took the stairs in the corner all the way to the top floor, then walked down the long hallway lined with windows on one side. Something about Paris just smelled like Paris, he thought. Violets and cigarette smoke. Their door was ajar. "Hello," he called, pushing it open.

"Ro!" Parvati said. A flurry of whirling limbs and long dark hair descended upon him. "I'm so happy you're here." They hugged. "Where's Connor?" he asked.

"Over here," a voice with an Irish lilt said to his left. Connor came over and hugged him. "Ro, it's been far too long."

Ro placed his bags on the daybed to the left of the door. "I assume I'm sleeping here?"

"Yes." Parvati looked concerned. "Is that OK?"

"Perfect. Anyway, you know me, I can sleep anywhere."

"That's for sure. Narcoleptics Anonymous." Connor turned to Parvati. "You ordered the pizza, right?" Parvati nodded. "Good. We're all cued up."

They moved across the room to a sofa facing a white wall. A projector perched on a small wooden shelf above their heads.

Connor bent over his laptop. "What are we thinking?"

Parvati paused, one finger on her chin, considering. "I don't know why, but I feel like 80s. Maybe Madonna. Early Madonna."

"Nice," Connor said. "Start with 'Borderline'? But let's cue some others. Ro, any requests?"

" 'Burning Up?' " Ro suggested. He smiled to himself. "Maybe not 'Live to Tell,' though."

"Yeah, that's not a great video." Connor pressed a button on his phone, then sank back down on the sofa beside them.

* * *

They chilled for a while, watching music videos, eating pizza, speaking, not speaking.

"Oh, guys, I have my tarot cards," Ro said, remembering. "If you have any questions."

"Which deck?" Parvati asked.

"Smith."

A light flashed in Parvati's eye. "Hold on, actually. I just remembered something."

She crossed the room to a wooden bureau in the corner and rummaged through a drawer for a moment. Then she stood back up, holding something in her hand.

"My cousin came to visit a few weeks ago and gave me a pendulum. Let's try it," Parvati said, flopping back down.

"Which cousin?"

"Not one of ours. On Dad's side."

"I have some emails to send. I'll be over there." Connor stood up, flashing them the Peace sign. There was only so much of Parvati and Ro's spiritualism he could take.

"Let's sit at the kitchen table," Parvati said.

They moved over and sat facing each other under a dangling bare lightbulb. Parvati pulled the pendulum out of a velvet pouch.

"Can I see it?" Ro said.

"Of course." Parvati started to pass it over.

"Wait." Ro held up his hand instinctively. "If it's yours, I'm not sure if I'm supposed to touch it. Can you just hold it up?"

"Of course."

Ro leaned over and peered at it. It was nothing special to look at—a simple chain made of steel links, ending in a clear, diamond-shaped quartz crystal. Something you could find in any mall for $10.

"How does it work?" Ro asked. "We can ask it yes-or-no questions?"

But even as he spoke, the pendulum began moving forward and backward, clearly answering his question.

Ro's jaw dropped. "Oh my God."

Parvati stared at her own hand, which was perfectly still.

"Wait," Ro said firmly. "Stop."

The pendulum obediently stopped moving.

"I didn't mean you," Ro said to the pendulum. It slowly began to sway again.

"Actually, yes. Everybody. Just stop for a second." Ro looked at Parvati. "I think this is serious. We need to figure out how to do this properly. And with the appropriate amount of respect."

The pendulum hung from Parvati's hand, waiting.

"How should we start?" Ro asked Parvati.

Parvati thought about it. "It's always good to start with gratitude. Dear Pendulum, thank you so much for being here with us tonight."

"Thank you," Ro repeated. "And please guide us so that we can access your wisdom in the most appropriate and respectful way."

The pendulum gave a luxuriant counterclockwise swirl.

"OK. The basics. Can you please show us yes?"

The pendulum swung backward and forward gently.

"And no?"

The pendulum gently swung from side to side.

"Hmm." What had that luxuriant counterclockwise swirl meant? Then Ro had an idea.

"Could you please show us a strong yes?"

The pendulum gave another luxuriant counterclockwise swirl.

"Yes is to the left," Ro said. "Counterclockwise."

"Interesting," Parvati said. "Why do you think that is?"

Ro thought for a second. "I think it's because the pendulum is the opposite of conventional logic." He leaned forward. "Could you please show us a strong no?"

The pendulum responded with a perfect clockwise circle.

"Sweet." Ro leaned back, satisfied.

"Dude." Parvati leaned forward. "Can we call you Pendy?"

The pendulum began to swing counterclockwise. Enthusiastically.

"Cool." Parvati sighed, satisfied.

Pendy calmed down. Both Parvati and Ro had instinctively known not to ask any personal questions about him. The gamble had paid off. Relieved, he gave a brief counterclockwise swipe.

"I have a couple more baseline questions, if that's OK," Ro said. "Can you show us what 'not sure, we'll see' would look like?"

Pendy considered for a moment, then swung diagonally from back left to front right.

"Got it," Ro said.

Parvati leaned forward. "Can you show us what 'do not ask that question' looks like?"

Pendy swung diagonally from back right to front left.

"Understood. I think we're ready." Ro looked at Pendy. "Do you think we're ready?"

Pendy circled counterclockwise once, lazily.

Ro looked at Parvati. "What do we want to ask?"

They were silent. Neither of them could think of anything.

Finally, Parvati spoke, hesitant. "Should I buy that Marni sweater?"

Pendy swung clockwise in a well-defined circle. A clear no.

"I wasn't sure," Parvati marveled. "Thank you!"

Pendy hung from her hand, modest.

"Maybe this is an opportunity to ask questions we never thought would be answered," Ro suggested.

Pendy sprang to life and spun a very hard yes. The hardest they'd seen so far.

"Whoa," Connor remarked from the daybed.

"OK. Alrighty then." Ro paused for a moment. "Was my third-grade teacher actually a total bitch?"

Pendy swirled confidently a couple of times to the left, then stopped. Yes, she was a total bitch, actually and definitely, but it wasn't worth wasting more time or energy on it.

"Wait," Parvati said, thinking about something. She leaned in. "Was my tenth-grade English teacher a pervert?"

Pendy took a hard left. Yes.

"It wasn't just in my head," Parvati said, pleased.

"Wait a second." Ro leaned in, suspicious. "Was mine a pervert too?"

Pendy swung another very hard left. Yes.

"I should have known." Ro looked at Parvati. "Why didn't anyone try to molest me?" He became pensive. "Maybe I just wasn't a cute kid," he concluded sadly.

"I'm sure you were the kid most likely to call the police," Parvati responded, crisp. "In the entire school, probably."

Waking up, Pendy swung frantically to the left. True.

"What next?" Parvati asked, unsure. Then she had an idea and leaned in. "Can we ask you questions about history?"

Pendy moved briefly to the left. Yes.

"There's something I've always wondered." Parvati's voice was thoughtful. "Was Marilyn Monroe murdered?"

Pendy bounced up and down, gathering strength, then swung a hard left. The hardest they had seen so far.

Parvati gasped. "I knew it somehow," she whispered.

Pendy came back to center.

"Wait," Ro said. He leaned in, his brow furrowed. "Was Wallis Simpson intersex?"

Pendy swung an even harder left. The hardest yet. Totally horizontal. Almost hitting Ro in the forehead.

"Thought you'd never ask," he seemed to be saying.

"Well, that's that," Ro muttered.

They were silent for a moment. Pendy swung, lazy.

"OK," Ro said finally. "I have a question about a family rumor." He leaned in again. "Am I descended from Genghis Khan?"

The pendulum hung from Parvati's hand, utterly and completely still.

"What does this mean?" Parvati whispered.

Ro thought furiously. Then something came to him. "Does hanging still mean it's absolute truth?" he asked Pendy. "Like, there's no doubt whatsoever?"

Pendy began to swing in a perfect counterclockwise circle, then kept going, quickly gathering speed and force.

Both Parvati and Ro recoiled. Parvati looked at Ro.

"Guess that explains my moral compass," he muttered.

The two of them were silent for a long moment.

"This is a lot to process," Parvati said with a sigh. "I think, now that we know about Pendy, we should think long and hard before we ask him more questions. And I don't think we should ask anything else tonight."

Ro nodded. "I agree." Then something occurred to him. "Although, before we stop, maybe we should ask Pendy if he has anything else he wants to tell us."

"Pendy, do you . . ."

But before Parvati could even finish asking the question, the pendulum started to describe a deep, wide circle to the left. Faster and faster.

"All right, then." Parvati's voice faltered slightly. "A message for me?"

Pendy swung to the right.

"Oh." Parvati turned to look at Ro. "The message is for Ro, then."

Pendy hung dead still.

It was meant to be.

Ro closed his eyes, steeling himself. Maybe he had always known. "I think you should hold the pendulum," he heard Parvati say.

He opened his eyes. Pendy was swinging decisively to the left.

Yes.

Ro reached out, clasping Pendy in his hand. "Here we go, I guess," he said, to no one in particular. He held Pendy up. Pendy jerked slightly. They were ready.

Do I need to speak to you out loud? Ro asked in his head.

Pendy swirled to the right. No.

"Whoa," Parvati said. "Are you asking him questions in your head?"

Ro looked at Parvati. "I think this might be personal. I'm so sorry."

"All right. I get it." Parvati moved away, uncharacteristically subdued.

Ro looked back at Pendy. They sat together for a moment.

Do you have a message for me? Ro finally asked.

Yes, Pendy said, with a definite circle to the left.

But I have to figure out what it is, Ro said.

Pendy jerked briefly, then went still.

They paused for a moment.

Did I do the right thing? Ro asked. With Alex and all that?

Pendy nodded.

You're sure? Ro asked. Even though anyone else would say it's the wrong thing?

Pendy nodded again. Vigorously.

Ro exhaled. He bowed his head. Am I supposed to go to India right now?

Yes. You are.

Ro closed his eyes. Do you have a mission for me there?

Yes, Pendy said.

Will I know what the mission is?

Yes, Pendy said. You'll get a sign.

Will I know why?

No, Pendy said. Decisively.

Ro winced. He hadn't been expecting that.

He regrouped.

But I will know when?

Yes. Pendy gave a desultory swirl to the left. I mean, knowing when's the least of things, no? And you'll know why soon afterward. I promise you that.

I'm in your hands, Ro murmured. But I have one last question.

What? Pendy replied, swaying gently.

Am I going to be all right?

Pendy's heart filled with sorrow. He hung still and looked at Ro. Yes. He slowly began to swing to the left. Yes, he repeated, gaining speed. You will be all right.

Ro opened his eyes. Do you promise?

Yes. Pendy whirled like a left-handed pinwheel. I promise.

Thank you, Ro whispered. He didn't believe it, though.

* * *

Ro arrived at the airport pretty much at the same time that the Radetzky Center gala was getting underway, about a thousand kilometers due east of him. But he studiously tried not to think about that. He sailed through check-in and the priority line at security. Once on the other side, he stopped at Relay and took his time, eventually picking up *Voici*, an SAS novel he hadn't read, and a magazine with Taylor Swift on the cover. Ro really loved Taylor Swift.

Then he headed downstairs to the lounge, where he passed the time the way he always did. He put down his bags, picked up a plate, peered at the buffet, put the plate back, untouched, sampled the new brand of champagne Air France was using, found it satisfactory, paged through the thick, shiny real estate magazines, decided that most of the houses were vulgar, picked up *Le Monde diplomatique*, made several startlingly strong French 75s, put *Le Monde diplomatique* back down, unread, read the horoscopes in *Voici*, ate a small cucumber sandwich with the crusts cut off, and spontaneously took a shower, because the shower was there.

He studiously turned his mind blank and tried not to think about lots of things: explanations given for his absence, the latrine's shrill laugh, which he did not plan ever to hear again, whether the colleagues he had worked so hard alongside were hurt that he wasn't there, or if they'd even noticed he wasn't there, and if they had, whether they thought he was outrageously rude for not showing up, or assumed he just didn't care about them, or the Radetzky Center, or about anything else, for that mattter, when the truth was that he cared so very, very much.

Le sigh.

He also kept a wary eye on the screens. Ro missed flights all the time.

Finally, the flight to Delhi flashed red for boarding. He walked unhurriedly toward the gate, occasionally glancing at the huge arching windows that reflected everything in the terminal, including himself. He decided that the energy at CDG before night flights was actually pretty calm and nice, all things considered. Bypassing the snaking line of passengers, he entered the lane on the left and handed over his documents again. "Merci," the man said.

Ro took the first left from the jetway and entered the plane. A smiling woman held a tray of beverages. Ro held out his passport and boarding card. "Bonsoir, M. Krishna," the woman said. "Pourrais-je vous offir quelque chose à boire?" she added, indicating the tray with her head. "Merci," Ro smiled, taking a glass of champagne.

* * *

And, now, a word from our sponsor.

The last years haven't been that easy for God. We all used to have plenty of time to take a break from milking a cow, or whatever, gaze upward, let our minds wander, and get messages from Them. Because it was so much more difficult for humans to communicate among ourselves.

But God is like a gas. They'll fill any openings They see. When communications started getting easier—telegrams, planes, fax machines, cell phones—is also when other things kind of stopped making sense.

Think about abstract art. Modernism. Song lyrics.

Song lyrics definitely stopped making literal sense at some point. These days, most songs don't tell a simple story, instead dealing in pseudo-poetry and fractured images. I mean, what the heck is a "wonderwall," anyway?

But perhaps these garbled messages (no disrespect intended) are God talking. God is efficient, so They kill many birds with one stone. Everyone has different visceral reactions to a song. Every song brings up different memories, feelings, images, associations, for every one of us. Every time we hear a song, we get our own personal, individualized message.

And then, when technology improved, God found a terrific new place to play. Algorithms! Now They can play you any song They want! You might think that algorithms are random. But maybe, just maybe, They aren't random after all. Perhaps every time an algorithm chooses a song, There's a message in it. For you!

Ro would get two such messages over the course of the next eleven days. He would not recognize either of them.

* * *

Ro stored his bags in the overhead compartment, placing what he needed in the compartments around him. An eye mask, ear plugs, magazines, two books, melatonin, Xanax just in case, a cheese sandwich, a bottle of water, gummy bears—an indulgence he allowed himself only when flying. Settling into his seat, he adjusted his headphones and set Spotify to play at random.

And a song began to play.

* * *

"This Orient" by Foals is a curious song.

The word *Orient* refers to the East. Everyone knows that.

But the song "This Orient" only ever refers to the West. Strange!

Thus does "This Orient" disorient.

Once, when Foals were asked about the song's meaning, the band nonchalantly responded that the song didn't mean anything in particular. Not to them, anyway.

But maybe, just maybe, the song did mean something after all.

Or even many things.

Maybe the song was always intended to transmit a message to Ro that night.

The pilot came over to say hello, just as the song started playing through Ro's headphones.

Directly into his brain.

"Bonsoir, Monsieur Krishna," the pilot said. (The pilot always came to say hi to Ro on Air France flights, probably because of his status. It was still a little weird, though.)

"Bonsoir," Ro said, sitting up a bit.

"Juste que pour vous le sachiez, on prévoit un vol tout à fait normal. Pas d'orage," he continued. "Vous allez pouvoir vous endormir tranquillement."

"Très bien," Ro responded.

The pilot looked at Ro's half-empty glass of champagne. "Vous avez besoin de quoi que ce soit? Une autre coupe, peut-être?"

Ro thought for a second. "En fait, est-ce que je pourrais avoir un jus vert? Je sais que c'est un peu bizarre."

"Nous pourrions arranger ça, je crois." The pilot smiled and went back to the cockpit.

Moments later, an attendant appeared with a glass of green juice. "Merci," Ro said.

And now it's just gone after dark
And we move to the other part of it
Secret part
Of your restless heart

To glide past every city light
Like a satellite
Careering through the sky
This color, this summer night

It's your heart
It's your heart
That gives me this Western feeling

It's your heart
It's your heart
That gives me this Western feeling
Do you know, you give me
You give me this Western feeling

Now look back see how far
you've come
Will you unravel in the sun?
But come undone
Find your place

Held up high said from string as well
No return to that restless place
You've reached it, you've found your grace

Placing the glass on the table in front of him, Ro leaned back and closed his eyes, although he had no plans to fall asleep immediately. The right time to fall asleep would happen, but it hadn't happened yet.

(The murders hadn't started happening yet, either.)

Sitting there, on the plane, en route to India, Ro knew that he was about to cross the Rubicon. A die had been cast. His life was going to change forever. That much was certain. But for the first time, he realized he had absolutely no idea how. Or how much.

I suppose you never do.

It's your heart, it's your heart
That gives me this Western feeling

It's your heart
It's your heart
That gives me this Western feeling

Oh do you know, you give me,
You give me this Western feeling

It's your heart, it's your heart
That gives you this Western feeling

It's your heart that gives you
That gives you this Western feeling

It's your heart that gives you
That gives you this Western feeling

It's your heart, it's your heart
That gives you this Western feeling

Oh do you know, what gives me,
What gives me this Western feeling?

Oh do you know, what gives me,
What gives me this Western feeling?

INDIA

(Ten Days to a New You)

DAY 2

December 24

R o woke up and had no idea where he was. He remained placid. This
had happened to him before. Many times before.

Experience had taught him to begin his investigation by searching
for clues using his senses. For starters, he looked down at himself in bed. He was
wearing a pair of white kurta pajama that he knew for a fact did not belong to
him. Their heavy, crisp white cotton perfectly matched the bed's heavy, crisp white
cotton sheets, making it look like Ro had no body. Just forearms, hands, and feet.

He moved all of them. They wiggled back at him, disembodied.

He turned his head back and forth, scanning the vicinity with his eyes.
He was in a hotel room, that was for sure. A very nice hotel room, even. Probably in the countryside, given the room's size.

Raising his head slightly, Ro looked past his feet to see a solid, expensive-
looking mahogany chest at the foot of the bed. Then two armchairs. One
was rounded, one more angular, but both were upholstered in the same soft-
looking, cream-colored fabric. The angular one carried a pashmina of fuchsia
with hints of gold; the other's was of a vivid grass green. A rough slab of black
stone served as a coffee table.

To his left was a mahogany bedside table, upon which sat an ornate silver
tray containing a porcelain teapot and cup. Sleep tea, the housekeeper had
said with a smile. Ro smiled. He knew where he was, and the small statue of
Ganesha next to the tray confirmed it. He was in India. He was at Samsara.

Closing his eyes again, Ro fell back onto the pillowy mattress, totally relaxed. Then he remembered the date, December 24, and he convulsed. He lay
for a moment on his side, collecting himself. He had to get it over with. He
picked up his phone from the floor next to the bed as if it were an unexploded
bomb, then unlocked it with his face. No new notifications or messages from

Alex. Of any kind. He exhaled deeply. Then again. He had to trust that everything had gone as planned. Pushing off the covers, he stood for a moment, running his hands through his hair. Then he walked to the sliding door and stepped out onto the balcony.

He rested his elbows on the wooden railing and looked out over Samsara. The bright green lawn beneath him gradually dissolved into a whitish-grey fog. He took a deep breath. He recognized herbs, and a hint of grass, and perhaps a touch of wood-burning smoke somewhere. Ro was reminded of Thanksgivings during college. He had always spent them with the Ziemssens in Vermont. Del Mar had been too far to go home.

He shivered and hugged himself. The late December air was chilly, and he wasn't wearing much. The war was now firmly in the past, he told himself. It was over, and he'd won. Today was the first day of the rest of his life.

Going back inside, he opened his laptop and paid a couple of bills that had come due. Then he put the laptop on a shelf in the closet. He hoped not to need it again for a while.

He walked into the bathroom and got into the shower. Then he turned the water on as hot as his skin could bear.

* * *

Scrubbed as clean as a newborn, Ro had just put on a fresh pair of kurta pajama when his eye fell upon a small brass button next to the door marked TEA. Amused, he pressed it, then was startled when the doorbell rang almost immediately.

A man with a mustache stood at attention, effortlessly carrying a heavy-looking wooden tray. His kurta pajama was similar to Ro's, but with full-length sleeves, and was topped with an orange, knee-length embroidered vest. He placed the tray on a desk. "Thank you," Ro said, smiling at him. The man smiled back. Rolling up his sleeves slightly, he crossed the room and lit the wood-burning stove in the corner, which Ro hadn't yet noticed. The sight of the brightly burning fire made Ro smile. Then the man picked up the tray on the bedside table and left the room.

Ro inspected the freshly arrived tray with increasing delight. It was divided into two parts of unequal size. The larger part contained a heavy-looking brass teapot, a white thermos of boiling water, a small jug of cream, a brass bowl with cubes of brown and white sugar, a small pot of honey, and a plate on which to place the used tea strainer. The smaller part of the tray contained an ironed copy of *The Hindu*, a folded sheet of paper stamped with "Today at Samsara," three small, cream envelopes of the highest-quality stock Ro had ever seen, each hand-addressed to him, and a grass-green paper box tied with a white ribbon.

The box contained the stationery he had ordered a few weeks prior, using a list of options provided by the hotel. Ro unfolded the tissue paper delicately to find "Ro Krishna" returning his gaze from the top note card, in marine blue, in a typeface Ro now knew to be Didot. He smiled, utterly enchanted.

Setting the note cards aside, Ro examined the envelopes nested underneath them. They were of the same heavy cream stock as the other envelopes on the tray. Turning one over, he saw they were blank except for a small, emerald green § on the back lower-right corner. Clever, Ro thought. If one were to use this stationery in real life (as was almost certainly the intention), only the initiated would know where it came from.

Mmm. The tea was delicious.

Ro turned his attention to the three envelopes addressed to him. Opening the left drawer of the desk, he found a steel dagger with an ornate handle. He gingerly tested the tip of the dagger with his finger and flinched.

Ouch. They weren't messing around.

Slicing open the first envelope, Ro was pleased to see JOSS ZIEMSSEN written across the top of the card, in brick red and all caps. "Welcome!" Joss had scrawled. "Come to yoga nidra at 8:00 and then we'll have breakfast with Chris and Catherine. Or else just come to breakfast, we'll be there by 9:30. J. So happy you're here!" Looking down at his left wrist, Ro saw that it was 7:40 and smiled. He would just be able to make it.

Although of the same stock, the second envelope looked slightly different, with emerald green edging and a large § in the same green on the envelope's

flap. The accompanying card had a green deckle edge and another green §
where the name would otherwise have been. "Dear Mr. Krishna," the card
began, "Please come to the spa at 10:15 this morning for orientation. Please
pick up the phone to your right and dial 1 should you have any questions." He
turned. A phone was, indeed, on his right.

"Ro Krishna" was written on the final envelope in confident, flowing cur-
sive. Probably female, he thought, but not definitely. He sliced the envelope
open. Amrita Dey had chosen turquoise script for her name. "Hello! So happy
you've arrived. I unexpectedly have to go to Mumbai today but will be back
tomorrow morning. I hope you'll join me for lunch tomorrow at 1 p.m. Send
me a note if you can't make it. Otherwise, see you then and there!"

Amrita was a very interesting person, Ro thought, as he stood up, stuffing
the card back into the envelope. Compelling, certainly. Also faintly malev-
olent, perhaps. But regardless, Amrita seemed to have grasped something it
had taken Ro a long time to realize himself. In the end, every person on Earth
wants the same thing: not to be loved, but to be liked. Amrita's note made Ro
feel liked. It was a nice feeling, and he looked forward to their lunch.

* * *

Ro walked out of the building that housed his room (which, according to a
discreet plaque, was called "The Residence"), carrying an ancient Dartmouth
tote bag with the day's schedule, a book, some blank note cards and envelopes,
and a bottle of water. He had deliberately left his phone behind.

Coming outside, he found himself on a path bordering a wide, perfectly
mowed lawn. The lawn ended, some distance away, in a line of dark, closely
planted trees, above which the mountain loomed, still largely hidden by
clouds. A couple of monkeys cavorted in the bushes next to him.

As Ro had arrived after dark the previous day, he had not yet taken in much
about his new surroundings. He now realized that Samsara was situated on a
plateau a good way up the mountain he was currently facing. He walked out
a few yards onto the lawn and then turned around. The Residence looked

Bauhaus or Art Deco: a longer and lower version of a building one might see in South Beach, or in Tel Aviv, or in which Hercule Poirot might live. Somehow, it gave off an impression that was both clinical and reassuring, perhaps because of the warm wood of its terraces and the charming pale yellow of the curtains behind them. The ground-floor rooms were shielded by low, discreet hedges, their gates opening directly onto the lawn.

He continued along the path for a few dozen meters. There, a tree-lined walkway turned off, leading to a smallish Indo-Saracenic building of sandstone. This, Ro remembered from his brief arrival tour, was Samsara's restaurant.

From there, the main path turned sharply to the right. First edging a line of trees, through which Ro could glimpse a large rectangular swimming pool, the path continued alongside the façade of a gleaming white-and-glass building that made Ro think of a cruise ship. The spa. The path ran on toward the line of trees at the far edge of the lawn, then, upon meeting it, disappeared.

That was when Ro realized he had no idea where he was going.

As if on cue, a golf cart screeched to a halt next to him. "May I assist you, Sir?" a smiling man in uniform said.

"Um, yes," Ro replied, startled. "Could you please tell me where the yoga classes are?"

"The Palace, Sir," the driver responded. He gestured to the empty seat behind him. "Please, allow me."

Ro clambered on.

* * *

A thick morning mist covered Samsara. Visibility was poor. Ro was a confident and enthusiastic driver, but even he would have proceeded cautiously given these conditions.

The driver of the golf cart had other ideas.

After careering around the hard bend next to the spa, the driver whizzed through the next few curves, cavalier, while Ro uneasily noted the morning dew still slick on the path. Then the path took an unexpected sharp descent. Ro fell forward. He braced himself, one hand against the seat and the other against the roof.

Then the path went flat again, sending Ro momentarily into the air. He could barely see anything through the mist. Something about it gave him the creeps. Adding to the eeriness were a few determined guests making their way to the Palace on foot, in white from head to toe, abruptly appearing in the mist, then disappearing just as quickly. Suddenly, the path took a jarring turn uphill, and Ro was flattened against the backrest of the golf cart while the driver somehow maintained his pace. Bracing himself against the seat and the roof once more, Ro closed his eyes. An interminable thirty seconds or so later, Ro felt the texture of the path under the golf cart change. Gravel. Making a sweeping turn, the driver came to a stop. "The Palace, Sir," he announced. "Your yoga class is downstairs."

After a brief, silent prayer of thanks, Ro opened his eyes. "Thank you," he said.

The driver sped off. Looking up at the Palace, Ro realized this was where he had checked in the night before, although he hadn't paid any attention to it at the time.

The Palace tapered like a wedding cake. Wide stairs led to the raised ground floor, the first of three floors, then two smaller floors were set back at the top. Although not especially large, the Palace had perfect proportions. Its façade was covered with ornate, intricate detailing. It was not a building that could have been constructed today, Ro thought. The Palace had been built for someone for whom money was no object, at a time when artisans still took real pride in their work. Perhaps late Victorian. It was a real bijou.

* * *

A number of guests were already in the room. Some were speaking in low tones. Others were under blankets, eyes closed. Everyone was in the same, identical kurta pajama. Choosing a mat, Ro sat down.

A tall woman entered the room through an inconspicuous door at the far end. She moved through the room with the deliberate, offhand grace of a dancer, her hair in a messy chignon, until she arrived at the teacher's spot at the head of the room. Pushing up her sleeves, she undid her chignon and unhurriedly shook out her long, glossy dark hair, then rearranged it in a low bun. Ro couldn't guess her age. Indian genes. The gravity of her movements, though, made him guess she was in her mid-thirties.

She stood up and waited as the room's low background murmur was gradually replaced by an expectant stillness. Ro was just wondering where Joss was when he appeared at his side, flopping onto the mat next to him. "You're here!" He leaned over and squeezed Ro. "We'll catch up after."

"Hello. My name is Fairuza, for those whom I haven't yet met. I'll be leading you through yoga nidra this morning. For those of you who aren't familiar with yoga nidra, it's quite different from our usual morning classes. The aim of yoga nidra, or yogic sleep, is deep relaxation while remaining fully conscious. Some of you will almost certainly fall asleep," she continued, to polite laughter. "That's fine too." She smiled briefly, although her face retained its gravity.

"Please lie down in a comfortable position. Your palms facing upward."

Ro lay down and wriggled until he was more or less comfortable.

"Now, please soften the muscles of your face and allow your eyes to close," the instructor continued.

Ro closed his eyes.

The instructor paused, allowing the stillness to grow in the room.

"Today, I will be guiding you to the state of consciousness between wakefulness and sleep," she said. "Occasionally, I will ask you to shift your awareness to various parts of your body, to bodily sensations, to emotions. Do not concentrate too much when I do." She paused. "Your goal here is relaxation."

Her footsteps moved slowly up and down the room.

"Now, without opening your eyes, visualize this room. Visualize the ceiling, the walls, the floor." She paused. "Then visualize your body on the mat. See how you are positioned. What you are wearing."

Ro saw himself from above, wearing white cotton, half-covered by a blanket. He looked like a corpse, he decided. A peaceful one at least.

"Become aware of the existence of your body. Here, lying on this floor."

Ro's visualization zoomed out. The whole room looked like a morgue, now that he thought about it.

"Now become aware of your natural breath. Your unconscious, spontaneous, regular breath. It moves through your body so easily. Without any effort at all. It flows in through both nostrils."

And all of a sudden, Ro felt a sneeze coming on.

"Notice how the air feels cool, fresh, as it comes in through your nostrils."

Somehow, he managed to swallow it.

"And warm coming out. So warm."

The sneeze began to come back. Desperate, Ro flipped onto his side. The rustling sound made by his blanket reverberated around the room.

The instructor paused. Hearing nothing further, she continued.

"Feel the coolness as you inhale the breath. Follow the feeling. Starting from your nostrils."

The feeling came back.

"Then up your nose."

It was hopeless.

"Into your sinuses."

"AH-CHOO!" It was like a grenade had gone off.

But then it was over. The instructor paused, then decided to continue.

"Then feel the coolness. It goes up your nostrils. Into your sinuses. Then down the back of your throat."

He was going to sneeze again. He knew it.

There was nothing else to do. Blindly, he sat up, blinked his eyes open, and walked-ran to the end of the room and up the stairs, hunched over like Quasimodo. He almost managed to make it out of the room. Almost.

AHH-CHOOO!

Pushing the door open, he leaned against it from the other side, finally safe. And then, suddenly, it came back. He sneezed again.

Then again.

And again.

And again.

He waited for the next sneeze, his whole body clenched tight. But it didn't come.

It was over.

* * *

His feet were cold.

Ro looked down and saw his bare feet on the marble floor. In his haste, he hadn't taken his things. He looked at his wrist. Forty-five minutes to kill before class was over.

Or to explore. He padded up the stairs, arriving in a grand, empty hallway with an enormous chandelier and carpeted stairs leading upward. The building was ominously quiet. To his left was a lounge with some large sofas, a few chairs, and a fireplace. On his right, he now remembered, was Samsara's front desk and reception. Hearing murmurs from the office, he crept past its door, then quietly began to climb the stairs.

The four rooms at the top of the Palace appeared to be used for storage as much as for anything else. Then Ro remembered the two smaller floors at the very top of the building. Finally, he found an elevator hidden behind a curtain in the corner. He pressed the button, but nothing happened. Then he saw the keyhole next to the button. Oh well.

He moved down one flight. Here, at least, the rooms appeared to be in use. A meeting room. A formal dining room, with a table for at least twenty. Another reception room. Then Ro arrived in the final room and smiled. It was a library. Ro's all-time favorite pastime was combing through hotel libraries, examining the books other guests had left behind.

Then he heard a commotion outside. Forgetting the books momentarily, Ro moved to the front window and peered out from behind the curtain. A grand old Rolls-Royce, two-toned in hot pink and sky blue, was pulling up in front of the Palace. A retinue, seemingly comprised of the hotel's entire staff, stood at attention. A uniformed chauffeur stepped out of the driver's seat and opened the rear door of the car. A woman emerged. Startled, Ro saw that her sari was the exact same pink and blue as the car. She swept majestically into the hotel, some staff hurrying after her, before Ro was able to catch a glimpse of her face. The remaining staff began unloading matching hot pink Goyard luggage from the car. Ro was fairly sure this was not a standard Goyard color.

Glancing at his wrist, Ro was surprised to see class would end in a few minutes. He began to make his way downstairs. Hearing voices from the office, he tried to slip past it unnoticed, but as he was passing the door Amrita walked out of it, almost colliding with him.

"Oh," Ro said, startled. "Hello there." He saw that Amrita was wearing kurta pajama. "Aren't you traveling today?"

"This afternoon."

He could sense something was off. Then he realized what it was: she wasn't making eye contact. "Is something wrong?"

Amrita sighed. All of a sudden Ro could see how upset she was. "You're not going to believe this, but I've lost my watch."

"Oh no!" Ro inhaled sharply. "That's awful. What happened?"

She shook her head, distressed. "I don't know what happened. When I went to put it on this morning, it wasn't there." She saw Ro's confusion. "It's always on my bedside table."

"I'm sorry." Ro paused, delicately. "You're sure you had it when you went to bed?"

"I think so, but can one ever be sure?" Amrita shook her head again. "I always take it off just before bed. I do think I'd have noticed if I hadn't had it on."

"Maybe you left it in the spa?" He immediately realized how lame this sounded. "It's just that I can't imagine anyone here stole it." Particularly when there's so much else to steal, he thought, eyeing her massive diamond drop earrings.

"I can't either." Amrita exhaled, annoyed. "It's all very baffling. Anyway, they've promised they'll look everywhere."

"You know, I have a feeling it'll turn up," Ro said, meaning it somehow.

"From your lips to God's ears." Amrita yawned. "It's all so exhausting. Why aren't you wearing shoes?" she continued, looking down at his feet.

"Oh." Ro looked down at his feet too, sheepish. "I had a sneezing fit during yoga nidra. Had to jam."

Amrita laughed, then laughed some more. "Thank you. I needed that."

"Oh!" Ro remembered something else. "By the way, who was that woman who just arrived?"

"You don't know her?" Amrita sounded surprised. But before she could continue, they started hearing noises from downstairs. The class was over.

"Go get your shoes." Amrita poked Ro in the chest.

"Jawohl. See you tomorrow. And safe travels." Amrita nodded. "And fingers crossed for your watch."

But seeing Amrita's remarkable eyes immediately cloud over, he chided himself. She had been smiling and happy. He shouldn't have reminded her about it.

* * *

Head down, Ro made his way through the bustling room toward his abandoned mat. Seeing him, Joss burst into peals of laughter. "Dude. Seriously rugged."

The woman on the other side of Ro laughed as well. "Poor you. I'm always terrified that will happen to me."

"Well, you can rest easy. Today's bullet had my name on it." He leaned down to roll up his mat, then looked up and caught her eye again. "Which is Ro, by the way." He stood up and reached out his hand.

"I'm Lala." She smiled, shaking it. Ro tried not to stare at her gigantic emerald earrings. Every person in the room was dressed identically, he mused, but some people were more identical than others. Lala put on a fur headband, obscuring the dazzling earrings, and turned to the man next to her. "This is my husband, Sanjay."

"How do you do." Ro extended his hand again. Sanjay waited a beat, then accepted Ro's hand with a thin smile. Ro tried not to shiver. Immediate bad vibes. "This is my friend Joss," he added hastily, to cover any emotion he had involuntarily shown.

Joss waved, unusually chilly. "Hello."

Sanjay turned to Lala. "Let's go to breakfast."

"Yes." Then Lala turned to them, impulsive. "Would the two of you like to join us?"

"Unfortunately, we have plans," Joss replied smoothly. Ro looked at him, surprised. "Chris and Catherine. The Forresters. Remember?"

"Oh," Ro said. "Yes, of course."

"Thanks." Joss turned back to Ro. "Shall we?"

Ro nodded. But then he turned around. "What about lunch?" he asked Lala out of nowhere.

There was an awkward pause.

"Sure," Lala said unsurely. She looked at Sanjay.

Sanjay shrugged. "Why not," he replied, unenthusiastic.

"Right," Ro said, already regretting it. He decided to double down. "Why not. At 1:00?"

Lala nodded.

"Let's go. Actually, wait a second." Ro wanted to apologize to the teacher, but scanning the room, realized she'd already left. He turned back to Joss. "Never mind."

* * *

Joss began descending the steep path by foot. "Wait," Ro said. "What are you doing?"

"Going to the restaurant. What are you doing?"

"Let's take a golf cart." Ro waved at a uniformed man in front of the Palace, who then muttered something into a radio. "It's kind of far, no?"

"I just feel bad making them drive me around," Joss admitted.

"Why would you feel bad?" Ro replied, puzzled. "If you didn't use them, they'd be out of a job."

A cart glided toward them. Relieved, Ro saw it wasn't the same driver he'd had that morning. They got on board and began to descend at a moderate pace.

"So what are they like? Chris and Catherine, I mean."

"They're great. You'll see. Not at all like you'd expect. Catherine went to Dartmouth, actually."

The clouds had begun to lift. Ro saw for the first time that both sides of the path were covered in trees and plants in every shade of green. Birds chirped and flew from tree to tree, while some small grey monkeys frolicked in the undergrowth.

"What's your plan for the next few days?" Ro asked.

"Well, tomorrow's Christmas. Chris has rehearsals because he's doing a dance performance at the big dinner tomorrow night." Joss looked at Ro. "That's a surprise, by the way. Don't tell anyone." Ro nodded. "Then he'll be training, of course, and I'll be location scouting." He sighed. "The shoot'll probably take a full year."

"A year?" Ro replied, surprised. "That's unusually long, no?"

"It's going to be the biggest US-India coproduction of all time." Joss looked at the driver, then leaned over and whispered into Ro's ear. "I think we're going to get . . ." He named two huge Bollywood stars.

Ro whistled. "I'm so proud of you. But a full year? So you're basically going to have no personal life?"

"Guess not. Life's easier once you've given up on love."

Ro laughed. "No interesting guys on the horizon?"

"None. I mean, it's fine. I don't care. Otherwise, I wouldn't exactly be able to peace out for two years." He looked at Ro searchingly. "What about you? Are you still speaking to Charlotte?"

Ro shook his head.

"Good."

"It's hard, though." Ro paused. "So many things happen where she's the only one who would understand why it's funny. Pretty much every day."

"Nobody since? It's been, what, almost three years? Or more?"

"Not nobody." Ro thought about it. "No one serious, I guess."

"Why not?"

"I mean, Joss, look at me," Ro said. "I'm a nightmare dressed like a nightmare."

Joss sighed, clearly exasperated. "Honestly, Ro, you're so weird sometimes."

The golf cart pulled up in front of the restaurant.

"I'm glad you're not speaking to her anymore." Joss got off the cart. "It wasn't good for you."

"Life isn't good for you," Ro replied. He got off the cart too.

* * *

Ro and Joss walked down a dark hallway toward the host stand. "Good morning, Mr. Ziemssen. And welcome, Mr. Krishna," the host said, smiling.

"Oh," Ro replied, startled. "Thanks."

The host turned to Joss. "Mrs. Forrester is inside. At her usual table."

"Great, thanks. We'll find our way." Joss pushed open the double doors. Ro, following, was blinded by the dazzling light in the room. The building's Indo-Saracenic exterior had concealed a large, contemporary atrium filled with skylights.

Ro stood for a moment, blinking, trying to get his bearings. The restaurant's decor felt almost Scandinavian, with white walls; blond wood; and clean, simple fixtures. The center of the room was a large, multilayered buffet covered with pastries, chafing dishes, bread, fruits, cereals, and plenty of other things Ro couldn't make out yet. A chef prepared eggs to order at a station on his left, while another prepared dosas at a station on his right. Everything was exactly as it should be.

So why did he feel a little . . . nonplussed?

Then he realized. It was because every single guest in there was wearing the same thing. A white cotton kurta pajama.

Including him.

People pouring themselves coffee, inspecting unfamiliar fruit at the buffet, leaning over tables to chat, buttering toast, reading newspapers, cracking the shell of soft-boiled eggs, eating dosas, signaling waiters, all dressed identically.

And then, unprompted, a question seared into Ro's brain.

Were they in an insane asylum?

He lost himself there for a few seconds. When he came back to his senses, Joss was looking at him quizzically. "You OK?"

"Of course." The smile Ro gave Joss felt extremely forced, but Joss didn't seem to notice anything.

* * *

Ro had the opportunity to observe Catherine Forrester as they approached the table. At first glance, even in kurta pajama, she did not look the way one would expect a major movie star's wife to look. Perhaps in her early fifties, she wore no makeup that he could see and was, in fact, a little disheveled. Her drugstore reading glasses were crooked. The long black hair streaming over her shoulders was streaked with grey. Seeing them arrive, she put down her copy of *The Atlantic* and stood up.

"You must be Ro," she said, shaking his hand firmly. "I'm Catherine." Up close, Ro saw the gigantic diamond studs in her ears. They made her look a little bit less disheveled.

"Joss, Chris wants to talk to you in the gym for a sec. Training stuff."

"Ah, OK." Joss turned to Ro. "The gym's just next door. BRB." He jogged away as Ro and Catherine sat down facing each other.

Catherine looked at Ro appraisingly. "Joss was right. You do have amazing hair." She turned to the smallish brindle French bulldog on the seat to her left, whom Ro hadn't yet noticed. "This is Mango," she said, nuzzling him. "Say hi, honey." Mango barked, obliging.

Ro leaned over and scratched Mango's neck. "Hello, Mango." He looked around. "Have you eaten yet?"

"No, I'm going to order off the menu." She moved around some newspapers on the table to reveal two menus, one of which she handed to Ro.

"Thank goodness," Ro said. "I hate buffets."

"Me too. If I wanted to take a cruise, I'd take a cruise. Not that I've ever actually been on one."

"I've never been on one either!"

A server came to take their order. "Thank you." Catherine smiled up at him. Then, as she turned back to Ro, something in the distance caught her eye. Immediately, she crouched in her chair, staring fixedly at the floor.

"Is something wrong?" Ro leaned over, concerned.

"I'll explain later," she hissed. "For right now, just look really busy. Don't look up."

Ours not to reason why, Ro thought. He leaned over, pretending to rummage through his tote bag. A few seconds later, someone paused close to him, casting a shadow. The shadow hesitated briefly, then moved off. Ro waited a good twenty seconds before raising his head. He caught Catherine's eye. She nodded. Slowly, they resumed their normal positions.

"What was that?" Ro asked in low tones.

"This guy." Catherine paused, then closed her eyes briefly. "The Visiting Light."

"What do you mean, Visiting Light?" Ro was baffled.

"There's a guest teacher here every month, for yoga or meditation or whatever. That's what they call it. Visiting Light." Catherine shuddered. "Anyway, he just seems like the worst kind of social climber, and he keeps trying to sit with us. I mean, it's great that the yoga and meditation teachers eat with guests here, but not that one." She considered. "There's just something off. If cultural appropriation were a crime, that guy would get death."

"Sounds more like a Visiting Blight," Ro quipped. Catherine chuckled.

Their food arrived.

"So, is this your first time in India?" Ro asked, neatly cutting into his dosa with a fork and knife.

"Oh, Heavens, no," Catherine replied. "I lived here for a couple years in my twenties." She registered Ro's surprise. "I was at State. From right after school until I got married."

"Very cool. I always wanted to be a diplomat. Where else were you posted?"

"Oh, all over the place." Catherine replied, waving a hand indiscriminately. "But my last post was Djibouti. Consular."

"Why was it your last one?" Ro asked. "Was the food that bad?"

"Ha." Catherine's laugh was more like a bark. "No. I met Chris in Djibouti. He was shooting there. I got assigned to be their minder."

"Was that an assignment you wanted?"

She gave another short bark-laugh. "Ha. Not in the slightest. I was livid. It was sexist. But then I met Chris." Catherine's face softened. "Which was the last thing I ever could've expected." She looked toward the door, and her entire face lit up. "And there he is," she said, waving.

Ro had met celebrities before, but he had never been in close contact with as big a star as Chris Forrester. Even dressed in his kurta pajama, Chris Forrester glowed almost radioactively.

"Great meeting you, Ro," Chris said, shaking Ro's hand warmly and immediately putting him at ease. Ro couldn't help but smile at him. Chris leaned over and pecked Catherine on the lips. "I'm starved. Gonna hit the buffet."

Ro and Catherine continued eating. "So what do you do, Ro?"

"I do my best," Ro replied. He had thought up this response to the inevitable question a month prior and had consistently been using it since then.

Catherine smiled, amused. "I remember now. Joss told us you left your job recently."

"Yep. Now just enjoying life for a bit. What about you? Do you work?"

"Sort of. I keep myself busy, anyway." Catherine took a bite of her omelette. "Where'd you grow up?"

"San Diego. I live in London now, though. What about you?"

"I'm from Boston, but we're mostly in Brooklyn now." She took a sip of her coffee. "And what does your family do in San Diego?"

Ro smiled, amused at how blatantly she was trying to place him. "My dad's a surgeon," he replied, as Joss and Chris came back to the table with full plates. "My parents moved there from London, actually. He got a fellowship. They were only supposed to stay a year, but when they got to San Diego, they changed their plans. Fast."

"San Diego versus Thatcher's England," Joss said, making a balancing movement with his hands.

"My father still talks in hushed tones about a radiator into which he had to feed coins," Ro said.

"And your mom?" Catherine asked, cutting into a piece of cantaloupe.

"She's an economics professor. At UCSD."

"Ro's mother is Lalitha Krishna," Joss interjected.

"Your mother's Lalitha Krishna?" Catherine leaned in eagerly.

Exasperated, Ro dropped his fork and knife down onto his plate with a clatter.

"Sorry," Joss mouthed.

"I met her in Davos a few years ago," Catherine continued. "Please say hello for me."

"How funny," Ro said politely.

"You've met his mother?" Chris asked Catherine.

"His mother's probably the worldwide expert on demographics and population control. She was on *Oprah*."

"Wow," Chris replied. He sounded impressed. Ro tried not to sigh.

Catherine took another bite, then turned back to Ro. "Do you have brothers and sisters?"

"One of each," Ro replied. "Because not having children wasn't really an option women had in the eighties." He took another bite of his dosa. "Yum. That's what Mother talked about on *Oprah*, actually. I'm the middle, obviously. You?"

"I have a twin sister. She's a beatnik." Catherine speared a piece of fruit. "Did your siblings also go to Dartmouth?"

"Stanford. Yours?"

Catherine shook her head. "My whole family went to Princeton. I rebelled."

"Yeah, me too," Ro replied. "Everyone kept trying to shove Stanford down my throat, but I thought it looked like a Taco Bell. And I like Taco Bell, but that's not the point." He glanced down at his watch. "I gotta motor, actually. Orientation. At the spa."

"Make sure you get time with Mahesh, Chris's trainer," Joss said. "He's incredible. He has a Ph.D. in yoga."

"And don't forget to add a one-on-one with the VB," Catherine added.

"VB?" Chris asked.

"I'll explain later," Catherine replied.

Ro stood up. "See you guys. And I'll see you at lunch," he added, turning to Joss.

"Oh." Joss smacked his forehead. "I forgot to tell you. I can't make it to lunch after all."

"Why not?"

"I have to do something in some other location," Joss replied. They'd been using that phrase since college.

"Fine," Ro sighed, rolling his eyes. "Whatever."

* * *

"So, Mr. Krishna," Dr. Menon began abruptly. "You look exhausted."

He took off his glasses and polished them on the ruby-red sleeveless vest that signaled his status as one of Samsara's Ayurvedic doctors.

Ro was taken aback. "It was a long journey."

"No, Mr. Krishna." Dr. Menon shook his head brusquely. "I mean more profoundly exhausted than that." He peered at the computer on his desk. "It's a good thing you came here," he continued, pecking away with two fingers. "Better here than the hospital, anyway. Do you enjoy spicy food?"

"Yes, I love it."

"I knew that." Dr. Menon consulted a file on his desk. "You won't have spicy food here. I'll be placing you on a special diet. Simple food. Vegetarian. Very bland." Dr. Menon seemed to take particular pleasure in pronouncing the word "bland." He peered into Ro's eyes. Ro shrank back.

"You get heartburn?"

"Yes," Ro admitted.

"I knew that too." Dr. Menon turned back to the keyboard. He pecked at it absently for a moment, then suddenly looked up again. "How was your childhood?" His tone was accusatory.

"Fine!" Ro squeaked.

Dr. Menon examined Ro for a moment, dubious. "When you have heartburn, try to think about an unpleasant memory from childhood. As unpleasant as possible."

"Pardon?"

"Heartburn is often merely the brain trying to avoid unpleasant things. And thus forcing you to think about something else. Such as heartburn. Please try it." Dr. Menon smiled thinly. "Most people find their stock of unpleasant memories to be more than ample." He looked down again. "How is your sleep?"

"Excellent."

Dr. Menon frowned. "I wasn't expecting that," he muttered.

"My father thinks it's hereditary. All of us can sleep and sleep and sleep." Ro smiled, a little smug. "If sleep were an Olympic event, I think I would medal," he added, not without pride.

Dr. Menon removed his glasses and looked at Ro again, but this time with a hint of approval. "You know, this is a great blessing."

"A blessing?" Ro leaned forward, curious.

Dr. Menon turned back to his screen. "We are all born with varying degrees of guilt," he replied. "Sleeping well is a sign of innocence." The printer emitted a sheet of paper. Dr. Menon handed it to Ro. "Your treatment schedule for the next week."

Ro scanned the page, uncomprehending. There were days and times, but the names of the treatments were transliterated from Sanskrit. "They are mostly various kinds of massage," Dr. Menon said, to forestall Ro's question. "Most of them quite pleasant. But it's probably best not to look them up in advance."

He paused, for quite some time.

"Or to panic. You must never miss your daily steam," he continued, before Ro could interject. "You will spend one hour in the steam and sauna area every afternoon. It is crucial to flush your system. And for you to slow down, Mr. Krishna."

Dr. Menon looked Ro in the eyes.

"Please do not undertake more than a minimum of physical activity. Or mental activity."

"Can I do yoga?"

"Certainly not if it's cloudy." Dr. Menon paused. "Mr. Krishna, you are in grave need of rest. Particularly mental rest." His gaze turned serious for a moment. "Please rest your mind as much as possible."

"Sure thing," Ro replied lightly.

Dr. Menon gazed at Ro for a long moment, then turned back to his computer, shaking his head. "Perhaps you could have a steam now," he suggested. His tone made clear it was an order.

* * *

Ro stepped out of the elevator into a dimly lit room lined with wooden lockers. Stacks of fluffy white towels were everywhere. The floor was made of small tiles in innumerable shades of blue and green.

"Good day, Mr. Krishna," a smiling attendant said. "You may remove your garments and place them in a locker of your choosing."

Ro undressed. Opening a locker, he found a robe of the thickest white terry cloth he had ever felt, with emerald green piping and a matching § on the left breast. He put it on. It felt like a weighted blanket.

"Please allow me to orient you."

The first room they entered contained an enormous, fan-shaped jacuzzi of sapphire-blue tile. Jets of water were prepared to pummel guests from every direction, but nobody was there. "Where is everyone?"

"Guests tend to come in the morning and evening, Sir."

Ro followed the attendant through another door into what looked like an anteroom. A glass door on the left led out to a terrace facing the forest at the back of the property. The steam billowing out of another door indicated the hammam. Then Ro noticed a spiral staircase in the corner.

"The sauna is upstairs, Sir. And here is our hammam."

The hammam was a gorgeous room made mainly of pale green glass tile, with a fountain in the middle and several long benches. A wooden bucket and chain in the corner served as a cold bath.

Ro smiled. Spending an hour a day in here would not be a burden.

* * *

Ro sat across from Lala and Sanjay, a noncommittal expression on his face. Internally, however, he was cursing Joss for having bailed so brutally. He was also wondering why he was sitting there himself.

Then he remembered. This lunch had been his idea.

Sanjay had grunted his way through the pleasantries—yes, they lived in Delhi; no, this wasn't their first time here—before spending the remainder of lunch on his phone. Although Ro would normally have found this abhorrently rude, in this instance he was grateful. It meant he did not have to speak to Sanjay, and Sanjay was a jerk.

Sanjay had ordered lamb, while Lala and Ro both had vegetable curry. Bland, as promised, but delicious. "No spice for you," the waiter had said to him.

"Are you vegetarian, Ro?" Lala asked, smiling a little shyly.

"I'm not," Ro replied. "Although I do probably eat vegetarian most of the time. What about you?"

"Same. I eat fish every now and then."

"I used to be vegetarian, but my body just runs better when I eat meat. I totally believe in vegetables." Ro bit into a carrot. "Carrots help your eyesight. Etcetera."

"I have amazing eyesight," Lala replied. "Especially in the dark. I could be a fighter pilot."

"Me too. Well, nothing crazy," Ro said. "I sometimes wonder what it means karmically when someone has terrible vision."

"Sanjay has terrible vision," Lala pointed out.

Ro turned back to Sanjay, still on his phone and absently stuffing lamb into his mouth. In the distance he saw the Forresters talking and laughing animatedly with a model-handsome man in a wheelchair, about Ro's age, with a head of hair to rival Ro's. The man turned his head to reveal a glossy natural silver streak in his hair. Ro was immediately racked with envy. Then Joss sat down with them too. Traitor.

Ro turned back to Lala. "I just don't think humans are supposed to be vegetarians," he confessed. "That being said, though, when I started eating meat in my twenties, it was a lot harder than I thought. Getting used to the idea of chewing on and ingesting flesh."

Lala shuddered, visibly disgusted.

"But that's exactly it. That's the truth of it." Ro leaned in. "When I started eating meat, I began to accept the visceral realities of the food chain. Of life and death." He laughed. "I was in law school then and making lots of arguments."

Sanjay looked up. "You're a lawyer?"

"Oh," Ro said, surprised at Sanjay's sudden interest. "I was. Technically still am, I suppose."

"And where did you study?" Sanjay asked, a little accusingly.

"Law or generally?" Ro sat back in his chair. "For law, Oxford and the Sorbonne." He paused. "Oh, and Columbia. I always forget." He smiled sweetly at Sanjay. "And you? Did you study law somewhere?"

"No. I studied economics. Here in India."

"Interesting," Ro replied, pleasant. "I'd ask where, but I'm afraid I don't know the universities here too well."

Lala bit her lip, also smiling.

Sanjay looked down at his phone, then back up at the two of them. "I have to go back to work."

"On Christmas Eve?" Lala said. "You're a public servant. What work could you possibly have?"

"Some of us actually have things to do." Glancing at Ro, Sanjay registered that he'd made a mistake. He made a point of giving Lala a kiss on the cheek. "I'll see you later." He turned to Ro. "Goodbye."

Ro smiled faintly. Sanjay left.

They sat for a moment.

"He has to work? Is he going back to Delhi?"

"Oh no." Lala looked puzzled. "He took another room that he's using as his office while we're here."

"He's a public servant?"

"Yes. He's in politics." She looked at him, still puzzled. "You didn't know?"

"No. Why would I?" And why would I care, he thought.

A server approached them. "Would you like tea or coffee?"

Ro looked at Lala, who was looking down. "Why don't we get something to go and take a walk?"

She thought about it. "All right."

* * *

They sat on a bench, gazing at the lawn, both in pajamas. Ro felt a little awkward.

It was chilly outside. Steam rose from their porcelain mugs.

"Mrs. Banerjee mentioned you," Lala began. "She said you were a family friend."

"Who's Mrs. Banerjee?"

Now Lala was really surprised. "Mrs. Banerjee," she repeated, looking at Ro, wary. "The owner of the hotel. She said she knew you."

"Oh!" Ro remembered. "My father said his friend owns the hotel. Vijay someone."

"That's her son-in-law." Lala nodded, reassured. "You'll meet her, at any rate. I think she's arriving today or tomorrow."

"Actually, hold on. Does she have a huge old Rolls-Royce? Pink and blue?"

Lala smiled. "She does."

"Ah." Ro sat back, satisfied. "She got here today. I was wondering who that was."

Lala turned toward him, her gaze unexpectedly sharp. "You really don't know who Sanjay is?"

"Why would I? You said he's in politics, but I've hardly ever spent any time in India. I don't know who anybody is." He paused. "You're making me curious, though."

Lala thought for a long moment, biting her lip. Ro waited.

"I'm going to take a big risk," Lala finally said. "I don't know why, but I have a feeling I can trust you. Can I?"

"For future reference, never ask anybody that again," Ro joked. Then, looking at Lala, he turned serious. He somehow felt that, under her cool, discreet surface, she might be in real trouble.

"I have an idea. You know, I really am a lawyer. I'm still admitted to the New York Bar, although I haven't practiced in ages. Why don't we say this is a client consultation?"

Lala nodded slowly, beginning to understand.

"If so, whatever we say is protected by client confidentiality. And if I repeat any of it, I'd be disbarred."

"All right." Lala smiled, her first real smile.

She remained pensive. Ro waited.

"So. Mrs. Banerjee told me that you were acquainted with Amrita Dey."

"No." Ro was surprised. "I mean, not really. I'd met her once before I got here."

"So you don't know her well?"

"Not at all. Why?"

"Because I think she's having an affair with my husband."

"Oh," Ro said, startled. "My, my."

They sat in silence for a moment.

"What makes you think that?" he asked gently.

"I don't know." Lala shook her head. "There are lots of things that don't add up. Sanjay insisted we come here. To a spa. As you saw, he's not exactly the relaxing type."

"No," Ro replied, shaking his head. "No, he doesn't seem to be."

"He transfers money every few months to a bank account in Switzerland." She stopped. "I can really trust you?"

"This is a privileged conversation."

"My father's security team has looked into it. The money is going into a numbered account. One that belongs to a Swiss citizen."

Security team? Ro thought.

"I don't think we've ever even met any other Swiss people." She wiped a tear from her face. "But there's one reason I'm sure, though. That something's going on."

Ro waited.

"It's how she looks at me." Lala turned to him. "As I said, I have perfect vision. When she looks at me, she's smug. She looks at me with pity. And nobody looks at me with pity."

Ro took a moment to reflect on everything Lala'd said.

"Look. I'm not going to argue with you. People's intuitions for this sort of thing are usually pretty solid."

He took a deep breath. "So. I don't know why, but I just don't think it's true. I don't know her all that well, but it just doesn't seem like her somehow."

Lala looked unconvinced.

"Also, no offense, but he's a jerk." Lala began to laugh. "Why would she want to have an affair with him?" Ro looked at her. "Seriously, no offense. But is he, like, super rich or something?"

"No." Lala smiled, shaking her head. "He isn't."

"And even if they're having an affair, why would he send her money? Particularly if he's not super rich? Because I really don't think she needs it." Ro shook his head again. "Listen, I think you may well have a real problem here. But I'm not sure this is it." He glanced at his watch. His next appointment was coming up. Plus, this was a good place to end. "I have to go. But you can speak to me whenever you want from now on. I'm your lawyer. My fee is one rupee an hour."

Lala laughed.

* * *

Before Ro could even enter the spa building, he heard a voice behind him. "Mr. Krishna?"

Ro turned around. The man who had spoken was perhaps a few years younger, wearing a long-sleeved kurta pajama and a royal blue tunic. He was slight of build, but Ro suspected that this belied his strength. "My name is Mahesh."

"Mahesh! The Forresters told me about you."

Mahesh smiled. "We have a room reserved, but it is such a lovely afternoon. Shall we go outside? We'll go through the spa." He held the door open for Ro. "Please."

* * *

Mahesh led the way through a set of swinging doors.

Ro saw plenty of things about which he might have had questions—hydrotherapy rooms, a solarium—but Mahesh was walking ahead of him, and very briskly at that. They quickly approached what appeared to be a dead end until Mahesh abruptly pushed open a door on his right, revealing another corridor. This corridor looked different, with cement floors and fluorescent lighting.

"Where are we?" Ro asked Mahesh's back.

"This is the operations area."

"Am I supposed to be back here?"

"It's fine." Mahesh waved a hand above his head. Ro followed him, almost breathless, feeling like Alice in Wonderland. Then Mahesh stopped, pushing open a door on the right. "The laundry." Ro's eyes were immediately dazzled by the fluorescent light and the white walls. Giant vats were washing what looked like hundreds of kurta pajamas. A wall of tumble dryers was completing the process. Turning, Ro saw that the room's walls were stacked with freshly pressed kurta pajamas in every size. Signs indicated that staff pajamas were to the left and guest pajamas to the right. "What's the difference?"

"Sleeves," Mahesh said, walking to a shelf on the left. "And fabric." He took down some yoga blankets. "There," he said, satisfied.

He turned around and raced back into the corridor, Ro once again struggling to keep up. The corridor continued for only a few more meters before dead-ending into what looked like a white brick wall. Ro turned to his right to see a steel fire door marked WARNING: ALARMED. "Don't worry. There's no alarm." Mahesh pushed the door open, revealing a ramp leading upward. Ro followed Mahesh up to the top of the ramp and then stopped, bewildered, seeing a snaking, tree-lined path in front of them. "Where are we?"

"You don't know? This is the main path to the Palace."

"I only arrived last night."

Mahesh disappeared down an unobtrusive trail between the trees. Ro followed more cautiously, pushing branches out of the way. A few feet later, the trail unexpectedly opened into a meadow that was like something out of a dream.

Ro went silent, trying to register all the beauty around him. The grass was mint-green and strewn with wildflowers. The meadow was partially bordered by the mountain behind them and partially by the trees to the left that lined the path. Mahesh was already putting down blankets. "Don't go close." He waved toward the far end, where there appeared to be a sheer drop. "That is a cliff."

Ro shivered. He'd never had a good head for heights.

Mahesh sat down. "Let's start with some breathing."

* * *

The two hours with Mahesh—breathing, yoga, meditation, more breathing— left Ro both exhilarated and exhausted. A slightly weird combination.

The spa lobby hummed with activity. Guests were getting in their last treatment of the day. Ro spied Joss on an overstuffed sofa, chatting with the man in the wheelchair who had the silver streak in his hair. He walked over to them.

"Nice hair," Ro said. It came out more coldly than he had intended.

The man shrugged, apologetic. "It's a gift."

"Ah, there you are," Joss said. "This is Amit. We're going to have dinner at 7:00 if you want to join."

"Sure," Ro said automatically. Then he paused. It was his vacation. He could do what we wanted. And what he wanted to do, he realized, was ab- solutely nothing. "You know what? Actually, I think I'm just going to order room service. Take a bath. Get to bed early."

"Sounds good," Joss said. "Come to morning stretch tomorrow."

Then, to his own surprise, Ro yawned. A full-body yawn. For several seconds.

"Wow." Amit whistled. "I'm impressed."

Ro was having a full-on nap attack. "I gotta go." He somehow made it back to his room and into a hot shower. He was sound asleep and snoring within minutes.

Ro didn't miss anything, either. Death hadn't arrived at Samsara just yet. He was planning to check in tomorrow.

DAY 3

(December 25)

R o woke. For a moment, he didn't know where he was. Then he remembered he was at Samsara. He stretched luxuriantly in his bed.

He turned and picked up his personal schedule, which the housekeepers had left next to the bed during turndown. The schedule informed him it was Christmas Day and that a gala dinner would be held in the restaurant that evening. As for the weather, it called for intermittent clouds and scattered showers. A high of twenty-one degrees.

Ro shrugged. Even after all these years, he was useless in Celsius.

Morning stretch was at 8:00 a.m. The classic brass-and-mahogany clock on the wall showed 7:40. He'd have to hurry up. He rang for tea.

Within moments, the uniformed server arrived with a tray containing nothing except a note on official Samsara stationery. "The doctor asks that you not eat or drink anything except water until after your first treatment today."

Ro looked down at his schedule. Right after morning stretch was "Kunjal Kriya." Whatever that meant.

* * *

Morning stretch was held in the state-of-the-art gym upstairs from the spa. Nobody was there. "Weird," Joss said, looking around. "It's usually pretty busy."

A spectacularly handsome man, perhaps in his late twenties, arrived a moment later. "Good morning. I'm Anwar."

"Hello," Ro replied, smiling.

Crickets from Joss. Ro turned around. Joss was staring at Anwar, his mouth slightly open. Ro elbowed him.

"Hello," Joss said, recovering.

"Ganesh is away this week, so I'll be taking over today's class," Anwar continued, seemingly unaware of his effect on Joss. "As you are only two today, perhaps I will stretch you out myself."

"Sounds good," Ro said.

"Which of you would like to go first?"

Ro looked at Joss, who was already flushing from the neck up, then looked down at his watch ostentatiously. "You know, I don't really have much time before my next session. I'll leave you to it." He winked at Joss as he left the room.

"Please lie down on your left side," Anwar said.

* * *

Ro moved down the stairs. A few guests sat on the massive overstuffed couches in the middle of the glass atrium, idly flipping through magazines.

He walked up to the spa desk. "Hello. I'm a bit early for a meditation class?"

"Oh yes, Mr. Krishna. Your teacher will collect you shortly."

"Thank you." As Ro turned away, his eye fell on a piece of paper in a clear plastic frame posed on the desk. "December's Visiting Light: Mitchell Charney," the sheet said in script, under a photo of a white man in profile. Maybe in his mid-thirties, the man gazed into the middle distance, a little smile playing on his lips, the sun setting over the ocean in the background. He wore a mandarin-collared linen shirt and a string of wooden beads around his neck. His hair, which was too long, made wings over his ears in a way that reminded Ro of Farrah Fawcett. Smaller print underneath advised that private meditation and yoga sessions with him were available. Those whose interest was piqued should enquire at the spa for further details.

Suddenly, Ro shivered, as if an ant had just run down his shirt. Catherine was right. This Charney person gave him the ick.

"Mr. Krishna," a cool female voice said behind him.

Ro turned and was discomfited to face the previous morning's yoga teacher. "Oh dear. I'm so sorry about yesterday."

She smiled briefly. "Please, don't worry." Her smile didn't quite reach her eyes, Ro observed. "It gets dusty in there. I'm Fairuza."

"Please, call me Ro," Ro said, taking her outstretched hand.

"We're in Room 3 today."

"Sounds good."

As Ro turned to follow her, he accidentally caught another glimpse of the VB's photo. Fairuza followed his gaze and shuddered. "The Visiting Blight."

"Where'd you hear that?" Ro replied, surprised.

Fairuza smiled. "Word gets around."

"How did this dude even end up here?" Ro mused, half to himself.

"He was probably in the white place at the white time. Shall we go?"

Ro nodded, unsure whether he'd misheard her.

Fairuza took a last look at the VB. "So unfortunate," she murmured.

* * *

The room had a wooden massage table in the middle. One corner held a large sink and in another corner was a shower. A table near the window held a large pitcher and a glass.

"Please, have a seat," Fairuza said to Ro.

There wasn't actually anywhere to sit, so Ro perched on the side of the massage table, his legs swinging like a schoolboy's. Fairuza remained standing.

"So, how familiar are you with yoga?" Fairuza began. "You do it regularly?"

"Yes," Ro responded. "Well, sort of."

"As I'm sure you'll know, the word 'yoga' simply means the meeting of the body and the mind," she continued. "Lots of things are yoga. But one major part of yoga is cleansing. Specifically, the cleansing of various organs."

Ro started to get uneasy.

"Because you have a history of digestive problems, such as heartburn, we must clean your digestive tract to remove any mucus or plaque."

Fairuza nodded toward the pitcher and glass.

"That pitcher contains salt water. Today, you're going to swallow its contents as fast as you can and then regurgitate them."

"Are you serious?" Ro said.

Fairuza returned his gaze, neutral.

"All right. Fine." Ro sighed, resigned to his fate. He stood up and moved toward the sink. "Do you want to bring the pitcher and the glass over here?"

Fairuza wordlessly brought them over.

Ro stood next to the sink and turned on the tap.

Fairuza handed him a glass of salt water. He drank it down as quickly as he could and handed her back the glass.

She filled it again. Already Ro's stomach was rumbling. He knocked back the second glass of salt water. By now he was feeling quite nauseated.

As she started to refill the glass, he stopped her. "Just give me the damn pitcher." He began to empty the pitcher into his mouth and almost immediately was gushingly, roaringly, tumultuously sick into the sink. Over and over again. In waves. Like a boat on the sea.

When he had recovered consciousness, more or less, he was completely drenched. His hair was wet from the water running out of the faucet. His face and stubble were covered in salt water and mucus and whatever else he had spewed out of his mouth, the salt water still dripping from his nose. He propped his hands on the sides of the sink.

"Hectic," he muttered.

Fairuza brought him several towels.

* * *

They sat in silence in a small lounge area in the midst of the massage rooms. Fairuza had brought Ro tea.

"That was like a horror movie," Ro said finally. "At least my day can only get better."

"There are far more intense practices," Fairuza said. "This was just the esophagus. There are yogas where you drink a gallon of salt water and then stand and do yoga poses to make the salt water flow through your intestines."

Ro shuddered slightly. "Is that what's in store for me later this week?"

"No." Fairuza smiled. "Don't worry. We don't do that one here. We want repeat visitors."

Ro looked closely at Fairuza for the first time. She had coiled her beautiful black hair into a bun. She had simple gold studs in her ears. Her eyes were so dark that it was difficult to see where the pupil met the iris. She was tall and slender, with delicate joints. Like any serious yoga teacher, all of her body movements were casually precise.

"How long have you been working at Samsara?"

"A couple of years." She shifted in her seat, tucking her legs up under her.

"How'd you start doing yoga?"

"I trained as a dancer. But then I fell in with a bad crowd." She smiled slightly. "One day I woke up and decided to come to Rishikesh. I don't know where the idea came from. God, I suppose. You know Rishikesh is a very holy place, yes? The Beatles studied meditation here."

"I'm aware."

"When I got to Rishikesh, I began to learn yoga. And then I learned to teach yoga, and here we are."

They sat, silent.

"It's funny," she continued. "I know this is the path on which I'm meant to be, but it's not the same path on which I was born."

"You're always on the path on which you were born."

Fairuza looked up at Ro, surprised. She nodded slightly, then stood up.

"Stay a moment to relax. I'll see you later."

Ro reclined on the couch, lazily gazing at the ceiling fan. Then, out of nowhere, he was reminded of Pendy. Ro realized, a bit uneasy, that he still had no idea what his mission was. Then he remembered: Pendy would give him a sign at the appropriate moment. He reclined further and closed his eyes.

* * *

Amrita was alone at a table for two at the back corner of the restaurant. Ro began to move toward the table, then stopped. Someone else was moving toward the table too. A blandly handsome man was rushing up to Amrita, a rictus grin plastered onto his face. Amrita looked up at him with a smile, the practiced smile of someone frequently fawned over. The man bent and whispered something into her ear, running his hand through his blondish-brown too-long hair. Ro disliked him immediately. Once again, Ro began to advance toward the table, his gait now somewhat grim and determined.

"Hello, Amrita."

"Oh, hello, Ro." Amrita turned to face him with a radiant smile. "So lovely to see you again. Have you met Mitchell?"

"No." Reluctantly, he turned around. "How do you do," he said, involuntarily frosty.

"Hi there, Ro," Mitchell grinned. "Pleased to meet you." Pushing up his sleeves, he started to reach out his hand, enthusiastic, before realizing Ro hadn't done the same.

Amrita was nothing if not perceptive. "Let's catch up this afternoon," she said to Mitchell, blowing him a kiss.

"Let's walk to the Palace for tea later," Mitchell said to her. "Dartmouth," he added, looking at Ro's tote bag. He smiled at Ro. "I went to Middlebury. Sort of the same thing."

"Not really," Ro said. Turning his back, he sat down and faced Amrita, whose eyebrows were raised. "You walk back and forth from here to the Palace?" he asked her.

"Bye-bye," she mouthed over Ro's right shoulder, giving a little wave. "I think it's good to get some exercise," she replied, turning back to Ro. "Mitch and I have gotten into the habit of doing it together." She looked at him mischievously. "You should join us sometime. I have a feeling you two might have a real connection."

"Yes, he seems great. And by great, I mean awful," Ro replied. "Who on earth was that?"

"He's one of the meditation teachers."

"Oh, I thought he was a guest. Since he's white." Ro remembered Mitch's long-sleeved kurta pajama. He should have realized that Mitch was staff. And then it dawned on him. "Wait. Is he the . . . ?"

Amrita nodded. "Visiting Light."

"Oh." Ro sank into his chair. His mind groped for the analogy, then found it. "It's as if he were entirely made of gluten," he murmured. He looked at his watch. "Wow. I saw his picture, like, an hour ago, but I still didn't recognize him." Looking back at Amrita, he saw her wince. "I'm so sorry. Your watch still hasn't turned up?"

"No," she replied, still clearly distressed. "I can't think what happened. I never lose anything."

"I'm terrified of losing mine. I don't usually travel with it." Ro paused. "I used to wear this Casio when I was traveling, but since that Shakira song . . ."

Amrita shuddered. "Say no more."

A waiter arrived. Amrita looked up at him with her dazzling smile. "Please tell the chef I'll have whatever he chooses for me." She turned to Ro. "What are you having?"

The waiter was still staring at Amrita, captivated.

Ro cleared his throat. "Ahem. I'll have the Pitta meal, please."

The waiter snapped out of his reverie. "Of course, Mr. Krishna." He paused. "No spice. Doctor's orders." Bowing smartly, he walked away.

Amrita looked at him, sympathetic. "Do you have Dr. Menon?" Ro nodded. "He's all gloom and doom. Thinks everyone's going to die tonight. Don't listen."

"Good advice," Ro replied. "How was Bombay?"

"It was fine. Quick. I just had to run some errands." She took off her fur headband and shook out her luxuriant hair, practically in slow motion. Tucking her hair behind her ears, she revealed Cartier earrings in the form of panthers. The panthers were made of pavé diamonds, with sapphire eyes.

"I like that headband. Looks warm."

"They sell them in the gift shop here," Amrita replied, putting the headband into her turquoise Goyard tote bag. The bag perfectly matched her eyes. Ro noted that the bag's monogrammed R.D. also perfectly matched Amrita's bright red nail polish.

"Why an *R*?" Ro asked. "Instead of an *A*?"

"Actually, my real name is Rita. After Rita Hayworth." She laughed. "But almost nobody calls me that. Amrita's a family nickname that stuck somehow."

"I've never seen that color before," Ro said, pointing at her bag.

Amrita laughed again. "Mrs. B. has them run up custom colors sometimes. Oh!" she exclaimed, leaning over and touching Ro on his forearm. "You saw her arrive yesterday. Mrs. Banerjee. She gave me this for my birthday. That's why it says *R*, in fact. Mrs. B.'s the only person who calls me Rita."

Another waiter materialized, pouring chai into the porcelain cups on the table. "You know, I was thinking of going to Bombay after," Ro said, taking a sip. "Where do you usually stay?"

"Well, usually at the Oberoi. But this time at the Soho House, because it's so convenient to the airport. I also stay at the Taj sometimes." She smiled. "The location is actually terribly inconvenient, down in Colaba, but I stay there just to show the terrorists they can't win." She reached into her bag and pulled out her lipstick.

"I'm sorry, I'm sure you're so sick of talking about them," Ro said, leaning forward. "But your eyes are remarkable. Is there a story behind them? Do they run in the family?"

"They do. My father had the same eyes as me. My brother too. They pop up every now and then. My sister has brown eyes." She looked at Ro, scrutinizing him. "How is it that we hadn't met one another before? How long have you been living in London?"

"Only about four years," Ro said, leaning back in his chair. "In any event, I try to keep a low profile. You've heard of FOMO? Fear of missing out?" Amrita nodded. "Well, I've always said I have HOBI."

"What's HOBI?"

"Horror of being included," Ro said, as two waiters arrived with their food. "Thank you," he said, smiling at them.

"Where were you before London?" Amrita asked, taking a delicate forkful of vegetable curry.

"Los Angeles, but only for a couple of years. I spent most of my adult life in France." Ro took a bite of his food. Also vegetable curry, but for Pittas like him. "Where did you grow up? You went to school with Alex?"

"Yes. In Switzerland. But I was actually born and raised in Brussels."

"Oh, yes," Ro said, nodding. "I remember now. But you live in London? Whereabouts?"

"My family has a flat in Mayfair. But I don't know that I'd say I live in London," Amrita said, considering. "Although I'm probably there more than I am anywhere else. I'll go back to London after Samsara."

Ro took another bite of his food. No spice in sight. "Did you spend much time in India growing up?"

"Not at all, actually. I think my father just felt much safer in Belgium than in India. He was in the jewel trade, you know. Where security is a major problem. My father lost everything during Partition. I don't think he ever felt safe here again."

"I'm so sorry. It's funny. I'm from the South. As far as I know, Partition didn't affect my family at all." He shook his head. "We were so lucky. Are."

"It's unimaginable, really." Amrita shuddered briefly. "Anyway, my father left and never looked back. So I grew up as a Belgian Indian. Someone from nowhere." She looked at Ro for a long moment. "Like you."

"I'm not from nowhere," Ro said. "I'm from San Diego."

"So you're American. But also British?" Amrita asked. "And anything else?"

"Yes, I'm British," Ro said, although he couldn't remember having told Amrita that. "I was born in London but moved to the US when I was three. Oh, and I have an OCI, of course." Ro decided not to mention his French passport. At least, not right then. He took another bite, then grimaced. "This needs salt," he said, adding some. "And you?"

"Well, Belgian. And Swiss through marriage. Plus an OCI, of course."

Ro looked down at Amrita's hand. She wasn't wearing a wedding ring, although she was wearing gigantic diamond and sapphire rings on two other fingers. And a tennis bracelet made from what looked like marbles, but were in fact diamonds. Then he remembered. "Oh, yes. You mentioned you were divorced. Someone from high school."

"Widowed, actually," she responded breezily.

"Oh." Ro paused, awkward. "I'm so sorry," he added, feeling extremely lame.

"Don't be," she said, still breezy. "Things happen. So, what are you up to at the moment? Alex mentioned you're in a transition period." Ro shrank back in his chair, wary. Amrita hastened to reassure him. "That's all he said, by the way. Swear."

Ro chewed for a moment, thinking. Then, surprising even himself, he decided to tell her. At least a little. "My life's been sort of a roller coaster recently."

"What happened?" Amrita leaned forward. "Only if you want to talk about it, of course."

Ro looked around the room, at all the people who looked like him. He felt strange, but he couldn't put his finger on exactly why. Then he realized what it was. He felt safe.

"I had a dispute with my employer. And it dragged on and on."

"You fought back." It wasn't a question.

"You have no idea," Ro replied. "I don't think they'd ever seen anyone like me."

Amrita looked at Ro. Her gaze was warm, sympathetic, and encouraging all at once. It pierced him. He sat up a little straighter.

"Then it got resolved. Out of nowhere. And all of a sudden, I was free. It still doesn't feel real. I haven't really processed it, I guess."

"What kind of dispute?" Amrita took another bite.

"Bad manager," Ro replied, terse.

"You were treated unfairly?" Ro nodded. "And this manager, was he or she white?"

"Yes. She. We were around the same age. Which seems like an important detail, actually."

Amrita sat back, looking at Ro knowingly. "It always comes down to race, doesn't it."

"I guess." Ro put down his fork. "But it was a little more complicated than that."

"How so?"

"Because it was also about class." Ro sighed. "I really don't want to go into any more details."

"Come on." The look in Amrita's eye was somehow both mischievous and confiding.

Ro sighed again. "This was the thing. I actually thought we worked well together. She was extremely competent and professional. But then I found out she was spreading really horrible lies about me behind my back. I can't tell you how upsetting it was. I actually trusted her." Ro paused. "She just lied to everyone's face all the time, including mine. To advance herself, and to hurt others. And she was such an amazing liar. It was uncanny. Not to be melodramatic, but I think she's the closest encounter I've ever had with evil. Actual evil."

"There's nothing more dishonorable than liars," Amrita agreed. "So what was the class issue exactly? Was she envious of you?"

"She was from a very different world. But I never said bad things about her." Ro paused. "I hate the way I sound right now. I sound like such a snob. If anything, I said nice things about her. I was impressed she'd gotten so far. Given her total lack of education."

"Don't worry, I believe you." Amrita assured him, her cup of tea in her hands. "But between us, give me some examples of her different world."

Ro slumped back in his chair and thought about it, then shrugged. Fine.

"I'm warning you, these are going to be cheap shots, but whatever."

Amrita leaned in.

"We had this lunch meeting once with a super-famous architect—like a household name, almost—and she ordered in from Pret. It was wild. What else." He tried to remember more. "Oh. We had this team pub quiz, and she didn't know any of the answers. Like, to anything. She had no general knowledge. And actually, this one other time I mentioned *The Odyssey*, and she seemed to think I was talking about a minivan of some sort." He reflected. "I think she may have met her husband in Ibiza. And then they got married there. On a bank holiday weekend." He wrinkled his nose. "You know what, actually, that's a little too much. I think I made that last part up." He paused. "Also, she smelled like hospital."

"It may be about class, but it's still about race," Amrita said. "It's not just white people, by the way. Racism is a trait of the lower classes everywhere. They need at least one reason to feel better than someone else." She took a sip of her tea. "Did she get fired?"

"You know, I guess she did," Ro replied, considering. He put down his fork and knife. "Sort of, anyway."

"Why do you keep referring to her in the past tense, by the way?"

"Because she's not in my life anymore." Ro picked up his fork again and took a bite of his curry. "And that's enough. I never want to speak about it again. We're changing the subject."

There was a long silence.

Amrita hesitated.

"You know," she began abruptly, "you're very brave for what you've done. To have fought back, I mean. I had a lot of liabilities. I'm a woman. I'm an attractive woman. Whom people find 'exotic.' A perfect cocktail for no one to take me seriously." She paused. "I was forced to take those things and turn them into strengths. Thank God I had money." She took a sip of her tea, reflecting. "And I did it, and it was worth it. I absolutely refuse to live in fear."

"So do I," Ro said. "You know, I'm actually super easy to manipulate. If someone makes me think that I'm afraid of something, I run straight at it. To show I'm not afraid." He looked at Amrita and immediately regretted what he had said. He had given her ammunition.

"Yes," Amrita responded, her tone artificially light. Ro could practically see her filing away his statement for future use. "You have to take your chances. And then see your chances through. Plan. Know your strengths, and play to them. Force the world to be the version of itself that suits you best."

Ro nodded. It sounded like he and Amrita had a lot in common.

A waiter cleared their plates.

"Thank you." Ro looked back at Amrita. "Shall we?"

They stood up and walked outside.

"Oh, by the way," Amrita said, pulling on her fur headband. "I got you a birthday present. A reading with a brilliant Vedic astrologer. He's booked up almost a year in advance, but he'll be in touch to schedule something."

Ro was genuinely touched. "That's so kind of you. I've never had a Vedic reading before."

"It was the least I could do to thank you for that lovely dinner." She rearranged her headband for another moment. The panthers vanished. "Well, goodbye for now. I'm heading to the Palace. I assume you're not?"

Ro shook his head.

She kissed him on both cheeks and walked away. As Amrita disappeared around the bend, Ro realized he'd forgotten to ask her a single question about Lala and Sanjay. He also realized that he had told her a little too much about himself. He had an uneasy feeling that people often did that around her.

* * *

"Hello," Ro smiled as he walked up to the spa desk. "I have a massage now, I believe."

"Oh yes, Mr. Krishna," the woman behind the desk said, typing a few keys. She paused to peer at the screen for a moment. Then she recoiled.

"Is everything all right?" Ro asked, surprised.

"Oh yes," the woman said, recovering. "We have a message for you." She rifled through a drawer, then handed Ro an envelope. Ro noticed her hand was shaking. Only the tip of the flap was sealed, so Ro gently opened the envelope with his finger and pulled out a heavy card. "MRS. B." was written at the top in fuchsia capital letters.

Mrs. B. had stylish, firm handwriting with Greek E's and used a broad-nibbed fountain pen with blue-black ink. "Dear Mr. Krishna, I was wondering if you'd like to take tea with me in my suite at the Palace this afternoon at 16:00? If you don't have a treatment then, or another conflict, of course. Otherwise, we'll catch up another time."

As the owner of the hotel, Ro thought, Mrs. B. had full access to his schedule. She knew well and good that Ro had a treatment then. But, he grudgingly acknowledged, she was still leaving it up to him. Technically.

He turned back to the woman behind the desk. "Can I reschedule that massage?"

She nodded vigorously. "I think that's an excellent idea, Mr. Krishna."

* * *

As the golf cart pulled into the drive in front of the Palace, Ro saw a man at the top of the stairs, wearing a different uniform from that of the staff. "Mr. Krishna," he said, bowing. He indicated that Ro should follow him.

Ro then received the answer to his question regarding what was on the top floor of the Palace: Mrs. B.'s rooms. Mrs. B.'s butler turned a key and pressed the elevator button. The elevator rose and the doors opened directly into Mrs. B.'s lobby.

Ro smiled as he stepped into the lovely room. Unlike the rest of Samsara, it didn't feel like Switzerland. Drawings of Indian temples hung on the wall next to Kandinsky prints. Family photographs and porcelain vases rested on antique wooden tables. He sat down in an armchair covered in Liberty cloth. Suddenly, he heard a bizarre sound through the window. What was it? He listened more closely. Whatever it was, it was awful. Like a saxophone caught in a threshing machine.

Before he could investigate further, Mrs. B. swept in. If she was Vijay's mother-in-law, she must have been in her seventies, but her skin was unlined and she could easily have passed for twenty-five years younger. Her long dark hair was streaked with grey and tied into a loose ponytail. She wore no visible makeup except for a swipe of hot pink lipstick and matching nail polish that did not entirely go with her skin tone but somehow was all the more charming for it. She was casually dressed in kurta pajama except for a tennis bracelet on her left wrist, improbably made of emeralds, and blinding diamond stud earrings, each seemingly the size of a small rock. Ro tried to decide if Mrs. B.'s earrings were bigger than Amrita's, but couldn't.

Mrs. B. curled up on the pale pink satin couch and tucked her feet underneath her delicately. "Mr. Krishna, so lovely of you to come. I'm Mrs. Banerjee, but you can call me Mrs. B."

"My absolute pleasure, Mrs. B.," Ro said, charmed. "And please, call me Ro."

She nodded, seemingly to herself, and smiled at him dazzlingly. Ro felt he had passed an invisible test somehow. "So, what brought you to Samsara?"

"Everything," Ro said.

Mrs. B. laughed.

"It was a little bizarre." Ro paused. "A friend suggested it. Then my father mentioned he knew . . ." He paused. Instinctively, he knew not to use the word "owner." "Vijay," he continued serenely. "Your son-in-law?" Mrs. B. nodded. "And I had dinner with Amrita the very same night. Whom you know as well."

"Of course." She smiled. "Her mother and I were girls at school together."

A man wearing a cream-and-green embroidered kurta pajama silently entered the room. He placed a silver platter on the table in front of Mrs. B.

"Thank you," she said, beaming at him. "Oh, Sundar, this is Rohan." She looked at Ro and corrected herself. "Ro. I hope you'll be seeing a lot of him."

"How do you do, Sundar," Ro said, half-standing.

Sundar smiled. "Enchanted," he said. "Would you like anything further?"

Mrs. B. smiled and shook her head. She turned back to Ro. "I've met your parents," she confided. "At my daughter's wedding."

"Yes. Apparently, my father and your son-in-law were the two best tennis players ever to grace the Gymkhana Club in Madras."

Mrs. B. laughed. "I'm sure they thought they were, anyway." She poured more tea into Ro's cup. "They're well? Your parents, I mean?"

"Very well."

"Now remind me, what does your father do? He's a surgeon?"

"Yes. Orthopedic."

"Ah, yes." Mrs. B. paused, pretending to try to remember. "And high profile, yes? Olympic medalists and so on?"

Ro nodded. He wasn't surprised that Mrs. B. knew exactly who his father was.

"Have you ever heard that joke?" Mrs. B. leaned forward. "Where do you hide something from an orthopedic surgeon?"

"I don't know. Where?"

"In a book. Your father struck me as quite an arrogant man," she murmured, seemingly to herself. "Your mother seemed sensible, though." She took another sip of her tea and looked at Ro, her gaze unexpectedly piercing. "Which of them do you take after?"

Ro considered it. "Neither, I'm afraid. I don't look like either of them at all. In terms of personality, I could say I'm somewhere in the middle, but even that wouldn't be true."

"How so?"

"Well, perhaps I'm a bit less fussed about external trappings of success. I don't like it when anyone knows where I am or what I'm doing. To the point of paranoia." Ro reflected. "Which is obviously a luxury I'm only allowed because of their external trappings of success."

"They did strike me as people," Mrs. B. said, pausing delicately, "who don't mind attention." She looked at Ro to see if she had offended him. "Then again, that's probably an advantage over there."

Ro sprang to his parents' defense. "Well, you know, that's excellent for a child. Not to have adults hovering all the time. I think the best way to grow up is in an atmosphere of benevolent neglect."

Mrs. B. looked at him, then evidently decided to change the subject. "You trained as a lawyer?"

How did she know that, Ro wondered. "Yes, but I stopped practicing ages ago."

"Are you happy you studied law, though? All things considered?"

Ro hadn't had this many intense conversations in a long time, let alone in the same day. "Well, being a lawyer taught me two things, I suppose."

"Which are?"

"First, how to prevaricate," Ro replied. "I can't lie to save my life. I don't know where to look, I don't know what to do with my hands. But my legal training taught me how to construct a sentence where every word is true even if the implication is not." Ro paused. "It's not something I do often, but sometimes one has no choice."

Mrs. B. laughed with delight. "I also can't lie. I never could. I'm so gullible. I've never understood how people can lie."

"I'm gullible too!" Ro laughed. "I'm almost too honest. Then again, as one of my law professors once said, nobody thinks they're a bad person."

"What's the second thing?"

"What?" It took him a moment to remember. "Oh, just to shut my mouth. Basically, to treat every conversation like it's subject to attorney-client privilege." Ro was quiet for a moment. "I don't think there's anything in my life that has gotten me to where I am more than that."

"Trust," Mrs. B. said. "It means people can trust you."

"I guess so. I never really thought of it that way, but yes. I guess it's about trust."

"And what are you doing now? For a living, I mean."

"I'm doing my best," Ro responded smoothly.

Mrs. B. raised her eyebrows. "I won't pry right now, but I will pry later." She took a sip of tea. "How did you find your lunch companions yesterday?"

Ro admired her abrupt changes of subject. It was a tactic he used himself. "I hardly know them. She seems very nice." He paused. "But he's horrible, no? Speaking of trust, I wouldn't trust him to give me directions to the corner."

Mrs. B. cackled, then turned somber. "I hope she leaves him, to be honest." Ro was disarmed by her frankness. "She deserves better. You know who they are, right?"

Ro shook his head. "No. I don't really know anything about them."

Mrs. B. raised her eyebrows. "Well, he's a politician. A rising star. In the Lok Sabha."

Ro was astonished. "Really? Who on earth would vote for that person?"

"No idea. And you don't know who she is?" Mrs. B. leaned forward, almost in disbelief.

"No." He thought for a second. "I only know her first name. Lala."

"Yes. She's Lala Chola." Mrs. B. waited for Ro's reaction. When she didn't receive a reaction, she clarified. "As in Chola Communications."

Chola Communications. The Cholas were one of the richest families in India. Ro leaned back in his chair.

"Yes," Mrs. B. said, a satisfied smile on her face. "Her father's Srivastava Chola."

"I see," he said. That explained the security team.

"She's the youngest. I've known her father for forty years," Mrs. B. continued. "He's a lovely man. Very erudite. Not what you'd expect."

"How many children do you have yourself?"

"Two daughters. Veena's married to your father's friend Vijay. They built Samsara," Mrs. B. added as an aside. The "with my money" was all but audible. "They're at Reethi Rah for Christmas. Vasantha, my younger one, married a Frenchman. A count of some sort. Looks tubercular. They spend Christmas over there. Terribly cold house. I went once. Never again. Speaking of counts,

I'll tell you what I counted: three toilets for fifteen bedrooms. Shoes on inside."

Ro shuddered. He knew that kind of house intimately.

"Objectively, I suppose my daughters married well, but their husbands don't have what we used to call character," she mused. "That count for example. What *I* can count is the number of times he's shown any initiative or courage." She paused, hand on chin, reflecting. "Actually, I can't, because you can't count a negative number. Although I must say the children are beautiful. And at least they have money," she added. "I don't know why people don't like to talk about money. I love money."

"As do I."

"Veena and Vijay are greedy," Mrs. B. continued, musing. "I keep thinking Vijay will try to kill me one year. Cut the brakes on one of those Land Rovers or something. That's why I fly but bring my own car. My driver picks me up in Dehradun."

The unpleasant noise Ro had noticed earlier suddenly became louder.

"Good gracious," Mrs. B. said. "Is that a bagpipe?"

Ro looked down. "I think so," he said quietly.

Mrs. B.'s eyes widened. "Sundar?"

Sundar appeared as if by magic.

"Please call the front desk and have them stop that noise immediately. This is not Gleneagles."

Seconds later the sound died out, like an expiring cat.

"Thank you," Ro said, with feeling.

"Certain noises can really make your hair stand on end, don't you find?" Mrs. B. shivered slightly.

"Yes, absolutely." He paused. "For me, it's the song 'Love Touch,' by Rod Stewart," he continued abruptly. "It showed up in one of my Spotify playlists a few months ago, and . . ." He trailed off.

Mrs. B. shuddered. "I remember that song. Horrible."

They sat in silence. Mrs. B. seemed lost in thought. "Or that 'Piña Colada' song," she finally murmured.

Ro winced. "Awful." He considered for a moment. "Well, at least those two reprehensible people found each other. And piña coladas are disgusting. At least they didn't ruin the gin martini."

Mrs. B. nodded. "I hadn't thought of it that way, but it's true. Whenever I see a piña colada now I think of adultery. And that song 'Brown-Eyed Girl.'" She paused, her voice lowering. "Why is she still growing? After all that business in the green grass?"

They sat in silence, both gazing at the floor.

"I'm happy you're spending time in India," Mrs. B. continued, breaking the reverie. "We need people like you to come back." She mused for a second. "It's so idiotic that the government doesn't allow dual nationality. If they did, an Indian passport could be something fun. Maybe even something to brag about. Like a Swiss one you might acquire out of nowhere. But instead they make having an Indian passport a millstone around your neck, something to throw away at the first opportunity."

"I agree, it's not the same. I would be so proud to have a full Indian passport." He looked at Mrs. B. "I hope you'll forgive my asking, but I'm curious. Why do you come here alone for the holidays?"

Mrs. B. pressed her hands together and smiled. "My husband died many years ago. He loved the mountains. I like to spend the end of the year thinking of him."

"How lovely," Ro said. "How wonderful that someone made you feel that way." He looked outside. It had begun to rain. "Also, that 'Piña Colada' song really is completely stupid. Who wants to get caught in the rain?"

"So unpleasant. I think perhaps white people do. But I think this rain will stop before the evening. Wait," Mrs. B. said. "I just had an idea. Sundar?"

Once again, Sundar appeared as if by magic.

"I want to buy bagpipe kits for all my grandchildren for Christmas. And lessons. Can you please handle this?"

She cackled.

"Yes, Madam," Sundar nodded.

Ro smiled, admiring. She actually cackled! Vicious!

He stood up, and Mrs. B. did as well. She kissed him on both cheeks. "Lovely to chat."

* * *

Leaving the Residence after a long nap, Ro could already make out the music from the Christmas party. He walked toward the restaurant, shivering slightly. There was a nip in the air. As he approached the restaurant, he saw Lala headed there too, from the direction of the spa. He waved.

"Headed to dinner?" she asked, arriving next to him.

"Yep." Ro looked around. "Where's Sanjay?"

"Sick," Lala replied, terse. "Stomach bug."

Then Ro felt someone link their arm in his from behind. Proprietarily.

"Finally!" Amrita exclaimed. "Where have you been?" She steered him into the restaurant, ignoring Lala. Ro had no choice except to go with her. He looked at Lala over his shoulder, apologetic.

Lala's eyes went dark.

* * *

The hotel had gone all out with the Christmas decorations. A stage had been set up at the far end of the room near the terrace. Joss was standing right by the door. "Look! Your favorite." He pointed at the lavish buffet.

"I'm ordering à la carte," Ro replied. "You remember Amrita?"

"Of course we remember each other," Amrita chided him, amused. "We've all been here for ages. You're the only late arrival." Joss and Amrita kissed each other on the cheek.

Catherine had already commandeered a table for eight near the entrance. "Oh, hi, guys. So, Chris, Joss, Ro, Amrita, Amit, Catherine," she said, counting on her fingers. Ro couldn't place Amit for a second, then remembered: Amit was the one with the great hair. He pursed his lips. "And who else?"

"Mahesh?" Joss shrugged. "I don't know if he's coming, though."

"Great." Catherine frowned. "That leaves one place."

"Let's save it for Mitchell," Amrita said.

Catherine glared at Ro. He shrugged. Idly, he reminded himself to look up the meaning of the name "Mitchell" later. He hoped it meant something horrible.

Amrita took off her headband and, placing it on the table, shook out her luxurious brown hair. Ro saw she was wearing the same turquoise and diamond earrings she had worn in London. She winked at Ro and headed toward the buffet.

Then Fairuza appeared. "Is this seat," she began, but before she could finish, they both overheard a loud "Hello!" Amrita was near the door, kissing the VB on the cheek and pointing toward the table. The VB looked over and lit up when he saw Catherine and Joss. "Never mind," Fairuza whispered, vanishing.

"Hi, everyone," the VB said, taking the seat next to Catherine. Catherine turned away, examining her nails. "You know, it's so weird. I think this is the first time I haven't spent Christmas at home."

"Shame you're not there," Ro responded, polite.

Catherine cracked up.

"But I'm going to go FaceTime with them in half an hour," he continued. "Gonna grab some food. Looks great. I love a buffet." He left the table.

"You're literally just bullying him. Both of you," Joss said reproachfully. "I have half a mind to tell him to stay here while I get his food for him. Just to force you to hang out with him more."

"That's not funny. Do not stop him leaving." Ro grinned suddenly. "Don't stop the VB leaving."

"Streetlights. People." Joss rolled his eyes and stood up. "Gotta head back-stage." He saw Ro's puzzled look. "Chris's top-secret dance performance, remember?"

"I think pretty much everyone knows already," Catherine said, flagging down a waiter. "Could we order off the menu, please?" The waiter turned to the buffet behind him, looking baffled, but regained his composure. "Of course, Madam. What would you like?"

"Whatever the chef recommends for a Pitta tonight." She appraised Ro with a glance, then turned back to the waiter. "He'll have the same."

The waiter moved off. "How'd you know I was a Pitta?"

"It's not rocket surgery, as the Australians like to say. You're probably a Pitta-Vata. Like me. You and I are pretty similar, actually."

The waiter soon came back with two modest plates of curry and rice. "Perfect."

A moment later Amrita came back, radiant. "You won't believe it. They've found my watch."

Ro smiled. "I'm so glad. I really couldn't believe someone had stolen it. Where was it?"

"I didn't ask. Probably the spa. Anyway, it's at reception. I'm going to go get it right now." Amrita shuddered. "I'm so relieved. It's maybe the only thing I have that I would have been really very upset to lose."

"Godspeed," Ro said. "Hurry, there's a dance performance in . . ." He looked down at his own watch. It was 8:47. "Thirteen minutes exactly."

"Ah, yes, I heard about that." Pulling her fur headband back on, Amrita moved toward the door.

Ro and Catherine ate, alone at the table. "Where did everyone go?" Ro asked.

"Unclear."

"Hello!" Mahesh appeared behind Catherine with a plate of food. He looked back toward the buffet with mild distaste. "So much waste," he murmured.

Suddenly, the lights dimmed and loud bhangra music began to play. The staff started to clap in time with the music. The guests started doing the same.

A dance troupe came onstage. Spotlights turned onto them while the lights in the rest of the room continued to dim. Suddenly, Ro felt a stir in the room and craned his head to see better. Chris had arrived onstage. He began to dance good-naturedly, moving among different members of the troupe.

The troupe performed a couple of short skits in Hindi that led the Indian guests to dissolve into laughter. Someone nudged Ro's arm. "I can translate for you later," Amit whispered to him.

Another song came on. Ro clapped along to the beat. Chris obviously had an excellent sense of rhythm, displaying effortless physicality.

After some particularly intricate moves, Chris left the stage to much applause. He reappeared moments later on the other side of Ro, kissing Catherine. "Where's Joss?" Ro whispered. Chris shrugged.

The troupe continued for several more songs. New dancers in different costumes joined the dancers already onstage. Ro looked around the table. Amit, Mahesh, Catherine, and Chris were all clapping along with the whole room, fully absorbed by the performance.

Finally, after two encores and much cheering, the lights came on, revealing that the staff had set up a bar outside during the performance. Everyone in the room got up and started moving toward it, chatting.

Ro saw Lala standing near the door. She had clearly been crying. He looked around. Nobody could overhear him. "Are you all right?"

"Not really." She dabbed at her eyes with a handkerchief. "Where's your friend?"

"What friend? Oh." Ro realized she was talking about Amrita. "I don't know. I haven't seen her in a while. You guys have the same headband, though. That fur thing."

"This?" Lala unconsciously reached up. "I bought it in the shop here last year."

"I actually thought you were her for a second," Ro said. Lala shot daggers at him. "Sorry." Ro looked around. "Where's Mr. Lala?"

"Still not well. I offered to stay in the room with him, but he insisted I leave." She frowned. "Not too nicely, if I'm being honest."

"Fair enough. You said it was a stomach thing?" Lala nodded. "That's the worst. He's probably trying to preserve whatever shred of dignity he can."

Lala thought about it for a second, then nodded. "That could be true."

Catherine approached them, Amit in tow behind her. "We're going to go back to our terrace to look at the stars. Want to join? Both of you, of course."

Ro looked at Lala. She smiled.

"Yes. I'd love to."

* * *

In the end, seven of them began to move down the path toward the Forresters' villa. Lala, Amit, Mahesh, Catherine, and Chris were together, talking animatedly and laughing. Ro and Joss lagged slightly behind. Ro shuddered. The path really felt quite sinister at night. He turned to look at Joss, who looked even neater than usual. "Wait. Did you just take a shower?"

Joss flushed. "Yeah."

"Why? And when?"

"Oh, right after the performance," Joss said, not meeting Ro's eye. "It was hot back there. All those lights."

After following the path through the trees past a couple of sharp bends, Mahesh stopped. "Does your wheelchair work on the grass?" he asked Amit.

"Sure does," Amit replied. "It's an SUW." Lala giggled.

"Good." Mahesh pointed through the trees. "There's a meadow through here. Where we came yesterday," he added to Ro.

"Let's keep going," Catherine said. "We have a terrific view from our terrace."

"I really think the best view is in the meadow," Mahesh said. "There's no light at all."

"I'm cold, though," Joss said. "I'd rather not be outside lying on grass."

"Hold on." Ro turned to Mahesh. "Are we near that door we used yesterday?"

Mahesh nodded.

"What door?" Amit asked.

"Give me five. I have a surprise for everyone." Ro started jogging away.

"Wait for me!" Lala caught up with him. "What are we doing?" she asked, once the others were out of earshot.

"There's a hidden entrance to the spa here. We can get some blankets from the laundry." They walked behind the trees and down the hidden ramp. Ro pushed open the door.

The lights inside were dimmed. Admittedly, the corridor was a little eerie. Ro sensed Lala's hesitation. "Don't worry. It's right here somewhere."

He took a few steps down the hallway and stopped in front of a swinging door on his left. "I think this is it." He gingerly pushed it open and was dazzled. The fluorescent lighting in the laundry felt practically nuclear coming after the dimly lit corridor.

Ro paused, allowing his eyes to adjust. As he had remembered, the walls were covered with rows upon rows of kurta pajamas. In front of him was an enormous vat where more kurta pajamas were being washed. The room, understandably, smelled like bleach. "Look! They're over there." Lala pointed to a stack of blankets. They each took a few and headed back outside.

Now that his eyes had adjusted to the fluorescence, Ro found himself blind as a bat when they emerged outside. "We got blankets!" he shouted into the dark. The group cheered and applauded. "Lala? I think you'll have to guide me. I can't see a damn thing."

Lala didn't respond. Ro turned around.

Lala was behind him, still. She had let the blankets fall to the ground and was looking past the trees lining the path. Then she put her hand over her mouth.

Ro looked in the same direction, but couldn't see anything at all. "What is it? Lala? Are you OK?"

Ignoring him, Lala suddenly rushed over toward the trees. Ro sprinted after her. "What's going on?" he heard Joss call behind him, concerned.

"Look!" Lala cried out, almost in hysterics. Ro could just about make out patches of white, flashing in the undergrowth.

Lala screamed and screamed.

And then Ro finally saw what—or rather, who—was there.

Amrita.

Her neck at an unnatural angle.

Those gorgeous turquoise eyes, open. Staring at him.

Lifeless.

Ro heard someone running behind him.

"Stand back," Catherine ordered. "Everybody, stay exactly where you are." She moved toward the body and, crouching, began to examine it.

Catherine, Ro thought absently. Well, well. Then, for the first time in his life, he realized he was about to faint.

DAY 4

(December 26)

Ro lazily stretched in bed as he woke up, loose-limbed and relaxed. His eyes were still closed. He had no idea where he was, but he remained unruffled. This had happened to him before.

Half-opening his eyes, he registered he was in a bed made up with cool, soft sky-blue linens. Thick white piping edged the pillowcases and duvet.

Then he turned onto his back and was amazed. The room's paneled ceiling was painted the exact same sky-blue as the sheets upon which he was lying, and the ceiling's moldings and detailing were also picked out in white.

The thought came to him unprompted.

Am I dead?

He turned his head. Mullioned windows, behind which the tops of trees waved at him. Ever so gently.

He had not died and he was not in Heaven.

At least, probably not.

He turned his head the other way. White walls, also paneled.

Yet . . .

Where was he?

He had to sit up, he decided. As he did so, his eyes fell upon a painting on the wall facing the bed.

Was that a Matisse?

At that moment, there was a knock on the door. "Come in," Ro said automatically.

The door opened, and Sundar appeared, in uniform, carrying a silver tray. "Good morning, Sir." He walked across the room and placed the tray on an ormolu table that Ro hadn't yet noticed. Sundar turned to the windows to open the curtains and paused. They were already open. He clearly hadn't expected that. He contented himself by moving toward them and tying them neatly with the sash that Ro had left hanging the previous night.

Standing back up, Sundar turned toward Ro. "If it's convenient, Mrs. Banerjee would like to see you in twenty minutes. She apologizes for having asked you to sleep here."

And then Ro remembered. Amrita was dead.

"You will find any toiletries you need in the bathroom. There are fresh kurta pajamas in the closet." Sundar cleared his throat, a little embarrassed. "Other things you might need are in the drawer here," he added, indicating a small white wooden dresser painted with flowers. "But please let us know if you require anything else, at all."

"I'm sure it's all fine," Ro said, slowly getting out of bed. "And twenty minutes should be ample."

"I'll let her know." Sundar smiled and left the room.

What were the other things Sundar thought he might need? Ro ambled over to the dresser and opened the top drawer. It was filled with Calvin Klein boxer briefs in every color imaginable.

He unfolded a few. They were all size medium.

* * *

Mrs. B. sat on the sofa, one finger on her lips, her brow furrowed, visibly trying to decide where to start. Ro sat watching her. He liked her tremendously, he realized. So many people started speaking before knowing what they wanted to say.

"Thank you for sleeping here last night," she began, somewhat abruptly. "I wanted to be able to speak to you first thing this morning."

Ro nodded.

"I don't want you to think I'm coldhearted, but I want to leave the tragedy of Rita's death to one side for the moment." She looked down, shaking her head. "I am devastated that this happened at Samsara. Of all places."

She looked at Ro. "Ro, I like what I've seen of you very much so far. You seem sensible. And sensitive. Which is a rarer combination than it ought to be."

"Thank you," Ro said politely.

"And more concretely, you're a lawyer, and we know your family," she continued, taking a sip of tea. She put the cup back in its saucer and shrugged. "I'm sorry, I don't mean to be a snob. But that's just how the world works, I suppose."

"I'm very happy to help you however I can," Ro said, realizing as he said it that he meant it. "But I'm afraid I'm not sure what you're getting at."

Mrs. B. leaned forward.

"Ro, this is going to be tricky for us to navigate. For Samsara, I mean." She hesitated. "I'm not quite sure what I'm asking of you, because I'm not quite sure what is happening. But I'd like you to be involved in the investigation on our behalf."

Ro paused. He hadn't expected that.

Misunderstanding his silence, Mrs. B. rushed back in. "Of course, we will cover the cost of your stay. And invite you back for another two weeks whenever you choose at our expense."

Ro shook his head. "That's not why I hesitated, but thank you, that's very gracious. Let me think for a moment." He ran his hands through his hair, distracted. "All right," he said finally. "First of all, I need to know what the hotel's objective is."

Mrs. B. sighed, relieved. Ro had understood. "The most important thing is not to have a fuss. To make it go away."

"Will you tell the guests what happened?" Ro asked, curious.

Mrs. B. thought for a moment, then shook her head. "I don't think so. At least not yet. Preferably never." She saw Ro's look of surprise. "People die in hotels all the time. All the time. And nobody knows. And on planes. Planes have corpse cupboards. Did you know that?"

"You know, I think I'd heard that somewhere once," Ro said, nodding. "Corpse Cupboard would be a good band name. A heavy metal band, maybe."

He registered Mrs. B.'s puzzled look. "Sorry. I'm just not sure what is and what isn't appropriate right now."

"Don't worry." Mrs. B. went silent for a moment. "I don't want you to think that I'm only concerned about the hotel. About money. That isn't it at all." She shook her head. "I've known—I knew—Rita since she was born." She paused. "And I am fairly if not completely sure that this was not a random killing."

Ro considered for a moment, then nodded. Mrs. B. was almost certainly right, he thought, although he didn't yet know why.

"I know this phrase is overused with regards to those who have passed on," Mrs. B. continued, "but I do think she would have wanted the utmost discretion." Suddenly, Mrs. B. looked very sad. "And that's what Meena would have wanted. Her mother. I can assure you of that."

"I agree with you. I didn't know Amrita well, but she was so private. So self-assured. She would have never wanted a spectacle." He thought for a second. "Particularly a spectacle she couldn't control."

There was a long pause.

"So will you do it?" Mrs. B. asked finally. Ro was charmed by how vulnerable she sounded. Everyone likes to feel needed, he reflected. He had questions, but they seemed unimportant in the end. Also, he had liked Amrita tremendously, and was very sad that she was gone. He wanted to do his part.

He stared up at the ceiling fan, gathering his thoughts. And then he remembered something else.

"Yes," he said. "I'll do it."

Maybe, just maybe, this was Pendy's mission for him.

"Good." Mrs. B. stood up.

"Wait a second. We're not quite finished."

Mrs. B. sat back down expectantly while Ro collected his thoughts.

"OK," he said finally. "What does this investigation entail? And with whom?"

Mrs. B. exhaled violently. "How stupid of me. I should have started with that. I called the Police Commissioner in Delhi last night. He's sending up one of his men." She looked at her watch. "Actually, he should be here by now.

He'll run the investigation. We'll meet in the conference room downstairs at 10 o'clock."

"All right."

"What's your treatment schedule today?" Mrs. B. asked.

Ro opened his eyes wide. "I was just assuming that all of that is canceled."

"Nonsense," Mrs. B. said briskly. "Today might be busy, but we can certainly fit in at least one massage. Perhaps at lunchtime. I'll have Sundar organize it."

"Thank you so much." Then, shuddering, Ro remembered Dr. Menon. And his eyes that somehow wouldn't shut up. "I also have a doctor's appointment. And I need to spend an hour in the steam room. Doctor's orders."

"I'll make sure you have time."

"Thank you." Ro thought of something else. "There's another thing I need to tell you. But will you promise that this stays entirely between us?"

Mrs. B. nodded.

"Please say it out loud."

"I promise," Mrs. B. said, her eyes twinkling.

"I had a conversation with Lala yesterday. Lala Mehta." He saw the look in Mrs. B.'s eye. "Lala Chola, I mean. Anyway. I told her I'd be her lawyer. And that she could speak to me confidentially."

"Really!" Mrs. B. raised her eyebrows. "What on earth brought that about?"

"Well, obviously, I can't tell you. I'm just wondering if it's a conflict of interest."

"Would you like to enter into a legal agreement with Samsara?" Mrs. B. asked.

"I don't think that's necessary just yet." Ro paused. "But what about this thing with Lala?"

"I can't imagine it's a conflict," Mrs. B. said, musing. "That poor girl. She's lovely. She's already involved. She discovered the body. They'll want to keep this as quiet as possible."

Then Mrs. B. winced.

"Oh, dear."

"What's wrong?" Ro leaned forward.

"I forgot the worst part." Mrs. B. closed her eyes.

As a former lawyer, Ro had heard that tone before. "What's the worst part?" he asked dryly.

"Sundar," Mrs. B. replied. Ro was confused, but then Sundar appeared out of nowhere. "Please ask Mrs. Forrester to come by."

Mrs. B. looked back at Ro. She opened her mouth to say something, then stood up instead.

"I'll let her explain."

* * *

Ro had deliberately chosen Mrs. B.'s usual spot on the sofa as a power move. Catherine was standing by the window, trying not to pace.

"Mrs. B. has told me that you're going to represent the hotel during the investigation," Catherine began. "And your background check came back OK, so I'm trusting you here."

At first, Ro was surprised. Then he was furious at this invasion of his privacy. He was about to stand up and leave, but then he figured it out. "Oh," he said.

"Sorry. I'm not the best at explaining things," Catherine admitted.

"Like that you're CIA?"

"For example." Catherine paused. "How did you guess?"

"Come on, Catherine." Ro leaned back on Mrs. B.'s sofa and crossed his arms, a bit smug. "I wasn't born yesterday. Everyone in the Horn of Africa is CIA. And, for future reference, nobody ever specifies 'consular,'" he added, making air quotes.

"Fair enough," Catherine replied, tense.

They sat in silence for a moment.

"Sundar, could I have some coffee?" Ro asked the air. Sundar was nowhere in sight. "With milk."

Sundar appeared with coffee almost instantaneously.

Ro took a sip. "Yum. Blue Mountain, I think. Anyhow. A movie star's wife. The best cover ever."

"That's not why I did it." Catherine sat down abruptly.

"Did what?" Ro asked, demure.

She held up her hand. "Please. We're not here to talk about me. I'm not going to answer questions about my life. Or my background. They're not germane."

Ro tried to raise one eyebrow quizzically, but ended up raising both of them. He didn't particularly care. "Fine." He crossed his arms again and leaned back.

"The easiest way to describe it is that I occasionally get involved with things in an official capacity."

"How do I know I can believe a word you say?" Ro was genuinely intrigued. "How do I know you work for the US and not, like, Belarus?"

"If you want, I can have the director of the CIA scratch his neck at a particular minute on C-SPAN today." Catherine spread her hands and shrugged. "But haven't we all been through enough?"

Ro considered for a moment. "No, that's OK."

"Good." Catherine paused. "How well did you know Amrita?"

"I felt like I knew her, but I actually didn't know her at all," Ro replied. "What about you?"

"I knew her well enough to know that lots of people had lots of reasons to kill her."

Ro saw that Catherine was waiting for his reaction. He decided not to react.

Catherine stood back up.

"You'll find out more eventually. I guess we're in this together now."

"But why are we in this together?" Ro still wasn't sure what was going on. "Besides Go Big Green."

"Because I know you didn't kill her." Catherine began to pace.

"Well, as it happens, I didn't. But why are you so sure of that?"

"Because the two of us never left the dinner table," Catherine replied. "We didn't go to the buffet. And we didn't leave during the performance."

"Oh." Catherine was right. He hadn't left the table at all. "It's interesting. This is the sort of place where nobody has any idea where anybody else ever is. But this was the one time that everyone was in the same place."

He looked at Catherine.

"Will you be in the meeting with the detective? Are you going to be an official part of this?"

"Yes and no. He's supposed to be good, by the way. Oxford, apparently."

"One last question. Just so I know how to behave. How much does Chris know about all this?"

All of a sudden, Catherine looked very tired. "Not much."

Something else occurred to Ro.

"Actually, Catherine."

"What?"

"I just want to be clear." Ro paused, trying to figure out how to put this delicately. "You say you're sure I didn't kill Amrita because we were together the whole time. But I can't say the same for you. I think you were with me, but I can't swear to it. I wasn't paying attention."

Catherine smiled thinly. "You might end up pretty good at this."

With that, she left the room.

* * *

As he couldn't find the stairs, Ro took the elevator down one floor at a few minutes to ten. The semi-abandoned rooms he had visited just a few days ago were now unrecognizable. Uniformed police buzzed back and forth between the two rooms on the east side of the building.

Seeing Ro, a police officer sprang to attention, evidently on notice for his arrival. "Sir!" He pointed to the front room on the other side of the staircase.

"Thank you," Ro said, turning around.

The air immediately smelled different.

He sniffed at it.

Fresh paint?

* * *

The old furniture was gone. In its place were a couple of large Formica tables pushed together and several uncomfortable-looking plastic chairs that made Ro think of a high school cafeteria.

Mrs. B. sat expectantly at the end of the table, her coffee mug in her hands, looking for all the world like it was her first day of school.

Catherine was pouring herself coffee from an ornate silver urn on the side table.

Ro turned to the right. He did not recall having seen the large mirror on the far wall before. And there was still that weird smell of fresh paint.

He took the seat next to Mrs. B. "Hello," she said, beaming.

"Coffee?" Catherine asked him.

"Yes, thank you. Just milk."

She handed him a cup and sat down on his other side.

"Is the investigator here yet?" he asked them.

"Yes, he is," a voice said. A man entered the room and closed the door behind him.

He looked to be in his late thirties and was dressed in a black suit that looked neither cheap nor expensive, with a white shirt and a carelessly tied black tie. He looked at the three of them, and his face fell. Then, recovering, he walked to the far end of the room and stopped at the end of the table, his back to the mirror.

"I am Inspector Singh."

Ro looked at Mrs. B. and Catherine and, seeing no movement from them, decided to go first. "I'm Ro Krishna."

"I know who all of you are," the inspector replied briefly, setting his bag on the table and beginning to dig through it. "I think we should get started straight away."

He pulled some folders out of his bag and set them down on the table.

"I'll begin by interviewing every person who interacted with Miss Dey last night, including the three of you. For the moment, we are keeping the news of Miss Dey's death as quiet as possible."

He looked at Mrs. B.

"Per the information we received from Samsara, we have informed her sister as next of kin. Miss Dey was unmarried with no children. Her parents are deceased?"

Mrs. B. gave a brief nod.

"Actually, wait." Ro half-raised a hand.

The inspector looked at him.

"She was widowed."

"I'd forgotten about that." Mrs. B. sighed. "It was a long time ago."

"What happened?" Catherine asked, leaning forward.

"Wait, please." The inspector held up his hand. "I want us to have our procedures in place first."

Ro nodded admiringly. A man after his own heart.

The inspector took a moment to collect his thoughts.

"All right. I will be interviewing witnesses in this room all day."

He turned to the mirror.

"The hotel was kind enough to install this two-way mirror overnight so that you can watch from next door. There will be a microphone and an audio feed."

That's why it smelled like fresh paint. Ro turned to Mrs. B.

"I thought it might come in handy one day after all this is over," she explained, vaguely waving one hand. "Interviews and so on."

"Why didn't you just put in an actual video camera?" Catherine asked, unable to contain herself.

"You know, the thought didn't even occur to me." Mrs. B. paused. "But video would have been so much less fun, don't you agree?"

Catherine sighed. "What if one of us has a question for the person you're questioning?"

Inspector Singh sighed in return. "That's really not your place, but I will give you my telephone number so that you can text me. If absolutely necessary." He gave them his number. "I'll put my phone on silent except for notifications from the three of you."

"Thank you for being so cooperative," Mrs. B. said, demure.

Catherine, however, was visibly impatient. "Do you have the cause of death yet?"

Inspector Singh nodded. "She was hit on the back of the neck with a rock. The blow broke her neck. Death was almost instantaneous."

"Was it one of the rocks lining the path?" Ro asked.

"Yes. Miss Dey was killed on the path and then her body was dragged to where it was discovered. We found bloodstains."

Ro shivered. "How heavy are the rocks? Is there any indication of whether the killer is a man or a woman?"

"None whatsoever. The rocks are heavy, but a woman in good condition could have done this."

"What was she doing on the path at that hour?" Catherine asked.

"She told me that she always walked up to the Palace." Ro looked at the inspector. "You should check if any of the golf cart drivers remember seeing or driving her last night."

The inspector raised his eyebrows at him. "We already have, naturally. They do not."

"Sorry." Ro was a little abashed.

"Have you found any DNA evidence yet?" Mrs. B. looked at Catherine and Ro. "I watch *CSI*," she added, apologetic.

"The body has been taken to the police station in Rishikesh, and they are doing all necessary examinations there."

The inspector paused, then took off his rimless spectacles and polished them on his shirt. He stared out of the window for a moment, lost in his thoughts, before coming to and putting his glasses back on.

"Before we begin to speak to anyone else, I want to speak to the three of you. I want to have an idea of who this woman was. You all knew her well?"

Mrs. B. nodded.

Catherine half-shrugged.

"I barely knew her," Ro said.

"How would you describe her in one word?" Inspector Singh asked unexpectedly.

Ro had no idea, but then the word appeared. "Shrewd."

Inspector Singh looked at Mrs. B. "What about you?"

"I really don't know." But then she did. "Persuasive."

"And you, Mrs. Forrester?"

Catherine didn't need much time. "Calculating."

Inspector Singh paused for a moment.

"I've found, in general, that the most recent acquaintances have the most apt observations." He turned to Ro. "Accordingly, Mr. Krishna, I'd like to begin with you."

Ro looked at the others. They both nodded slowly.

"All right. Let me just get another coffee."

* * *

Inspector Singh paced in front of the mirror while Ro sat on one of the uncomfortable plastic chairs. Catherine and Mrs. B. were in the room next door checking the quality of the audio feed. Finally, the inspector perched, his hands on the table, and opened his mouth to ask Ro his first question. His phone buzzed. Annoyed, he looked at the message. He sighed and moved to the side of the table.

"What was that?"

"I was blocking their view." Inspector Singh opened a notebook that was on the table. "Mrs. Forrester has told me she believes you cannot have committed the murder. She says you were in her presence the entire evening."

"Yes. But I can't swear that she was always there. She probably was there. I just wasn't paying attention."

"She told me that too." The inspector looked at the notebook again, then looked at Ro. "Let's take our time, to the degree we can. Can you please tell me how you met Rita Dey?"

Ro considered for a second. "I first met Amrita in London, in November. A friend brought her to my birthday dinner."

"Amrita?"

"Yes." Ro shook his head. "I forgot. She told me her legal name was Rita. But I think she always went by Amrita."

"Her passport says Rita. Do you know why she went by another name?"

"I think it was a family thing. But, really, I think everyone called her Amrita. You know, you should probably call her Amrita too, because otherwise anyone you speak to is going to get confused. The only person I've heard call her Rita is Mrs. Banerjee."

"What was her connection with Belgium? She had a Belgian passport."

"Well, she was Belgian." Ro was slightly puzzled. "The same way I'm American. I'm not sure I understand the question."

"Of course." The inspector sounded contrite. "But did she actually live in Belgium?"

"I'm not sure," Ro said, considering. "She grew up there." He thought for a second, then shook his head. "She was maybe born there, actually. I can't remember. She told me she mostly lived in London."

The inspector made a note. "Who brought Miss Dey to the dinner?"

"It was a friend of hers from school whom I'd gotten to know recently." Then Ro's heart sank. "Oh, dear."

"What's wrong?"

"I just realized I'm going to have to tell him about Amrita. I think they were really very close. And he's totally unreachable right now."

Perhaps he should tell Bronya, he reflected, then decided against it. She probably wouldn't be able to reach Alex either.

"Did you spend much time with Miss Dey once you'd arrived here?"

"I mean, I only got here a few days ago." It felt like he had been at Samsara forever. "We had lunch on my second day here. The day she died, actually." Ro paused, shivering briefly. "But that lunch was the only time I ever had an in-depth conversation with her."

"What did you discuss?"

"Life, growing up, careers, family. Lots of things."

"What did Miss Dey do for a living?"

"I'm not sure that she did anything for a living." Ro shrugged. "My impression was that she had family money. They were originally in the jewel trade."

"Did she seem agitated or fearful in any way?"

Ro thought for a long second, then slowly shook his head. "No. On the contrary. She was one of the most self-assured people I've ever met."

He sat up a little straighter.

"You know, that's what's so strange. She was very, very astute. And aware. It's inconceivable to me that she wouldn't have known she was in danger." He shrugged. "Maybe she did and just didn't show it. I suppose anyone would feel safe at Samsara regardless of what was happening in the world outside."

"Were there any staff or guests with whom she seemed particularly friendly?"

"Hard to say. She interacted with a lot of people." Ro thought about it. "She spent a lot of time with that horrid visiting meditation teacher. Mitchell something. With me, I suppose. And the Forresters. She knew a lot of the staff, but I didn't notice anyone she was close to."

The inspector stood up. "Before we go into yesterday's events, is there anything else you think I should know?"

"I can't think of anything." Ro shook his head. He certainly wasn't going to mention his conversation with Lala. "But I'll let you know if something comes to mind."

Inspector Singh nodded. "All right. Please tell me what happened yesterday in your own words."

Ro thought for a second about where to start. "Well, it was Christmas," he began. "So the hotel had a big buffet dinner. And a surprise dance performance."

"Just speak about the evening at your own rhythm," the inspector interjected. "I'll ask you questions when I have them. When did you arrive at dinner?"

"About 8:15, I'd say. It started at 8."

"With whom were you seated?"

Ro counted on his fingers. "Me, Catherine, Chris, Joss, Amrita, Amit, Mitchell, Mahesh. Eight of us. But because it was a buffet I don't think all of us were ever at the table at the same time. And a couple of people showed up late or left early."

"We'll come back to this." Inspector Singh made a note of the names. "What was the schedule for the rest of the evening?"

"We ate from around 8:30 to 9. Then at 9 there was a surprise dance performance. Though everyone seemed to know about it in advance, so it wasn't really that much of a surprise. I'd guess that ended around a quarter to ten."

Ro paused, trying to remember.

"After that there were drinks outside, but someone had the idea to go look at the stars. I think it was Amit. So we started going down the path. I ran into the spa to get some blankets, and Lala came with me." He shivered. "Then Lala saw her body as we were coming back."

"Do you know what time that was?"

"Not precisely. Maybe 10, 10:15."

"Was the body hidden?"

"It was hidden from the main path and fairly hidden from the side door to the spa. And that door wouldn't have been used at night anyway." Ro paused. "I don't think most people know about that door, actually."

"How did you know about the door?"

"Mahesh showed it to me the other day when we did a session outside."

Inspector Singh made a note. "What can you tell me about Miss Dey's movements and demeanor at dinner?"

"She seemed normal. It was her idea for Mitchell to sit with us. Oh, wait." Ro literally slapped his forehead. "I forgot something very important."

"What?"

"Hold on a second." Ro collected his thoughts. "Amrita lost her watch a few days ago. She was very upset about it."

"Her watch?"

"Yes. That's why she was outside in the first place."

"How do you mean?"

Ro shook his head. "I'm explaining badly. Let me start at the beginning. Amrita wore a watch that had belonged to her mother. A Cartier Panthère. It had gone missing. She was quite upset, naturally."

Ro paused, remembering.

"I thought it would turn up because I didn't think this was the sort of place where things got stolen. Anyway, people are parading around much more expensive jewelry and watches than that. Including her."

"When did it go missing?"

"She wasn't sure," Ro replied. "She thought maybe at the spa the previous day, but she didn't know. I heard about it two days ago. But anyway, that doesn't matter. During dinner, she got a message that the watch had been found and was at the Palace. She left dinner to go get it straight away."

"What time did this happen?" the inspector asked, hovering over his notebook with a pen.

"I actually looked at my watch as it happened. It was 8:47."

"Why did you look at your watch at that moment?"

Ro shrugged. "I guess because we were talking about watches." The inspector nodded. "Also, weirdly, we had almost the same watch."

Ro held out his wrist. The inspector examined his watch briefly.

"And mine was—is—my father's. So I must have reflexively looked at mine."

"Did Miss Dey leave the table at all before then?"

"Of course she did. It was a buffet." He thought. "Actually, she got the message while she was away from the table. I don't know who gave it to her."

"And did you see her alive after that?"

"No, I didn't." Ro shivered.

The inspector paused for a moment while Ro regained his composure.

"I'm sorry," he said softly. "This must all still be quite a shock."

"It is." Ro closed his eyes, then reopened them. "Let's continue."

"Let's go back to the dinner. How many people were there?"

"I'd say pretty much everyone at the hotel. It was included in the cost of the room, so I don't know why anyone wouldn't have gone." He saw the inspector's mild surprise. "Rich people love free things."

"Indeed." The inspector gave a brief, wry grin. "Let's go through the list of people sitting at your table. I'll ask what you recall regarding their movements. Is that all right?"

"Of course."

"Catherine Forrester."

Ro shrugged. "As I said earlier, I think she was with me the whole time, but I can't swear it."

"Chris Forrester."

"Chris and Joss were with us at the beginning of dinner, but Chris was in the surprise dance performance. So they left early to get ready. Probably at around 8:30."

"They'd gone before Miss Dey left to get her watch?"

"Yes. Definitely. Actually, wait." A thought had occurred to him. "Did Amrita have her watch on? When she was found? It would be useful to know. In terms of timing."

"We'll check." Inspector Singh stood up, opened the door, and barked something at a junior officer in Hindi. He closed the door and came back to the table, sitting down. He consulted his notes. "Joss Ziemssen."

"Same as Chris. Left at 8:30, came back after the performance." Then he remembered that Joss hadn't come straight back. And the shower.

Ro took a sip of water to hide his unease.

Thankfully, the inspector seemed absorbed by his notebook.

"Amit Chopra."

"Oh!" Ro said, happy to be back on safe ground. "He arrived right after the performance started. Probably at, like, 9:05."

"Why was he late?" the inspector inquired.

"I think he had some work to do." Ro thought for a second. "Anyway, unless he's completely faked his injury, he couldn't have done it. He couldn't have picked up a rock while sitting in a wheelchair and then have hit Amrita on the back of her neck."

"You'd be surprised," the inspector responded dryly. He looked back down at the notebook. "Mitchell Charney."

"He also left dinner early. He said he was going to FaceTime with his family in the States for Christmas. Actually, wait." Ro turned to the mirror. "Catherine, did he ever even come back from the buffet? I don't think he did."

The inspector's phone buzzed. He consulted it. "No. She doesn't think he came back either."

"Huh." Ro slumped back in his seat. "So he must have left before Chris and Joss. Just before 8:30. Definitely before Amrita."

"Mahesh Subramaniam."

"Subramaniam?" Ro replied, surprised. "I didn't know he was Tamil." Ro tried to remember. "Mahesh was hardly at the table at all during dinner. But he's a yoga teacher, he knows all the guests. He was definitely there for the whole performance, though."

The inspector paused. "Isn't it unusual for the staff to socialize with the guests? To eat dinner together and so on?"

"Well, in general, the staff doesn't socialize with the guests," Ro explained. "But I think the yoga teachers are different. They're like our professors. I think most of them have graduate degrees. You should ask Mrs. Banerjee about that, though, I'm not sure."

"When did Mr. Subramaniam come back to the table?"

"Right before the performance started. So a couple minutes before 9, I'd say."

"Lala Mehta."

"I didn't see much of her during the evening," Ro replied truthfully. "Just before dinner and after the dance performance."

"And Sanjay Mehta?" the inspector asked, his pen hovering over his pad.

Oh. It slowly dawned on him.

"He wasn't there all evening."

The inspector pounced. "And why was Mr. Mehta absent?"

Every word Ro chose would be important. "I think he wasn't feeling well. An upset stomach."

The inspector closed his notebook and looked at Ro.

"In your opinion, is there anything else that you think I should know right now?"

Ro could think of a few things the inspector would probably want to know, but he didn't think the inspector should know them right now.

"No," he replied. Honestly.

The inspector's phone buzzed.

"Mrs. Forrester thinks I should interview her next. The audio and video connections are fine, by the way, so she suggests we reconvene in here."

* * *

Mrs. B., Inspector Singh, and Ro spent the next twenty minutes reviewing a lengthy and exhaustive confidentiality agreement that Catherine had had printed in advance of her interview. "I'm sorry, Catherine, but I refuse to be held responsible for things I might say in my sleep," Ro said, pushing the document away.

"Just cross that section out then," she replied, terse.

"I have to ask the Police Commissioner before I am authorized to sign this," Inspector Singh said a couple of minutes later.

Catherine showed him something on her phone. He raised his eyebrows. "Fine." He kept reading.

Once they had all signed, Catherine settled into her chair. "I am very limited in terms of what I can and cannot say here," she said, crossing her arms.

"Please feel free to ask me any questions you like, but I may not be able to answer them."

"Yes, I've understood that," Inspector Singh said. "How did you know Miss Dey?"

"I wouldn't say I actually knew her," Catherine replied. "But I certainly knew of her."

"And why did you know of her?"

Catherine shrugged.

Inspector Singh sighed. "What did Miss Dey do for a living?"

"How should I put this." Catherine thought for a moment. "I suppose one could say she was an opportunist. Because of her looks and her personality—and of course, her wealth—she had power over people. And she knew how to use it. She could get people to reveal things. To confide in her."

She thought for a second.

"More for fun than anything else, I'd heard. Nobody ever got the impression that she needed the money." She gave a brief and somewhat wolfish smile that vanished more or less upon arrival. "Although she was an excellent businesswoman."

Businesswoman? Amrita hadn't worked a day in her life, Ro thought. But another word had caught his attention.

"What do you mean by 'opportunist'?"

Catherine gave another brief smile. "In the basest terms, Amrita had a nose for finding out when someone had been in a compromising situation. And if not, she could create one. Or create the illusion of one," she continued, affectless. "She was very good at acquiring and wielding leverage."

Mrs. B. sat in the corner, looking vaguely horrified.

"So she was a blackmailer," Ro said.

"Let's not start using such big words straight out the door," Catherine replied. "My understanding is that she would never have done anything sordid or cheap." She paused. "Amrita was just good at finding out people's secrets. And then exploiting them."

Mrs. B. nodded. "You know, that makes sense."

"What makes sense?" the inspector asked, looking at her.

"Rita was spending more and more time in India," Mrs. B. said. "I never really understood why. She wasn't close to her family here." She hesitated. "I don't quite know how to explain this."

She looked at Catherine and Ro.

"It's not like the West here, you see. People have secrets. Things to hide." She looked a little frustrated. "I'm not explaining properly."

"No," Ro said, jumping in. "You are. Let me think." He paused. "In America, if there's a sex tape of you, it could make you rich and famous. Here, it would still ruin your life." He looked at Mrs. B. "Is that what you mean?"

Mrs. B. returned his look, grateful. "Yes. That's exactly what I mean."

"So there are more potential targets here," Ro said meditatively.

Catherine nodded. "Amrita was very good at finding out when people had something to hide. And she enjoyed it." She paused. "All of this to say there were plenty of people with a motive to kill her."

Ro leaned forward. "Like who?"

"Fair question." Catherine grinned at him unexpectedly. "We'll get to that."

"Looking forward," Mrs. B. said, her tone bright. "But what we still don't know is what all this has to do with you, Mrs. Forrester."

"I've worked for the US government on and off for most of my adult life."

"Are you on or off right now?" Ro interjected, curious.

Catherine smiled briefly. "On. For the most part." She looked at Mrs. B. "And please call me Catherine."

Mrs. B. smiled in assent.

"As we've established, I work with American intelligence." Catherine saw Mrs. B.'s grin. "And no, that's not an oxymoron. Nice try. Anyway, we occasionally collaborated with Amrita on certain matters." She hesitated. "This time they involved terrorism."

"What on earth did Rita have to do with terrorism?" Mrs. B. muttered darkly.

"Nothing." Catherine smiled again. "And that was the point. Amrita just really hated terrorists. A childhood friend of hers was killed in the Paris attacks."

"So, what were you and Amrita doing together here?" Ro asked, leaning in. "In as vague terms as necessary."

Catherine chose her words carefully. "State asked Amrita if she could find proof of a certain party's involvement in the financing of international terrorism. And she did." She paused. "At least, she said she did. State sent me to get it from her. It worked out perfectly. Chris needed somewhere to train, and she was coming here anyway."

"Did you get the proof?" Mrs. B. asked.

"No. We did not." Catherine smiled, a little grimly. "You've searched her room, I suppose," she added, turning toward the inspector.

"Yes. We'll get to that."

Amrita really hadn't seemed afraid, Ro mused. He looked down at his hands and, seeing his watch, immediately looked back up. "Was she wearing a Cartier watch? Do we know yet?"

"Let me ask."

Inspector Singh stood up and left the room. Many voices were heard. After a moment, he came back into the room consulting a piece of paper. "Yes. She was wearing a Cartier watch of gold and diamonds."

"Oh." Ro slumped back in his seat. Somehow, he hadn't expected that.

"What was found on her body?" Catherine asked.

The inspector consulted the list in his hand. "Besides the watch, a fur headband. A turquoise and mother-of-pearl necklace. White cotton kurta pajama. A Samsara robe. A room key."

"No phone?" Ro asked.

"No." Inspector Singh consulted another sheet of paper. "But there were two iPhones in her room, which seems odd."

"No, it's not," Mrs. B., Catherine, and Ro responded in unison.

They all looked at each other, a little sheepish.

Mrs. B. half-raised a hand. "I have two."

"Three for me," Catherine volunteered.

Inspector Singh looked at Ro.

"Three also," he admitted. "But that's not the point. What's important is that she had already picked up her watch from the Palace." He shook his head. "So she was walking back to dinner when she was killed."

"Right." Catherine looked at Inspector Singh. "Do we know when she picked it up?"

"I'll find out."

"And her room?" Catherine stood up and walked over to the window.

"We are still compiling the list of what was found there," the inspector replied. "The room was in quite a bit of disarray."

Mrs. B., Catherine, and Ro all looked at one another, dubious.

"What now?" The inspector sounded irritated.

There was a long pause.

"Well," Ro said, hesitant, "that seems out of character. From what little I knew of her, she seemed extremely on top of things. She hated being late, for example."

Mrs. B. nodded vigorously. "Rita was very organized."

Catherine was pacing by the window. "So someone went through her room." She turned to Mrs. B. "Can we find out who entered her room?"

Mrs. B. shook her head. "As you know, we use real keys."

"Ugh." Catherine sighed, exasperated.

Mrs. B. fixed her with a freezing glare. "If you'd prefer key cards, may I suggest the Hilton Garden Inn. I believe there's one close to the airport."

Catherine sat back down. "She's been coming here for years. Did she always stay in the same room?"

"Always." Mrs. B. thought for a moment. "You know, that's what's funny about all this. At her core, Rita really was a creature of habit."

"How well did you know her?" the inspector asked.

"I've known her since she was born," Mrs. B. responded, surprised. "I thought you knew. Her mother and I were girls together."

The inspector made a note. "I think it would be helpful to interview you next, if you don't mind."

* * *

"You had known Miss Dey for her entire life?" the inspector began.

"Yes." Mrs. B. looked down. "I'm sorry. It's still difficult to hear the pluperfect." She shook her head slowly before continuing. "I was at school with Meena. Rita's mother."

"Where was this?" The inspector's tone was gentle.

"Calcutta. Loreto."

He put down his pen. "First, can you shed some light on the question of her name? Was her given name Rita or Amrita?"

"It's a bit convoluted, I'm afraid, so bear with me. Rita was the youngest of three, by quite a bit. By at least ten years. Meena's oldest was a boy, Amar. He was killed. In a riding accident, soon after Rita was born. Still a boy, only just fifteen, sixteen." She shuddered. "Horrible. I don't suppose Meena ever really recovered. Not that many would have."

She paused again, remembering.

"I don't know how it happened, but somehow, gradually, Rita turned into Amrita. I think it was so that Meena could still say part of Amar's name."

Ro shivered.

Mrs. B. noticed. "Yes," she nodded. "Yes. I never liked it. It's eerie. I always called her Rita, as you know."

"Where was the family money from?" Catherine asked.

Ro saw the inspector tense, then visibly decide not to reassert control over the questioning. He was getting useful information.

"The money came from her father. It was quite a tragic story. His family were jewel merchants. They were all killed during Partition. He somehow managed to escape and ended up in Calcutta. He must have brought some of the jewels with him." She paused. "Meena was from a very good family but there were four girls. No boys. Not much money." She shook her head briefly.

"And it's a shame to say, but she was dark. I hate bringing it up, but it mattered in those days. Anyway. Mr. Dey was very rich. It was a surprise when he asked for her hand, but for her family it was a godsend."

"They lived in Belgium?" the inspector asked.

"Yes. They moved there soon after Amar was born."

"Do you know why they moved there?"

Mrs. B. paused. "It made sense for business. But it was also about security. Belgium was safer."

The inspector nodded. "How often did you see them?"

"You know, quite a bit," Mrs. B. said, thinking about it. "At least once a year, I'd say. We'd go to Europe once or twice a year. And then Meena came back to India almost every year as well. Nalini was even in school here for a year or two, I think." She saw the questioning look on the inspector's face. "Meena's elder daughter."

"How much older was she?"

"Much older. Ten, twelve years." She considered. "Meena and I must have been close to forty when Meena had Rita. I remember being horrified she was putting herself through that again. And Mr. Dey must have been nearing sixty. If not more."

"Both of Amrita's parents are dead?" Ro asked, leaning in.

"Yes." Mrs. B. nodded. "Meena died of cancer. Breast. Quite young. Mr. Dey died a few years afterward. I can't remember how, but you know, he was already quite elderly by then. I think an aneurysm, maybe."

"When was this?" the inspector asked.

"Let me think." Mrs. B. considered. "Oh, probably twenty years ago. Yes. Because Rita stopped university after her father died. She must have been nineteen, twenty."

"Where did she go to school?" Catherine and Ro asked in unison.

"One of those schools in Switzerland. I can't think which. Then the American University in Paris." She thought for a second. "Rita was always a very good student. A very bright girl. But also extremely efficient. Once her father died, she had things to do other than study."

"Who was her husband?" the inspector inquired.

"Ah. Yes. She married quite young. One or two years after her father had died. They'd met at school. He was Swiss." She paused. "Oh, dear. This is too awful, but I can't actually remember what he was called."

"Did you know him at all? What kind of person was he?" Ro was genuinely curious about the sort of person Amrita would have married.

"Leclerc," Mrs. B. said, hitting the table with a great deal of satisfaction. "Eric Leclerc. That's it." She looked at Ro. "Oh! What was he like. He wasn't like much, I'm afraid. He was handsome, of course. But also slightly odious. A sort of diet Thierry Roussel."

"But there was no one to stop it," Ro said.

"That's not quite right," Mrs. B. said. "I could have tried to stop it if I'd really thought it disastrous. But Rita was no fool. She knew what she was doing."

"How did he die?" Catherine asked curiously.

"Skiing," Mrs. B. said. "He fell out of a helicopter." She paused. "Landed like a plastic bag full of soup, from what I understand," she added.

Catherine, who had been taking a sip of coffee, coughed.

"There were no children?" the inspector asked.

"No," Mrs. B. said. "No inheritance either. He didn't come from anything." She paused, reflecting. "At least she got a Swiss passport out of it."

"Did you always stay in touch with her?" Ro asked.

"Yes," Mrs. B. said. "Yes. I made a point to. For Meena." She paused. "I wasn't like a second mother to her, or whatever people say in that sort of situation. Rita didn't need a second mother. But I did everything I could to make sure she knew she could rely on me. That she still had a family." She reflected for a moment. "And recently, over the last few years, I really did see quite a lot of her."

"I have a weird question," Catherine said, perching on the table. "Did you like her?"

"You know, I think that's an excellent question. And the answer is that I just don't know. She was extremely solicitous and well mannered and good company. But Rita was so"—she paused, searching for the word—"autonomous. Always so self-assured. I'd never thought of it this way, but I don't think I especially mattered to her. Frankly, I don't think anyone especially mattered to her. Which isn't a particularly endearing quality."

Ro nodded slowly. He knew what she meant.

"She was very clever. She could be quite fun." Mrs. B. thought for a second. "As long as your interests and hers were in alignment, all was fine. And you know, our interests were never in conflict. I think she liked seeing me because I reminded her of her mother. Also, I'm very rich. Being close to me is not exactly an inconvenience." She raised her hands and shrugged. Ro's eye was once again caught by the giant emerald tennis bracelet on her wrist. "I don't know that I liked her. Or admired her, even."

Such a complicated, intricate person, Ro thought. Such a complicated, intricate life. Vanished.

"Actually, I want to change all that," Mrs. B. said after a moment. "And to apologize for having said it. I did admire her. I do admire her. And I shall continue to admire her. She was strong. She went through the world doing exactly as she pleased. She acted like a man and was treated like a man. She had authority. And confidence. And courage. Lots and lots of courage." She paused for a second. "Of course, it's much easier to have courage if you're rich."

And that, Ro thought, was the truest thing he'd heard all day.

"Time for a short break, I think." Mrs. B. stood up.

The inspector was looking at his notes. "Actually, just a moment. Before we break, I do have a few more questions."

"Oh?" Mrs. B. asked, surprised.

"Only a few." The inspector's tone was mild. "But you may wish to sit back down. For your own comfort."

Mrs. B. looked at him for a moment. Then she sat down again.

A bit abruptly, Ro thought.

"You were not at the same table as the others during the dinner yesterday," the inspector stated.

"No," Mrs. B. said. "No, I wasn't."

"So where were you during dinner?"

Ro was surprised to see that Mrs. B. did not answer straight away. Then he saw that Mrs. B. was visibly struggling.

He and Catherine both leaned in, rapt.

Finally, Mrs. B. sighed. "I wasn't there," she confessed. Her shoulders slumped.

"What do you mean?" Ro said.

The inspector shot him a warning glance and held up his hand.

"Sorry," Ro mouthed, sitting back in his chair.

"This can't leave the room. You'll think it so awful of me." Mrs. B. hesitated. "But I didn't go to the dinner. I just didn't feel like it, I'm afraid."

The inspector sensed that this wasn't the whole story. "And what did you do instead?"

Mrs. B. paused and looked at them. Then she sighed again, realizing that resistance was futile. "I caught up on my shows. My television shows."

Unexpectedly, Catherine laughed. "What shows?"

"*Real Housewives*," Mrs. B. replied, with all the dignity she could muster. "*Ultimate Girls Trip.*"

They all processed that for a moment.

"Was anyone with you?" the inspector asked.

"Oh!" Mrs. B. brightened. "Well, Sundar was there, of course."

Great, Ro thought, mentally rolling his eyes. Sundar would say whatever Mrs. B. told him to.

"What happened in the episodes you saw last night? I haven't caught up yet." Catherine looked at Mrs. B., innocent.

This, Ro was certain, was a lie.

"Well, not much actually happened," Mrs. B. replied. "But that poor Brandi. She means well, but the others don't seem to understand." She paused, contemplative. "You know, the other women should just treat her as if she has Tourette's. Rather than getting so upset all the time."

"You're right," Catherine replied, nodding.

"Fine." The inspector shook his head. "I think that's all for right now." He looked back at his notebook. "I would like to speak to everyone who interacted with Miss Dey last night."

"I'd like us to start by interviewing Joss Ziemssen and my husband," Catherine said. "I don't want Chris's training regimen disturbed any more than it has to be."

"Well, really," the inspector began, but Catherine silenced him with a look.

"I showed you already," she said quietly. "Your government has given me the authority to run this investigation. If I want to."

"Fine." Inspector Singh sighed. "I'll ask Mr. Ziemssen to be here in fifteen minutes." He looked at his watch. "Let's take a short break. But everyone, please be in there in ten minutes."

Looking pointedly at Catherine, he jerked his thumb toward the mirror. "Maximum."

Ten minutes would be just enough time to start exploring the library, Ro thought. Perfect.

He hurried down the stairs.

* * *

Ro was mentally rubbing his hands together with glee as he walked into the library. Books surrounded him on all sides. The shelves stretched all the way up to the ceiling. While scrupulously clean, the library somehow still had a dusty aura. It did not feel used much, or appreciated much.

But it was time to get down to business.

He began to scan the shelves with a trained, expert eye. English-language books were, naturally, the most trafficked. Constant vigilance was mandatory. Blink and another guest would snatch them before you even knew they were there. The French books tended to hang around a bit longer, and Ro frequently ended up with the French translations of English-language blockbusters he had missed along the way. German was a mixed bag, although sometimes there was a classic mystery or two. The Scandinavian books generally lingered the longest, growing increasingly dour as they settled into the lower shelves.

Engrossed, he lost himself in the shelves for some time. His hand hovered for several seconds over *Greenmantle*, but then he spied an Agatha Christie whose dénouement he had forgotten. He gazed at the French-language title: *Le meurtre, est-il facile?* He'd find out, he supposed.

Glancing at his watch, Ro saw the ten minutes were over. He jogged back upstairs, Agatha Christie in hand.

* * *

To Ro's surprise and delight, the adjacent room had practically been turned into a screening room. Large reclining chairs faced the two-way mirror. Various tables were scattered with magazines and snacks. Mrs. B. was recumbent in a velour chair, her feet on a footrest, drinking a Diet Pepsi through a straw. Catherine was perched on a sofa, looking restless.

Ro flopped into a recliner next to Mrs. B. "What have you got there?" she asked.

"Just a mystery novel." He stuffed the book into his bag.

"I never read mystery novels," Mrs. B. mused. "They so rarely stick the landing, don't you find?"

They heard a knock on the door. Ro almost went to open it until he caught Mrs. B.'s eye.

"No," she said, pointing at the two-way mirror. "That was over there."

In the two-way mirror, the inspector opened the door. Joss walked in.

"Please," the inspector said, indicating where Joss should sit. The inspector then took a seat on another side of the table, ensuring that the three of them had a clear view. He'd learned his lesson.

Ro immediately felt uncomfortable watching Inspector Singh and Joss. He turned to look at Mrs. B. She was as engrossed as a small child at a Disney movie.

"Hello, Mr. Ziemssen," Inspector Singh began. "Thank you for agreeing to see me on such short notice."

"Naturally," Joss said. "What a tragedy. I want to help however I can. Not that I think I know anything that would be of interest to you."

"One never knows," the inspector replied, his tone mild. "I'd like to discuss what happened yesterday. And please allow me to say that I'm sorry you've had to go through this. It must have been quite traumatic."

"It was," Joss said quietly. Ro could see Joss was shaken under the polished exterior. "It was, and is, quite a shock."

"Had you ever met Miss Dey before coming to Samsara?"

"No."

Catherine leaned forward.

"Oh. No. Wait. Yes, of course. I met her in London in November. At Ro Krishna's birthday dinner. Ro, who's also staying here. But that's the only time I'd met her."

"Did you spend much time with her here?"

"Not really." Joss thought for a second. "In groups, a bit. I don't think I ever had a one-to-one conversation with her."

"What was your impression of her?" The inspector seemed genuinely curious.

"She was extremely intelligent and self-assured. Independent. Modern. I don't know why I chose that word, but it does fit her somehow." Joss paused. "Also beautiful, of course."

"Can you please describe to me what happened yesterday evening?"

"Well, I didn't see much of Amrita. I saw her right at the beginning of dinner. But we didn't stay long because we had to get ready for the performance."

"We?"

"Oh. Chris and me. Chris Forrester."

"Did you converse with Miss Dey at all?"

Joss thought about it. "You know, I don't think I actually exchanged a single word with her after we said hello to each other."

The inspector put down his pen and stood up. "What time did you leave the table?"

"About 8:25, I think," Joss replied. "We had to be backstage by 8:30 to get ready."

"And what did getting ready involve?"

"Hair, makeup, and costume for Chris. Nothing major, but it still took about half an hour."

"So you were backstage, with Mr. Forrester, from 8:30 to 9." The inspector sat down and made a note.

"Yes."

"And during the performance?"

Joss shifted, uncomfortable. "I watched it from the terrace behind the stage."

Ro leaned forward.

Now, Ro had known Joss since they were seventeen. And Joss had a tell. Whenever he was uncomfortable, or not telling the entire truth, his neck started to flush red. And his neck was flushing now.

Slightly.

"From the terrace," the inspector repeated. "Who else was there?"

"I don't remember." Joss shifted in his seat again. "There were a bunch of us. The sound engineers."

The flush was still there.

"Did you leave the backstage area at all?"

"No."

The inspector looked at his notebook, then back up at Joss. "The part with the singing, was that also rehearsed?"

Ro put his head in his hands.

Catherine whistled. "He's good."

"What do you mean?" Mrs. B. asked.

"There wasn't any singing," Catherine replied, absorbed.

Joss went still for a moment. "The whole evening went as planned," he said finally.

Catherine leaned forward, her elbows on her knees.

"And once the performance had finished, you rejoined Mrs. Forrester, Mr. Krishna, and the others?"

"Yes. We decided to go look at the stars."

"Did you see Miss Dey's body?" The inspector's question was abrupt.

Joss sat up straighter. "No. Catherine and Ro secured the perimeter pretty much immediately. Once Ro came to, at least."

"What do you mean?" the inspector asked, leaning forward. Ro winced.

"Oh. Ro passed the hell out when he saw the body. It was super dramatic." Joss smiled despite himself. "So at first I was making sure he was all right."

"Ah. I didn't know about that." The inspector made a note in his notebook. "Did you know about the side door to the spa, by the way?"

"No." Joss flushed again.

Either the inspector didn't notice, or he decided to ignore it. "Thank you, Mr. Ziemssen," he said, standing up. "I think that will be all for right now."

"What was that all about?" Catherine said. She knew Joss almost as well as Ro did. She leaned forward, her hands under her chin. "Where was he?"

"I don't know," Ro replied, thinking about it. "I just don't know. He had absolutely no motive, though."

"At least not that we know of." Catherine paused. "Well, in any case, I don't think any of us did it. If one of us had, we would never have let the group get so close to the body."

"I don't think I agree, Catherine. Amrita's body was pretty well-hidden. Most people didn't know about that entrance to the spa. It was just dumb luck that I knew about it and knew we could get blankets there." Ro shook his head slowly. "And it was dumb luck that Lala glanced in that direction when we were leaving."

"I don't know," Catherine said, a bit peevish. "Whatever." She sat back, crossing her arms.

* * *

"Happy to help however I can, Inspector." Chris smiled, relaxing effortlessly into one of the uncomfortable plastic chairs. "I'm afraid I don't think I know anything of relevance, but of course you'll be the judge of that."

"Thank you, Mr. Forrester," the inspector replied, consulting his notes. "By the way, my mother's a big fan."

Chris smiled thinly. "Thank you so much."

Catherine chuckled, her eyes sparkling. "God, he hates that."

Once again, Ro was charmed to see how much genuine affection the Forresters had for one another.

"Does he know you have anything to do with this?" Mrs. B. asked Catherine, sipping through her straw.

"No. Ugh." Catherine sighed. "I told him State asked me to keep an eye on the situation, but not like this. He thinks I'm getting a massage."

"Had you ever met Miss Dey before coming to Samsara, Mr. Forrester?"

"Yes," Chris replied.

Ro looked at Catherine, surprised. She avoided his look.

"Ah?" The inspector also sounded surprised. "Where was that?"

"At a spa in Thailand. Chiva-Som."

"That's quite a coincidence, no? That you'd run into her again here?"

"Not as much of one as you'd think." Chris laughed. "There seems to be a global class of pretty dubious rich people who spend their lives going from spa to spa."

"Did you know that Miss Dey would be here?"

"Oh no," Chris responded, surprised. "We didn't actually know each other. We chatted a couple of times in Thailand but certainly didn't become better acquainted than that."

Ro looked at Catherine again. She studiously continued to avoid making eye contact with him.

"So, please walk me through your evening yesterday," the inspector continued, standing up.

"Well, Mrs. B. had told me a couple of days ago that the hotel was having a dance performance on Christmas," Chris began. "She asked me if I wouldn't

mind doing a short routine with the performers. I thought it might be fun."
He shrugged. "I like to dance, and I always like to learn some local dance
where I can. Keeps you moving in different ways."

"What time did you arrive at the restaurant?"

Chris paused, trying to remember. "We got there around 8, so Joss could
grab a quick bite before we had to get ready."

"You weren't eating?"

Chris shook his head. "I was dancing right afterward."

"That makes sense. What time did you leave the table?"

"I'm not sure, but I'd guess around 8:15."

"Not later?" the inspector asked.

"I don't believe so." Chris thought about it. "We were due to start makeup
at 8:30, and I always like to be early. And things always end up taking a little
longer because people want autographs or pictures, and I like to oblige them
if I can."

Again, Ro was enchanted by Chris's simplicity and humility. There wasn't
a hint of ego in his words.

"After makeup, you went straight into the performance?"

"Yes. It lasted for maybe 20, 25 minutes. Then I spent some time taking
pictures while the other acts performed."

"Did you return to the table during the performance?"

Chris shook his head. "No. I ate a little backstage and rejoined my wife at
the end of the performance. A few minutes before 10, probably."

"I thought he came back earlier than that," Ro said.

"He did," Catherine replied. "He just doesn't remember. That's the problem with witnesses."

"Could you see the audience at all during the dance? Or while you were
backstage?"

"No," Chris replied. "I wasn't paying attention while I was onstage. And
backstage was, well, backstage."

The inspector paused. "Was Mr. Ziemssen with you the whole time you
were backstage?" he asked, his tone light.

Chris thought about it for a second. "I don't remember. There were a lot of people around, though."

"But you don't remember seeing him specifically?"

"No." Chris saw the look on the inspector's face and laughed. "But trust me, Inspector, Joss Ziemssen has nothing to do with this. He spent ten minutes trapping a spider in our villa yesterday so that he could release it outside instead of killing it."

Ro smiled.

"I'm sure you're right," the inspector replied smoothly. "But I'm sure you'll understand I have to verify everyone's movements."

"Of course."

Just then, the door in the other room opened and a junior officer hurried in. He whispered to Inspector Singh.

"What?" Inspector Singh said sharply.

The junior officer whispered something else.

The inspector responded in Hindi, loud and angry.

Ro turned urgently to Mrs. B. "What's he saying?"

"'What on earth do you mean? That's impossible,'" she replied, totally absorbed.

Inspector Singh and the other officer exchanged several more furious whispers. Finally, the junior officer left.

The inspector stood in the mirror, lost in thought.

"Is that all?" Chris asked. He began to rise from his chair.

"I'm so sorry," the inspector replied, turning back to him. "We're almost done. I just have a few questions about when you found Miss Dey's body."

"Of course, Inspector." Chris sat back down. "I didn't actually see her body, though."

"You didn't?"

"No. As soon as Lala started screaming, Catherine ran over and ordered us to stay where we were."

"Were you surprised that she did that?"

"No," Chris replied, a smile flickering on his lips. Catherine smiled back.

"She used to be a diplomat. She thrives on chaos." He looked at Inspector Singh. "You should see her in a souk."

The inspector shuddered, clearly picturing it. "Did you know about the side door to the spa?"

"I did. It's a shortcut to get back to our villa, which is sort of between the Palace and the restaurant."

"All right." Inspector Singh looked down at his notebook, then back up at Chris. "Thank you very much, Mr. Forrester. I'll be in touch if I have any further questions."

Chris smiled broadly at him and left the room.

After a few seconds, the inspector went to the door and peered into the hallway. Seeing that the coast was clear, he turned to the mirror and beckoned the three of them to come into the other room.

They dutifully filed in and sat down. "What happened?" Catherine said.

The inspector bent over, placing his hands on the table, his arms straight. "My inspectors have interviewed every front desk employee. They've confirmed that Miss Dey reported her watch as being lost, but they say it was never found. According to them, the watch was never turned in."

The four of them sat in silence.

"Do any of you know who gave her the message that her watch had been found?"

Ro and Catherine looked at each other. Catherine shook her head. "She got the message while she was at the buffet. She told us about it when she came back to the table."

"We'll interview the restaurant staff," the inspector said, pinching his nose between his fingers. "But the chances are that nobody will admit to it. They'll be too afraid of getting in trouble."

"Are we still keeping Amrita's death a secret?" Ro asked.

"Yes," Mrs. B. replied firmly.

Ro looked at Catherine, who shrugged. "It's normal to try to keep it quiet when someone dies at a hotel."

"To the degree possible," the inspector said. "But people talk. Especially staff."

Catherine abruptly stood up and began pacing.

"Who's next?" Mrs. B. asked brightly, rubbing her palms together.

The inspector looked at his list. "Amit Chopra."

"Is he coming here or will we go to him?" Ro asked. "He's in a wheelchair," he added, seeing the inspector's look of mild confusion.

"Ah. No, he didn't say anything about us going to him."

"He's very mobile," Catherine said, appreciative. Catherine had taken an obvious shine to the very handsome Amit.

* * *

Amit sat at the table in his wheelchair, the inspector at right angles to him to preserve the view. "Thank you for coming to speak to me, Mr. Chopra," the inspector began. "This is an informal conversation."

"Of course. It's so shocking."

Amit's hair settled in natural, effortless waves all over his head. His silver forelock fell over his forehead. It was perfect.

Ro pursed his lips.

"Could you please tell me a bit about yourself? Where you were brought up, what you do for a living, and so forth?"

Amit nodded. "I was born in India, but I moved to the States with my mother when I was very young. I mostly grew up over there, in Ohio. My father stayed in India, though, so I traveled back and forth a lot."

"And where do you live now?"

"I live in Hyderabad, but that's fairly recent. I moved to India for my job a few years ago."

"What sort of work do you do?"

"I'm one of the associate general counsels of a consumer goods corporation." Amit named a brand known throughout the world. "I handle all of our EMEA subsidiaries."

"Did you know Miss Dey well?"

"Not well at all," Amit replied. "I knew her slightly because we both come here at Christmas. But I don't think we ever engaged in anything more than small talk, if that."

"You always come here at Christmas?"

"For the last few years, at least. I started coming here after my parents died."

"And Miss Dey was generally here at Christmas as well?"

"Yes." Amit paused. "She's family friends with the owners, I believe."

"What was she like? As a person."

Amit seemed to close in on himself.

Ro leaned forward.

"Very sociable. Extroverted. Polished but charming."

Inspector Singh looked down at his notebook, but somehow Ro knew the inspector had registered the change in Amit's energy.

All of a sudden, Amit seemed . . . guarded.

"I think he's hiding something," Mrs. B. said. "He knows something about Rita."

Ro noted that Amit and he were probably around the same age. Amit was maybe a little younger. Then something occurred to him.

He turned to Catherine.

"Both of his parents are dead. That's unusual for someone his age. Do you know how they died?"

Catherine shook her head slowly. "No. But I'll find out."

"Let's talk about last night," the inspector continued casually, flipping through pages of his notebook.

Amit relaxed.

"Can you please describe the evening's events, in your own words?"

"Well, I was stuck on work calls right up until dinner."

"So you arrived at dinner late."

"Yes. I probably got there a few minutes after 9," he replied. "Maybe 9:10. The dance performance had already started, so I stayed near the back with Catherine and the others."

"Could you give us the names of some of the people who were on the video calls with you?"

"Sure, but why would you need that?" Amit looked puzzled.

"Of course, you understand that we need to confirm everyone's movements."

"That won't be a problem. I was on calls nonstop from 6 to 9."

Amit paused. He still looked puzzled.

"But I'm still not sure why you need to confirm my movements before 9."

Inspector Singh put down his pen.

"What do you mean?" he asked, his tone light.

"Well, because Amrita was still alive at 9," Amit replied. He registered the surprise on the inspector's face. "I saw her when I was leaving my room. Just after 9."

The inspector's next words were slow and deliberate. "Is there a way to determine the exact time you left your room? For example, the time at which your last call ended?"

Amit thought about it. "I sent an email right after the call." He pulled up his sent messages and handed his phone to the inspector. "It was 9:03. I left my room pretty much immediately after."

"You saw her. Can you please describe what happened?"

"Of course." Amit nodded vigorously, on surer ground now. "I'd just left my room. When I turned to lock the door, I happened to see Amrita going into her room. It's down the hall from mine."

"Did she see you?"

Amit considered. "I don't think so. Her back was to me."

"Are you sure it was Miss Dey?"

"I assumed so." Amit seemed somewhat startled by the question. "But yes, I am fairly sure. It certainly looked like her. And she was wearing that fur headband thing she always had on."

"You saw her actually enter her room?"

Amit nodded. "Yes. I saw her turn the key, go into her room, and shut the door."

Ro grabbed his phone and frantically texted the inspector.

They heard the phone buzz in the other room. The inspector picked it up, visibly irritated. Then, nodding briefly, he turned back to Amit.

"Did you happen to see whether she was wearing a watch?"

Amit looked puzzled, but didn't ask why. He closed his eyes, thinking, then shook his head, regretful. "No," he replied, opening his eyes. "No, I don't remember. She was a few doors down. And of course, I wasn't paying any particular attention."

"Her back was to you the whole time?"

"Yes."

"And she was definitely going into her room? She wasn't leaving?"

"Yes. Definitely. I saw her go into her room."

"Did you see Miss Dey alive after you saw her in the hallway?"

Amit shook his head slowly. "No."

The inspector paused, then visibly decided to move on. "Then you went to the restaurant. What time did you arrive?"

"Well, it's only a couple of minutes away. I'd say I was definitely there by 9:10. Maybe even before."

"What did you do when you arrived?"

"The performance had already started." Amit shrugged. "But I saw some friends at a table right by the door, so I just joined them."

"Then you remained there, at the table, until the performance was over."

"Yes, I did."

"You were in the back of the restaurant by the exit. Did you see anyone leave during the performance?"

Amit looked up and to the side.

Both Ro and Catherine hunched forward.

"No. I didn't."

"He's lying," Mrs. B. said.

"Then, after the performance, some of you decided to go look at the stars."

"Yes."

"Whose idea was that?"

"Probably mine." Amit smiled, a bit rueful. "I've become very interested in stargazing since my accident."

The inspector softened. "May I ask you what happened?"

"Of course. I was in a car accident when I was 19. I'm paralyzed from the waist down." He saw the mildly skeptical look on the inspector's face. "I'm happy to provide you with my medical records, Inspector. But please be assured, I could not have killed Amrita Dey. At least not like this."

At least not like this? What was that supposed to mean, Ro thought to himself.

"Do you know how she was killed?" the inspector asked lightly. "Did you see her body?"

"No. But from what I understand her neck was broken."

"Please remind me, who all was with you when you went to look at the stars?"

"Chris, Catherine, Ro, Joss, among the guests. Then Mahesh, one of the yoga instructors."

"And Mrs. Mehta," the inspector added.

"Oh yes, of course." Amit looked up to the side. "We saw her as we were leaving and someone invited her. I think Ro."

"I think he saw Lala leave during the performance," Catherine said, still engrossed in the mirror. "But then she came back. That's why she was standing by the exit when we left."

"That's pure speculation, Catherine," Ro replied.

"You started walking . . ." The inspector paused, flustered. "Apologies."

Amit smiled and waved it off.

"Toward the meadow off the path," the inspector continued.

"Yes. Then we waited while Ro and Lala Mehta went to the spa to get us blankets."

"How long were they gone?"

"A couple of minutes at the most."

Ro sighed with relief, even though he hadn't done anything wrong.

Catherine looked at him, amused. "Don't worry. I know you didn't do it."

"Were you already aware of that entrance to the spa?"

"No." Amit suddenly looked annoyed. "And they should have told me about that entrance years ago because it makes the spa more accessible. It would have saved me a lot of trouble."

"So Mrs. Mehta entered the building with Mr. Krishna."

"Yes. They came back up the ramp a couple of minutes later. But I didn't see Lala when she came back. I only heard her when she started screaming."

"So you never saw the body?"

"No," Amit said, firm.

The inspector paused, making a few notes. He stood up.

"Thank you, Mr. Chopra. I think that will do for now."

Inspector Singh opened the door for Amit to leave, then sat down, poring over his notebook.

The three of them in the other room saw Amit hesitate. He looked at the inspector.

His mouth opened as if he were about to say something.

Then he thought better of it, turned his wheelchair around, and left the room. A few seconds later, the inspector left that room and entered theirs.

He stopped for a moment, looking at the mirror they'd been watching him through, then shook his head silently.

He sat down, choosing the most upright chair in the room. "Thoughts?"

"He knows more about Amrita than he's saying," Ro said. "Not necessarily about her death. But about her. I think."

The inspector nodded. "That was my impression as well."

Catherine stood up and began pacing.

Mrs. B. was lost in thought. "Why did she go back to her room? What does that mean?"

"What time did he see her?" Ro asked. "9:05, approximately?"

The inspector nodded.

"And she left the table at 8:47. My watch is always accurate."

"This doesn't make any sense." Catherine shook her head. "If she had decided to go to her room before going to the Palace, it would have taken her five minutes. She would have gotten there at least 10 minutes before Amit saw her there." Catherine paused. "Could she have gone to the Palace before going to her room?" Then she answered her own question. "There's no way. Not unless she took a golf cart. It's at least 15 minutes each way by foot."

"I think it's time for a break." Mrs. B.'s tone was firm. No one disagreed with her. "And you, young man, have a doctor's appointment," she added, looking sternly at Ro.

"And I have a massage." Catherine looked at the inspector. "Who's next?"

The inspector consulted his list. "As you can imagine, it's been quite difficult to schedule something with Mr. or Mrs. Mehta. So I think we'll speak to this Mitchell Charney person."

Ro inwardly groaned. Mrs. B. looked at him, her eyes twinkling.

"Let's meet back here in 90 minutes," Inspector Singh said.

* * *

Catherine and Ro took a golf cart down to the spa in silence, both lost in their own thoughts. Ro shivered slightly as they drove past the spot where they had found Amrita's body. Which reminded him of something.

He turned to Catherine. "You never said that you'd met Amrita before."

"You never asked," Catherine responded coolly.

Ro thought for a moment and nodded. Fair enough.

"Anyway, it's like what Chris said," she continued. "Spas are always filled with the shadiest people."

Catherine looked at Ro.

"Check out the Wörthersee sometime. It's pretty much SMERSH Homecoming Weekend."

* * *

"I like to do a quick check-in on Day 4," Dr. Menon said briskly, settling into his seat behind the desk. "Sometimes the initial release can be quite intense. How did you sleep last night?"

He peered at Ro. Instinctively, Ro shrank back in his chair.

"Very well," Ro replied. It was the truth. Ro generally slept well no matter what. But he didn't know whether the doctor was aware of what had happened the previous night.

"Hmm." The doctor looked at him, dubious. "Did you have any dreams?"

"I'm not sure." Ro thought about it, then remembered. "Actually, I did. I dreamt I ran into my friend Yvonne. On Lex. We got a coffee."

He looked up. Dr. Menon was looking at Ro like he was an extraterrestrial.

"Lexington Avenue," Ro explained, apologetic. "In New York."

Dr. Menon opened his mouth to say something, then closed it. His gaze wandered to the tote bag on the chair next to Ro, then stopped on something.

"Mr. Krishna!"

Dr. Menon glared at Ro, accusing.

Ro shrank even further back into his chair.

"Are you *reading*?"

"Yes," he said, feeling guilty.

Then he sat back upright.

"You never told me not to, Dr. Menon." His tone was equally accusing. Offense is the best defense, Ro always thought.

Dr. Menon gave a theatrical sigh.

"This isn't a game where you find the loopholes, Mr. Krishna. Stop reading. Immediately. Are you resting?"

"I was resting, but . . ."

Ro paused, then decided he had to bring it up. Doctor-patient privilege, after all.

"I'm not sure if you heard, but there was an . . . incident here yesterday."

Dr. Menon's eyes clouded over. He sank back in his chair and stared into space for several seconds. Then he came back to the present.

"Yes. I know what happened."

"Horrible," Ro said flatly. "Just horrible."

They sat there, silent.

"Anyway," Ro continued, "Mrs. Banerjee has asked me to help the hotel with the investigation."

A split second of terror flashed over Dr. Menon's face, so fast that Ro wasn't sure whether he had imagined it. Ro noticed, though, that Dr. Menon's hand continued to shake for a few moments.

The doctor stayed silent, thinking about something far, far away. The look gathering in his eyes made Ro increasingly uneasy.

"I want to help you, Mr. Krishna," he finally said. His voice was unexpectedly soft. "I think your nervous system is under extreme strain. Severe, extreme strain. And I don't like it."

He paused.

"Mr. Krishna. I beg of you. Please take as much rest as you possibly can. And please come to see me every day."

"All right." Ro shifted uncomfortably in his chair. "All right."

"Good." The doctor turned back to his computer. "I'll ensure you're booked in."

* * *

After cycling through the steam room and ice bath twice, Ro still felt unsettled by what the doctor had told him. He felt like the murder was still physically in his body, and that he hadn't yet purged it.

Perhaps the sauna would help.

He walked up the short set of stairs and opened the wooden door to be met by a blast of hot air straight in the face. He recoiled slightly, then stood up straighter and went in.

The sauna was gorgeous, built out of warm-colored wood. It was rectangular except for one corner that jutted out. Moving closer, he saw that the corner contained an ice-cold shower, operated by a simple chain with the water tank above his head. The shower was tiled in white and had chest-height windows on three sides.

Ro placed his towel on a wooden headrest and lay back, allowing his body to sweat, to excrete whatever toxins it needed to excrete. It felt fairly horrible for a few minutes. Then he sensed something foul, something noisome, begin to approach his skin from inside his body. He was sweating, but not sweating enough. His body was still resisting. For a moment, Ro thought he might pass out, or vomit, or both.

Then the dam burst. Sweat flooded from Ro's forehead, his arms, his thighs, his neck. He lay there slumped like an empty box of wine. But then, gradually, he began to realize that he felt good. Really good. Like a million dollars.

He stood up and went to the shower. Jerking the chain, he gasped as the flood of icy water cascaded onto his head. Letting go of the chain, he stood for a moment, eyes closed, allowing the cold water to course over him. He turned back into the sauna for another round of heat, but his eye was caught by the windows.

He moved closer.

Through the left window, he could just about see the spot where they had found Amrita's body, although the trees blocked the meadow beyond. The center window looked squarely over the main path at the spot where Amrita had been murdered. Shame the spa was closed at that hour of night, he thought, and that nobody had been here to witness what had happened.

Then he smiled at his own stupidity. You wouldn't be able to see anything at night anyway.

* * *

After the sauna, Ro approached the spa desk. "Could you please call Mrs. Lala Mehta's room for me?"

The man behind the desk began to dial and handed Ro the receiver.

An unfamiliar male voice answered the phone brusquely. "Yes?"

"This is Ro Krishna calling," Ro said politely. "May I please speak with Lala?"

There was a long, uncertain pause. Muffled voices. Then the sound of movements.

"Ro?"

"Hello, Lala," Ro said. "Can we speak for a few minutes? Perhaps you could come outside. We could go for a short walk."

"I'll meet you in front of the restaurant in five minutes."

* * *

Ro was surprised to see Lala approach the restaurant from the main hotel building. "You're staying in the Residence?" he asked her, handing her one of the porcelain mugs of masala chai he had waiting.

"Thank you," she said, accepting it. They began to walk onto the lawn. "Yes. There are only two villas on the property. One's being refurbished, and the Forresters have booked the other one." She shrugged. "Anyway, Papa always thinks it safer to be around other people. I suppose he's not wrong, considering what happened with your little friend," she added, a bit gratuitously.

"Speaking of which," Ro said, "I wanted to talk to you for a second. To start with, everything I said yesterday stays the same. I'm bound to you by attorney-client privilege. I will never repeat anything you have said or will say to me."

Lala nodded slowly.

"The hotel has asked me to be involved in the investigation on their behalf." He paused. "The one thing that Mrs. B. knows is that I'm already representing you. She was fine with that. Because they want to hush it up."

"Why are you telling me this?"

Ro looked at her quizzically. "Well, because what you told me the other day gives you a motive."

Lala started. "Oh. I hadn't thought of that. But you're right, of course."

They stopped for a moment.

"How is Sanjay, by the way?" Ro asked, remembering.

Lala frowned. "He actually seems to be very ill. He can't keep anything down. He's in the bathroom every few minutes. Which at least means I don't have to speak to him. Why are you protecting me, by the way?" she asked, cradling the porcelain mug in her hands.

"Oh," Ro said, surprised. "Well, first of all, because I gave you my word. I really am your lawyer now."

Lala smiled.

"I mean, obviously, at the time I didn't think we'd be heading into a murder investigation, but there we have it." He considered. "But also, there's another thing. This wouldn't have made a difference because we'd already entered into our agreement. But I know you didn't kill her."

"How do you know that?"

"Because if you'd killed her, you wouldn't have gone out of your way to discover the body. You'd have wanted it to stay hidden for as long as possible."

"Oh." Lala nodded slowly, then more vigorously. "I suppose you're right."

"That being said, I don't want anybody to get the wrong idea," Ro continued. "So I do think you should speak to the inspector who's up here investigating. Inspector Singh."

"Why?"

"It looks suspicious if you don't want to help," Ro said. "Also, he's a pretty smart guy. All you have to do is tell the truth about what you saw. You don't actually know anything."

Lala paused, thinking about it. "Would you be in the room with me?"

"No." Ro shook his head, decisive. "I don't think anybody should know about our arrangement for the moment, other than Mrs. B." He thought for a second. "You should absolutely have a lawyer there with you, though."

"Did you have a lawyer with you?"

"No, but I didn't do it." Lala glared at him. "Sorry. But you know what I mean."

"Fine. Anyway, Papa's already sent one up. Apparently one of the top criminal law professors in the country. It was he who answered the phone when you rang." She laughed. "He didn't want me to come meet you, but then I told him I had you on retainer."

"Great." Ro exhaled. It was so rare and such a relief when people knew how to behave in their own best interest. "Just tell the truth and nothing but. If you have any doubts, say, 'I don't recall.' And give as little information as possible without looking suspicious. If Inspector Singh asks you if you have the time, you should just answer 'Yes.'"

He remembered something else.

"Here's an old trick from when I used to prepare witnesses. Tell your lawyer to put his hand on the table when he thinks you're saying too much."

She giggled. "All right. I'll do it. I'm sick of all this coddling anyway. And thank you. I'm in a much better mood now." Lala paused to readjust the fur headband over her ears. India, the land of fur-wearing vegetarians, Ro thought. "See you soon."

It was funny how similar everyone looked from behind in their identical kurta pajama, Ro mused, watching Lala walk away. How much easier it was to commit a crime in a place where most people looked like one another.

Then something occurred to him. "Wait," he barked.

Lala turned around, startled.

"I just thought of something." He walked toward her in long strides. "Listen. I know it's very unlikely, but I just realized, the killer might have thought Amrita was you."

He saw the horror in her eyes and immediately regretted having been so blunt.

"I'm sorry. I didn't mean for that to come out so brutally. But I just noticed. You and Amrita are around the same height, and you both have that fur headband." He continued, his tone more gentle. "Look. I'm sure it's not the case. But I don't think we can take any chances here."

"Why would anyone here want to kill me?"

"Are you serious? Mrs. B. told me last night that you're one of the Chola kids. Although I didn't know that yesterday when we spoke."

Lala stared at him, goggle-eyed. "You didn't know?"

"I had no idea. But yes. I'm sure people have motives that you'd never even know about."

Lala shuddered. "I'll have Papa send security."

"Please do. And call Mrs. B. Have her send hotel security right now, before his security gets here."

He looked at her.

"And for the meeting with Inspector Singh, don't forget everything we talked about. Grande dame. Regal. Grace Kelly. Vague. Truthful, but not helpful. You got this."

"I got what?" Lala replied, puzzled.

"Never mind."

* * *

Mrs. B., Ro, and Inspector Singh sat in the interview room. Catherine was dialed in to the speakerphone on the table.

"I'm sorry, guys, but I have to do a yoga class with Chris. He's about to smell a rat. He can't know how involved I am with all this."

"That's fine," the inspector said. "Mrs. Mehta has unexpectedly agreed to speak to me. I've asked her to come to the Palace in an hour."

"Good. What about her husband?"

Inspector Singh smiled grimly. "He's entitled to all sorts of protections as a member of Parliament. He's refused to come in so far. I'll likely have to go to his room to get his statement."

"All right." Catherine paused. "What's happening now? The VB?"

"The VB?" the inspector asked, puzzled.

"I'll leave you to it."

She hung up.

* * *

"Much more relaxing without Mrs. Forrester, don't you think?" Mrs. B. popped open another Diet Pepsi and sat back in her recliner. "At least we don't have to have that little dog in here with us too. I told her I was allergic."

Ro poured himself a cup of coffee and settled in as well.

They heard a knock on the door in the other room.

Through the mirror, Ro and Mrs. B. watched the VB shuffle in, red-eyed, looking thoroughly defeated.

"Are you feeling all right?"

"I'm sorry." The VB somehow managed to shake his head and nod at the same time. "I think I'm still in shock. I had no idea what had happened to Amrita until your officer called me."

"You knew Miss Dey well?"

"Yes. Well, yes and no. We only met here, but we spent a lot of time together."

He began to sniffle.

Inspector Singh mechanically handed him a tissue.

"Thank you," the VB said, wiping his nose.

He paused, collecting himself.

"She was a remarkable woman."

The inspector bowed his head respectfully for a moment.

Ro bowed his head too. Amrita had been a remarkable woman. No doubt about that.

"I understand that you're not a guest here," the inspector continued smoothly. "But not a staff member either. Would you mind explaining your role to me?"

The VB sat up a little straighter. "I'm a visiting meditation teacher here."

"Not so distraught when he gets to talk about himself," Mrs. B. snickered.

"Where do you live full-time?"

"Well, I don't really live anywhere. I spend most of the year visiting and working at various spas and hotels. At their invitation."

"So he's basically a grifter," Ro concluded.

Mrs. B. shushed him.

"How exactly did you come to Samsara?"

"Samsara has visiting experts all year round. People who display mastery in their fields."

"So Samsara contacted you?"

"Well, not exactly." The VB shifted in his seat. "I wrote to Samsara about a year ago asking if they'd consider me. They wrote back a few months ago."

"So difficult to get someone around the holidays," Mrs. B. confided, turning to Ro.

"You should have just picked someone at random out of the phone book," Ro replied.

"This is the . . ." Looking down at his notes, Inspector Singh paused, dubious. He looked back up at the VB. "The Visiting Light program?"

The VB nodded.

"And is this your first time in India?"

"Yes," he replied. Then the VB visibly tensed. "Well, actually, no."

"Wait, what?" Ro leaned forward, suddenly alert. "What's this all about?"

"He lied for some reason, and then realized how easily he'd get caught," Mrs. B. said. "I wish we had popcorn." She picked up the phone and said a few words in Hindi.

"When were you last here?" the inspector continued, mild.

"A few months ago. Just to Mumbai. Visiting friends." The VB looked at the inspector. "I'm sorry. I'm still in shock."

He looked less in shock than when he'd walked in, Ro thought.

Ro's eyes narrowed.

The inspector paused, then decided to move on. "How did you come to know Miss Dey?"

The VB visibly relaxed. Ro was totally absorbed. He'd never before realized how much people unconsciously give away with their bodies.

"I hold a sort of open house twice a week to talk about my work. Amrita came to one and then booked some private sessions with me."

"Private sessions of what kind?"

"Breathwork and meditation."

The inspector paused. "I'm sorry to ask this question so directly, but were you and Miss Dey involved romantically?"

"No," he replied. "We weren't. But I would have liked to be." He struggled to keep his composure. "I had never met anyone like her."

Suddenly, he started to gurgle.

"I was falling in love with her." Tears began to stream down his cheeks.

The popcorn arrived.

Inspector Singh handed the VB another tissue. "Did you plan to stay in touch with Miss Dey after she left Samsara?"

The VB nodded. "Yes. She had invited me to come stay with her in London on my way back to the US. She had some people she thought I should meet. To raise my visibility." He swallowed. "I thought she was going to change my life forever. As if I could start over."

"Ah. I understand why he's so bereft now," Mrs. B. said, nodding. "He's just lost his golden ticket."

Ro almost felt sorry for the VB for a moment. Almost.

But then he wondered. What on earth did Amrita have up her sleeve with this guy?

The inspector picked up his notebook. "When are you planning to leave India?"

"I'm planning to travel around for a month or two after Samsara. So maybe in February."

"Huh." Ro shook his head. "First he's never been here before, then he has been here before, and now he's staying here for a few months?"

The inspector made a note. "All right. Could you please walk me through your movements last night?"

"Of course." The VB sounded mechanical. "I was just in my room, doing some work, until dinner. I got to dinner just after 8."

"Did you see Miss Dey?"

"Yes, but only for a minute. I left to call my family for Christmas."

"Father was some sort of rural pastor," Ro informed Mrs. B. "Mother died of cancer. Or diabetes, maybe. First wife cheated on him and peaced out. Then he found meditation. Love and light. Lucky us."

"How do you know all that?" Mrs. B. asked, impressed.

"I Googled him out of disinterest," Ro replied.

"Do you know what time you left?" the inspector continued.

"Around 8:30."

"Did you eat with the Forresters?"

"No." The VB shifted uncomfortably. "I just grabbed a quick bite standing at the buffet."

It was plausible.

"Where are you staying here, by the way?" Inspector Singh asked.

"In the staff quarters. The wing with the yoga instructors."

"What time did you finish the call with your family?"

"Probably around 9:15. I can check."

"Did you go back to the dinner afterward?"

"No."

"Why not?" the inspector asked casually. "It was still quite early."

"I had some work to do."

He saw the look on the inspector's face.

"Administrative stuff. Bills. You know." He sounded a little defensive.

"So you did not see Miss Dey alive again after that," the inspector said bluntly.

"No." The VB's eyes started welling up again, as if on command.

"Can you think of anything that might be useful for us to know? Did she confide anything to you?"

The VB began to flush again. There was a long pause. "I really can't think of anything." He sounded insincere.

Ro turned to Mrs. B. "Why on earth is this guy here? And I'm sorry, but why do you have a white person teaching Indian people how to meditate?"

"At Samsara we are color blind," Mrs. B. responded with dignity. "We had a lovely white man last month. From Boston. He stretched out my QL muscles, whatever they are. Or QF muscles. I didn't even know they existed." She sighed. "I don't know that this one's all that much worse than anyone else, though. Yes, it's now obvious that he's a fiasco, but we are admittedly in an unusual situation."

Ro nodded, a bit unsure. He could well imagine that the VB wasn't all that much worse than past Visiting Lights. But somehow, something about this guy just got under his skin.

"Perhaps we should cancel the program," Mrs. B. continued, meditative. "Or at least change its name. It really is rather silly. We had one very unfortunately unattractive man a year or two ago whom everyone called the Visiting Fright. But it's hopeless. If it were a Visiting Master, there would be a Visiting Disaster. A Visiting Scholar could become a Visiting Horror. Etcetera."

Ro suddenly yawned. "It's been a long day."

"And we still have Lala ahead of us." Mrs. B. gave Ro a meaningful look.

Ro squirmed uncomfortably. But the thought of Lala still made him smile.

* * *

Lala sat in the interview room, cool and collected, a cup of coffee on the table in front of her. Her lawyer, an older man, wore glasses and a well-cut suit that had aged along with him.

"Thank you for coming to speak with me, Mrs. Mehta," Inspector Singh began, rather formal.

"Of course," she replied quietly. "It's one's duty in a situation such as this."

Ro tried his best to suppress his grin.

Catherine, who had come back for Lala's interview, eyed him with interest.

"You must still be in shock," the inspector said. "Do you feel ready to discuss what happened last night?"

Lala's lawyer looked at her warily. She nodded at him.

"Mrs. Mehta will answer your questions, but I'll ask you to stop this interview at any moment if it becomes too much for her," her lawyer said.

"I understand."

The inspector marked a brief pause.

"How well did you know Miss Dey, Mrs. Mehta?"

"I hardly knew her at all."

"When did you first meet her?"

"Here, at Samsara. Last Christmas."

Lala slowly removed her fur headband, folded it, and placed it on the table. Massive earrings of black pearl and diamonds glinted from her ears.

Ro sat straight up. "Wait a second. I just thought of something."

"What?" Catherine asked, turning toward him.

"Not now. I'll tell you later," he replied, absorbed by Lala's interview.

"Fine, but for goodness' sake, write it down so you don't forget it."

She tossed him a copy of *Hello!* magazine and a pen.

"Did you spend much time together?" the inspector asked.

"Only the way one does with fellow hotel guests."

"Did you keep in touch with Miss Dey after you left Samsara last year?"

"How do you mean?" Lala asked, polite.

"Did you socialize with her over the course of the last year?"

"Not really." Lala put her finger to her lips, thinking. "I may have seen her at a couple of parties, but I can't be sure. I wasn't really paying attention, you see." She smiled at the inspector and shrugged. "She lived in Europe in any case, didn't she?"

Lala's lawyer put his hand on the table.

"Do you know where in Europe?"

Lala shook her head. "I'm afraid I don't," she replied with a wan smile.

"Apologies. I know this will be difficult for you to discuss, but my understanding is that you discovered Miss Dey's body."

"Yes," Lala replied. "Yes, I did."

She closed her eyes briefly.

Inspector Singh allowed her a moment.

"Can you please tell me a bit about the circumstances?" he continued, gentle.

"We'd all left to stargaze. Ro Krishna and I stopped in the spa to get everyone blankets. And then, when we were leaving the building, I turned, and I saw . . ."

Lala's voice began to falter. Her lawyer put his hand on her arm.

She turned to him. "It's all right," she said, brave. "I can keep going."

He looked her intently in the eye, then removed his hand and sat back.

Catherine chuckled.

"I saw something white. Something that didn't belong there."

"It was very dark, and the body was actually quite covered."

Inspector Singh leaned in slightly.

"How did you manage to see it?"

"I have unusually good eyesight." Lala leaned back in her chair, now on familiar ground.

"Did you know it was a body?" the inspector asked.

"No. But I knew something was wrong." Lala shook her head and closed her eyes. "I felt it. Something was very wrong."

"Are you all right?" her lawyer asked.

Lala opened her eyes and turned to him. "Thank you," she said simply.

Mrs. B. leaned in, rapt.

"But you moved toward it, whatever it was," the inspector continued. "Weren't you afraid?"

"Yes," Lala replied, surprised. "Of course I was afraid. But whatever I saw wasn't moving, I suppose, and I wasn't alone."

She went quiet.

"I'm sorry. I've never seen a dead body before."

Inspector Singh paused, respectful, then continued.

"Did you touch the body?"

"No." Lala shook her head vigorously. "Absolutely not. Anyone would know they shouldn't. And Mrs. Forrester took control almost straight away, regardless."

"Because you passed out," Catherine remarked, turning to Ro.

"Bite me."

"Why wasn't your husband with you last night?" The inspector's tone remained light.

Lala started. Her lawyer tensed.

"He had a stomachache. He decided to stay in the room to rest."

"Why didn't you stay with him if he was ill?"

Lala raised her eyebrows at the inspector. "Have you ever had a stomach bug? The last thing you want is a witness. So you can try to preserve at least a shred of dignity."

"True," Ro said, proud. Mrs. B. nodded too.

"In any event, I checked on him all evening to see how he was feeling."

"Did he leave the room at all last night?"

"I wouldn't have thought so. He was really quite unwell." Lala paused. "He still isn't entirely better, to be honest. Sanjay might be many things, but he isn't a hypochondriac."

The inspector looked down at his notebook, then back up at Lala. "Whom did you sit with at dinner?"

"With Ro Krishna and the Forresters."

Catherine and Ro both inhaled sharply. She hadn't sat with them.

"But I only sat down once the performance started," Lala continued, tranquil. "Everyone was milling about the buffet until then. I'm not even sure that Ro and the others saw me sit down. They probably didn't, actually, as they were facing the other way."

Catherine looked through the mirror, admiring.

"Mrs. Mehta, if you'll forgive me, I'd like to ask you a somewhat unorthodox question."

The inspector paused.

"How would you describe Miss Dey in one word?"

Lala thought about it. "Overconfident."

"Overconfident? That's interesting."

"But I might only be saying that because she got herself murdered. Which means she wasn't quite as clever as she thought she was."

The lawyer put both hands on the table.

"I'm sorry. I'm still quite shaken by last night." Lala gave the inspector another wan smile. "Is that all for now?"

"Just one last question." The inspector paused. "You said you messaged with your husband all evening. Did you see him again at any point during the evening before you discovered Miss Dey's body?"

Lala paused. "I'm sorry, Inspector, I feel quite dizzy."

The lawyer immediately took Lala's arm and glared at Inspector Singh. "We'll have to continue this later."

And with that, they left the room.

"Brava," Mrs. B. said.

"What's she hiding, do you think?" Catherine sounded genuinely curious.

"Well, she's certainly not hiding that she seriously disliked Rita," Mrs. B. mused.

"Whatever." Ro sat back, crossing his arms. "Anyway, she obviously didn't do it."

Mrs. B. and Catherine looked at him, curious.

"If she'd done it, she wouldn't have discovered the body."

The inspector entered the room.

Catherine turned to Ro. "What was that thing you thought of earlier?"

"Oh." Ro looked down at the issue of *Hello!*, then back up at the inspector. "This is important. Did you find earrings on Amrita's body? I don't remember any mention of earrings."

"Hold on," the inspector said. He left the room. Through the mirror, they watched him pick up his notebook and leaf through it. He came back in. "No."

Ro stood up and began to pace. "She was definitely wearing earrings when she left dinner."

"Are you sure?" the inspector asked.

"Absolutely." Ro turned to face Inspector Singh. "I remember because they were the same earrings she was wearing when I met her in London. They matched her eyes. Turquoise and diamond." He paused. "Were they in her room?"

"We don't have the final room inventory yet. We should have it by the end of the day." He looked at Mrs. B. "Along with the results of our examination of her body."

Mrs. B. nodded approvingly. "I wonder what you'll find."

The inspector remembered something.

"Actually, one last question. Why do you call Mr. Charney the VB?"

The three of them looked at one another, a little embarrassed.

"It stands for the Visiting Blight," Ro admitted.

The inspector shook his head, disapproving. "That's sophomoric. Shall we plan on meeting back here tomorrow morning at 9?"

"Agreed," Mrs. B. said, clapping her hands and pressing a button to bring her recliner back upright. She turned to Ro. "Let's call you a golf cart."

Ro couldn't wait to take a hot shower and get into bed. "Thanks. I certainly wasn't planning to walk."

* * *

Scrubbed clean and wearing a freshly ironed pair of kurta pajama, Ro was about to get into bed when the phone in his room rang. He took his time, sitting down on the bed and pouring himself a cup of sleep tea, then answered on the fourth ring.

"Yes?"

"Mr. Krishna? This is Inspector Singh."

There was a long and pregnant pause.

"Inspector," Ro said, hesitant. "Is everything all right?"

"I'm afraid Miss Dey's body has disappeared," the inspector said, affectless.

Ro gasped. "What do you mean?"

Inspector Singh paused. "Miss Dey's body was picked up this morning to be transferred to the police morgue. But her body never arrived."

For a long moment, neither man spoke.

"I don't know what to say." Unlike her watch, Ro had a feeling Amrita's body wasn't going to turn up.

"We will discuss this in the morning." Inspector Singh paused for a moment. "I don't like this at all," he muttered, seemingly to himself.

Then he hung up.

DAY 5

(December 27)

R o woke up and knew exactly where he was. It felt the same as when he didn't, he realized, suddenly jaded.

He looked down at himself. His white kurta pajama perfectly matched the crisp white sheets, making it look like he had no body: only forearms, hands, and feet.

Rolling out of bed, he stood up, then stretched a little. His body and mind both felt heavy and dull, but that was understandable. It was no wonder that the previous two days had left him feeling hungover.

Tea would help. He buzzed and, as always, heard a knock on the door an impossibly short time later. A smiling man came in and put the tray on the usual table, clearing Ro's sleep tea on the way out.

Ro went to examine the tray. Three envelopes today. He didn't recognize the handwriting on any of them.

He took the dagger out of the desk drawer and sliced open the first one at random. Taking out the card, he was amused to see that the hotel had ordered note cards for Inspector Singh, who had unsurprisingly chosen what looked like Times New Roman in black capital letters for his name. Which was, apparently, "INSPECTOR SINGH." The note asked him to be at the Palace at 9:00 a.m. for the morning meeting.

The second envelope was on official Samsara stationery. Ro opened it, then shivered.

The note was from Dr. Menon. The underlined date at the top of the note, at least, reminded Ro that it was his father's birthday.

"Dear Mr. Krishna," the note began disapprovingly, "I have been informed that you will not be able to attend our scheduled consultation today. I would ask that you reschedule it as soon as possible. In the meantime, please take your steam today after your Udwarthana treatment this afternoon. Please take as much mental rest as you can."

More words were at the bottom of the card. Ro scanned down.

Under his illegible signature, Dr. Menon had added, "I hope you are not reading anything besides this note."

Ro dropped the note into the wastepaper basket, then sliced open the final envelope and pulled out the card. Then he did a double take.

The card was from the Honorable Sanjay Mehta, MP, who had opted for a sober charcoal grey and who had stiff up-and-down handwriting.

"Mr. Krishna, I should be grateful if you could spare me a half hour of your time later this afternoon. I propose 5:30 p.m. in my office (Room 605), but do feel free to suggest another time if that time is inconvenient."

Ro's eyebrows rose. This was a curveball.

He looked at his schedule. 5:30 would actually work perfectly. He dashed off a note to Sanjay accepting the appointment. Then, spontaneously, he pulled out his phone to check the meaning of the name Sanjay. He was quite displeased to find it meant "triumphant" or "victorious."

"I don't know about that," Ro muttered to himself.

He took out another blank card and hesitated for a second, his pen hovering over the card.

"Your husband has asked to speak to me later today. Just wanted to let you know. Please leave a note for me in the spa if necessary. Will be in touch afterward." He sealed the envelope and addressed it to Lala. Finally, he jotted a note to Joss suggesting that they meet for lunch. He'd barely seen Joss, he realized, suddenly a bit annoyed.

Leaving the room, he searched for someone in the hall to whom he could give his notes, then came upon a small service area, hidden by an unobtrusive curtain.

"Hello?" he called, gingerly pushing it open.

The uniformed man from earlier that morning sprang up from his seat. "Sir?"

"Hi there. Could you please arrange to have these notes delivered?"

Ro handed over the ones addressed to Sanjay and Joss, then hesitated.

"Could you please ensure this one is given to Mrs. Mehta when she is alone?"

"Yes, Sir. Of course."

As he turned to leave, Ro saw the shelves of the service area were labeled with room numbers. The upper shelves contained trays of morning tea, while the lower shelves contained trays of evening tea. All ready to go.

Ro smiled. He liked it when things were well-organized.

Another thought occurred to him as he left the Residence. Why hadn't Amrita been murdered with one of the daggers?

They were certainly sharp enough. It would have been so much easier than with a rock.

* * *

The inspector looked tired and drawn when Ro arrived at the Palace. Catherine was standing, drinking coffee and staring out the window.

"Joss can't make lunch, by the way," she began abruptly. "He wanted me to tell you."

"Oh," Ro replied, a bit vexed.

"And Mrs. B. wants us to fill her in later," Catherine continued, without turning around. "She said she needs a spa day."

"Good for her." Ro sat down, then looked back up at Catherine. "Does Chris even know what you're up to right now?"

"Ugh." Catherine flopped into a chair. "No. He thinks I'm getting tons of treatments. He's starting to get a little weirded out, to be honest."

"Don't you think you should just tell him what you're doing?" Ro was puzzled. "I mean, he's going to find out sooner or later, isn't he?"

"Let's burn that bridge when we come to it." Catherine sighed. "He's going to be so pissed. I promised him I gave all this up. Years ago."

"Are they out scouting today?"

"No." Catherine motioned toward the inspector. "They're not letting anyone leave the hotel today."

"So we're telling the guests?" Ro replied, surprised. "Has Mrs. B. agreed?"

The inspector shook his head. "As it happens, there were no departures scheduled today, so we're saying there was a road accident and that the road down the mountain is closed. The road's certainly dangerous enough for it to be true, in any case. Let's get started."

He took a seat.

"As both of you know, we discovered last night that Miss Dey's body was missing." He paused, his face grim. "We have since learned that a false morgue truck picked up the body at Samsara yesterday before the real truck arrived. The driver of the real truck assumed there had been a duplication of orders somehow."

Ro's jaw dropped.

Catherine turned her head and looked at the wall. "You should check the local crematoria," she said quietly.

"We've already done so." Inspector Singh paused. "A body matching the description of hers was cremated near Haridwar yesterday morning."

"Oh, my God." Ro stared at the inspector in disbelief, mouth wide open.

"Wow," Catherine muttered, shaking her head. "Had you gotten any samples at all yet? From the body?"

The inspector shook his head. "All that was to be done at the morgue. We have no physical evidence beyond the brief initial examination."

Catherine stood up suddenly and went back to the window. She started pacing.

"Have you told her next of kin?" Ro asked.

"I was coming to that. We spoke to Mrs. Acharya yesterday. Her sister."

"Is she on her way?"

Inspector Singh shook his head. "Her family's in Thailand for the holidays. She did, however, help us contact Miss Dey's lawyers in London. We will speak to them later today."

"How did her sister seem?" Catherine abruptly turned around. "Did she seem upset?"

"She seemed more put out than anything else, I'd say."

Catherine turned back to the window.

Ro remembered something else. "What about her earrings? Were they in the room?"

"Ah, yes." Inspector Singh rummaged through the papers on his desk, then handed a few stapled sheets to Ro. "Here's her room inventory."

Ro looked at Catherine. "Aren't you going to take a look?"

"Already seen it," she said, waving her hand dismissively. Evidently, it hadn't been helpful. At least not to her.

Ro began to scan the pages. He was initially surprised by how many clothes Amrita had brought with her, but then remembered she was planning to go to Bombay after Samsara. That reminded him of something.

He raised his head. "You know she went to Bombay for a day last week, right?"

"Yes," the inspector replied. "She stayed at the Soho House and used hotel cars throughout her stay. We're verifying her movements, but nothing of interest has come up."

"All right," Ro replied, a little deflated. He looked back down at the list. Amrita certainly wasn't the kind to travel light, he thought, raising a mental eyebrow at the truly startling number of Loro Piana scarves she had brought with her. He flipped past a lengthy list of beauty products to arrive at the section headed "Jewelry." He scanned the list carefully, following the text with his index finger. Some beautiful pieces. Sundry Cartier earrings and rings in Cartier boxes, including the panthers he'd met at lunch. More Alhambra. Bulgari. Boucheron. JAR. A diamond-and-emerald earring and necklace set, in a Harry Winston box. Once he'd gotten to the end of the list, he sat back up, disappointed.

"No. They're not here."

The inspector shook his head, puzzled. "You're sure she was wearing them?"

"Absolutely." He looked back down at the list. There was something off about it. "Where was the jewelry?"

"All her jewelry was in the safe. Besides what she was wearing."

"She fit all those jewelry boxes into the safe?" Ro asked, puzzled.

Inspector Singh nodded. "They put an especially large safe into the room for her. She always stayed in the same room."

"Oh. Interesting." Ro paused. "Was anything else in the safe?"

"No," Catherine said. She turned to the inspector. "You were going to check when the safe was last opened, yes?"

The inspector went to the door, opened it, and called something out in Hindi. They heard a faint voice reply. He closed the door again and stood against it, thinking.

"The safe was opened at 9:07 p.m. and closed again at 9:13 p.m."

Ro whistled. "So she went back to her room to open the safe."

Catherine stood, her brow furrowed, thinking furiously. "But that was 20 minutes after she left dinner. How could she have gotten her watch back? She couldn't have gotten to the Palace and back in 20 minutes. On foot, anyway."

"But we don't know that she had her watch then. And we also don't know when exactly she was killed."

Ro paused, thinking about it.

"She could've left dinner, then done something during those 10 minutes— we don't know what—and then have gone to her room. Then, sometime after 9:10, she went to the Palace, got her watch, and was killed on her way back down."

"But nobody on staff will admit to giving her the watch," Catherine replied.

"Or to telling her during dinner that her watch had been found, even." Ro paused. "But that call happened. There's no doubt in my mind. She had definitely lost her watch, and she was definitely thrilled that someone had found it." Ro turned back to the inspector. "Can I see the list of what was found on her body again?"

The inspector nodded. He searched on the table briefly, then silently passed the piece of paper to Ro.

A fur headband. A Cartier watch. A turquoise and mother-of-pearl necklace. White cotton kurta pajama. A robe. A room key.

Ro shook his head. "I really don't like that her earrings aren't here." He paused. "Maybe the murderer took them."

"But left behind a gold-and-diamond Cartier watch?" Catherine asked.

"Wait a second." Ro was still looking at the list. "This definitely isn't all the jewelry Amrita had with her."

He looked up at them.

"I'm sure I saw her wear things that aren't on this list. She was wearing these gigantic diamond drop earrings the other day. They're not here." He closed his eyes, trying to remember. "And a diamond tennis bracelet." He shook his head, frustrated. "Other things too, I think."

Catherine took the list from him. "She was wearing these ginormous ruby earrings a few days ago. They're not on here."

"Maybe she took some jewelry to Bombay with her."

"It's plausible." The inspector looked at Ro. "You didn't ask why she was going, by any chance?"

"No," Ro replied firmly. "I never would have asked her that. We weren't on those kinds of terms."

He looked down and scanned the inventory once more, trying to make a mental checklist of what he usually brought when traveling. He ticked them off the list. Noise-canceling headphones. Travel wallet. Chargers. Laptop. Two iPhones. Passport. OCI. Then he realized. "Keys." He leaned back, satisfied. "There aren't any keys here."

"She had her room key with her." The inspector looked at Ro and understood. "Oh. You mean her house keys."

"Yes. Wouldn't she have had her house keys with her somewhere?"

"Um. Not necessarily," Catherine volunteered, half-raising a hand. She sounded a little sheepish.

They looked at her.

"When you have staff, you don't carry keys. Someone opens the door."

"So you don't have keys?"

"No." Catherine paused. "Well, I mean, I have keys. Of course I have keys. But I don't carry them around, and I wouldn't be surprised if Amrita didn't either."

"You're saying you don't have keys to your house with you here?" the inspector asked, sounding dumbfounded.

"No. Well, actually, yes. That is what I'm saying."

There was a long pause.

"What do we do now?" Ro asked finally. There was still something about the inventory that bothered him, but he let it be. It would come to him if it was meant to. Also, he had a posture assessment scheduled in twenty minutes.

"Well, we'll keep moving forward. I'll keep looking for links between Miss Dey and guests here. Looking for possible motives."

Inspector Singh smiled, briefly but not unpleasantly.

"Please go enjoy your day. I'll be in touch with any updates."

* * *

Ro and Catherine sat in a golf cart on their way down to the spa, each lost in their own thoughts.

As they neared the place where Amrita had been killed, Ro hesitated. "Actually, Driver, could you stop for a second?"

"What are you doing?" Catherine asked.

"Hold on a sec."

Ro got off the golf cart and stood on the path for a moment, looking around. A couple of monkeys playing nearby saw them and scattered.

The morning mist hadn't yet entirely lifted. Ro sniffed the air. It smelled fresh, like pine. A hint of wood smoke came from somewhere. The spot was eerily silent except for the occasional chirp of a bird and some rustling in the leaves.

He looked to the left and right, then above. Nothing but trees.

Catherine got off too, and stood next to him, expectant. "Are we having a moment of silence?" she asked dryly.

Ro looked at her. "No, but now that you mention it, perhaps we should."

Catherine opened her mouth to say something, but Ro turned his back to her and closed his eyes.

For a moment, he simply stood there, eyes closed, allowing himself to be present. He inhaled and exhaled slowly, feeling the air fill his lungs and the oxygen go to every corner of his body. He bowed his head out of respect.

And then, suddenly, he felt Amrita's presence. He let his head hang, his eyes still closed.

He was filled with sadness. Had Amrita really been meant to die so young?

There's something you want me to do here, Ro asked her suddenly. What? He knew not to promise to seek justice for her. He wasn't even sure what justice would mean.

He waited. And then, all of a sudden, he understood.

Amrita wanted to know why she had died.

Because she did not know why she had died.

I'll try to find out, Ro whispered. I'll try to find out.

He raised his head again and opened his eyes. Catherine was looking at him. "She will be missed," he said simply.

Ro looked over to the side of the path and saw the rocks lining it. They were all big and black, fairly uniform. Choosing one and picking it up, he was surprised by its weight. The rocks were much heavier than they looked. Bending his knees slightly, he lifted it over his head. He winced a little.

"This isn't that easy," he said, looking at Catherine. "These rocks are pretty awkward."

"You're complicating things," Catherine replied, brusque. "It's easy as pie."

She felt around the back of Ro's neck.

"Just hit anywhere around here. Hard. And then hope for the best."

She grabbed the rock from Ro and grasped it with both hands at chest level, facing him.

Then she tossed the rock back onto the side of the path.

"Let's go."

* * *

Ro's posture assessment did not go well.

A tiny woman in a tracksuit and sneakers had dissected him as if he were an earthworm in an eighth-grade science class. Ro skulked out of the room, having been diagnosed with a too-forward head and neck; rounded shoulders; internally rotated arms; an upper body tilted toward the right, yet a right pelvis higher than the left; an anterior pelvic tilt; and two externally rotated legs.

He wandered back into the atrium, dazed, to wait for his private yoga class, and was very happy to find Mrs. B. in the reception area of the spa. She was curled up on one of the overstuffed couches, flicking through a magazine, her reading glasses on.

"Hi," he said, sitting down next to her.

"Oh, hello," she said, absently turning a page of *Hello!* "How was this morning?"

Ro considered. "Well, you heard about Amrita's body, of course."

"No?" Mrs. B. said idly.

"Her body disappeared. It got picked up by a fake morgue truck and cremated straight away." Ro looked at Mrs. B. "So there won't be any DNA evidence."

"Well, that's a piece of luck," Mrs. B. replied. "Better for us if there's as little fuss as possible. And frankly, I can't bear the idea of people picking apart Rita's body and swabbing everything." She shuddered. "Poor Rita. And poor Meena. So undignified."

Ro was surprised at her cavalier attitude, but decided to let it slide. "Are you planning to cut your trip short?"

"Why would I do that?" She sounded surprised.

"I don't know?" Ro shrugged. "I mean, maybe you feel unsafe here? Considering there was a murder?"

Grimacing, Mrs. B. made a gesture with her hand for Ro to keep his voice down.

Ro winced. "Sorry," he half-whispered.

"Why would I feel unsafe here? My life isn't exactly as glamorous as Rita's was." She paused. "I suppose it's true that my sons-in-law wouldn't be too sad to see me dead, though. They'd finally get their hands on the money." She looked at Ro, who was visibly embarrassed, and smiled. "You know, I'm always convinced they're going to cut the brakes on one of those Land Rovers while I'm in it. Why do you think I bring my own car every year?"

"That's the second time you've brought up the brakes being cut," Ro said. "That's quite specific, no?"

There was a long pause. Mrs. B. turned back to her magazine. "I had a dream once," she replied, a bit too casually.

"If you don't mind my asking, who actually owns the hotel?"

"Technically, some little man in Liechtenstein, I expect." She flipped another page of *Hello!* "But my daughter and my son-in-law built it with my husband's money. And mine. You know, it's quite irresponsible that they didn't come back from the Maldives after all this mess, but I suppose I did tell them not to bother." She turned to Ro and leaned in, confidential. "Also, it's too awful, but I'm enjoying myself. Just a bit. Aren't you?"

"I know what you mean." Ro wasn't enjoying himself, not exactly, but he did feel more himself than he'd felt in a long time. He felt more awake. And, ironically, more alive.

"It's so interesting, isn't it?" Mrs. B. continued. "I'd planned to spend New Year in Rougemont, but this is much more fun."

Rougemont, Ro thought. Switzerland again. "Why is everyone in Switzerland all the time?" he muttered, half to himself.

Mrs. B. nodded, taking the question seriously. "Yes. It's strange. When I went to the top of the Jungfraujoch some years ago, there was an Indian restaurant. Right there, at the top of the mountain. Most unexpected."

Ro looked up to see Fairuza walking toward them. "Not you," he said involuntarily.

Fairuza grinned at him. "Shall we begin?"

"Depends on what we're doing," Ro muttered, shrinking into the couch.

She laughed. "Just yoga. Or meditation. Promise."

"Fine." Grumbling, Ro extricated himself from the sofa. He stood up and made to follow Fairuza, then thought of something.

"Actually, would you mind giving us one second?"

"Of course." Fairuza stepped a discreet distance away.

"Have you spoken to Lala?"

"That poor girl." Mrs. B. immediately turned serious. "I think the shock is only just hitting her."

"I know it's unlikely, but I'm concerned the killer could have mistaken Amrita for her. They were dressed the same and wearing the same headband." Mrs. B. shuddered. "She has security now? 24 hours a day?"

"Yes," Mrs. B. replied. "Even when her husband is there. Especially. Oh, here you are, Rishi."

She beamed at the handsome masseur who'd appeared at her side.

"One last thing. Do you carry your house keys with you when you travel?"

"No." Mrs. B. sounded puzzled. "There's always someone home. Why do you ask?"

"Never mind."

* * *

Ro followed Fairuza down a hallway, admiring her posture and elegance, the way the kurta sleeves hung around her delicate wrists. They arrived at a door with a "5" on it. Fairuza pushed it open.

Ro and Fairuza entered an empty white room. He could see the overcast sky through the windows placed high on the walls. An alcove contained yoga mats, blocks, and blankets. They each took a mat and, moving back to the center of the room, rolled them out. Fairuza sat, gesturing to Ro to do the same. He sat, crossing his legs, unconsciously pulling his right foot onto his left thigh.

"So, we will have two private sessions together to focus on yoga or meditation, or a mix of both. As you know"—she smiled briefly—"because you signed up for them. Do you have a sense of what you'd prefer?"

"Not really." Ro thought for a second. "Maybe meditation, just because I'd be less likely to take a meditation class in normal life."

"Excellent," Fairuza said. She tucked her legs behind her. "Do you meditate regularly?"

"It's funny," Ro said, musing. "I feel like I'm actually meditating a lot of the time. I don't actually think that much. My brain is sort of in neutral unless I have to think about something. I think it must be genetic."

"It's possible," Fairuza said. "I'm quite similar."

"I remember when I found out white people think all the time," Ro said, reflecting. "It was in college. I was in line for a movie with my friend Joss— who's with me here, by the way—and he asked what I was thinking about. I was so surprised. I was like, 'Nothing. We're standing in line.' Then I looked at him and asked him, 'Are *you* thinking about something?' And he was. So hectic."

"What was he thinking about?" Fairuza said.

Ro paused, trying to remember. "You know, I don't think I asked." He turned back to Fairuza. "Actually, do you think that's why Indian people age so well? Because they can stop thinking whenever they want?"

"We," Fairuza said. "Not they."

Ro grimaced. Yikes, he thought to himself.

"But yes," she continued. "It's an idea. Anxiety is very aging. And indecision."

"And lack of clarity," Ro said, thinking. "Only a white person could have written *Ulysses*."

"Only a white person could have read it," Fairuza replied.

Ro giggled. "How did you get into meditation?"

"I started meditating when I started doing yoga seriously. I can honestly say that meditation changed everything about my life."

Ro was intrigued. "How so?"

"It's so difficult to say without sounding like a cliché, but I suppose it is one. I realized that you have the solution to every problem inside yourself. And that made me calm down."

Ro nodded.

"The key to a happy life, I feel," Fairuza continued, "is to eliminate anxiety. Anxiety adds nothing. It does not make you perform better. It only makes things worse. Ultimately, anxiety is nothing more than an excuse."

"Have you actually eliminated anxiety from your life?" Ro asked.

"Of course not. I'm only human. But I've made a lot of progress. And I've found other things that help."

"Like what?" Ro asked.

"I always tell the truth," Fairuza said simply. "Or at least, the truth as I see it to be. It makes life so much simpler."

"Yes," Ro said. "I actually can't lie. At all. If I try to say something that isn't the truth, I get all flustered. I don't know where to look."

"Knowing what's yours and what isn't," Fairuza continued serenely. "Recognizing the energy in objects. And respecting them. When you behave with honor, life is simple. Problems fall away."

Ro nodded. "Also, just doing your best. It's that simple. As long as I tried my best, I'll forgive myself if I made a mistake. Just knowing I made the best decision I could at the time is enough. And learning a lesson from it."

They sat for a moment.

"Where do you think the solutions come from? The solutions you find?" Ro asked, curious.

"God," Fairuza said. "What about you? Are you religious?"

"I am," Ro said. "I don't understand how anyone isn't. I mean, it's not like every single person in the history of humanity until the invention of Wi-Fi was a moron." He paused. "People built temples, and churches, and cathedrals for a reason. It's not just because they had nothing better to do." He thought for a second. "Every time you have an idea, God is putting it there. Where else is it coming from?"

"That was nicely put," Fairuza said. "Most people just pat themselves on the back for being clever."

"Oh, I do that too. They're not mutually exclusive," Ro said. "I also think God lives in algorithms on the internet. In randomizers. But that's another story." He paused. "I was never good at science. You don't have to prove something for it to be true. The relationship between science and the truth is a Venn diagram, it's not just a concentric circle." He reflected for a moment. "I loved math, though. And you? What did you study?"

"I studied French and philosophy," Fairuza laughed. "Very practical."

"Here in India?"

"Yes. I grew up mostly in Delhi." She fiddled with her hands. "But I'm going to spend the winter in Europe this year."

"Oh, really?" Ro said, interested.

"Yes. I'm going to teach yoga at the Gstaad Palace."

Switzerland again, Ro thought. "Have you taught there before?"

"No," Fairuza said. "But I know it reasonably well. My brother lives in Switzerland."

"Banker?" he asked, sympathetic.

Fairuza nodded. "Did you come to India often as a child?"

"No," Ro said. "My parents left for university and never came back. I don't really know if that was their intention."

"Immigration is hard," Fairuza said. "It cuts off family stories. And family energy. It's almost impossible not to lose the richness, the texture."

"Yes. It's a total reset. Everything becomes antiseptic," Ro said.

"Where in India is your family from?" Fairuza asked.

"We're Tamil." Ro thought for a second. "I hadn't thought of it this way before, but I'm one of the first people in hundreds of years, if not more, of my family not to have been born within the same few hundred square miles. On both sides."

Ro considered for a moment.

"But immigration isn't the only kind of reset. I suppose Partition was trauma that reset things as well." He looked at Fairuza. "My family was lucky. Partition didn't really affect us. Not directly, at least. But it seems just . . ." He paused, at a loss for words. "Unimaginable, I guess."

"Yes," Fairuza responded. "Partition here was a very violent jolt. It also cut off family stories and family energy. It was the biggest trauma this country ever went through. People don't talk about it." She paused. "But those stories are still here. It's not just a reset, the way immigration can be."

"Was your family badly affected?" Ro asked.

"Yes," Fairuza said. "I think almost every family in northern India was, in one way or another. My grandfather lost everything."

"It's inconceivable how much suffering there was then," Ro said, shaking his head. "Like the Second World War. But your grandfather, he rebuilt his life?"

"In a way. He could never get over what happened, though. There was a bitterness inside him that never went away."

Ro nodded. "I suppose that's one good thing about immigration. You get to focus on the future," he mused. "I've never thought of it this way before, but immigration still has a real cost. You might be able to escape the bad stories, but you also get rid of all of the good fortune. You have no roots."

"You have roots," Fairuza said. "You're Indian. Do you feel Indian?"

"No," Ro said.

He thought for a second before continuing.

"It's partly language. I speak five languages. Tamil is not one of them." He paused, realizing the absurdity. "For hundreds, if not thousands, of years, my ancestors—every single one of them—spoke a language I don't really speak. I wouldn't even be able to communicate with them if I saw them. If I wrote a book, they wouldn't be able to read it. If they had anything they wanted to say to me right now, I wouldn't understand it."

"Firstly, you should buy some crystals while you're here," Fairuza said. "Crystals from India. But secondly, there are many ways to communicate."

They sat in silence for a moment.

"Let's begin," she said. "Let's connect you to your roots. Even on a super-ficial level, not feeling your roots can cause all sorts of health problems. Your kidneys. Lungs. Any paired organs. Your feet."

She looked at him.

"The left side of your body is linked to your mother and her ancestors, and the right side is linked to your father and his ancestors. Did you know that?"

Ro shook his head.

"Families take many different forms today," Fairuza said. "And that's a very beautiful thing. Love is love. Every person remains the product of two biological parents. Regardless of whether you were raised by them, or if you even know who those two people are, your ancestors on both sides wish the best for you.

"You get your life force through those two people," Fairuza continued. "But you only get it if you let go of any judgment about the circumstances sur-rounding it. You have to say yes to the gift of life exactly how you received it. The gift of life was given to you in the precise way it was given to you for a reason."

Ro nodded.

"There's a trick I always tell people," Fairuza continued. "One of the fast-est ways for anyone to turn their luck around is to put photographs of their grandparents on the walls."

Ro looked surprised.

"Yes," Fairuza said. "It's true. Your grandparents only want the best for you. Things with parents can be complicated. Your grandparents, and all your ancestors further back, only wish you the best. They only want you to succeed."

Ro nodded.

"I have an idea," Fairuza said. She smiled at Ro, and he smiled back. "Let's do a meditation on your ancestors. Where you visualize them, and you visual-ize them giving you love. Did you know your grandparents well?"

Ro thought for a minute. "Neither yes nor no." He paused. "I think my grandmother on my father's side never understood why my father left India. He had everything here."

"Things happen," Fairuza said simply. "In the end, it was what he was supposed to do, because he did it. Are you comfortable like that?" She indicated Ro's legs. He was sitting cross-legged.

"Yes, I prefer to sit cross-legged," he said. He laughed. "I guess genetics count for something after all."

"They count for a lot," Fairuza said. "You can close your eyes."

Ro closed his eyes. Immediately, he realized how much he relied on his eyes for information, to the point where it was a crutch. With his eyes shut, his hearing immediately became more acute. He could feel and smell the air.

Fairuza stood up and began walking around the room. "Breathe through your stomach. Think about a ball of bright, shining light," she said. "Just above your head."

Ro adjusted his legs and then focused.

"The light serves your highest good. Now inhale it. Let it fill your body." She paused. "From head to toe."

Ro could hear her pacing softly around the room. He found the sound oddly soothing.

"Now exhale everything you want to release. And everything that does not serve you. Everything that does not serve your highest good. Release it now."

Ro exhaled and a noise came out of his vocal cords, as if he was clearing his throat. It felt good. He did it again. And again.

"Sense the light above your head. Now breathe the light into your heart. And again. Until you see a glowing ball of sunlight filling your heart."

He breathed. Again he heard her slow, rhythmic footsteps.

"Now visualize your parents standing right in front of you."

Ro summoned up an image of his mother and father.

Not for the first time, he was struck by how little he looked like them. There was no resemblance at all, in terms of facial features. And Ro was much darker than either of his parents were.

"Keep feeling the light in your heart. How brightly it shines." More footsteps. "Register how you feel. What emotions surface. And then say Yes, to them, and let them be."

Ro said Yes.

"And then any emotions that do not serve your highest purpose evaporate. Keep breathing the light into your heart."

Ro kept breathing.

"Bring happy, beautiful moments you've shared with your parents to mind. Look at your mother and father with love. And thank them. You may have to repeat this several times until it feels completely true and sincere. That is all right.

"If you sense any blockages here, simply imagine bowing your head in front of your parents. Humbly recognize the gift of life. The life they created. That they gave you. Thank them."

Ro thanked them.

"Each time you thank them, feel more and more love inside your heart. If you wish, you can say, 'Thank you. You gave me the greatest gift. The gift of life.'"

Ro thanked them for the gift of life.

More footsteps.

"There is a beam of light streaming from your parents' hearts into your heart."

A few more footsteps, then Fairuza paused.

"This light is love. All you have to do is open your heart and receive it."

Ro breathed.

"You may thank them for it," she added.

Ro thanked them.

"Now see your grandparents. Standing behind your parents."

Ro breathed.

"They love you. They support you. They strengthen you, and they bless you.

"Acknowledge them. Your mother's mother. Your mother's father. Your father's mother. Your father's father. Thank them. For the gift of life.

"Now their hearts open and streams of love, light, joy, and blessings stream from their hearts into your parents' hearts. They mix there, and then they stream into your heart. The stream is love. Open your heart and receive it."

Ro received it.

"You may say Yes, and also thank them."

Ro said Yes, and thanked them.

"Now the parents of your grandparents join. The mothers of your two grandmothers. The fathers of your two grandmothers. The mothers of your two grandfathers. The fathers of your two grandfathers. Your 16 great-great-grandparents.

"Each of these people sends a stream of love into the heart of his or her child, that then goes into the heart of his or her child, that then goes into you. Open your heart."

Ro opened his heart.

"Now see more generations joining in. 32 ancestors."

Ro started visualizing them. More footsteps.

"Now 64.

"Now 128.

"Then 256.

"Now 512. 1024. 2048. 4096 ancestors. And so forth. And onward.

"And onward. All of these people are sending you their love and their blessings. Every one of these people wishes you luck. Open your heart and receive their wish. And their love. And their blessing.

"And now, if you'd like, Ro, you can say Yes."

"Yes," Ro said.

"If you'd like, you can say thank you."

"Thank you," Ro said.

They sat in the room, silent.

"Thank you," Ro said.

* * *

Mahesh was standing in the spa lobby as Ro left his session with Fairuza. He broke into a big smile when he saw Ro.

"Hello, Sir," Ro said, grasping him by the shoulders warmly. "How are you today?"

Mahesh looked around to make sure no one was within earshot. "Very shocking about Miss Dey," he said in a low tone. "I had a bad feeling."

"Yes." Ro became solemn. "It is shocking."

"Her eyes," Mahesh continued, shaking his head.

"Right." Ro got a little sad. "They were remarkable, weren't they."

"No. Bad blood," Mahesh said, grim. "They were a sign of bad blood."

Ro looked around. Still nobody in earshot.

"Mahesh, I have a question for you," he said, leaning into Mahesh's ear. "I'm so sorry to ask." The trust was somehow implicit.

Mahesh nodded.

"Someone answered the phone in the restaurant that night and gave Amrita a message. That her watch had been found. But nobody will admit to doing it. They don't want to get into trouble. Which I understand."

Ro made his voice even lower.

"Do you think you could try to find the person who answered the phone? I don't need even to know who it was. I just have two questions."

Mahesh looked at Ro, intent.

"First, was the call in Hindi or English? And second, did the voice sound like it was a man or a woman?"

Mahesh nodded. "I will try to find out. Hello!" he exclaimed, looking over Ro's shoulder. Ro turned around.

Chris and Catherine were walking into the spa. Mango sat placidly in the L.L. Bean bag on Catherine's shoulder.

"Mahesh!" Chris called. "What unspeakable things have you planned today?"

"Torture," Mahesh replied with a smile. The two of them moved off.

Catherine seemed restless. She nuzzled Mango.

"What's up?"

"You play squash, right?" she asked, her face still buried in the nape of Mango's neck.

"Uh, yeah." Ro was caught off guard. "I used to, anyway. Not anymore." He paused. "Did Joss tell you?"

"Yep. He said you were really good."

"Well, I don't know about that," Ro replied, cautious. "I used to play all the time, but I haven't really played in years. I broke my shoulder snowboarding and had to stop."

"Did you play for Dartmouth?"

"No. I only started playing seriously in college. I played a ton back then, though."

He paused.

"Did you play for Dartmouth?"

Catherine nodded. "Want a game?"

Ro was startled. "They have a court here?"

"Yep," she replied, terse.

Ro looked down at his body, clad as per usual in a white kurta pajama. "I literally don't have anything," he said, raising his arms. "I don't think I have gym clothes with me, even. Let alone squash shoes."

"I checked already. They have everything here." Catherine looked over at the gym desk, where Joss's hot trainer from morning stretch was sitting.

The trainer waved. Catherine flushed a little. "He can borrow gym clothes from you, right?" she called out to him.

The trainer smiled, giving two thumbs up. "So handsome," Catherine murmured girlishly.

She turned back to Ro, all business. "What size shoe are you?"

"Oh," Ro said. "US 10."

"I thought so. You're the same as Chris. You can borrow his shoes and racquet."

"You guys brought squash shoes and racquets with you?" Ro said, disbelieving.

"Let's go back to the villa and grab everything." Catherine began to move toward the door.

"Hold on."

Catherine turned back toward him.

Ro looked at her wrists. She wasn't wearing a watch.

"Are you left-handed?"

"No. Why?" Catherine sounded amused.

"I don't play against lefties," Ro replied. "It's no fun."

"I'm not left-handed." Catherine turned around again. "Let's go."

* * *

Ro hadn't yet been to Chris and Catherine's villa. The villa was situated about halfway between the spa and the Palace, at almost the lowest part of the path, up three flights of stairs.

"Must be annoying with luggage," Ro observed.

"There's an elevator on the side," Catherine replied. "I take it when I'm being lazy."

The stairs led to a rectangular terrace with a sitting area, a dining table, and sunbeds. A wall of glass separated the terrace from a large living room.

"Mind if I explore a little?"

"Of course not. Feel free."

The villa really was built like a treehouse, a treehouse made of beautiful dark wood. The living room was wide and shallow. The idea clearly was that the occupants would spend most of their time on the terrace.

Ro took a spiral staircase in the corner to find a charming lofted bedroom perched under the eaves. The pitched ceiling contained skylights on either side. Another wall of glass faced out in the same direction as the terrace downstairs, with a balcony just large enough for a small table and two chairs.

Coming back downstairs, he saw that Catherine was still rummaging around for the racquets, goggles, and whatever else they needed. He ambled back onto the terrace and leaned on the railing, looking out.

The villa was built more or less at the top of the treeline. Ro could see the roofs of the spa and the Residence, but that was all.

He looked down. He could barely even make out the path directly in front of the villa.

He walked to each side of the terrace. Really, you could see only the tops of trees, waving gently in the breeze. You couldn't even see the Palace. He closed his eyes and inhaled. The air smelled incredible. Fresh, light, a hint of mint, unexpectedly.

"It's great, right?" Catherine said, materializing next to him.

"Yes," he replied, opening his eyes. "So peaceful. Like being on the ocean, but with trees. It's so simple, but I can't remember ever having seen something like this before."

"It's pretty special." Catherine turned back around to leave.

Ro thought of something. "Since we're up here, I just wanted to check. We can't see the spot where Amrita was killed from anywhere on the terrace, can we?"

"I don't think so." Catherine walked to the edges of the terrace. "No, we definitely can't." She pointed. "It would be over there, but the trees are in the way."

She paused, thinking.

"You know, I wouldn't be surprised if whoever killed her checked every blind spot on the property first."

"Yes. Also, this is the only villa in use right now. The other one's being renovated." He stopped, realizing something. "Whoever killed her was a planner. I also wouldn't be surprised if that dinner is pretty much the only time all year when everyone at Samsara is in the same place."

"That's true. I'm really not happy about any of this."

They were silent for a moment.

"You know, I can't stop thinking about something this guy at the FBI said to me once."

Ro turned toward her. "What was it?"

"He said that murder's like potato chips," Catherine replied, her tone flat. "Because it's pretty hard to stop after just one."

* * *

Objectively, Ro was a more than creditable squash player. It was true that he hadn't played for Dartmouth, but he had in fact been good enough to play for his college at Oxford. It was only when getting into the golf cart to return to the spa that Ro saw the Heights Casino tags on Catherine's squash bag. At that moment, he realized he was in for it.

They walked through the spa and down a corridor Ro hadn't noticed before. Catherine pushed open a door to reveal two regulation squash courts, perfectly outfitted.

He might as well have been at the Yale Club in New York.

"Spin for service?" Catherine said. "I'll take up."

Ro nodded.

Catherine spun the racquet. It landed right side up.

She picked it back up with her right hand.

Then, deliberately transferring the racquet to her left hand, she prepared to serve.

"You're a jerk, Catherine," Ro said.

Catherine served.

The serve was unreturnable.

* * *

They sat outside the spa near the pool, still in their gym clothes. It hadn't been a total massacre, but Catherine had still won in straight sets. 11–7, 12–10.

"I didn't lie, by the way. I really am right-handed. My coach made me learn how to play lefty because he knew it would be a huge advantage."

"It doesn't matter. You're still a jerk."

They sat in a comfortable silence. Unexpectedly, Ro realized that he enjoyed Catherine's company a great deal.

"It's crazy about Amrita's body going missing."

Catherine frowned. "I don't like that at all."

"Yes." Ro shivered. "I know what you mean. It was very"—he searched for the word—"effective."

Catherine nodded.

"That reminds me," Ro said, pulling his phone out of his bag. "I've been meaning to check if her name means something. Rita."

He opened his browser and did a search.

"Oh. It means 'pearl.' That feels appropriate. For someone who came from a family of jewelers."

"What about Amrita?" Catherine asked idly.

Ro did another search, then paused for a long moment. "Oh."

"What?" Catherine leaned over.

"It means 'immortality.'"

An awful sort of silence descended over the table.

"Yes, well," Catherine finally muttered.

Unasked, the hot trainer brought out a tray with a pitcher of water with lemons and cucumber and two glasses.

Catherine smiled girlishly. "Thanks."

Ro looked at her, surprised at the change in tone.

The trainer smiled and went back inside.

"Whoo!" Catherine laughed, embarrassed, beginning to fan her face with one hand. She really was blushing now. "It's getting hot out here."

Ro looked at Catherine, then looked at the trainer walking away, then suddenly went quiet. A thought had occurred to him. For the first time.

Probably because he now had the strength of all of his ancestors behind him.

"Are you OK?" he heard Catherine say. He realized he had been staring into the distance.

"I'm not really sure how to say this," he began slowly.

Catherine waited.

"That trainer. Yes, he's very good-looking. But it's not just that. It's that he was allowed to know it. I'm explaining myself badly."

Ro shook his head. Catherine knew not to interrupt.

"The confidence that guy has. That unquestioning certainty that he's hot. It was never even an option for me. I guess I'm realizing that for the first time."

"How do you mean?" Catherine asked gently.

"It's so hard to describe." Ro stopped to try to collect his thoughts. "It may be different now. I'm pretty sure it is, at least in some ways. But when I was growing up, in America, as an Indian person, there wasn't a single public figure I could aspire to be who looked like me. Not a single one. Nobody in the newspaper. Nobody on TV."

Ro swallowed. Catherine looked at him, intent.

"But it wasn't just public figures," he continued. "It was every single day in school. Or on television. The jock didn't look like me. The cheerleader never looked like me. Even the student body president never looked like me. These archetypes." Ro stopped, allowing the feeling to enter him. "They weren't even possible."

Catherine sat, silent.

"And, you know," Ro said, turning toward her, "even if it is better now, in terms of movies and TV or whatever else, it's still so fundamental."

He paused.

"Imagine loving to read more than anything. Then imagine, with every single book you read, that you know with absolute certainty that, if they were going to make a movie of the book one day, you wouldn't be able to play a single role in it. Because of the color of your skin. You're just out of the running. Disqualified. It's not about how good you are. It's just not even an option."

Ro gazed at all the people he could see around who looked like him. Doing all sorts of different things.

"You have to force yourself to stop dreaming. To stop pretending you could be the person you're reading about. Because you can't."

There was a long pause. Catherine placed her hand on Ro's and squeezed it.

"I'm not saying this to be funny. But how'd you get through it? I mean, get through it seemingly totally unaffected?"

"I'm not sure I understand the question."

"Look. Not to downplay anything you went through. But nobody would ever think you'd ever faced the slightest challenge. In your life. At all."

"Oh!" Ro was surprised. "I've never thought about that."

He considered.

"I suppose it's quite simple," he said finally. "There are only three steps. First, never register what anyone thinks of you. Ever. Second, be perfect. All the time. And, finally, make it look effortless."

"I see," Catherine said quietly.

Ro hesitated.

"Of course, none of that means I got through it unaffected."

He looked at Catherine and smiled at her.

"I'm starved. Lunchtime."

* * *

The afternoon massage consisted of Ro's body being covered in sticky red powder. He felt like Sedona. Afterward, he was instructed to sit in the steam room for at least thirty minutes for the minerals from the red powder to sink into his skin. The cold shower afterward, during which he washed away the remainder of the powder, was one of the most pleasurable he had taken in some time. Passing a window, Ro saw it was already dark outside. He decided to double-check.

As usual, the sauna was totally empty. Ro went over to the shower area and peered out the windows.

He had been right. You couldn't make out anything whatsoever at night.

* * *

As Sanjay opened the door, Ro immediately noticed how tired he looked. He seemed to have aged several years since they'd had lunch only a few days prior.

Something else seemed off. Then Ro realized. Sanjay was dressed in street clothes, a button-down shirt and a pair of dark trousers.

Sanjay smiled thinly, registering Ro's surprise. "I've been on videoconferences the whole day."

At first glance, the room appeared identical to his own. Then Ro glanced through the windows and inhaled sharply. The room's wall of windows looked out over the side of the mountain, giving a perfect view of the snaking silver Ganges and, far below, the lights of Rishikesh. It was magnificent.

"Wow. I hadn't been in a room on this side of the building yet."

"Please, have a seat." Sanjay waved toward the chairs. "Would you like something to drink?"

"Just water. Thanks."

Sanjay put a bottle of water and two glasses down on the table, then poured each of them a glass.

Ro took a sip.

There was a pause.

Ro waited for Sanjay to speak. This meeting had been his idea, after all.

Sanjay coughed. "So, Mr. Krishna," he began. "Thank you for coming."

"Please, call me Ro," Ro replied politely.

A look of mild distaste appeared on Sanjay's face. "I don't know that we're quite familiar with each other enough for that, are we?"

He raised his eyebrows. Ro scowled.

"We've already been introduced with our first names," he replied, curt. "I'm not calling you Mr. Mehta. But if you want to call me Mr. Krishna, please feel free."

Sanjay smiled briefly. "Are you always this difficult?"

Ro thought about it for a second.

"Yes."

Looking at Sanjay, Ro noted that he really did look quite ill. His left hand was shaking slightly, and he had bags under his bloodshot eyes.

Ro softened a little, despite himself. "So, what brings me here?"

Sanjay thought for a moment before speaking.

"I was hoping to get your point of view about a difficult situation. Perhaps in an ongoing manner. You're a lawyer, yes?"

Ro was a little jarred. First Lala, then Mrs. B., now Sanjay.

Were there no other lawyers in India?

Then he remembered. Lala's family had already flown one in.

For her. Not for him.

"Yes. I am, technically. But I haven't practiced in years." He looked at Sanjay, puzzled. "But why would you want my point of view?"

"Well, first of all, you're a foreigner. Which is a not insignificant factor." Sanjay paused. He really did look very ill.

"But otherwise, it's a feeling, I suppose. That you might see things differently. And, potentially, that you aren't too troubled by rules."

Ro's eyes narrowed. "I'm not sure what that's supposed to mean."

"I wasn't insinuating anything by that." Sanjay raised his hands. "I just meant that you converse in an unusual way. You must know that."

"I didn't think you were listening to me."

Sanjay paused. "You're actually very strange, you know. It's not exactly a compliment."

Fair enough, Ro thought. Grudgingly.

They sat for a moment.

"What kind of situation?"

"I think you can guess."

Ro thought about it. He could guess.

"I would pay you, of course."

This was a misstep.

Ro waited a beat before responding. "What makes you think I'm for hire?" he said, in a half-strangled whisper he'd picked up from *The Godfather*. It came in handy more often than one might have thought.

Sanjay hesitated for a long moment. It had clearly been a while since he'd met someone who wasn't openly for hire.

"In any event, even if I were, I don't know if you could afford me," Ro continued in the same half-strangled whisper. He looked at Sanjay. "Aren't you a public servant?"

Sanjay flushed, irritated. "Can we please stop playing games?"

"I'm not playing games." Ro switched back to his normal voice, puzzled. "I'm just at a total loss as to why I'd ever agree to help you."

"Look," Sanjay said, leaning forward. Ro noticed once again that Sanjay's hands were shaking. "I'm going to put my cards on the table. Can I have your word that this conversation will remain confidential?"

Ro thought about it for a moment, then slowly shook his head.

"No. I'm not trying to be difficult, but I can't promise that. I have no idea what we're talking about. But as a general rule, I'm pretty discreet. That's all I can say."

For whatever reason, Ro's answer seemed to give Sanjay a boost. He sat up a little straighter.

"Fine. I'll be direct."

He swallowed, steeling himself.

"I had a motive to kill Amrita Dey. And I have no alibi for the time when she was killed. But I didn't kill her."

"Hold on."

Ro held up his hand.

"I think it's best if you give me as few details as possible. Let me think for a second."

He closed his eyes.

An image of Pendy in Parvati's apartment in Paris came to him, unbidden.

"Perhaps I should just ask you questions," Ro continued, reopening his eyes. "Yes-or-no questions."

Sanjay nodded.

"I'm not going to beat around the bush. I don't want to waste either of our time."

"All right."

"Was Amrita blackmailing you?"

Sanjay spluttered. He opened his mouth, then closed it.

"Yes or no?" Ro asked, stern.

Sanjay took a moment to regain his composure.

"Yes," he finally said. Some fine beads of sweat began to appear on his temples.

"All right," Ro said crisply.

He thought for a moment.

"Did she have some sort of physical proof of what you had done? Like a photo or bank records?"

Sanjay nodded. "Yes."

"Was the underlying issue sexual in nature?"

"No." Then Sanjay stopped. "Well, not involving me, anyway."

What was that supposed to mean? Ro decided he didn't want to know. He pressed on.

"Did you have an affair with her?"

"No."

Ro thought for a moment, then had an idea.

He leaned forward and looked directly into Sanjay's eyes.

"On a scale of one to ten, how bad is what you did?"

Sanjay's mouth fell open, and his eyes went blank.

All of a sudden, Ro realized that Sanjay was terrified.

Sanjay struggled for a moment, then made up his mind.

"Eight," he whispered.

Ro sat back.

There was a long silence.

"I don't know what to tell you," Ro said finally. "If Amrita had physical proof, I have a feeling the police are going to find it. That's exactly what they're looking for."

He saw the terror in Sanjay's eyes and, despite himself, again softened a little.

He leaned forward. "I'm still not sure what you want from me."

"I want you to help me defend myself," Sanjay replied, his voice rising. "I didn't kill her."

"Hold on." Something had flashed into Ro's brain. Intuition, maybe. "You did do something, though."

Ro leaned over and peered at Sanjay. His eyes narrowed.

"You killed someone, didn't you. Or had someone killed."

A flare of pure panic surged behind Sanjay's eyes.

"Actually, stop." Ro immediately held up his hand, shielding his own eyes. "Stop. Stop." He turned his head away. "I don't want to know about this."

There was a long pause.

"I didn't kill Amrita Dey," Sanjay repeated. "I didn't."

"Then don't be afraid," Ro responded coolly. "The truth has a tendency to come out."

Sanjay looked down, his fists involuntarily clenched.

"What is it?" Ro asked. His tone was not unkind.

Sanjay took a moment before responding.

"I think I'm being set up to take the blame. For her murder. I can't explain it. I feel the walls closing in."

"Who do you think could be setting you up?"

Sanjay looked down. "My father-in-law," he replied quietly.

There was another long silence.

"You know, I don't think that's right," Ro said abruptly. "I don't know why, but I just don't. Anyway, I don't think there's anything I can do to help you here."

"Why? Do you not believe me?"

"That's really neither here nor there," Ro replied. "It's not about whether you did it. I would help you if you'd done it, but done it for reasons I respect."

He paused.

"I don't know if you're guilty. Of this crime, anyway. I don't know if you killed Amrita Dey or not. But even if you didn't kill her, I know you did something really, really bad. And I'm pretty sure it wasn't for any reasons I'd respect."

Sanjay shrank in his chair.

"There's something else too." Ro hesitated. "This is so pretentious, but I don't know how to say it in English. Just in French."

"Then say it in French."

"Ta gueule me revient pas."

Sanjay paused. "Can you at least try to translate it?"

Ro thought about it. "I guess it means that I just don't like your face."

Sanjay snorted. "That was simple enough to say in English."

"You're right," Ro said, considering. "It was, wasn't it."

He stood up.

"I'll see myself out. By the way, I don't anticipate having to repeat anything we've said to each other tonight." Ro paused. "I hope you understand this isn't personal."

Sanjay nodded at him. Ro made his way to the door.

"Oh. One last thing. Consider it a friendly tip. That visiting meditation teacher. I'd watch out if I were you. She might have told him what you did."

He left, closing the door behind him.

Ro was deep in contemplation as he descended the stairs to his own room. On balance, he did believe Sanjay.

If Sanjay had killed Amrita, she would have known why she had died.

* * *

At 8:30 p.m. precisely, 7:00 a.m. in Del Mar, Ro picked up his phone and dialed.

"Hello," said a booming voice at the other end of the line.

"Father," Ro said. "Happy birthday."

There was a slight pause.

"Ro!" His father recovered, sounding surprised but pleased. "I'm so happy you called." His voice trailed off at the end of the sentence, though.

Ro smiled, a little sadly. "Did you think I wouldn't?"

There was another pause.

"How is everything?" his father asked, hesitant.

"The hotel's great. You have to come here sometime."

"Mmm," his father replied, noncommittal. "Have you seen Vijay?"

"No, they're in the Maldives. But his mother-in-law is here. Mrs. Banerjee. She says she's met you before."

His father was silent for a moment, then cleared his throat.

"Yes," he finally said. "Not the easiest woman in the world."

"Oh, really?" Ro was genuinely surprised. "She's been perfectly lovely to me."

"Ah? Well, it's been a long time. Let me see. How would I describe her?"

Ro smiled, picturing his father in his favorite old chair.

"I've got it, I think," his father said, satisfied. "Rude, dismissive, and lazy."

Ro laughed. "Funny. That's not at all my impression. She certainly doesn't seem lazy, at any rate."

"She had very strange eyes," his father continued, remembering. "I'm sure you've noticed. I always got the impression that she was X-raying everyone to calculate their inner value."

Ro was curious now. "Where did you think your inner value fell on her scale?"

"I'm not answering that. It's my birthday."

Ro laughed. "What are you up to today?"

"Not much. Just took a walk on the beach. How's Joss?"

"They're really excited about the new project." Ro thought about it. "I've hardly seen him. It's weird. I've been so busy."

"Busy?" His father sounded mildly curious.

There was a silence. Perhaps a longer silence than either of them had expected.

"Ro?" his father said sharply. "Is everything all right?"

"Yes, Father, I'm completely fine," Ro replied automatically. "But some funny things have been happening here. Funny as in strange," he clarified.

"Oh?"

"Yes." Ro sighed. "A woman here was killed. Someone whom I'd met before, in fact. In London. A month or so ago."

"What happened?" His father sounded alert now.

"Nobody really knows yet."

"But Ro, are you OK? Are you safe?"

"Yes. Father, I'm completely fine. Really. I mean, obviously it's been a little traumatic."

"Did you know this person well?"

"Not really," Ro said, honestly. No reason to go into detail.

"Do they know who did it? I'm sorry. I don't even know what questions I should be asking."

"No, no," Ro reassured him. "So far, these are the appropriate ones. But no, they haven't caught anyone yet."

"I don't like this at all." His father paused, debating what to say next. "Why don't you just leave?"

"I'm fine, Father. I promise."

Ro took a deep breath to calm himself down, in hopes that it would also calm his father down.

"This wasn't some random killing. At least I don't think so. And I don't know anything about it. So I'm perfectly safe."

"OK. I trust you, but please leave the first minute you sense anything suspect." His father sounded skeptical. Understandably. "Is everyone kicking up a tremendous fuss?"

Ro considered. "Not really. It's a little surprising, actually. The hotel's trying to keep the whole thing under wraps. As much as they can, anyway. But everything's sort of business as usual."

"Well, don't be surprised if nothing comes of it. Life's cheap in India. Easy come, easy go." He paused for a moment. "Unless revenge is involved. In which case the police will probably take one of the suspects into a field for a 'reenactment.' Then they'll kill him and say it was an accident."

Ro giggled, amused. "That sounds like more of an 'enactment.'"

"As I said, easy come, easy go." His father cleared his throat. "It's actually our country's great strength, you know. The fact that we aren't afraid of death. Because we know it's not the end."

Ro was silent.

"The West keeps dabbling in Indian traditions and repackaging them with new faces attached. Yoga. Meditation. I wish they'd appropriate that one instead." His father cleared his throat again. "It's quite annoying, actually."

* * *

After they'd hung up, Ro called Inspector Singh.

"So, I had an idea," Ro began without preamble. "I think we should do a reenactment."

"A reenactment? Already?" the inspector replied, surprised. "That's a bit extreme at this stage, no?"

"A reenactment of when Amit saw Amrita in the hallway."

There was a long pause.

"Oh," the inspector said. "I thought you meant something else."

"Anyway, I don't think it would take long, and I don't think it would hurt. But let's do it right away if possible."

"All right. I'll call Mr. Chopra. Who will play Miss Dey?"

"I'm sure Mrs. B. would love to." Ro thought of something else. "Also, you should probably warn Amit the three of us are helping out with the investigation."

They hung up. Ro immediately picked up the phone again.

"Hello?" Lala said.

"Hi, it's Ro," he said casually. "So, this is really random, but can I borrow your fur headband?"

* * *

Inspector Singh, Catherine, Mrs. B., and Ro were in the hallway on the ground floor of the Residence. Rooms lined both sides of the hallway, a plate glass window at each end of the corridor.

It had already gotten dark. Farther down the hall, maids were doing turndown service, ferrying pots of sleep tea.

Amit's door was open. He sat in his wheelchair in the doorway.

Mrs. B. stood across the hall in front of what had been Amrita's door. She had taken her hair down and it was hanging in a lush curtain halfway down her back. She easily looked twenty or thirty years younger than she was.

"I almost forgot." Ro fished into his pocket and pulled out Lala's headband. Crossing the hallway, he handed it to Mrs. B. She smiled at him.

"Where'd you find that?" the inspector asked.

"It's Mrs. Mehta's."

Mrs. B. grinned. She put it on and turned to face the door, the room key in her hand.

"Showtime." Catherine slouched against the wall, her arms crossed.

Amit wheeled himself out of the room and turned, seeing Mrs. B.'s back. "No," he said immediately. "She was turned more to the left."

A sergeant entered the hallway and whispered something to Inspector Singh. They began to confer in low tones.

"Could you see her profile?" Catherine asked.

Amit scratched his head, then shook it. "No."

Ro remembered something. "Mrs. B., are you wearing a watch?"

Mrs. B. looked abashed. "No. I forgot."

"Here." He passed her his.

She started buckling it onto her left wrist.

"Actually, hold on. Amrita wore her watch on her right wrist."

Mrs. B. dutifully buckled the watch onto her right wrist. The sergeant left.

"All right," the inspector said. "Let's begin."

Mrs. B. turned toward the door, key in hand. Then she mimed opening the door. Her watch moved back and forth.

"Anything coming to mind?" Catherine asked Amit.

Amit paused, thinking. "For the moment, not really. There's nothing that seems totally off."

"What about the watch?" Ro asked. "Can you remember if she was wearing it?"

"Sorry." Amit shook his head. "It's not ringing a bell."

"What if she opened the door with her left hand?" Catherine asked.

Mrs. B.'s right hand dropped to her side. The kurta pajama fell just below her elbow, highlighting the watch on her wrist. She mimed opening the door with her left hand.

Amit closed his eyes, reflecting. "I just can't remember. I wasn't really looking." He looked up at them. "If I had to guess, I'd say no, because I think I would have seen it."

"Was she wearing earrings?" Ro asked Amit, then answered the question himself. "The headband would have covered them."

"She had that headband on the whole time. I'm sure about that, anyway."

Ro turned to Inspector Singh. "She took her headband off at dinner. She was definitely wearing earrings. I'd swear to it."

Everyone was silent, thinking about next steps. Finally, the inspector spoke.

"If anything else does come to mind, please let us know."

"Of course. I'm sorry this wasn't of more use."

Mrs. B. came over to return Ro's watch.

"Oh, thanks." He began buckling it onto his wrist.

"Wait a minute." Catherine's eyes narrowed. She turned to Inspector Singh. "Can you check which wrist Amrita's watch was on?"

Inspector Singh's face turned grim as he processed the question.

"I don't need to check. Her watch was on her left wrist."

They stood there for a moment, registering the importance of what Inspector Singh had just said.

Ro opened his mouth to add something, then closed it again.

Somehow, he sensed that they'd just made a mistake. But he didn't know what kind of mistake. At least, not yet.

* * *

Later that night, as he was getting ready for bed, Ro's phone rang.

"I don't like this at all," Catherine said without preamble. "Inspector Singh checked for fingerprints on the watch. There were fingerprints, but only hers."

"So?"

"There should've been someone else's too. Whoever found it. Whoever handed it to her."

"You know, I just got my watch battery changed. They polished it with a cloth before they gave it back. Maybe it was something like that."

Catherine sighed. "Anyway, there's nobody we can ask, because nobody will admit to giving it back to her in the first place."

"But wait." Something dawned on Ro. "Those fingerprints would mean she'd put her watch on herself. But if so, why would she put it on the wrong wrist?"

They were both silent.

"This is giving me a headache. Anyway, I'll see you in the morning."

"Oh, wait." Ro remembered something his father had said. "I think I figured out why Amrita was hanging out with the VB. Remind me to tell you guys tomorrow."

"OK. Why can't you tell me now?"

"Ugh. I'm not talking about that dude before bed. It would give me whitemares."

Catherine laughed. "Fine. A cliffhanger."

"A fairly mild one," Ro replied.

They hung up. Ro got into bed. But for once in his life, he couldn't fall asleep.

A strange feeling was blooming inside him, and although it was unfamiliar, he still recognized it.

He felt silly and melodramatic when he tried to put it into words.

But the fact remained that, somehow, Ro knew he was in danger.

DAY 6

(December 28)

That uneasy feeling was still there when Ro woke up. He felt restless right away. He didn't want to drink tea or to meditate. He needed to move, to use his body somehow.

He jumped out of bed and headed straight into the shower. First, he turned the water on as hot as he could bear, deliberately letting his mind go blank for a minute or two. Then he abruptly switched the water to ice cold, letting it pound down over his body for thirty seconds.

Turning off the water, he got out of the shower. Whatever was facing him, he was as ready as he would ever be.

* * *

"We've now spoken to Miss Dey's lawyer," Inspector Singh began. "And to her next of kin, her sister, Mrs. Acharya. A number of interesting things have come up."

He paused, visibly putting his thoughts in order.

"Such as?" Catherine asked, impatient.

He looked at her. "Please, Mrs. Forrester."

Catherine piped down.

Inspector Singh continued to think for a moment. "All right," he finally said. "We can begin with her testamentary dispositions."

He pulled a piece of paper off his desk.

"To begin, Miss Dey did not leave anything to Mrs. Acharya or to her family. She directed that all her assets be sold, the resulting funds divided among a number of charitable causes."

Inspector Singh consulted the piece of paper in his hand.

"The list is quite broad. A significant percentage is to go to the Loreto Schools for scholarships for girls' education in the name of her mother, Meena Dey."

Mrs. B. nodded approvingly. "Good girl."

"There are also significant bequests to elephant sanctuaries," the inspector continued. "Organizations providing birth control to women in rural areas worldwide. Several organizations that support divorced and widowed women in India. One to an organization called Americans United for Separation of Church and State." Catherine laughed, a short bark. "And finally, to the RSPCA in the United Kingdom."

Ro grinned involuntarily, remembering how much fur Amrita wore.

"I must say, that's a lovely list," Mrs. B. said. "I'm very proud."

"So, nothing at all to her family," Catherine mused. "What was the total value of the assets?"

The inspector smiled.

"This is where things become interesting."

He picked up another piece of paper.

"In terms of real property, she owned a flat in London, on Farm Street in Mayfair, and a small house in Italy, in Pantelleria. Then there were several bank and brokerage accounts. The total value of her estate is estimated to be £5,000,000."

"That seems low," Mrs. B., Catherine, and Ro all said in unison.

"What name did she use on her will, out of curiosity?" Ro asked, leaning forward.

"Rita Dey." The inspector looked at Mrs. B. "You knew her family. They were very well-to-do?"

"Yes." Mrs. B. nodded vigorously. "Rita certainly inherited much more than that."

The inspector nodded, satisfied.

"I spoke at length with Mrs. Acharya. When their father died seventeen years ago, his estate was divided between the two of them, his surviving children."

Ro leaned in. They were getting to the good part.

"The estate consisted of some real property," the inspector continued. "Primarily a house in Belgium, a house on Malabar Hill in Mumbai, and that flat in London. They sold the house in Belgium and divided the receipts. Miss Dey took the flat in London and Mrs. Acharya took the house in Mumbai, where she still resides."

He paused again. Ro leaned in further.

"However, the bulk of the estate consisted of raw and cut gemstones. Miss Dey and Mrs. Acharya had them professionally valued and then divided them equitably."

"How much were they worth?" Catherine leaned forward.

"According to Mrs. Acharya, at that time, the total value of the gemstones was in the vicinity of seventy million dollars."

Ro and Mrs. B. gasped.

"So," the inspector continued, affectless, "a significant part of her estate is potentially missing."

"Her solicitors don't know anything about this?" Ro asked.

"No. It seems that she deliberately hid assets."

"That makes two of us," Catherine muttered. "Her sister has no idea either?"

"No," he said. "Frankly, she was so furious to find out about Miss Dey's testamentary dispositions that she doesn't seem particularly inclined to help."

"Yes." Mrs. B. shuddered. "Nalini must have been beside herself."

"We're going to keep searching," the inspector said.

"What about other motives?" Catherine said.

"We're continuing to look into her affairs. And those of the guests here. To see if there are any connections. Do any of you have any other thoughts?"

Ro remembered what Lala had told him. And what Sanjay had told him, for that matter. But they had told him those things in confidence. He kept his face neutral.

"Oh," Catherine said, looking at Ro. "I found out how Amit's parents died."

"And?"

"His mother died of cancer. But his father died in a 'hunting accident' a few years ago," she replied, making air quotes with her fingers.

"Why the air quotes?"

"Nine times out of ten, a hunting accident means suicide. The gun went off while he was holding it to his own head. By accident, of course."

"Suicide could mean blackmail." Mrs. B. was thoughtful.

Catherine looked at Ro. "Didn't you have something to tell me about the VB?"

"Oh, yes." Ro slapped his forehead. He turned to the inspector. "I think Amrita was grooming him to be one of her sources of information."

The inspector was uncomprehending. "How so?"

But Catherine was already nodding.

"He's this perfectly pleasant and generically handsome guy, preaching this anodyne gospel of self-love and self-care," Ro said. "If you send him into the world, into the right places, people might confide in him. He's like a therapist. And he'd keep their secrets from everyone. Everyone except the woman he loves. Amrita had him wrapped around her finger."

He looked at the inspector.

"You know, I have a feeling the confidences went both ways. I feel like she told him things to make him trust her. And he somehow thinks that keeping her secrets is still the right thing to do."

"I'll speak to him again." Inspector Singh turned to Mrs. B. "At this point, we would like to search the guest rooms."

"No," Mrs. B. and Ro said simultaneously.

Mrs. B. beamed at Ro, then turned back to the inspector.

"That's out of the question," she said firmly.

"I thought you would say that," the inspector replied. "I can go to the chief magistrate of the district to get a warrant."

Mrs. B. smiled sweetly. "Oh yes, do speak to dear Ravi. That reminds me, I'm overdue to give his mother a call."

Catherine glared at her. She opened her mouth to say something, then thought better of it. She turned around, crossing her arms.

"In any case, Catherine," Ro said, "someone would have to be an idiot to keep anything incriminating in their room. They'd have buried it somewhere." Like the jewelry missing from Amrita's safe, he thought to himself.

"Any other ideas before we go down to breakfast?" Mrs. B. asked them.

Catherine shook her head. "I really feel like we're at an impasse. Let's go." She stood up.

Ro stood up too. "Well, maybe there'll be another murder and we'll get more clues," he said flippantly.

But as soon as he said it, the room went still.

Ro immediately knew what he'd done.

He had just invited Death back to Samsara.

And, as it would turn out, Death was all too delighted to accept.

* * *

Chris, Joss, Mahesh, and Amit were already seated at a table on the terrace.

"How lovely!" Mrs. B. exclaimed. "Is there room for us to join you?"

"Of course!" Chris leaped up and began moving another table next to theirs. "Thank you," he smiled at a distressed waiter who had just arrived to do the same thing.

They ordered from the waiter and sat down, Ro next to Mahesh.

"Hello," Mahesh said, in a totally normal tone of voice. "It was Hindi."

Ro nodded.

"Catherine, I was going to call you," Amit said. "Why don't we go down to Rishikesh today? I think we could all use a change of scenery. Do a little shopping and go to the ceremony."

"What ceremony?" Joss asked.

"Was it a man or woman?" Ro asked Mahesh, casual.

"The Ganga Aarti ceremony," Amit replied. "It's a prayer for the Ganges."

"He could not say," Mahesh replied. "The voice was low. And there was a great deal of noise."

Catherine looked at Chris. "What do you think, honey?"

Chris beamed. "I think this is just what we need."

"Just hold on a minute, everybody." Joss raised his hand. "I don't want to be a killjoy, but this sounds like a security nightmare. We can't have Chris randomly walking the streets of Rishikesh."

"Oh. You're right." Chris deflated slightly.

But Mahesh had an idea. "We could make him look like someone else. We could disguise him."

Joss still looked dubious.

Mahesh smiled at him. "People are easily fooled. They believe what their eyes tell them and don't listen to their other senses."

Ro was warming to the idea too. He turned to Catherine. "We could probably ask Inspector Singh for a police escort."

"Good idea." Catherine stood up and ambled over to the railing, looking out at the view. Then she turned to the left.

Her back stiffened for several seconds.

Ro went to join her at the railing. "What is it?" he asked quietly.

"Look," she muttered between pursed lips. She made a slight gesture with her head.

Ro turned and understood.

The terrace looked directly into the ground floor hallway of the Residence. The whole end of the hallway was a glass window.

"That means . . ."

"That anyone who was having dinner on the terrace last night would have seen the reenactment," she said quietly. Her face was grim. "I don't like this. I don't like this at all."

"We have to tell Inspector Singh," Ro whispered. Catherine nodded briefly.

They went back to the table, where the others were discussing ways Chris could disguise himself. "I'm still not wild about all this," Joss said.

"What, Joss?" Chris said. "Do you think I'm not a good enough actor to go unrecognized?"

Joss laughed. "I can't argue with that. Fair enough."

"I'll ask the beauty salon to come do a makeover," Mrs. B. said impulsively. "My treat."

"Will you come with us?" Ro asked her. "Please do!"

"No." She shook her head decisively. "I've been so many times. But perhaps I'll organize a cocktail party this evening when you return. I think we need to celebrate a bit."

"Yes," Amit laughed. "Celebrate being alive."

"Excuse me, Sir." A waiter came over and handed Ro a note card on Samsara stationery.

"Thank you," Ro said, puzzled.

He opened the note and shuddered.

"Dear Mr. Krishna, you are very overdue for our next consultation. Please schedule it immediately. Yrs." Then an illegible scrawl.

"No answer," he said to the hovering waiter. Ro tried to crumple up the note, but the stock was too heavy. He couldn't even fold it.

The VB walked in.

Ro audibly groaned. Catherine pinched his leg.

"Ow," Ro said. "That hurt."

"Can I join you?" the VB asked.

"Sadly, we were just about to leave," Catherine replied smoothly.

Joss gave them a stern look.

Just then, everyone's food arrived.

"We're just going to scarf this down and dash," Chris said, apologetic.

"That's all right," the VB replied. "I have to go work on my talk anyway." Nobody asked what the talk was about, so he continued. "I'm giving a lecture this afternoon at the Palace. On meditation through grief and trauma."

"So timely," Amit said, polite.

"Wait a moment." Mrs. B.'s tone was stern. She pointed a finger at Mitchell. "Do not mention the death of Miss Dey. On the orders of the police. Do not forget, her death is not general knowledge amongst the guests."

"Ah yes, of course." The VB looked slightly shaken.

"I'd advise you to choose another subject," Mrs. B. continued with asperity. "There are plenty of books on Indian spirituality at the Palace. I'm sure something will strike you on the head."

"But there's so little time. I'd already prepared." The VB fingered the beads around his neck.

Amit noticed. "Where'd you get those beads?"

"Oh!" The VB looked down at his fingers, surprised. "Down in Rishikesh. They're prayer beads."

Mrs. B. looked up at the VB. "We can move your talk. Perhaps to later this evening." She considered for a moment. "Maybe you can make it about falling asleep more easily. But that's just an idea."

"All right. I guess I'll go . . . meditate about it, or something." He moved off, his gait uncertain.

"Namaste," Ro said, bringing his hands to his heart.

"Did you purposely move his lecture to the same time as your cocktail party?" Amit asked Mrs. B.

"I didn't, you know," she replied, buttering a piece of toast, "but the subconscious mind works in mysterious ways."

"I'm sure Ro wouldn't miss it for anything," Catherine said.

"Yes, it's on my to-do list. Right after eating glass."

Joss looked at Ro. "What do you have against him? I don't think I get it. He's annoying, but he could really be a lot worse. I've met much worse, in fact."

Ro shrugged. "There's this expression in French: 'tête à claques.' It means someone whose face you just want to smack around. He has one of those." He took a sip of his coffee. "Born that way, I guess."

"Do you often smack people around?" Amit asked.

"I've never thrown a punch in my life." Ro's tone was a little smug.

Joss looked at Ro, his eyebrows raised, then looked at everyone else. "I don't know if that's true or not, but you certainly have a temper. Remember the cigarette story?"

Ro rolled his eyes.

"So, one time in college," Joss began, "some random guy started telling people that Ro had put a cigarette out on his arm at a frat party."

"Which I hadn't," Ro interjected. "By the by."

"Anyway," Joss continued, ignoring Ro, "a couple weeks later, Ro was driving around, saw said guy, and decided to try to run him over. The guy had to dive behind some bushes. And then when our friend Connie told Ro to stop acting so scary all the time, he just giggled and said, 'I'm only scary if you're afraid of death.'"

Ro couldn't help giggling again.

"Seriously?" Catherine said, looking at Ro.

Ro shrugged. "He wanted a story, so I gave him a story." He looked at his watch. "Mahesh, we have a session now, don't we?"

Mahesh nodded.

"Let's head down to Rishikesh around 3?" Chris turned to Mahesh. "And Mahesh, you're coming."

"Of course," Mrs. B. said. "Mahesh, we'll make sure your schedule is cleared for the afternoon."

Mahesh smiled. "In that case, I'd be very happy to join you."

* * *

Somehow, Room 5 felt different today, but in a way that gave Ro déjà vu. Bright, cool winter sunlight streamed through the windows. It took him a moment to realize that the room reminded him of Dartmouth. He felt a sudden, sharp pang of nostalgia.

Mahesh quietly set out two yoga mats to face each other and sat down cross-legged, not making eye contact.

"Is everything OK?" Ro sat down cross-legged as well. "Mahesh, I hope you know this already, but you can trust me. Is something wrong?"

"It doesn't matter what happened," Mahesh replied. "Whatever happened, God has given to me as a lesson. So now I have to discover what I am meant to learn."

"So tell me what happened, and we can try to figure out the lesson."

Mahesh's uncertainty was palpable.

"Oh, by the way." Ro remembered something. "I just found out your last name is Subramaniam. I'm Tamil too."

"You are?" Mahesh looked up and broke into a wide smile. "Your family name is Krishna, so I didn't know. I was meaning to ask. From where is your family?"

"Mostly Madras, but my grandmother's family is from near Tirunelveli."

"No!" Mahesh's mouth fell open. "I'm from Tirunelveli also."

Ro beamed. "That's wonderful."

"Unakku Tamil theriyuma?"

Ro shook his head, a little sadly. "I can understand it, but I don't really speak it at all," he admitted, embarrassed. "But it would really please me if you spoke to me in Tamil."

"Seri." Mahesh smiled.

"So tell me what happened. And we can figure out the lesson."

Mahesh's face immediately fell. "The lesson is about ego," he said, reverting to English. "I should not think I have the right to boast about all that I know."

Suddenly, it dawned on Ro. "Is it because that moron is giving a talk today and you're not?"

Mahesh looked down, avoiding Ro's eyes.

"You've been studying for years," Ro continued, almost on autopilot. "Then this idiot shows up here, walks into the library, copies some Indian ideas, and then passes them off as his own while people admire his wisdom."

He heard a noise above him.

The ceiling fan in the room had clicked on. It began to turn.

Counterclockwise.

Ro snapped to attention.

"Did you turn that on?" he asked Mahesh sharply.

Mahesh shook his head.

The fan began turning faster and faster.

Pendy? Ro thought to himself.

Mahesh sat up straighter, still not meeting Ro's eyes. "Let's do a meditation on the elimination of desire from our lives. Is it all right if we do meditation instead of yoga today?"

"Of course." Ro shook his head to try to snap out of it and turned his attention back to Mahesh.

"Please arrange yourself into a comfortable seat and close your eyes."

Ro obediently rearranged himself and closed his eyes.

Then he reopened them.

"No, Mahesh. I'm sorry. I'm not going to be able to do this. I'm too angry. So, every month you have these foreigners, these Visiting Lights, giving talks here as if they're experts on Indian wisdom? While the real experts here don't give talks?"

"Yes," Mahesh replied simply.

"I'd like you to use this half hour to meditate on the fact that you deserve recognition for what you've accomplished. You have a Ph.D., right?"

Mahesh nodded.

"Or whatever else you want to meditate on. Really, Mahesh. I mean it."

Ro stood up, feeling almost as if he were in some sort of trance. It was time for his mission, he realized. And just as Pendy'd said, he knew what he had to do, even if he didn't know why.

"I'll go start my steam early."

He started walking away, then turned back and looked at Mahesh.

"Things are going to change," Ro said quietly. "I promise." Then he left the room.

* * * * * * * * * *

Some time later, Ro emerged from the spa after his daily steam, scrubbed to within an inch of his life, in new pajamas, his mind a blank. He realized he wasn't sure what to do or where to go. Then he remembered. The trip to Rishikesh. He had to go put on actual clothes.

He went back to his room and, noticing that he was still sweating a little, took another shower. Then he went into the closet and got dressed. Vuori joggers, a T-shirt with the name of a surf company in Encinitas printed on it, an ancient North Face grey-and-black-paneled jacket. He put on socks from H&M and then pulled on his black-on-black Nike Air Force 1s.

He missed his kurta pajama already, he thought, as he threw them into the laundry basket and covered them with two used towels. He had never realized how exhausting it was to wear labels all the time.

While buckling his watch, he happened to feel his pulse. It was significantly more erratic than usual, and the skin under his fingers felt clammy to the touch.

* * *

He walked up the stairs to the Forresters' villa and into a flurry of activity. For all intents and purposes, a magazine shoot was in progress. Chris sat in the middle of the living room in front of a panel of mirrors, wearing a robe. All the lights in the room had been dragged into the center. One person worked on his face, another worked on his hair, and yet another worked on his body. They appeared to be making Chris look tanner and older. Joss stood next to him, his hand to his chin, offering suggestions. A table on the terrace held coffee, drinks, and snacks. Ro was grateful to see a bottle of green juice. He grabbed it and downed it in a few gulps.

Turning, he was surprised to see Lala in a corner chatting with Mrs. B. Like him, Lala was dressed to go into town in low-key athleisure. For once, she wore simple gold studs in her ears.

"Such fun!" Mrs. B. said, still in kurta pajama, waving at the people working on Chris. "I'm not coming along, but I didn't want to miss this."

"You're coming with us?" Ro said to Lala.

"Yes. I absolutely need a change of scenery."

"What about Herr Lala?"

Lala darkened. "No. It's not like him to mix with the people. Although it's his job."

"I'm sorry," Ro said, meaning it sincerely. He lowered his voice. "You have security?"

She nodded toward a large but previously inconspicuous man in the corner.

"Good." Ro exhaled. "I'm glad about that."

Lala looked at him searchingly. "What's wrong?"

She really was unusually perceptive, Ro thought. He didn't like it one bit. "Actually, that reminds me," he said, turning to Mrs. B. "Can I borrow you for a moment?"

"Of course," she said, surprised. They moved onto the terrace.

"I'm a little upset about something," Ro said. "I don't think it's fair or respectful that someone like the VB is being held out as an expert and giving lectures to guests when staff members like Mahesh and Fairuza aren't. They know so much more than he does." He paused and shook his head. "I'm just so sick of all of this."

Mrs. B. looked taken aback. She put her finger to her lips, contemplative. Then she spoke. "You're absolutely right. We just hadn't thought of that. It was only because they're visitors. Special attractions, of sorts. Not for any other reason. I wish I had a better response than that to give you, but I'm afraid I don't."

"It's great to have visiting teachers spreading new ideas. But don't let them overshadow the wonderful people you already have."

"Honestly, I'm embarrassed." Mrs. B. shook her head. "I'll take care of it."

"Mrs. B.," Chris called from inside. "Come tell me what you think."

Mrs. B. gave Ro another smile and went inside.

Ro moved over to the railing and leaned onto it, his arms crossed. He stood for a moment, breathing, looking out at the sea of trees, losing himself for a moment in the innumerable shades of green. He looked to his right, then to his left. He couldn't see anything but trees. A few monkeys playing. He began to calm down.

He closed his eyes. Inhale, exhale. Inhale, exhale. The air smelled like pine.

"Having a moment?" a voice said behind him.

Ro opened his eyes and turned around to find Joss. He couldn't quite read the look on Joss's face.

"I guess. I was just realizing I've been through a lot. Today has gotten to me."

"I'm worried about you," Joss replied simply. "I know you're good at not thinking about things you don't want to think about, but Ro, you found Amrita's body. You must be in shock." He paused. "You're actually trembling right now."

Ro looked at his hand and consciously stopped it from moving. He noted, dispassionately, that his nails were dirty. "Joss, this isn't the time or place."

"Fine," Joss said. "But I want to have a talk with you. Soon."

Ro looked back up and noticed that Joss wasn't in street clothes. "Aren't you coming with us?"

"No. I mean, I've been down there scouting a bunch already." Once again, Ro saw that weird flush rising in Joss's neck. "And I have lots of other work."

Joss ran his hand through his hair. It was covered in scratches.

"What happened to your hand?" Ro asked him suddenly.

Joss instantly turned bright red. "I was, er . . . outside. Got too close to a bush."

Ro was suspicious, but before he could ask another question, noises started coming from inside.

The elevator doors opened. Amit wheeled himself in. "Cool elevator!" Then, seeing Chris, he whistled.

Walking back inside, Ro too, was impressed at the transformation. Chris now actually looked his age, which was probably early fifties. The makeup artists had made his skin several shades darker. He wore a wig. Padding inside his cheeks had completely changed the structure of his face. Rectangular, wire-framed glasses completed the look.

"Very impressive," Joss said, solemn, coming up behind Ro. "I approve."

Everyone applauded. Ro felt his mood start to lift slightly. Then he noticed Catherine for the first time that afternoon. She stood at the back of the room, looking pensive.

"Are we ready? Who's coming? Me, Catherine, Ro, Amit, Lala." Chris looked around. "Where's Mahesh? Oh, there he is."

Ro turned to see Mahesh. He'd just arrived on the terrace.

Lala pointed at her security guard.

"All right. Mr. Big too."

Catherine looked at Ro. "Should we invite the Visiting Blight?"

Ro stiffened. But it was just a joke, he thought. "You're a poet, and you didn't even know it," he responded lightly.

Catherine smiled back.

"Anyway, the Blight is busy," Mahesh said sweetly. "We walked up to the villa together. He is going to the library to prepare his lecture."

Ro looked at Mahesh, surprised.

The sound of breaking glass startled everyone.

"Sorry." Catherine looked vexed. A water glass had fallen from her hand and shattered. "I don't know how that happened."

"Don't worry." Mrs. B. moved briskly to the phone and dialed. "Hello, this is Mrs. Banerjee. Please send housekeeping to Villa 2. Also, I would like to host a cocktail party tonight. At seven o'clock, let's say. Please inform all the guests. Oh." She paused, remembering. "Please reschedule the Visiting Light's talk for tonight at 7:15."

She hung up and looked at Mahesh. "Mahesh, come speak to me tomorrow, by the way." She smiled, seeing his hesitation. "Only good things."

"Oh, Mahesh," Joss added. "Remember to get your passport from reception."

"I will."

Mahesh moved to stand next to Ro. Ro tried to process what he'd just heard.

"Why does Joss need your passport?"

"I can't tell you. But good things only."

"Wait. They keep your passport at reception?"

"Yes. The passports of the permanent staff."

They stood in silence for a moment.

"What was that about? You said you walked up here with the VB just now?"

"Kavalai padaidhe," Mahesh replied simply. Hakuna matata. Don't worry.

* * *

Two Land Rovers, one cream, one green, waited for them in front of the Palace. Catherine, Chris, and Amit piled into the cream one with Officer Chandra, a member of Inspector Singh's staff whom he had grudgingly lent them for the afternoon.

Lala and Mahesh got into the green one. Lala's security officer was already in the front of the car next to the driver. Ro paused next to the open door, looking up at the sky. The sky was mostly blue, but he thought he felt rain in the air.

"What is it?" Mahesh said, leaning out.

"I'm just wondering if it's going to rain."

"Does it matter?" Lala asked, puzzled. "We have umbrellas."

She pointed. There were, indeed, three very heavy-looking umbrellas in the car, made out of metal.

"It's not that. I'm just worried I left my laptop on my balcony."

Mahesh looked at the sky. "It will rain at the end of the day, I think. Don't worry."

Ro got in and closed the door.

The back of the Land Rover had been custom-fitted to have two comfortable pairs of bucket seats facing each other. Although the interior looked very stylish, Ro had some doubts as to its actual safety. There was a roll bar, but there were no airbags in sight.

Ro buckled his seat belt. At least the seat belt seemed relatively sturdy.

"I like what they've done with the cars." Lala buckled herself in too. "It's very safari."

"Yes, but safaris are generally on flat land. I'm not too sure about this Land Rover for going up and down a windy mountain road."

As if on cue, the driver started the car. He passed through Samsara's gates. The Land Rover began going downhill almost immediately.

Ro was on edge, but tried not to show it.

"Well, they've been doing it for years. I'm sure they know what they're do-ing," Lala replied, casual. "Anyway, if something happens, just open the door, curl into a ball, and roll out of the car."

Mahesh laughed. "How do you know that?"

"I had to do kidnapping training."

There was a long silence.

Ro changed the subject.

"This is the first time I've left Samsara since I got here."

"Me too," Lala said. "It feels funny, doesn't it?"

Ro had arrived at Samsara in the dark and didn't remember the journey up the mountain, but he'd certainly remember the journey down. The guardrail seemed . . . nonchalant. He decided to stop looking out the window.

Then they hit a couple of jarring bumps.

"Jesus." Ro gripped his armrest.

"Don't worry." Mahesh gave Ro a reassuring look. "We will be all right. You will be all right."

Ro turned to Lala. "Have you been to Rishikesh before?"

"Yes, a couple of times," she replied. "Once when I was a child, then again last year when we came here."

They sat in a companionable silence for a few moments, their bodies shift-ing in tune with the Land Rover's movements.

Lala smiled. "You know, it's funny." She looked at Ro and Mahesh. "I hope you don't think this is a strange thing to say, but I feel like myself around the two of you. Like a real person."

Mahesh nodded, clearly aware who Lala was. "It must be so draining. In every interaction just take, take, take. Everyone takes."

"Yes." Ro paused. "I feel so lucky that I grew up with what was, in retro-spect, the perfect amount of money."

"What's the perfect amount of money?" Lala leaned forward, curious.

Ro thought about how best to phrase it. "Enough that I never had to worry about it, but not enough that trying to do something with my life felt pointless."

Lala laughed. "That feels right."

"I love money," Ro continued, musing. "Money is great. Money is energy. But like any energy, it can turn destructive. You shouldn't hoard it. Because it corrodes anything it touches for too long."

He paused.

"Money wants to go out and play. It wants to be used generously. To make people happy. Not to be thrown away in a casino like it's valueless. Or to be spent on a mausoleum of Birkins in every color."

"That's true." Lala reflected. "Think about the words that have to do with money. Money wants to deepen experiences. To enrich. To create luck. Texture. In the end, money wants to be good fortune."

Ro nodded, impressed.

"I always think of money as food," Mahesh said. "You must consume it at the right moment. You should not waste it. And if you keep it for too long, it goes bad."

Finally, the road flattened out, and the Land Rover entered the outskirts of Rishikesh. They followed the other car into a parking lot and parked side by side.

Everyone clambered out of the Land Rovers. "The drivers will wait here," Mahesh said, herding everyone together. "And we all will walk." Then his eye fell on Amit. He blushed.

"Or roll." Amit flashed a peace sign.

The central part of Rishikesh was pedestrianized. Lots of people were around, everyone going about their business. Considering that they formed a group of seven people, including one person in a wheelchair, Ro worried that their saunter through Rishikesh would feel cumbersome. But everything felt surprisingly fluid and easy somehow. The crowds moved with a serene flow.

Mahesh saw Ro checking out the many signs offering yoga teacher training. "Rishikesh is the yoga capital of the world," Mahesh said, with some pride. "Did you know that, Ro?"

"Nope. That's rad, though."

"You do know that the Beatles studied meditation here?" Lala said.

"I think I'd heard that somewhere. Where did they stay?" Ro asked Mahesh.

"That way." Mahesh waved his hand above his head in no particular direction.

They continued to make their way down the path, the green snaking Ganges flowing placidly on their right.

Then Ro spied a store selling jewelry and crystals. "Guys, let's go in here!"

* * *

"Ro! I didn't know you were coming down to Rishikesh today."

Ro turned his head to see a woman in the store smiling at him. At first, he didn't recognize her. Then he did a double-take.

"Fairuza! Hello! Yes, we decided this morning." Ro had only ever seen Fairuza in kurta pajama. Now out of uniform, she was stylish and glamorous, in white jeans and an aquamarine silk top with large sunglasses perched on her head. "That's so funny. I came into this store because of you, actually. To buy crystals."

"Perfect timing, then."

The rest of the group entered the store.

"So many of you came down!" Then Fairuza hesitated. "But who is that?" She lowered her voice and nodded toward Chris.

Ro whispered a few words into her ear.

Fairuza giggled, delighted. "That's great. Hello, everyone!" She waved at them, and they waved back. "And hello, Amit."

"Hi, Fairuza." Amit's voice sounded weird. Ro turned to look at him. He was blushing.

Fairuza moved off to chat with the Forresters.

"Did you know she was coming to Rishikesh?" Ro asked Amit. "Is that why you suggested coming down here?"

"I have no comment," Amit responded, dignified.

Ro approached the counter. Fairuza came and stood next to him, saying a couple of words to the shopkeeper in Hindi.

The shopkeeper took out a few trays of crystals.

Ro bent over them. Unlike in crystal stores in California, the crystals weren't tagged with their names and properties. He'd have to fly blind.

He turned to Fairuza. "What do you think I should get? Can you help me choose?"

"Absolutely not." Fairuza shook her head, decisive. "Look at them. Feel them. Hold them. You'll know which ones to choose."

Ro began to explore. She was right. Different energies emanated from every one of them.

He took his time selecting a few, choosing some with his eyes open, some with his eyes closed.

Eventually, he took five crystals to the till. The shopkeeper rang him up, putting the crystals into a small yellow zippered pouch. Ro handed over much less money than he had imagined and put the pouch in his pocket.

Then the shopkeeper handed Ro another small fabric pouch. This one was orange, with an "Om" printed on it.

"Gift with purchase," the shopkeeper said, smiling at him.

The pouch was heavy in Ro's palm. There was something inside it.

"Gift with purchase?" Fairuza said behind him, surprised. "I've never gotten one."

Ro opened the pouch. Whatever was in it, it slid onto his hand, then dangled from his palm, languid.

A pendulum.

Pendy? Ro asked silently. Is that you?

The pendulum swung ever so slightly to the left, then ever so slightly to the right.

Yes. Now shut up.

* * *

They made their way through the bustling town in a leisurely manner toward the pedestrian Lakshman Jhula Bridge, a suspension bridge made of steel.

Ro stopped and looked up at it, impressed.

"When was this built?" he asked Mahesh.

"The 1930s, I think. Look at the monkeys."

Looking more closely, Ro saw that monkeys were using the structure as a jungle gym. He smiled.

They paused halfway across the bridge to admire the thirteen-story orange Trimbakeshwar Temple, dedicated to Lord Shiva. The temple looked like it was in perfect condition, but Amit informed Ro that it was actually over four hundred years old.

Once they had crossed the Ganges, they made their way toward the outdoor temple where the daily ceremony honoring the holy river took place. Chris wheeled Amit down one of the aisles.

Ro found himself seated between Catherine and Mahesh. Catherine still felt off to him somehow. "Are you all right?" Ro asked her.

Catherine met his eyes. "I'm good, thanks for asking." She turned her gaze back to the Ganges. "What about you?"

Ro considered for a moment. "I'm getting there. I hope."

"Good." She didn't make eye contact. "I'm glad."

"What's going on with Joss, by the way? Why isn't he with us?"

Catherine suddenly became more animated. "You know, I don't know. I'm not sure what's going on." Then her face tightened up and she turned back to face forward.

Ro tried to focus on the preparations for the ceremony. A number of boys in robes were acting the way boys do, jostling one another while also helping the priests, the Ganges moving inexorably in the background.

The ceremony started. A fire was lit. The priest said something in Hindi and then began chanting.

Ro couldn't understand him, but he didn't feel too bad, because his parents wouldn't have been able to understand him either. As if on cue, Mahesh whispered into his ear, "Yenaku puriyavai illai." I don't understand him at all.

Ro closed his eyes and let the sounds wash over him. But he soon realized that, even though he couldn't understand what the priest was saying, he recognized a lot of words. Names. First names, last names. Names of family, names of friends. Before they were just random sounds. Now they belonged somewhere. He still didn't know what they meant, but he saw that they meant something. He heard his own family name. Again and again.

He let the sounds make their way through his body. He asked God to forgive him for everything he had ever done wrong. All his life, Ro had generally done what he thought was the best thing to do at the time, even if in the end sometimes it wasn't. But he was only human, and he felt the light enter his heart.

He didn't realize he was crying until Mahesh whispered into his right ear. "I will protect you." He said it in Tamil. And then, one second later, Catherine squeezed his left knee and whispered into his left ear. "Don't worry. It's all right. It's going to be all right." She said it in English.

* * *

Everyone was contemplative after the ceremony. Unhurriedly, they began to make their way back to the cars. Ro and Amit were behind everyone else. For whatever reason, the crowds of people were flowing primarily in the other direction, making Ro feel like he was walking into traffic. But everyone parted for them with a smile.

"Can I push you?" Ro asked.

"It's electric," Amit replied. "But you can push me if you want to."

"OK," Ro said impulsively. "I will."

Unhurriedly, they began following the others through the streets.

"The ceremony's wonderful, isn't it? That's at least the third time I've seen it, but I can't imagine ever getting tired of it."

Ro didn't respond. He was thinking about something.

"What's up?" Amit looked up over his shoulder at Ro.

Ro hesitated. How to phrase this.

"I have a question for you, Amit," he finally said, staring straight ahead. "And it might come as a somewhat unpleasant surprise. But I really do think responding honestly is in your best interest."

He kept pushing Amit up the street, parting the steady wave of people flowing the other way.

"What was your connection with Amrita Dey? Because there was one. That much is obvious."

Amit was silent.

The two of them continued to push forward, crowds streaming in the other direction, both looking straight ahead.

"I'm not sure what you mean," Amit finally said.

Ro sighed. "You're good at plenty of things, Amit, but you're not a good liar. Your voice goes up by a full octave whenever Amrita's name comes up."

"How would you even know that? We've never talked about her."

"You know I'm involved with the investigation," Ro responded quietly.

Amit was silent. They kept moving forward.

"She had something to do with the death of your father, didn't she," Ro continued. "Was she blackmailing him?"

Amit tried to stop the wheelchair, alarmed. "How did you know that," he hissed.

"Shhh." Ro kept pushing forward, waving subtly toward the rest of the group. "Keep it down."

Amit was silent for a long time.

"I'm not talking about this."

"Amit, it's going to come out. You're going to have to talk about this."

"Then we'll talk about this when it does."

Amit pressed a button and stopped his wheelchair dead in its tracks. Ro stopped too.

"I didn't kill her," Amit said quietly. "And I couldn't have killed her. At least, not like that. That doesn't mean I didn't want to, though."

He turned his head to look at Ro, his eyes filled with truth.

"To be honest, someone else just beat me to it."

"Let's keep going," Ro said quietly. They started moving again.

"Do you know who that person is?" he asked, his tone gentle.

Amit hesitated for a long time, then shook his head. "No. I don't."

They had almost reached the spot where they'd left the cars. Looking up, Ro saw Mahesh lagging behind the rest of the group, waiting for them.

"It will rain tonight, Ro." Mahesh pointed to the sky. "For your laptop, I mean."

"Thank you, Mahesh," Ro replied, feeling an unexpected flush of happiness. That was excellent news about the rain. And he was very pleased that both Fairuza and Mahesh were finally calling him by his first name. It made him feel like he belonged.

* * *

The cocktail party was in full swing when they got back to Samsara. Guests milled around the lawn in front of the Residence, all still in kurta pajama, but with jewelry and makeup. Ro was amused to see that Mrs. B. had accessorized her kurta pajama with what looked like the entirety of the Cartier Tutti Frutti collection.

The group headed over to Joss, who was standing by the bar. "You missed out," Catherine said. "It was pretty spectacular."

"Yeah, I've heard," Joss replied. "I had a good day here, though."

It was dark, but Ro could swear he saw Joss blushing.

"Get up to much?" Ro asked him casually.

"The usual, I guess. Some work. A couple of massages."

Lala came over. "Where have you been?" Ro asked.

"I went to the Visiting Light talk, but no one was there." She sounded puzzled.

"Well, that's not surprising," Amit said. "Everyone's here."

"That's not what I meant." Lala shook her head. "He wasn't there either. The room was empty."

"The VB wasn't there?" Joss replied, surprised. "That's a little weird. I can't imagine he'd miss his own talk."

"Perhaps his talk was rescheduled," Mahesh said firmly.

Chris looked around. "Do you know if there's a bathroom around here? Time to get this makeup off."

"Probably fastest to go over to the restaurant," Joss said.

"Oh, don't bother." Amit pointed toward his room. "Use mine. It's right there. The terrace door is open."

"Cool, thanks." Chris walked off.

"I'm ready for bed," Mahesh said. "It's been a very long day."

"Indeed it has," Catherine said, yawning. "Me too."

"Me three." Ro yawned too. His muscles ached with exhaustion. He'd definitely be sore tomorrow. Ro turned to Amit to say good night, and then he stopped dead in his tracks.

Sitting in his wheelchair, Amit was staring at something. With a very strange look in his eye.

Ro turned to see what Amit was staring at.

Catherine and Mahesh, chatting with each other.

Ro turned back to Amit. Amit still had that strange look in his eye. A look of fear. And, maybe, of comprehension.

All of a sudden, Ro was terrified.

"I need to talk to you," he said to Amit quietly. "Let's go into your room."

They entered the room through the terrace. Ro closed the door and exhaled. "It looks like you've thought of something."

"I don't know." Amit was clearly in distress. "Something's up. But I don't know what it is."

"Oops," Chris interjected, exiting the bathroom. "Passing through." He smiled at them and left the room through the sliding door.

Ro closed the door behind Chris and checked the room to make sure no one else was there. He came back to Amit's side.

"Can you try to think what it was?" Ro's voice was low. "You were reminded of something?"

Amit seemed like he was about to speak, but then he shook his head.

"There's something there, but I don't know what it is."

"Fine." Ro sighed, frustrated. "Try to relax. Maybe it'll come to you in your sleep."

Amit nodded.

"And Amit, do not leave your room. Lock the doors. I don't know why. But I'm worried you're in real danger."

Amit swallowed.

"I'm going to call Inspector Singh and get police protection for your room." Ro opened the sliding door onto the terrace and moved through it.

He turned around.

"Call me if you need anything at all. And lock this door. Right now."

From the other side of the window, Ro saw Amit lock the door.

* * *

After calling Inspector Singh, Ro sat in a chair in his room.

Pendy hung from his hand, languid.

"Can I ask you . . ." Ro began, but Pendy immediately began to move to the right.

No.

"But did I . . ." Ro continued.

Yes. Pendy moved to the left, then the right. Now stop asking.

"Fine," Ro sighed.

He stood up, walked five feet, and got into bed, more exhausted than he could remember ever having been in his life. It had been quite a day. He stretched, then grimaced. His arms and ribs were really very sore. And he, too, had some scratches on his hands. Which made him think about Joss again. Why on earth was Joss being so shady?

Then something in the air changed. Ro heard the sound of rain.

The sound of the rain got heavier and heavier.

Then, suddenly, he remembered his laptop. He sat up and looked to his right.

The laptop was sitting on the floor, where he'd thought it would be.

Breathing a sigh of relief, he sank back onto his pillow. The rain sounded quite heavy indeed. The world, he reflected, would be a cleaner place tomorrow.

He was relieved, as the rain sounded quite heavy.

DAY 7

(December 29)

Ro tossed and turned all night. When he slept at all, he had dreams both boring and stressful, mostly set in the corporate world. He finally gave up and staggered out of bed at dawn.

Stepping onto the terrace, he shivered, hugging his arms around him. The rain had been heavy. The ground was covered in mud, and the air was still filled with mist. He went back inside.

Ro knew it was far too early to call another guest room, but he couldn't help it. He needed to check on Amit. He picked up the phone and dialed.

The phone rang and rang. No response.

He hung up and dialed again.

It just rang and rang.

He hung up again and called Inspector Singh. "I'm sorry to wake you."

"You didn't wake me." The inspector sounded exhausted.

"I'm worried about Amit. I just tried his room and there was no answer. Can you check with your officers?"

"Hold on." He heard the inspector say a few words in Hindi. "The officers didn't leave their posts all night," he said, coming back to the phone.

"I'm sorry, but can you please have someone go in and check on him? I just have a horrible feeling. I can't explain it."

The inspector sighed. "All right."

They hung up.

Ro sat, uneasily waiting for the phone to ring again.

It didn't.

The minutes kept passing, filling him with more and more dread.

Finally, there was a knock on the door, and Ro knew he had been right.

Inspector Singh looked more tired than Ro had ever seen him. "He's dead."

Ro shook his head, tears prickling the backs of his eyes. He'd tried his very best to save Amit, but he had failed. "Do we know what happened?"

"We don't know yet. But I suspect poisoning." The inspector's face was grim. "I have three officers guarding the body. There will be no hanky-panky this time."

Ro almost grinned at this unexpected choice of words, but managed to stop himself. Then he remembered his conversation with Amit in Rishikesh.

He became somber once more.

"I'm going to call Mrs. B. and Catherine. We should all sit down."

* * *

They regrouped in the interview room. Everyone was in shock. Catherine had been crying and was puffy-eyed.

"We haven't received the full toxicology report, but we believe his sleep tea was poisoned," Inspector Singh said. "In any case, there is no indication that his death was anything other than peaceful."

Ro half-raised his hand. "There are a couple of things I should mention straight away. First, on the way back last night, Amit more or less admitted to me that Amrita'd had something to do with his father's death. He swore he didn't kill her, though, and reminded me he couldn't have killed her that way anyway."

Inspector Singh nodded. "He put me in touch with his doctor without my asking. His doctor confirmed the extent of his paralysis."

"But here's the interesting thing," Ro continued. "He said that someone beat him to it. And he said he didn't know who, but I got the feeling he did. Or at least, that he had an idea."

They all paused, registering the implications of Amit's words.

"What was the other thing?" Catherine said abruptly.

"So that first conversation was in Rishikesh. But something else happened at the cocktail party, once we'd gotten back. Amit was deeply disturbed by something he saw there. I tried to get it out of him, but he couldn't put it to-gether for me . . ." Ro trailed off, feeling pretty lame.

"That's not very helpful," Catherine muttered.

"I know." Ro paused, embarrassed. "And there's one last thing. Also not helpful, I'm afraid. Anyone could have killed him."

Ro leaned forward. The others were listening intently.

"The party was just in front of his room. He had left the door to his room open, and people were going in and out to use the bathroom."

The inspector shook his head, pinching the bridge of his nose between his thumb and index fingers.

He looked at Mrs. B.

"Unfortunately, I think we may now need to lock down the hotel and in-form the guests."

Ro turned to Mrs. B. "I'm afraid I agree."

"Yes," Mrs. B. nodded. "The situation is different. Rita's death was one thing. It's another thing entirely if people are being killed for things they might have seen or known."

"In the meantime, though," the inspector said, looking grimly satisfied, "we have one strong lead. We've become aware of financial transactions in-volving Miss Dey and Sanjay Mehta."

Ro exhaled, leaning back in his seat. So they had found out after all. He hadn't been able to tell them personally because of attorney-client privilege, but Ro had to admit he was relieved.

"Wow," Catherine said. "I can't say I'm surprised. There's something wrong with that guy."

"Poor Lala." Mrs. B. looked at the inspector. "How will you proceed?"

"Delicately. He's a member of Parliament, after all. We're examining the records now." Inspector Singh looked at Ro and Catherine. "Did either of you see Mr. Mehta at the cocktail party?"

"I did, actually," Catherine said. "Right when I arrived."

Just then, a junior officer burst into the room without knocking. Inspector Singh looked at him, angry.

The officer ran up and urgently whispered to the inspector in Hindi.

"What?" Inspector Singh replied sharply in English.

The officer frantically whispered several more words.

Mrs. B. gasped, placing her hand to her mouth.

Catherine leaned in. Her brow was furrowed.

"What happened?" Ro said.

"The Visiting Blight is missing," Inspector Singh said grimly. "Mitchell Charney, I mean. Sorry. He did not attend his own talk last night."

For the second time that morning, Ro had a truly horrible feeling, right in his gut. He wanted to stand up and go to the window, but felt glued to his chair.

"Oh, yes," Catherine said. "We'd heard he didn't show up."

"And his bed hasn't been slept in." The inspector looked at the three of them. "When did you last see him?"

"I last spoke to him in the restaurant. Yesterday morning." Ro turned to Catherine and Mrs. B., his heart pounding in his chest. "With both of you."

"Yes." Catherine sat up a little straighter. "Same."

"Me too," Mrs. B. echoed.

"What time was that?"

"Probably around 11:15 or 11:30," Mrs. B. said.

"Did any of you see him afterward?"

Catherine and Ro paused.

Mrs. B. reflected. "No, but Mahesh saw him right before you all left for Rishikesh." She looked at Catherine and Ro, who nodded. "Remember?" She turned back to the inspector. "That must have been right around 3. Mahesh Subramaniam. One of our yoga instructors."

"Yes," Catherine said, thoughtful. "Mahesh said he walked up the path with him." That reminded Ro. He wasn't sure whether to ask some questions about that.

"Was he at the cocktail party you had yesterday?"

"No. That's probably why we had such a nice time," Mrs. B. mused absently, as if to herself. She looked back up at Inspector Singh. "Do we have to inform the American embassy? Always such a hullabaloo when Westerners go missing."

"I'm afraid so," he replied.

Mrs. B. sighed theatrically. Then she thought of something and brightened. She turned to Ro. "Do I remember correctly that his family is poor?" she asked, hopeful.

"I don't know about poor," Ro replied, startled. "Modest, maybe."

"Oh, good," Mrs. B. said, relaxing back into her seat. "They won't be able to cause too much fuss."

She turned back to Inspector Singh.

"Let's search his room."

"I'll search his room," the inspector replied, frowning. "You will all stay here."

"No," Ro replied.

"I own this property," Mrs. B. said simultaneously.

"Fine." The inspector sighed, exasperated. "But you're not to touch anything."

"Promise." Mrs. B. nodded her head vigorously. "Let's get the key from downstairs."

* * *

Just before the hidden entrance to the spa, their golf cart turned right, down a path Ro had never noticed before. He was reminded once again of how disorienting Samsara's geography was. The tree-lined curves and rolling hills distorted actual distances in an unnerving way. As they passed two small, derelict wooden buildings, Ro flinched. The buildings looked straight out of the movie *Deliverance*.

Continuing through the forest, they finally pulled up to the pleasant-looking staff quarters. "His room would be over there in the wing to the right," Mrs. B. said, pointing. "That's where the yoga teachers and visiting staff stay."

As she was pointing, Mahesh unexpectedly came out of the door, dressed in his work uniform, adjusting his sleeves. He stopped, startled, when he saw all of them. "What's happening?"

Ro looked at Mrs. B., who shrugged.

"The Visiting Blight's gone missing," Ro said to him.

"Oh, really?" Mahesh replied, interested. "Is he now the Visiting Flight?"

Mrs. B. giggled.

The inspector glared at her. "That's not funny."

* * *

The staff quarters were white and spare, but still quite stylish in a minimalist way. The floors were covered in marine blue tile.

They turned down a hallway lined with windows on one side and doors on the other. Officer Chandra was already waiting outside one of the doors halfway down the corridor.

Reaching into his pocket, the inspector pulled out the key, then unlocked the door to the room and opened it wide.

"The room is small," the inspector said sternly. "You will wait here, in the hall."

They all nodded.

The inspector and Officer Chandra put on gloves. Officer Chandra picked up his evidence bag. They went into the room.

At first glance, it was neat and in good order, with white walls and the same blue tile floors as the hallway. The room contained a double bed, a built-in wooden wardrobe, and a small desk, upon which a laptop sat. A couple of stairs at the back of the room led to what Ro assumed was a bathroom.

The three of them watched, absorbed, as the officers began methodically to search the room. Officer Chandra opened the wardrobe and started to go through every item of clothing, checking each pocket before placing it on the bed.

The detritus of a life, Ro thought.

Inspector Singh opened the desk drawer and pursed his lips. He called out something to Officer Chandra in Hindi.

"What is it?" Ro asked, turning to Mrs. B.

"They found his passport," Catherine replied, absorbed.

Ro turned to her, surprised. "You speak Hindi?"

A sudden flash of irritation crossed Catherine's face. "Yes. A little. I told you I used to be stationed here."

"Yes. You did." And now you're annoyed because you just made a mistake, Ro thought to himself.

Mrs. B. had been following the action. "They found his wallet too," she said without turning her head.

Inspector Singh was, indeed, placing a wallet in an evidence bag. Turning, he said something else to Officer Chandra in Hindi.

"What did he say?" Ro said, turning to Catherine.

She struggled, clearly not wanting to admit she'd understood, but also realizing that lying was futile. "Something about a toothbrush," she muttered.

"He told him to go to the bathroom and take anything that could be used for DNA evidence," Mrs. B. responded. "Like his toothbrush."

The search continued. Inspector Singh stripped the bed piece by piece. He examined the pillows carefully. Then he crawled under the bed.

He stayed there for quite some time.

When he came back out, he went straight to Officer Chandra's bag. He rifled through it for a moment, then removed a small knife.

Then Inspector Singh ducked back under the bed.

After a while, Ro realized that he was holding his breath.

Finally, Inspector Singh came back out. In his hands were two hard drives and a thumb drive. "These were taped to the bottom of the bed," he said, a grim smile on his face. "I'll go back to the Palace straight away to look at these. Officer Chandra will continue here."

Mrs. B. looked at Ro, who shrugged. It didn't seem like any more excitement would happen there, so they followed Inspector Singh out of the building.

* * *

It had started to drizzle again. They stood in front of the staff quarters. Unaccountably, their golf cart had left. "Staff these days," Mrs. B. muttered darkly to herself.

"Let's just walk to the main path," the inspector said. "I'll radio for someone to pick us up."

They followed the path into the forest. The ground was still muddy from the heavy rain overnight.

They arrived at the two derelict wooden buildings Ro had noticed from the golf cart. In size, they were somewhere between a shed and a barn.

Ro shuddered. There really was something sinister about the buildings in the misty grey light.

Inspector Singh felt something too. He stopped. "What's in these buildings?" he asked Mrs. B., his tone unexpectedly sharp.

"I've no idea," Mrs. B. replied, shrugging. "Gardening tools, perhaps."

Inspector Singh moved to the door of the first building and, with a bit of difficulty, removed the piece of wood barring the door. He pushed the door open and peered inside.

"What's in there?" Catherine asked, trying to look over his shoulder.

"Nothing of interest, I think. Old paint cans. And yes, there's some gardening equipment. It's mostly empty."

He closed the doors and replaced the piece of wood, then turned and looked at the second building.

The piece of wood barring the door of the second building came off much more easily.

Inspector Singh pushed open the doors.

He peered in, then turned back around to face them.

"Stay here," he ordered, holding up his hand, in a tone that brooked no argument. He went inside.

Ro peered in from outside the door.

The building was filled with antiquated gardening equipment. Inefficient-looking tools made of rusted metal, used to keep a garden tidy in a place where human labor is cheaper than machinery.

The inspector cautiously made his way through the room. He disappeared behind a menacing-looking metal contraption with rusted teeth.

"Every single thing in there could kill someone," Catherine muttered behind Ro. She wasn't wrong.

The inspector was gone for several minutes. When he finally reemerged, he looked grimmer than Ro had ever seen him.

"There's any type of poison you could imagine in there. Cyanide for wasps. Every kind of weed and insect killer."

He turned to Mrs. B.

"We need to lock this building immediately. I will send an officer to guard it twenty-four hours a day."

"Dear, oh dear." Mrs. B. had a grave expression on her face. "How careless."

Easy come, easy go, Ro thought, looking at his watch. "Sorry, guys, but I have to run."

He had a massage in ten minutes.

* * *

Ro was uncharacteristically pensive as he lay there in the steam room, postmassage. So much had changed since the last time he'd been in there. Only the day before.

He suddenly felt something extremely icky inside him. He shifted, startled.

The icky thing grew and grew. What was it?

Ro was almost sick. Then a great burst of sweat came out of him, and the icky feeling flowed out of his body with it.

To his surprise, Ro realized that what had just passed out of him was the latrine. That awful situation was now truly and definitively in the past.

He felt lighter now. The universe felt right again. With regards to that, anyway.

But emotions caused by other problems started to mix inside him, filling the chasm left by the latrine's final exit.

Unease about the VB's disappearance. Real, genuine grief about Amit's death.

And, perhaps above all, a new, profound sense of peace, of acceptance, after the Ganga Aarti ceremony in Rishikesh.

There was something about Amit's death that felt particularly unfair to Ro. Something that felt deeply wrong. And then he realized it was because Amit's life had been reduced to collateral damage. Amit was an ancillary victim.

Probably, anyhow.

Ro sat up. It was time to get out of there.

He paused at the door to the terrace but decided not to go out there that day. It was still a little too soon. Instead, he went upstairs and took a freezing shower. Then he went into the sauna to sweat some more, just in case any last traces of the latrine were still lurking inside him.

* * *

After another icy shower, Ro ambled out to the terrace by the pool. Catherine, Chris, and Joss were at a table at the far end.

Ro flopped down on a lounge chair next to them. "That massage was exhausting."

He closed his eyes for a moment.

"Silent Night" was playing through the pool speakers.

"Why are they still playing Christmas music?" he asked, sitting back up.

"I think it's pretty much open season on holiday music until New Year's," Chris said.

"Silent Night" finished. The next song began. It was "Do They Know It's Christmas?"

Ro sighed. "This song is so unfortunate."

Chris laughed. "How so?"

"Where to start?" Ro asked rhetorically. "Perhaps with the video. Have you ever seen it? They've clearly taken so many drugs, it looks like their heads are on springs. Anyway."

He paused to listen to the lyrics and shook his head.

"Also, I was at Kilimanjaro at Christmas with my parents a few years ago. I can confirm there's snow in Africa at Christmastime."

Catherine laughed.

"What's so funny?" a new voice said.

Ro opened his eyes again. Fairuza had just come through the side doors from the spa.

"We were just talking about inappropriate songs," Chris responded. "Like this one." He waved toward a speaker.

Joss was silent, his brow furrowed, thinking about something. Finally, he nodded briefly to himself.

"You know, I've always been baffled by one song. Because it's by an artist for whom I have a tremendous amount of respect. But it starts with a sample that's so"—he paused, grasping for the word—"distasteful, that I'm"—he swallowed—"baffled."

Ro sat up, pleased. Joss looked more like himself than Ro had seen him in a while. "What's the song?"

"'XO.' By Beyoncé."

"That's a good song!"

"I know it's a good song."

Joss paused. Everyone was silent, waiting for him to continue.

"But have any of you ever listened to it from the beginning?"

"No," Catherine said. "I don't know the song, in fact."

"Let me play it for you guys." Joss fished around in the tote bag on his lap and pulled out his phone. "I'll turn the speaker up as loud as I can."

Everyone was quiet as Joss started playing the song. The beginning flew by. Ro could hear some spoken words. Then the song began.

"I couldn't hear anything," Chris said.

But Ro was ahead of him. "Hold on." Something was dawning on him. Something so grim that he couldn't even believe it. "Can I have your phone?"

Wordlessly, Joss handed it over.

Ro restarted the song, the phone's speaker now glued to his ear. He gasped, horrified.

"Wait. Is that from the *Challenger*?"

"Yes. She sampled a statement from NASA right after the *Challenger* disaster. 'Flight controllers here looking very carefully at the situation.'" Joss paused, his face crumpling as he realized how truly awful the whole thing was. "'Obviously a major malfunction,'" he concluded quietly.

There was a long pause.

"What's the song about?" Chris finally asked.

"Not that," Joss said.

"No song is about that," Chris said. "What the actual."

"Chris, that might not be true," Ro said, pensive.

"What do you mean?"

"I hate to say it," Ro continued, "but I can think of a couple of songs where maybe, just maybe, that sample would have been appropriate."

He corrected himself.

"Actually, no. It would never have been appropriate. Under any circumstances. But at least it would have been logical."

"Like what?" Joss asked.

"Like 'Leaving on a Jet Plane,'" Ro responded.

Fairuza burst out laughing. Everyone looked at her.

"Sorry," she said, collecting herself.

"Slow clap," Joss said.

"Or 'Rocket Man,'" Chris said, considering.

"You know, I thought of that," Fairuza said. "But no. It wasn't a long, long time."

"'It's Raining Men,'" Joss offered, to collective moans.

"'Free Fallin','" Chris responded with a grin.

"How about 'Space Oddity'?" Ro said. "Or 'The Final Countdown'?"

"Or 'Under Pressure,'" Fairuza suggested.

"Ch-ch-ch-ch-changes," Joss sang.

Startled, Ro swallowed the wrong way and began to cough.

"If we're going eighties, I propose 'I Melt with You,'" Catherine said.

There was a long pause, during which Ro tried and failed to figure out how to work in "Wind Beneath My Wings."

"Do you know what song's definitely not about the *Challenger*?" Catherine said suddenly. "'Nothing's Gonna Stop Us Now.'" She paused. "By Starship," she added, realizing.

"Or 'I Will Survive,'" Joss said.

Ro grinned. "Or 'The Safety Dance.'"

"Or 'Stayin' Alive,'" Fairuza added.

"I've got one," Chris said. "How about *Cloudy with a Chance of Meatballs*?"

"That's disgusting, honey," Catherine said affectionately, taking his hand. "Also, it wasn't cloudy that day. And that's a movie."

"I think movies are fair play."

Ro glanced down at his watch.

"Anyway, this has all been very, but I've gotta motor if I'm going to make it to lunch. I'll be *Gone in Sixty Seconds*."

Everyone groaned again as Mahesh wandered out. He smiled and perched on a chair.

"What are all of you laughing about?"

They all looked at each other. "Um . . . do you remember the *Challenger*?"

Mahesh nodded. "The space shuttle? The one that exploded?"

"Yes," Joss said. "We're thinking of song and movie titles that could be about the *Challenger*."

Mahesh looked puzzled.

"It's kind of a long story."

"Hmm." Mahesh thought for a moment. "How about 'Skyfall'?"

* * *

Ro ran into Lala as he was entering the restaurant. She was leaving.

"Hello," he said. "You've eaten?"

"Yes."

They stood there for a moment.

"Shall we get some tea and go for a walk?"

* * *

They walked slowly, both carrying large, steaming mugs of masala chai.

"So do they think the VB killed Amit, then ran for it?" Lala asked.

"I don't think so."

Lala looked at him.

"They found his passport and his wallet," Ro said. "He couldn't have gotten very far without them."

"Unless he's some sort of international man of mystery and had a fake passport and wallet ready to go," Lala suggested.

Ro considered. "If that's the case, then he's the best actor I've ever met. Chapeau."

They walked in silence.

"I have to tell you," Ro said finally. "The police know about the financial transactions between Sanjay and Amrita."

"I know," Lala responded coolly. "I told them."

Ro reeled for a second, genuinely surprised, then recovered. "Good for you."

"He's a jerk," Lala said, dismissive. "I was very young when we got married. I thought he could be Barack Obama. Turns out he was more of a Ted Cruz. It's a shame. I'd much rather be a widow than a divorcée," she added inconsequentially.

What was that supposed to mean, Ro thought to himself.

"Anyway, I think everyone thinks that Sanjay did it."

"I know." Lala hesitated. "Papa's on his way here to bring me home."

"You know, that's very nice of him. Even if you don't need him, it's nice that he would do that."

"He's a good man."

Ro noticed a slight disturbance in the trees in front of them.

"What's going on over there?" Ro said.

They approached. A couple of monkeys were fighting over something.

"Wait a minute," Lala said sharply. "What are they fighting over?"

Ro suddenly remembered her exceptional eyesight.

Lala strode over toward the monkeys. One dropped whatever it was holding.

Both monkeys ran away.

Lala bent over, peering at something on the ground.

Then, in the most polite, discreet, and ladylike way possible, she turned her head to the side and vomited.

Ro rushed over and looked down too.

The monkeys had been fighting over a human finger.

It was a thumb.

A white thumb.

DAY 8

(December 30)

Ro was in Switzerland. In Davos, if we're being precise.

In an austere room where he'd spent a few weeks, during the summer when he was nineteen.

Ro went to the wood-framed window and gazed at the magic mountains outside for a moment. Then, turning his head, he glimpsed a mirror and began to glide toward it.

He looked at his reflection and was surprised to see his eyes were turquoise.

Like hers.

He also noted dully that he was wearing earrings. Magic Alhambras. Made of turquoise and pavé diamonds.

Like hers.

But then, as he peered more closely at his reflection, he saw that his eyes were dead, actually. Unreadable. Flat.

Like hers.

Then the phone rang and he woke up.

"We've found Mr. Charney's body," Inspector Singh said without preamble. "We need to talk. I think you had better come to the Palace straight away."

Ro's stomach dropped. He didn't know what to say.

"Mrs. Forrester is already here, for reasons that I'll explain," the inspector continued. "I will also inform Mrs. Banerjee."

Ro exhaled. "I'll be there as soon as I can."

He got up, rang for tea, and went into the shower.

When he emerged, the tea was in its usual place, along with an envelope. He sliced it open.

It was from Joss.

"You and I are having breakfast tomorrow," Joss's note said. "We have things to discuss. TOMORROW. OR ELSE," it concluded ominously.

That was a bit unfair, Ro thought. If anything, he'd been the one trying to pin Joss down, not the other way round. But in any event, he agreed. It was high time that they caught up. He dashed off a quick note to Joss and left it on the table for housekeeping to deliver.

As he was dressing, he spied his phone on the bedside table and spontaneously picked it up in order to check the meaning of the name Mitchell. To his consternation, he learned that it meant "gift from God."

Ro scowled, then brightened. At least, he reflected, the gift had been returned to sender.

* * *

The previous day's drizzle had turned into a steady rain that showed no signs of abating. Ro could hardly see five meters ahead of the golf cart as it slowly wound its way toward the Palace. He'd never come across the maniac driver again, he realized with a sigh of gratitude.

He jogged up the stairs and began to enter the investigation room.

Then he paused in the doorway. The energy in the room felt strange. Different from how it felt after the deaths of Amrita and Amit.

Inspector Singh and Catherine were sitting together at one end of the table. Mrs. B. sat facing them.

"What's going on?" Ro said to Catherine and Inspector Singh. "You actually look"—Ro searched for the word—"pleased?"

"Wait till you hear this, Ro," Catherine said with a brief, wolfish grin that instantly disappeared.

Ro entered the room and flopped into a chair. "So it was his thumb?"

"Yes," the inspector responded. "We matched his fingerprints to his passport. His thumbprint, anyway. But in any event, we found his body this morning. Halfway down the cliff near the spa."

Ro tried not to react. He got up, turning his back to the others, and went to the coffee urn. He slowly poured himself a cup while waiting for the inspector to continue.

"Was it suicide?" Mrs. B. asked hopefully.

"Not unless he beat himself to death with a rock, strangled himself with his own necklace for good measure, and then threw himself off a cliff."

Inspector Singh paused.

"But something even more serious has arisen."

Ro turned around, surprised. He went back to the table and sat down.

"We decrypted the drives found under Mr. Charney's bed," Inspector Singh continued. "It took us some time because they were very heavily protected."

The inspector paused again, seemingly enjoying the tension he was creating.

"And?" Mrs. B. asked. "What did you find?"

Inspector Singh smiled grimly. "The drives contained child pornography."

"What?" Mrs. B. and Ro both exclaimed in unison.

Catherine looked at Ro, once again with that wolfish grin.

"What on earth do you mean?" Ro was flabbergasted.

"It appears that Mr. Charney was at the center of a major child pornography network based in the United States," the inspector responded, settling back into his chair. "And there were indications that he was planning to expand his activity into India. He was setting meetings up in Mumbai next month. I cannot believe I am saying this, but this is a lucky day for our country. We found really vile things. Shocking."

He looked at Catherine.

"It's also fortunate that Mrs. Forrester happened to be here."

"Yes," Catherine said, nodding. "It's huge. I've already been in touch with Justice. There's tons of data. Emails. Records of cryptocurrency transactions. We've already started coordinating with the Indian government."

Ro sank back in his chair, his mouth hanging open. "But this is absolutely astonishing."

"It sure is," Catherine said.

All of a sudden, the energy in the room changed. A dark, gross spirit had lifted. The room felt clean and light.

"Did the rain just stop?" Mrs. B. asked. She moved toward the window.

"Do you think that's why he was killed?" Ro asked.

"We don't know yet," the inspector said. "But the fact that he was killed in the same way as Miss Dey would suggest that the two murders are linked somehow."

"Yes, I agree," Ro said, ignoring Catherine's Cheshire cat grin.

"How exactly did he die?" Mrs. B. inquired, moving back to the table. "I didn't quite catch everything you said earlier."

"It was the same as Miss Dey," the inspector said. "He was hit over the head with one of the rocks from the path. But there were more injuries. He took quite some time to die."

He paused. Ro shuddered.

"And then, to make sure, the killer throttled Mr. Charney with Mr. Charney's own necklace. Wooden prayer beads."

"And where did you find the body?" Ro asked, sipping his coffee.

"He was killed in the meadow near where Miss Dey was murdered," the inspector said. "But then the killer pushed the corpse off the cliff."

"Could you get any evidence from the body?" Mrs. B. asked, breathless.

"No. There was heavy rain last night. And, in the meantime, the animals got to Mr. Charney's body." The inspector shook his head. "There are all kinds of animals in the forest here."

"Closed casket," Catherine smirked.

Ro, who'd been taking another sip of coffee, swallowed the wrong way and began to cough.

"Could you tell when he died?" Mrs. B. continued.

"Sometime yesterday afternoon," the inspector said. "The rain and the condition of the corpse make it difficult to say. But probably late afternoon, given Mr. Subramaniam's testimony."

"While we were in Rishikesh, Ro." Catherine turned to Mrs. B. "So we all have alibis except for you," she added, half-jokingly.

"I suppose I don't have an alibi," Mrs. B. mused. "But you must believe me when I say that I would never have bothered." She paused, thinking. "Sanjay Mehta was here all afternoon."

"He refuses to cooperate. But we are continuing to gather evidence. I just wish we had more."

"Maybe we should do another reenactment?" Ro suggested, taking a croissant.

"That's inappropriate," Catherine said.

Mrs. B. sat in the corner, looking somber. "If Sanjay Mehta is arrested, it will be an enormous scandal," she murmured.

"I apologize, Mrs. Banerjee," the inspector responded formally, "but at this point, regardless, scandal is probably unavoidable."

Mrs. B. nodded. "I think I should go back to Bombay." Then she froze for a moment. "I just remembered something. Did you know that Rita went to Bombay for a night or two just before she died? She told me she had to run some errands there."

The inspector nodded. "Yes, we knew. We've spoken to her driver and to the staff at the Soho House. Nothing of interest has come up."

Ro looked at Catherine. "Have you found what you're looking for? That link to the terrorists? Or whatever that evidence was?"

"No." Catherine shrugged, resigned. "I've pretty much given up hope. You win some, you lose some."

She stood up and stretched her arms.

"Want to get breakfast?" she asked Mrs. B. and Ro.

"Yes," Ro replied. "I'm starved."

They walked downstairs. Something Catherine said had jogged Ro's memory, but he didn't know what it was. Then, as the golf cart was about to leave, it dawned on him.

"Wait for me for a minute." He ran back upstairs.

"What is it?" Inspector Singh asked as Ro reentered the room, slightly out of breath.

"Check the Taj Hotel in Colaba," Ro said. "See if she left anything there."

The inspector frowned. "We checked all her movements with her driver from the Soho House. She did not go to Colaba."

"I'll bet you she did. Amrita told me she stayed at the Taj sometimes. Just to show the terrorists they couldn't win."

* * *

As they arrived at the restaurant a few minutes later, the host handed the phone to Ro. "Inspector Singh would like to speak with you straight away."

"She left an envelope in the hotel safe at the Taj," the inspector said to him. "It contained keys to several different safe deposit boxes. At two different banks."

The inspector paused.

"And, by the way, thank you."

"I'm so glad I could help," Ro replied.

He hung up the phone, feeling very pleased about everything. It was perhaps the first time Inspector Singh had seemed like a normal human being.

Actually, now that Ro thought about it, he really didn't know anything about Inspector Singh at all.

* * *

After breakfast and a massage, Ro sat with Mahesh, drinking tea in a quiet anteroom of the spa.

"Mahesh, I'm so sorry to bother you, but I have another very important question," Ro began.

Mahesh nodded.

"The night that Amrita Dey was killed. I think someone came upon her body and didn't tell anyone. A member of the staff. And took her earrings."

Mahesh nodded slowly, processing the information. "All right."

"I mean this person absolutely no harm," Ro continued. "They will get into no trouble at all. I don't even need to know his or her name. And I'll actually buy the earrings from them," he added impulsively. "In cash. That way they won't have to worry about having to sell them."

He paused for a moment.

"I just have a couple of questions to ask the person. That's all. I promise that's all."

"I will see," Mahesh said.

*   *   *

Somehow, Ro knew it was all over.

The energy had shifted. The wave had crested.

He didn't feel the need to follow the events minute by minute, or even to ask for an update. He just knew that whatever was supposed to happen had happened.

Then Catherine called, asking him to come to her villa.

*   *   *

Ro walked up the stairs and onto the terrace. Catherine was inside. He entered the living room through the open sliding door.

"So," he said.

"So," she replied. She had a quietly satisfied air about her.

"Did they find the safe deposit boxes?" Ro asked, sitting down.

Catherine nodded. "Yes. And everything they needed. The proof that she was blackmailing Sanjay Mehta."

"What was it all about?" Ro leaned forward, curious.

"Well, it was pretty sordid." Catherine reflected. "Turns out when he got elected, it was partly because of a sex scandal involving the incumbent."

"Oh?"

"One that Sanjay arranged. He'd paid the woman to do it." Catherine paused. "And once he'd been elected, he had the woman killed."

Ro winced. "That's pretty bad."

Sanjay'd been right. That was at least an eight, Ro thought. Maybe even a nine.

"And what about you? The proof you were looking for. About financing terrorism, or whatever it was. Did you find it?"

"Yes," Catherine replied, rearranging her legs on the sofa. "We did."

"Good," Ro said. "I'm glad."

They sat for a moment.

"Well, I guess that's that."

Ro paused.

"So they've arrested Sanjay?"

"There was no need," Catherine replied. "He killed himself this afternoon."

"Oh wow. Wow." Ro took a moment to process the information. He hadn't seen that one coming. "What happened?"

"They think he took cyanide."

"From the shed?"

"Not sure. Probably, I guess." Catherine shrugged and nodded simultaneously. "He left a note on his iPhone. Pretty formal. 'I, Sanjay Mehta, hereby confess to the murders of Amrita Dey, Mitchell Charney, and Amit Chopra.' Etcetera, etcetera."

Ro opened his mouth, then closed it again. He realized he didn't know what to say. His mind was furiously processing a number of things.

"And asking for it to be kept as quiet as possible," Catherine continued. "For Lala's sake."

"Poor Lala." That much was definite, anyway.

"Her father's here," Catherine added casually. "I'm sure it'll all be hushed up. Nobody wants a scandal."

"No," Ro said. "They don't."

There was a long pause.

"Did he say why?" Ro finally asked.

"Why what?"

"The other two. Amit and the VB."

"No. The note just said he did it. It didn't say why. And you're right, it is a little strange." Catherine paused, looking at Ro. "I mean, why would he have killed the VB?"

"Oh," Ro said, remembering something. "Oops."

"What?"

"I may have told Sanjay to watch out for the VB," Ro admitted. "That Amrita might have confided in him."

"Seriously?"

"Yep. My bad." Ro paused. "I should probably tell Inspector Singh, shouldn't I."

Catherine looked at Ro for a long time. "You're a real piece of work."

Ro shrugged. "You should meet my sister. Compared to her, I'm a cupcake. What about Amit?"

He paused, thinking about it.

"You know, Amit got to the dinner late. Maybe Sanjay saw him on his way to kill Amrita and was afraid that Amit had seen him too."

Catherine thought about it for a second, then nodded. "I suppose that's plausible."

"I guess we'll never know for sure," Ro said. "Good thing he confessed."

They were silent for a moment.

"Well, I guess that's that," Ro said again, stretching his arms above his head languidly.

"Yes," Catherine said. "I'm done, anyways."

"And life goes on." Ro rubbed his hands together. "Dinner?"

"You go ahead. I'm not hungry yet."

Neither of them moved.

"Are you satisfied?" Catherine asked him.

"How do you mean?"

"With the resolution. That Sanjay killed them. All of them."

"I'm satisfied." Ro thought about it. "It feels right, on balance."

"I know you're satisfied," Catherine said dryly. "And I agree that it feels right. Too right, almost. That's the problem."

Ro sighed. "I wish rich ladies wouldn't keep looking for problems all the time. You'd be much happier if you didn't."

Catherine gasped.

"Anyway, as the hotel's representative, I'm glad it's over," he continued, serene.

"You don't have any questions?" Catherine asked him, her eyes narrowing.

"No. Not really." Ro shrugged. "Do you?"

"Objectively, there are a lot of things that don't make sense."

It was high time to change the subject, Ro thought. "Objectivity," he replied, "is white subjectivity."

They processed that thought for a moment.

"Aren't you curious?"

"No," Ro said. "I'm not. It's macabre."

"Men don't poison people," Catherine continued, as if Ro hadn't said anything. "Sorry to be sexist, but it's a truism. Also, murderers don't generally choose a painless poison for their victims, then off themselves with a different poison that's particularly brutal."

"Come off it, Catherine. I mean, people light themselves on fire sometimes." He yawned.

"Do you think Mrs. B. was really a family friend of Amrita's?" Catherine asked suddenly.

Ro froze mid-yawn. He hadn't considered that possibility.

Then he remembered. "Yes, you know, I think she was," he said, a little reluctantly. "I seem to remember Amrita telling me that. Shame. It would have been cool if she had been all Keyser Söze."

"And what about Lala?" Catherine said, pressing on. "She actually seems like the strongest suspect to me."

"Don't be stupid. If Lala had killed Amrita, there's no way she'd have discovered the body. We've been through this." Ro stretched his arms over his head and arched his back. One of his vertebrae cracked. "Ooh, that felt good."

"Stop being silly," Catherine said crisply. "Lala could so easily have killed her, then decided to find the body herself to be in control of the narrative."

Actually, Catherine had a point. Then Ro shook his head. "I still don't think she did it. I don't know why, but I still don't think she did it."

"Who *do* you think did it?" Catherine leaned forward.

"Your mom," Ro said.

He yawned again, stretching his arms.

"It's a good ending, Catherine. Let sleeping jerks lie. Particularly because."

"Particularly because what?" Catherine raised her eyebrows.

"Particularly because I think Chris knows a lot more than he's letting on."

This wasn't exactly true, but he thought it would make Catherine clam right up.

It did.

"Don't let the perfect be the enemy of the good," Ro concluded.

He stood up.

"When are you leaving, by the way?" Catherine asked casually.

"Oh. I just decided," Ro responded. "New Year's Day."

"What time? I might hitch a ride down to Rishikesh with you. Do some shopping."

"Early afternoon. My flight's at around 4." He shivered. "Not looking forward to the drive down. That road's a little scary."

"I agree," Catherine said, nuzzling Mango. "It certainly can be."

"Feel free to join me. It would be nice to have some company." Ro bent over to scratch Mango on the back of his neck, then walked back out through the sliding doors onto the terrace.

"Ro," Catherine called out.

He stopped.

"We never did figure out what happened with her watch. I know that bugged you. It bugs me too."

Ro stayed there for a moment, turning this over in his head. He did not turn around.

Then he kept moving across the terrace and went down the stairs.

Once he reached the bottom, he spontaneously decided to take a little stroll before dinner. He was curious to see whether the shed of horrors was still being guarded now that everything had been resolved.

* * *

Ro got into bed that night doing the opposite of what he had advised Catherine: He was not just allowing, but encouraging, the perfect to be the enemy of the good. He didn't actually think Sanjay Mehta had killed Amrita Dey. Like Catherine, he had many reasons to think that both the suicide and the note were suspect. In fact, he just knew it somehow.

And this meant he still hadn't figured out why Amrita had died.

He remembered that moment on the path where he'd felt her immortal spirit. He'd told her he would try to find out.

He decided to let his mind wander. Maybe divine inspiration would come.

He picked up his phone and mindlessly read messages for a moment. Then, out of nowhere, he remembered something he'd been meaning to check. So he checked it.

Wait. What?

This didn't make any . . .

And how?

Even if . . .

Would he ever even want to . . .

And then . . .

and this was important . . .

Could he even prove it?

Ro shook his head and put the thought out of his mind.

If it was meant to crystallize, it would crystallize.

He began drifting off.

Last night's dream came back. Eyes.

Other images.

Keys. Eyes. Eyes.

Earrings. Passports.

Eyes. Unreadable eyes.

Ears. Watches. Fur.

Switzerland. Keys.

Passports.

Wrist. Fur.

Passports.

Passport.

Then Ro sat straight up.

DAY 9

(December 31)

R o woke up in a great mood. He stretched languidly in bed, smiling. He looked down at himself. The heavy, crisp white cotton of his kurta pajama perfectly matched the heavy, crisp white cotton sheets, making it look like Ro was composed only of forearms, hands, and feet.

He moved them all. They wiggled at him, delighted.

It was New Year's Eve.

He called Mrs. B. "Are we all meeting this morning?"

"Well, I don't know, but I think it would be nice, yes?" Mrs. B. said. "Closure and all."

"Agreed." Ro paused. "Also, I have a favor to ask you. Do you have a picture somewhere of Amrita's family? Especially her brother and sister?"

He could sense Mrs. B.'s hesitation.

"Don't worry, it's not to cause any trouble," he said, to reassure her. "Trust me. It's just a question of personal curiosity."

"I do trust you," Mrs. B. replied. "But thank you for saying that, because I think the faster we move past this business the better. Let me think. I'm sure I have one somewhere in Bombay. I'll call my housekeeper and ask her to look."

"Thank you," Ro said. "Let's find some time to talk later today, just the two of us. I think we deserve a debrief." Ro did want to debrief with her, but he also knew he'd be asking her for another favor later that day.

"I wholeheartedly agree," Mrs. B. said. "See you in a few minutes."

He picked up a note card to jot a message to Joss, then put it down and grabbed his phone instead.

"Let's meet at the restaurant at 11?" he texted.

"Roger," Joss texted back immediately.

* * *

The inspector looked sharp and well rested. Both he and Catherine glittered with vitality. Everyone, in fact, was in a great mood. The sun was shining and cottonwool clouds were sailing slowly through the sky.

"Everything is settled," the inspector said. "Mr. Mehta's body will be transported to Delhi today."

He looked at his watch.

"In fact, the body should already be on its way. Officially, Mr. Mehta will have died in his sleep in Delhi. I don't know if they've decided on a cause of death yet. Perhaps epilepsy."

Catherine nodded. "That's always a good one."

"And what will you say about Amrita's death?" Ro enquired. "If it's all being hushed up."

The inspector looked at Mrs. B.

"I've spoken to Nalini. The family will say it was caused by unexpected heart failure. Most deaths are, I suppose."

"And Amit's?"

"Also unexpected heart failure," Catherine chimed in. "Amit actually didn't have next of kin. His parents were dead, and he didn't have siblings. But we've already informed his lawyers and a few of his close friends."

"Lala's father is going to endow a scholarship in Amit's name at the University of Michigan," Mrs. B. added. "I spoke to Mr. Chola this morning."

"That's a really nice idea." Ro stood. "Anybody want coffee?"

Mrs. B. nodded.

Ro went over to the urn and poured each of them a cup. "Oh, what about the Visiting Blight?" he added casually.

Catherine smirked at him. "Official cause of death is that he fell off a cliff."

"Seems fair," Mrs. B. mused.

Ro nodded, thoughtful. "This really does seem to have worked out astonishingly well," he mused. "How are you going to prevent the other guests from saying anything?"

"Well, the murders never became general knowledge among the guests," the inspector pointed out. "Thankfully, we managed to corner Sanjay Mehta first."

"In any case, we will ask for every guest to sign an NDA," Mrs. B. added. "In exchange, we will waive all charges for their stay here."

"We're saying that the NDA is because of Chris's movie," Catherine interjected.

"That's very generous." Ro was impressed.

"Mr. Chola is a generous man." Mrs. B. winked at Ro.

That reminded him. "How is Lala?"

"It's a major shock, but she's all right. She will leave this morning. You should call her after this."

Mrs. B. turned to Catherine.

"And you? You have found what you were looking for?"

"Yes." Catherine smirked again. "I have."

"I'm organizing a party tonight," Mrs. B. informed them. "For New Year's Eve. We should celebrate."

"Great idea," Ro said.

"I was thinking of fireworks but ultimately decided against them," Mrs. B. added.

Probably the right call, Ro thought. It was a little too soon.

After nonchalant goodbyes, Mrs. B. and Catherine left the room.

Ro lingered for a second.

"We haven't gotten the chance to get to know each other," Ro said, "but I wish we had. I've been very impressed by you."

"Thank you." Inspector Singh looked Ro in the eyes. "And likewise. You're extremely competent."

Ro smiled. He knew the inspector meant this as the highest praise imaginable.

"In fact, working with all three of you was a pleasure," Inspector Singh continued. "Shockingly. I expected an absolute nightmare."

"Yes," Ro agreed. "It really should have been a nightmare, all things considered. The look on your face when you walked in and saw the three of us for the first time . . ."

Inspector Singh gave Ro a wry grin.

"Can I ask you? Where did you grow up?"

"I was born in the UK but came back to India when I was five," Inspector Singh replied. "Then I returned to the UK for school."

"And you were at Oxford, Catherine said?"

"I was."

"I was too. For graduate school." Ro hesitated. "I have to ask. How did you end up in the Indian Police Service?"

The inspector smiled, a bit rueful. "That's a long story."

Ro nodded. "Well, I do hope I get to hear it sometime. Please look me up if you're ever in London."

"And please look me up if you're ever in Delhi, Mr. Krishna," the inspector replied, reaching out his hand.

"Please, call me Ro," Ro said, shaking it.

"All right," the inspector smiled. "You can call me by my first name as well."

"Thank you."

"Which, as it happens, is Ro." The inspector actually giggled at the look on Ro's face. It was like the sun had come out. "Rohit."

"I'm Rohan."

They both laughed for a second.

"Well, hope to see you soon, Ro," Ro said.

"Likewise, Ro," Ro said.

Ro closed the door and went down the stairs. He smiled to himself. He'd never met another Ro before.

It was a funny feeling.

A nice one, though.

* * *

Ro arrived five minutes early to brunch with Joss. He had just sat down when Joss entered the dining room, early as well. Ro stood up and waved.

Joss came to the table. "Good evening," he said.

Ro mock-bowed.

They sat. A waiter brought over two menus.

"Joss. I wanted to start by thanking you for suggesting this. Or, rather, for insisting upon it."

"We have a lot to catch up on, no? I'll have the buffet," he said to the hovering waiter.

"I'll have the Pitta menu," Ro said.

Joss stood. "BRB."

While Joss inspected the buffet, Ro looked around the room. Guests were milling about, all wearing their kurta pajama.

He remembered what Alex had said to him the day before he'd left for India.

People had been born. People had died. The world had kept turning. And yes, now it was another day.

That day in London felt like a hundred million years ago.

Samsara still looked like an insane asylum, though.

* * *

Ro's Pitta meal had just arrived when Joss came back with a plate piled high. Joss began to butter his toast.

Ro looked at Joss's hands and forearms. The scratches were healing, but were still visible. Now that he knew for sure that Joss wasn't the murderer, Ro could be direct. "What happened to your hands and arms? Why are you all scratched up?" he asked bluntly.

"Oh," Joss replied, his mouth full of toast. He swallowed. "I was sort of wondering when you'd ask."

"Joss! I did ask!" Ro exclaimed. "Right before we went to Rishikesh. You deflected."

"Why didn't you push me?"

"Because I did not want to risk becoming an accomplice to murder," Ro responded crisply.

Joss abruptly dropped his fork and knife, looking completely shocked. He immediately flushed all the way up to his forehead. "You thought I might have had something to do with this?"

"Joss!" Ro said. "You randomly went and took a shower while Amrita was getting murdered, then showed up later covered in scratches." He paused. "Obviously, I didn't think you killed her. But I wanted to find out who did first."

Joss's flush gradually began to descend. "I know you and Catherine were involved with the investigation, by the way." He took a bite of his omelette. "Catherine told us. Chris was furious."

"I would've told you too, if I'd had the chance. But anyway, what's with the scratches?"

Joss finished chewing, swallowed, then wiped his mouth delicately. "Anwar."

"Anwar?" Ro repeated, baffled. "Who's Anwar?"

Joss looked briefly irritated. "Anwar. At the gym. The trainer."

"The trainer?" And, suddenly, it all dawned on Ro. "Oh. The hot trainer! You've been having a thing with him?"

"Yes," Joss replied, curt. "And he doesn't want anyone to know about it."

Ro looked at the scratches again, then up at Joss, who was putting a brave face on it. "So you'd meet outside. When nobody was around."

"And I accidentally fell into a very thorny plant."

Ro smiled despite himself, then turned serious again. "Anwar's a very handsome man. But so are you, Joss."

Ro looked at Joss. Joss was sitting ramrod straight, looking to one side, evidently trying to keep it together.

"You're the best catch I know, Joss," Ro said quietly. "Anyone who's lucky enough to be with you should be shouting it from the rooftops."

"It's hard," Joss said simply.

"You know, I've really loved being back in India, but there's one thing about India that makes me furious. The homophobia. Because somehow I'm sure it's because of the English. Because of colonial morals. Not because of anything that's actually in Hinduism. Homophobia is, purely and simply, letting the colonizers win."

Ro peered intently into Joss's eyes, which were bright with tears that hadn't quite started to spill.

"I know that doesn't help you. But are you OK?"

"I am," Joss said. He swallowed, then nodded. Gathering himself, he looked directly into Ro's eyes. "Ro, are you OK?"

Ro was taken aback. He hadn't expected that, but he knew he had to answer honestly. "I don't know."

"What happened to you? What happened to the extreme extrovert?"

"He slammed his bike down the stairs," Ro responded casually. He took a sip of his coffee.

Joss looked down at his plate.

"What happened at your job, Ro?" he asked quietly.

"Oh, my God. Wow." Ro was a little stunned to realize he'd completely forgotten about all that. He smiled at Joss. "That's all fine now. Forgive me, but I don't want to relive it. Let's just say I had a bad manager. But it's all been completely resolved."

"Then let me just say that I'm sorry." Joss turned back to his food. "Did this manager get fired at least?"

Ro thought about how best to answer. It was true that he never lied, but that didn't mean he always told the truth. "Yes, in a manner of speaking. Anyway, I've moved on."

"To what? Do you know what you're going to do now?"

"No idea." Ro looked down at his plate. "I've decided to give myself six months before I even think about that."

"Good," Joss said, nodding. "Take as much time as you need. Figure out what you really love. Then do that."

"Well, I'm not quite sure that would work. If I did what I loved, I'd spend all my time lying down."

Joss laughed. "What are you going to do in the meantime?"

Ro considered. "I think I'll stay in India for a while, actually. Then I don't know. Maybe the Caribbean. I'm looking forward to being part of the do nothing club."

"So you're just going to travel around by yourself?" Joss sounded skeptical.

"I guess. I mean, it's not like I have anyone to go with." Ro paused. "Actually, scratch that. I prefer traveling alone anyway. You get to do whatever you want."

They ate for a moment in silence.

"I'll tell you one thing, though," Ro continued. "I'm going to keep traveling around places where I blend in. Where I don't stick out in a crowd. Which, thankfully, is most of the world."

He paused, thinking about how best to phrase what he wanted to say.

"I never realized that before India. Just blending in here makes me more relaxed than I think I've ever been."

Joss put down his fork and knife and looked at Ro, intent.

"You know, it's like I sailed through life like a white person, but at what cost?"

Ro hesitated again.

"I finally see that I've spent my entire life sticking out. I'm almost always the only person in any given room who looks like me, so people look at me more. Which is totally understandable. I'm not blaming anyone, but it's still exhausting." Ro shrugged. "I'm realizing now that the only thing I've ever wanted is to disappear. To blend into the background. For nobody to notice me. So I'm going to disappear for a while. I think I've earned that."

Joss looked down at his plate for a long time. He shook his head.

"Ro, I don't think you know how devastating it is for me to hear that. I know you're living it, not me. But you have to be a little bit more gentle with how you express yourself sometimes. Because other people care about you too."

Ro nodded, acknowledging Joss's point.

"I'm sorry." Joss shook his head again. "I just want you to be happy, so if that's what makes you happy, go for it. Disappear. One thing, though. Disappear all you want, but promise that Connie and I will know where you are. At all times."

Ro smiled. "I promise."

"We're both in our late thirties, and our lives haven't progressed in a normal fashion," Joss continued. "From now on, I think we need to commit to being each other's family. Explicitly."

"You are my family," Ro responded, curt. "You've always been my family." He was almost beginning to get angry. "And you should know that."

Joss looked at Ro for a long time. "Are you lonely?" he asked softly.

"I don't know what that means." Ro suddenly felt exhausted. "And it's not just about whether I'm single, by the way. In general, I actually think married people and people in relationships are much lonelier than single people. When you're in a relationship, you engage with the world so much less. I don't think I've ever been lonelier than I was during the last couple of years Charlotte and I were together. I'd completely lost sight of myself. I was gone. It felt like the rest of my life was just going to be one long march to the grave. At least I'm me now."

Ro reflected.

"I have my answer. No, I'm not lonely. Because I feel like I'm constantly engaging with the world."

He took another bite of his food.

"Are you lonely?"

Joss looked away. "I'm only lonely when I'm at home. As soon as I have a change of scenery, everything's great. And the Forresters make me feel like part of the family."

"Are there moments in your day when you feel more alone than others?"

"When I go to sleep," Joss said quietly. "And when I wake up. What about you?"

"I'm alone when I'm awake," Ro replied. "But never when I'm asleep."

Joss looked at Ro, hesitant.

"Ro, we've never talked about this, but I've shared hotel rooms with you. You thrash in your sleep all night. Every night. You know you have a sleep disorder, right?"

"Yes." Ro looked down and sliced up some fruit. "I'm aware."

They ate in silence.

"Do you feel loved?" Joss asked, sounding sad.

"Once again, I'm not sure what that means," Ro replied, thinking about it. "I don't know how to handle it when people are nice to me. I don't want to get dependent on it. What about you? Do you feel loved?"

"Yes," Joss said.

"Good for you."

"This is worse than I thought." Joss paused. "What about your family?"

Ro thought about it.

"You know, I think they do love me. I just don't know that they've ever liked me all that much."

Joss sighed. "I'm not trying to invalidate your feelings, Ro, but I think that's completely ridiculous. I know your family. I know they love you."

"Yes, Joss. You're right. They love me. But I can't explain it." Ro shook his head. "They're always very kind to me, but almost too kind. It's like there's something wrong with me." He shrugged. "I don't know. Maybe they're right, given that we're purportedly descended from Genghis Khan. Who knows."

Joss still seemed a little sad. "Do you know what actions by others make you feel supported? Do you know the answer to that?"

"I do, actually," Ro said, relieved to be on safe ground. "None."

Joss looked stricken.

"Don't look at me like that. It doesn't help either of us." Ro looked down at his plate. "I guess I'm finally realizing that I've had to turn myself into a soldier. To get through life." He looked back up at Joss. "And a good soldier doesn't need emotional support."

They chewed, both of them contemplative.

"Are you sure you still have to be a soldier?" Joss asked gently.

"I don't know," Ro replied. "But I'm afraid I may have forgotten how to be anything else."

"You haven't. I promise you." Joss hesitated. "Does anything at all make you feel supported?"

Ro thought about it for a while. "You know what? Being here does. In India. I feel like everything's changed. I've never felt closer to my family than since I got here."

He took a sip of his coffee, choosing his next words with care.

"Mmm. This is great coffee. There have been times here when I really feel like I've been guided by a spirit. By an impulse I can't describe."

"I understand, I think," Joss replied, nodding. "That day you went to Rishikesh. You've seemed different since then."

"What do you mean by that?" Ro asked, now suspicious.

"Was it because of that ceremony? At the Ganges?"

Ro thought about the day they'd gone to Rishikesh.

Had all those things really happened?

Easy come, easy go.

He smiled at Joss. "Yes, Joss. You know what? Yes. To quote Dartmouth's most famous alum, I think my heart grew three sizes that day."

"Good," Joss said. He took the last bite of his omelette. "Connie reminds me of the Grinch more than you do, though."

Ro laughed a little. Then he laughed a little more.

Then Joss joined in too.

* * *

Lala and Ro walked up the lawn from the restaurant in silence, holding porcelain mugs of masala chai.

"I feel like a weight has been lifted," Lala said. "It's awful to say. Of course I think I'm still in shock."

"I think I know what you mean," Ro said.

"Or even that a curse has been removed, maybe," Lala said. "I don't know."

"You're leaving today."

Lala nodded.

"Where are you going?"

"Delhi," Lala replied. "What about you?"

"I'm leaving tomorrow. Bombay." He sipped his tea.

"How long will you stay there?"

"I don't know," Ro answered honestly. "At least a couple of weeks. But then I'll travel around India for a while, I think."

"I'll be in Bombay next week."

"Good," Ro replied. "I hope to see you there."

He had a feeling he would, one way or another.

"I did have something I wanted to tell you. I think you should take over Sanjay's seat in the Lok Sabha."

Lala processed that for a moment.

"I hadn't even considered that."

"I just have a good feeling about it, somehow."

Lala looked at him. "I don't know if anyone else sees it. But why are you so sad?"

"Right now?" Ro replied, uncomprehending.

"No. All the time."

At first, Ro was taken aback. Then he nodded slowly.

She did have supernatural vision, after all.

"I'm not sure." He hesitated, realizing this wasn't entirely true. "But I think it's getting better." And it was, actually.

"It does seem to be," Lala said.

There was a long pause.

"I don't know anything about politics."

"You know, that'll probably be a major advantage."

Ro smiled at her.

"You know how to learn, and you also know when something isn't true. In fact, in every way, you see very clearly. Promise me you'll think about it."

Lala laughed, surprising even herself. "I promise. I'll think about it."

But Ro thought, from the hint of a smile lingering on her lips, that she might have already made up her mind.

* * *

"So, Mr. Krishna," Dr. Menon said acidly. "You finally deign to see me."

"I don't think that's exactly fair, Dr. Menon," Ro replied, startled. "You know about what was going on."

"That's no excuse."

There was a long, uncomfortable silence.

"I'm not very happy about this, Mr. Krishna," Dr. Menon continued. "I think you're leaving without having gotten the rest you badly needed."

"Do you think I should stay longer?"

"No," Dr. Menon responded.

Ro was surprised. "Why not?"

Dr. Menon looked at Ro for a long time. "Because I fear it's already too late."

Ro didn't understand. "Why is it too late?"

He looked into Dr. Menon's eyes for the answer. The brief flash of smugness Ro saw there made him spiral into a cold fury.

Somehow, Dr. Menon knew something.

Time to shut this down. Once and for all.

"Actually, do you know what I think, Dr. Menon?" Ro continued conversationally, leaning forward. "I think you should wipe that face off your head."

He was satisfied to see that Dr. Menon's face did, indeed, wipe itself blank.

Ro continued to lean forward until their heads were only inches apart.

Dr. Menon shrank back.

"I'm going to complain to Mrs. B. about you," Ro said with a soft smile.

He watched the terror bloom in Dr. Menon's eyes for a long, pleasurable moment.

Then he stood up, turned around, and left the room.

* * *

Mahesh was waiting for Ro in the reception area of the spa. He looked Ro in the eye meaningfully. They went outside.

"I have found her," Mahesh said, his voice low. "She is very frightened."

"Please make sure she knows I mean her no harm. I don't even want to know her name."

Mahesh nodded.

"If you can, please bring her to my room in about fifteen minutes. And, once again, she has my word. Nothing bad will happen to her because of this."

"Seri." Mahesh headed off in one direction, Ro in the other.

* * *

Ro was sitting on the sofa in his room. Mahesh stood next to him. A young, terrified chambermaid was in front of them. Ro thought she couldn't have been more than sixteen.

"Mahesh, you can translate for me?" Mahesh nodded.

Ro exhaled. "First of all, please thank her for being here. I am very grateful to her. And please tell her she is very brave to have come forward."

Mahesh repeated what Ro said in somewhat halting Hindi.

The girl visibly relaxed a little.

"Please tell her she has nothing to be afraid of. And that no one outside this room will ever know about this conversation."

As Mahesh translated, the girl calmed down a bit more. "Thank you," she said in slow English.

Ro smiled at her. He turned to Mahesh. "Does she have the earrings?"

Mahesh spoke to the girl. She nodded.

"Please tell her I will buy them from her." Ro named an amount of money. "Is that all right with her?"

Mahesh spoke to the girl. She nodded again.

She took something wrapped in fabric from her pocket and gave it to Mahesh. Mahesh passed it to Ro.

The earrings were just as Ro remembered. Gorgeous. Magic Alhambra drop earrings from Van Cleef & Arpels, made of pavé diamonds and turquoise.

When he looked at them closely, he realized they were probably worth a little more than the amount they had agreed upon. He felt guilty for a moment.

But then again, she shouldn't have been going around stealing earrings off dead bodies.

Ro looked at Mahesh.

"Please tell her that I will transfer the money to your account, then you can withdraw it and give it to her. Is that all right?"

Mahesh spoke to the girl. She nodded again.

"I have one question for her. Was Amrita wearing the fur headband when she found the body?"

"I don't know how to say headband in Hindi."

"Improvise."

Mahesh said a few words to her. The girl shook her head. No.

"All right," Ro said. "That's all." Then a thought came to him. "Actually, there's something else."

Mahesh looked at him, expectant.

"I would like her to do one more thing for me. Tonight. During the New Year's Eve party."

Ro said a few words to Mahesh.

Mahesh's eyes widened.

Then he turned his head and told the girl what Ro had asked. The girl turned to look at Ro.

"Yes," she said.

* * *

Mrs. B. and Ro sat in her living room drinking masala chai. "Oh, I have the photo you asked for," she said suddenly. Ro had almost forgotten.

Getting up, she went to a desk on the side of the room and picked up a physical photo. She walked back to the sofa, handed the photo to Ro, then sat back down.

"How'd you get this here so fast?"

"I had it flown here. I thought it might be important."

Ro examined the photo. The colors were faded.

"Where was this taken? And when?"

"Belgium," Mrs. B. replied, tucking her legs under her. "Probably in the early 80s."

Five people stood in front of what looked like a very grand brick house. Ro wasn't the best at dating buildings, but he would have guessed the house was late 19th century.

Mrs. B. was in the foreground of the photo, in profile, looking at a laughing, green-eyed boy. Her hand was on the boy's shoulder.

A dark-haired woman stood next to Mrs. B., her hands on the shoulders of a thin, dark-haired, dark-eyed girl who looked remarkably like her. The girl was scowling.

A tall, handsome man stood behind the women, a warm smile on his face. He wore a dark coat. A green scarf was tied precisely around his neck.

Ro glanced back up at Mrs. B. She'd hardly aged since the photo. Indian genes.

"Thank you for getting this. It looks like a lovely house."

"Yes, it was a lovely house. A bit too grand for my taste, though. And very drafty."

"Her brother looks like he had a lot of personality."

"Yes. But he was very spoiled."

Ro looked at the girl. "Nalini doesn't look particularly happy."

"She never looked happy. Still doesn't. But in fairness, it must have been rather difficult. Amar always hoovered up all the attention."

"You said Nalini mostly grew up in India, right?" Ro asked Mrs. B., casual. "And Amar mostly in Europe?"

"Yes. I don't ever remember seeing Amar in India, actually." Mrs. B. considered for a moment. "You know, perhaps that's why Meena came back here. So that Nalini could be out of her brother's shadow. But I never thought of that before. It might not be true."

"They look so alike. Meena and Nalini, I mean."

Ro looked down, examining the photo more closely.

"And that's Amrita's father?" He pointed at the man behind the two women.

"Oh, no," Mrs. B. replied, surprised. "That's my husband."

"Oh!" Ro looked back down at the smiling man and smiled too. The man in the photo looked warm and friendly. He reminded Ro of someone. Maybe Ro's own father, actually. "I should've guessed. He has great energy. Even just from the photo."

Mrs. B. smiled.

"Why isn't Mr. Dey in the photo, by the way?"

"He rarely came outside. I think sunlight had some sort of effect on his eye condition."

"Right." Ro handed Mrs. B. the photograph. She placed it on the table next to her. "So Mr. Dey didn't come back to India much?"

"No," Mrs. B. replied, thinking. "Hardly ever. Maybe never, actually. You remember, he lost his whole family during Partition. Perhaps he wanted a clean break with the past. I'd probably want the same."

"Makes sense," Ro said. "Do you have any photos of him?"

Mrs. B. considered for a second. "You know, I'm not sure that I do. Now that I think about it, he never liked having his picture taken. But shall I have someone check?"

"No, that's all right." It was.

She took a sip of tea. "So, did you find what you were looking for?"

"I did." Ro took a sip of tea himself. He was acquiring a taste for it.

"I think it's for the best if I don't ask questions." Mrs. B. suddenly turned serious. "More importantly, what's to become of you, life's problem child?" She looked at Ro, her look somehow both appraising and concerned.

Ro felt his heart warm up and expand. He really had become extremely fond of Mrs. B.

He smiled at her. "I'm not really sure. I'll go to Bombay for a week or two and take it from there."

"Come stay with me. I mean it. I have plenty of room."

"Thanks so much," Ro said. "But I'll stay at the Soho House. I think I should discover the city on my own. To a degree, anyway."

"Fine. I understand. But come to dinner. Are you free on Saturday?"

"I have no plans whatsoever."

"Perfect," Mrs. B. clapped her hands. "I'll get a group together."

Ro smiled again. "I'd love that. Thank you."

"I think Lala might be in town," Mrs. B. said meaningfully.

Ro didn't reply, but he was still smiling.

"How long will you stay in India?"

"I haven't really thought about it." Ro shrugged. "I'm in a strange position right now where I'm inadvertently completely free. So I'll see how it goes. But I'll definitely stay for a while."

"Good. I think you'll find that you love it here." She poured herself some more tea. "I have to say, I don't understand why anyone would want to live anywhere else. It's ever so much fun here," she continued, sipping. "You can more or less do whatever you like. And you see the consequences of your actions so quickly."

A thought suddenly occurred to Ro.

"Did you have something to do with the disappearance of Amrita's body?" he asked her, leaning forward.

"Oh, dear."

Everything about Mrs. B. suddenly radiated guilt. Her voice, her face, her body.

Ro couldn't help smiling. She looked just like a little girl.

"It's OK. I promise I won't tell anyone. But what did you do?"

Mrs. B. sighed. "I bought a morgue truck and then arranged for it to come pick up her body first thing." She paused, shaking her head. "You must think I'm so awful."

"No evidence, no scandal."

"Well, I'd be lying if I said that wasn't part of it," Mrs. B. admitted. "But that wasn't really why. It was for her mother. And for her."

She hesitated.

"I know we talk about justice for the victim in situations like this, but Rita was nobody's victim. I didn't want her body being pried apart and scratched and tested. She would have hated that. Leaving her body in dignity is also justice for the victim. I wanted her body to depart so her soul could rest. I thought that was more important. Because I do believe her soul is still here. The soul of everyone who has passed on." Mrs. B. looked at Ro. "I know it, in fact."

Ro nodded. He knew it too.

"You know, I think that's why I could never live in the West," she continued. "It's fun for shopping and all, but this terrible, paralyzing fear of aging. Of death. This obsession with youth. It's permeated everything. And it's so backward. And corrosive. Aging is growth."

She shrugged.

"After birth, death is the only thing that every soul on this Earth has in common. Death is always all around us. Always. Everywhere. The same way life is. Perhaps even more so." She poured herself more tea and sipped from the cup. "You can't avoid it. You have to accept it. You have to plan for it. And be organized for it."

Unexpectedly, she giggled.

"If you really want to have some fun? If you really want to detox? Forget Samsara. Write your will. And be as detailed as possible."

Ro laughed.

"It's so much fun," she continued, her eyes twinkling. "Deciding whom you want to get every one of your possessions. Every single one. Who would be the happiest to receive what. And who would be the angriest not to get what they thought they were due. What they thought they deserved. And it's delightful to know that you decide what everyone deserves from you. Not them."

"I'm going to go back to my room and do this right now," Ro said, meaning it.

"Because in the end, it's going to happen," Mrs. B. continued serenely. "We have to give away everything we own. Everything that ever happened was what was supposed to happen. A cliché, but clichés generally become clichés because they're true, I find."

Ro nodded. She had a point.

Mrs. B. was still thinking. "Except for that song 'Love Touch.'" She shuddered slightly. "That should never have happened."

Ro giggled, delighted. He adored this woman. "I have one more favor to ask you."

"Anything, dear boy," she replied, beaming at him.

"I understand that the hotel keeps copies of the passports of all the guests. And the passports of all your staff."

"Yes, we do. Why?"

"Could you give me access to them tonight? Just for a minute. This is just to satisfy my own curiosity. I promise."

Mrs. B. narrowed her eyes at him. "What are you cooking up?" Then she shook her head. "Actually, I don't want to know. But yes. Of course. I'll arrange it."

"Thank you so much." Ro stood up and smiled. "And see you at the party tonight. And on Saturday in Bombay."

"And on Saturday in Bombay," Mrs. B. repeated, smiling back.

Ro left the room, absently whistling the horn call from *Siegfried* to himself.

He was very pleased to have learned about the morgue truck.

It was the one thing he hadn't figured out.

* * *

The party was lovely. Mrs. B. had spared no expense with the food and wine. The restaurant staff circulated with bottles of Pol Roger, Ro's favorite.

Ro saw Catherine talking with Fairuza and Mrs. B., but he didn't feel like socializing. He was looking for Mahesh.

He found him standing in a corner, chatting with Chris and Joss, laughing. "Excuse me, guys," Ro smiled. "Do you mind if I borrow Mahesh for a second?"

Ro led Mahesh away by the elbow.

"Would you mind coming to the Palace with me?"

"Of course not," Mahesh replied, surprised.

They stopped by a golf cart. "Could you get on the cart and tell the driver to pick me up just around that bend over there? I don't want anyone to see where we're going. I'll walk ahead."

Mahesh nodded.

Ro took his time ambling around the corner, stopping once he was sure he was no longer visible from the party. The golf cart arrived moments later.

They rode up to the Palace in silence.

Ro no longer shivered when they passed the place where Amrita had been murdered. He hoped Amrita's soul was at peace now that he might have figured out why she had died.

Anyway, in a few minutes, he'd know for sure.

They passed nobody along the way. All the guests were at the party.

When they arrived at the Palace, the receptionist nodded. "Mrs. Banerjee told me you would be coming. I've placed everything necessary in the back office," he said, pointing.

Ro and Mahesh walked into the back office, where a stack of papers and passports was mixed together.

"Let's split the pile and go through them," Ro said. "I'll tell you what I'm looking for."

"I think I know," Mahesh replied. "Because of what you asked the chambermaid to do."

Mahesh said a few more words. Ro nodded.

They went through their piles in silence.

After a few moments, Mahesh handed him something. "Here," he said quietly.

Ro looked at it and closed his eyes. "Thank you," he said.

He had been right.

* * *

Mahesh and Ro sat on the steps of the Palace, looking up at the sky, in a companionable silence.

"You're leaving tomorrow, Ro?" Mahesh asked.

"Yes, but I'm staying in India for a while." That reminded him. He was going to write to Parvati to see if she wanted to join him.

"I'm glad you're staying," Mahesh said.

"So am I. It just feels like the right thing to do."

There was a long pause.

"I was there," Mahesh said softly to Ro, speaking in Tamil. "Behind you, in the trees. You know that, yes?"

Ro turned this over in his mind for a few moments, then nodded. "I don't even know how to begin to thank you."

Mahesh looked at him and raised his hands to his heart.

They continued to sit, taking pleasure in the energy of the moment. Nothing needed to be said. They were just happy.

Midnight came and went without their noticing. There were no fireworks. No sounds. The year ended. The year began.

It wasn't, in fact, the first New Year's Eve Ro had spent in India, the place where his parents had been born, and their parents before them, and their parents before them, and their parents before them. But it was, he thought, the best one he'd spent there so far.

DAY 10

(January 1)

It was New Year's Day.

Ro surveyed his room. His travel clothes were laid out on the bed. He was more or less ready to go. He had never had an easier job packing. Except for the day in Rishikesh, he hadn't actually worn anything that he'd brought with him. Opening his carry-on, Ro came across the book he had been planning to read at Samsara—*The Transfiguration of the Commonplace*, written by a Scottish nun—and smiled a bit sadly. He hadn't even touched it. Maybe on the plane, he thought.

He had already had breakfast with Chris, Joss, and Mahesh to say goodbye. At least, goodbye for now. They would meet somewhere in a few weeks, now that Ro had extended his trip. With Mrs. B.'s blessing, Mahesh would take a leave of absence from Samsara and train Chris for the duration of production. Chris was already dropping heavy hints about relocating Mahesh to the US afterward.

Alex would finally be back from his retreat tomorrow. Ro would have to call him and, most likely, be the one to break to him the news that Amrita, one of his oldest friends, had died. Ro was not looking forward to it. He disliked speaking on the telephone at the best of times, and this would likely be a very long call.

He stepped outside, still in his kurta pajama, as he'd scheduled one last appointment at the spa. He stood for a moment in front of the Residence and closed his eyes, breathing in Samsara's air, willing himself to remember exactly how it smelled, exactly how it tasted.

Pine. Grass. A hint of wood smoke.

Then he opened his eyes and looked at the sky. It was a dazzling day. Only a few clouds were on the horizon.

* * *

Ro sat cross-legged on a yoga mat in Room 5, waiting. He had already placed another mat on the floor facing him. Sunlight streamed through the high windows.

The door opened.

"Hi, Ro," Fairuza said, smiling at him. "It's your last day?"

"Yes," he replied. "I'm leaving today."

"Did you have a good stay? Despite everything?"

"You know what, I really did."

Fairuza slipped off her sandals, sitting gracefully on the mat facing him. "So what shall we work on today?" she asked, tucking her legs underneath her. "Some yoga? Stretch you out before your journey? Or some more meditation?"

"Actually, I was hoping we could just talk and maybe take it from there."

He saw Fairuza hesitate.

"Talk?"

"Yes," Ro said. "I've learned a lot from our conversations. And now I have some things I'd like to get off my chest."

Fairuza nodded briefly. "All right," she replied, rearranging her legs.

Ro paused. Fairuza looked at him expectantly. Her expression was unreadable.

"I have a lot to say." Ro paused again. "It's so difficult to know where to begin."

"Start by saying whatever comes to mind first," Fairuza suggested. "The story will come together one way or another."

"You're right," Ro said, remembering something. "Yes, it will. Thank you."

Alex had used similar words back in Bermuda. How long ago that seemed. Many lifetimes.

He closed his eyes. Once the story had fully entered into him, he opened his eyes and began to speak.

* * *

"The resolution of Amrita's murder felt right to me at first," Ro began. "It seemed like the Universe had decided that Sanjay Mehta would be guilty of this crime. Perhaps because of other, unpunished crimes in his past. I still had some questions, though."

He closed his eyes again.

"For starters, some of Amrita's jewelry had been taken from the safe in her room. But not all of it. Some of her most expensive, name-brand jewelry was still there. That just didn't make any sense. Although nobody really seemed to care about that."

He kept his eyes closed, gathering his thoughts.

"Also, there were a couple of other things I would have expected the police to find in her room, but they weren't there. But we'll get to that."

He stopped.

"Also, why did Amit have to die? I really couldn't find a good explanation for that."

Ro opened his eyes. Fairuza was staring straight at him.

A basilisk stare.

"How did Amrita get her watch back?" he asked softly. "And why was her watch on the wrong wrist?"

Although Fairuza had almost total control over her body, she tensed. Ever so slightly.

Ro felt it.

"And the more I got to know about Amrita, the more I had questions about her. Who she was. Where she came from."

He stood up.

"Specifically, about her family."

He looked at Fairuza.

"There's nothing in this room, by the way. No phones, no recording equipment. No hidden cameras, for example. Feel free to check, but you can trust me on this."

Fairuza gave the slightest of nods.

"What was with the story with Amrita's father? And his eye condition?" Ro mused.

He began to pace.

"Why did he live abroad? Why did he only allow one of his children to spend time in India?"

He stopped.

"In fact, what did he have against India? Something just didn't add up to me."

Ro began to pace again.

"And there was something about Amrita. She was one of the most ob-servant people I've ever met. And she didn't think she was in danger. How could she possibly have had no idea that she was in mortal danger?"

He stopped to look at Fairuza.

"Because I really do believe that. She had absolutely no idea."

Ro stood still for a moment and turned away, debating how best to proceed.

He could feel Fairuza's eyes burning into his back.

He turned back around to face her.

"You know, I have this weird thing," he said, conversational. "I love words. Always have. They're probably the love of my life. And names. Where they're from. And sometimes I look them up. It's almost as if I collect them. To play with them." He looked at Fairuza. "I was a lonely child."

Ro abruptly sat back down on the mat. He crossed his legs, facing her.

"So I looked up your name," he continued. "Fairuza. Guess what?"

Fairuza remained still.

Ro closed his eyes briefly, then opened them and looked directly into hers.

"It means turquoise."

Fairuza tensed again.

Barely.

But Ro felt it. He nodded.

"So I started thinking."

He stood back up.

"Why would someone name their daughter Turquoise? Maybe because of her eyes? Can't think of many other reasons."

He looked at Fairuza. Her eyes narrowed.

"Particularly in India. Not much turquoise here. I mean, India's not exactly New Mexico."

"You can see for yourself that my eyes are dark," Fairuza responded.

"Perfectly," Ro said, admiring. "I know you never lie. Yes, every word you just said was true. But it's not the truth. And actually, for once, I can prove it. A couple of different ways, even."

"Really? How?" Fairuza crossed her arms.

"We'll get to that," Ro said. "But anyway, right now, for the sake of argument, let's assume that your eyes are, indeed, turquoise. Because of some weird gene that runs in the family. A mutation."

He remembered Mahesh's words.

Bad blood.

Ro placed his hand on his chin, thinking.

"So. Amrita's father showed up in Calcutta right after Partition. With a whole bunch of jewels. Saying his entire family had been killed. Father, mother. Brother. Everyone."

He paused.

"But what if his family actually hadn't been killed? What if he saw Partition as an opportunity?"

He closed his eyes.

"You could just take everything, disappear, then reappear with a new name," he said quietly. "It would have been so easy back then. It was chaos. But then you have a problem. A really big problem."

He opened his eyes again and looked at Fairuza.

"Your eyes. Because you have turquoise eyes. And everyone always remembers them."

Ro began to pace again.

"So you hide your eyes as much as you can. You tell everyone you have an eye condition. You wear sunglasses. You marry someone with dark eyes. You're a recluse. You say that you can't be outside. And then, eventually, you leave the country. You only allow one of your children to come back. The one with brown eyes. Oh, that reminds me," Ro added, rummaging in his pocket. "First piece of proof."

He pulled out a small package and tossed it to Fairuza. She caught it.

"Color contacts," Ro said. "I had housekeeping get them from your room."

Fairuza silently put the package into her pocket.

Ro sat back down. "I never could figure out why I couldn't read your eyes."

There was a long pause.

"So I think somehow you and Amrita are related, and all this has something to do with Partition," Ro continued softly. "You can trust me. I promise. But tell me. Was I right about what her father did?"

Another long pause.

Fairuza looked at him, considering.

Finally, she nodded. "No. You were wrong."

"I was?" Ro replied, very surprised.

"Yes," she said. "It was much worse than that."

They sat for a moment.

"He didn't lie when he got to Calcutta," she said. "His entire family really had been murdered."

She paused.

"But what he didn't say was that he'd murdered them. He slit all of their throats in the night. While they were sleeping."

Ro recoiled.

"Seven people. His parents. Uncle. Grandparents."

Ro's eyes flooded with tears. It hadn't occurred to Ro that Amrita's father had actually killed them.

"And his younger brother. My grandfather. He woke up and fought for his life until Amrita's father gave up and ran."

"Wait a second." Ro held up his hand, apologetic. "I just want to make sure I understand everything correctly. So your grandfather and Amrita's father were brothers?"

"Yes. She and I were a generation apart, although I'm only a couple of years younger than she was. Her father must have had her quite late."

"You're right. I think Mrs. B. said he was almost sixty when she was born." Ro paused. "So the two of you were cousins?"

"Yes," Fairuza confirmed. "She and I were first cousins, once removed. Not that she knew that, of course. It's a little confusing, I know."

Suddenly, Ro shivered. Parvati. He and Parvati were also first cousins, once removed.

But onward.

"So Amrita's father killed the whole family, but his younger brother—your grandfather—survived."

"Yes. My grandfather survived, but he had a scar from ear to ear. It happened on December 25th," she added quietly.

There was a long silence.

"I don't know what to say."

Fairuza nodded. "It was a terrible thing."

"Did you always know about this?"

"No." She shook her head vigorously. "Not at all. We knew that his family had all been murdered during Partition, and of course, he had that scar anyway. But he never talked about it. And that wasn't at all unusual, you know. Nobody ever talked about those times. Or talks about them now."

She looked away for a moment, biting her lower lip, thinking.

"It feels important to tell you this," she continued abruptly. "Ultimately, my grandfather led what I believe to be a very happy life. He started a construction company that was very, very successful. He worked all over the world. He made really quite a lot of money. And he and my grandmother always seemed so happy together. I think they really were."

"Do you think he was looking for his brother the whole time?" Ro asked softly.

Fairuza thought about it for a second, then nodded. "Yes. Perhaps not actively, but I'd imagine so."

"So, how did you find out?" Ro asked.

"It was a few months before he died," Fairuza replied. "He took my brother and me into a room and told us what had happened. He asked us to avenge his family. And to take back what was rightfully ours. And we promised we'd try." She shook her head. "I suppose it became more important to him as he looked back on his life."

"The injustice of it all."

"Yes." Fairuza nodded. "Also, don't forget, he'd never actually found his brother. He had no idea where he was, and, of course, neither did we. It was a purely theoretical question."

"So, how did you find them?" Ro leaned forward, curious.

Fairuza looked at Ro for a moment, visibly debating whether or not to tell him. Finally, she nodded. "Nalini's idiot son signed up for 23andMe."

"That's not fair." Ro couldn't stop himself from chuckling. "Their father was dead. They weren't living as recluses anymore. They didn't know about any of this."

He thought of Amrita and grew somber again.

"They had no idea they were in danger."

"No," Fairuza agreed. "She certainly wasn't hiding her movements."

"And she came here every year," Ro continued, meditative. "And so you got hired here. Last year, I believe you said."

Fairuza didn't say anything.

Ro stood up.

"So this is what I think happened."

He began to pace around the room again.

"I'm not sure how you got her watch, but it doesn't really matter. You work in the spa, so you could have gotten it out of her locker."

He saw Fairuza's eyes narrow.

"Anyway. Christmas Night. Everyone would be in the same place. Watching a surprise performance that you knew about. So the coast was clear."

His voice trailed off unexpectedly. Fairuza waited, her arms crossed.

"You called the restaurant and told them to tell Amrita to come to the Palace to get her watch."

His shoulders slumped a little.

"You surprised her on the path. Told her you thought you'd spare her a trip, maybe."

Fairuza tilted her head ever so slightly.

"Then you picked up a rock," he said softly.

They were silent for a long moment.

Abruptly, Ro sat back down. "Why'd you choose that way?" he asked. He was genuinely curious.

They sat for a moment.

"I've always liked rocks," Fairuza finally replied.

Ro's eyes widened. "Don't be flip," he said, his tone sharp. "The more I learned about Amrita, the more I admired her. Admire her."

"I'm not being flip," she responded quietly.

Then Ro remembered the crystals in Rishikesh. He suddenly understood.

Fairuza had killed Amrita using a part of India.

They sat in silence.

"You didn't get blood on your kurta pajama?"

He stopped.

"Oh."

"What?" Fairuza said.

"The place where you killed her is right next to the laundry. I knew that."

He remembered that moment on the path where he'd felt Amrita's spirit.

"She didn't know why she died, did she."

"No," Fairuza replied. "No, I suppose she didn't."

Ro shook his head. "It seems so awful that she didn't know why."

"Perhaps she does now," Fairuza offered, rearranging how she was sitting.

Ro nodded. He hoped so, anyway.

"Anyhow," he continued. "You took her headband and went to her room. Your hair and hers were pretty much the same length."

He thought of something and leaned forward.

"Weren't you worried about DNA? From the headband?"

"I'd tried it on earlier that day. In front of other people."

Ro nodded, impressed despite himself. "Then you went into her room. I assume you had a camera over the safe."

He leaned forward again.

"What was the combination? Something simple, I bet."

Fairuza raised an eyebrow. "8765."

"Wonderful." Ro shook his head, filled with admiration.

The world would be a far less interesting place without Amrita Dey.

"Speaking of the safe," Ro continued. "What was taken and what was left behind. It was all so very scrupulous. Even down to returning her mother's watch."

He looked at her.

"You only took what objectively could have been considered yours."

Fairuza returned his look, silent.

"And then some other murders." Ro shook his head. "I'm not sure where to start."

"I was in Rishikesh the whole day the VB was killed," Fairuza reminded him.

"I know. We'll get to that. But I'd prefer to take things in order." Ro suddenly stood up. "Amit's death was painless. A mercy killing, almost."

"When he was alive, he was always in pain," Fairuza said. "Always. But he never showed it."

"He was a good man." Ro looked at her. "Why did you need to kill him?"

Fairuza suddenly stood up too. She walked to the corner of the room and began going through the blankets and yoga mats.

"Feel free to look," Ro said. "Of course. But I promise. There are no recording devices in this room. Of any kind. At least, not that I've put in."

She nodded but nonetheless continued her cursory search. Once she'd finished, she sat back down.

"Did you see him when you were going into Amrita's room?"

"No," Fairuza replied. "But he told me about the reenactment."

Ro grimaced. "That wasn't very clever of him."

"No," Fairuza agreed. "No, it wasn't. He told me that nothing came of it." She shook her head. "I don't know why, but I still had a bad feeling. That I'd made a mistake. And that he'd realize it."

"You know, I think you were right."

"You do?"

"Hold on. I have to go further back." He paused for a moment, then shook his head violently. "The thing with Amrita's mother's watch just bugged me. I don't know why. Well, actually, I do."

He showed Fairuza his wrist.

"It's probably because I have almost the same one, and it's my father's."

Fairuza winced.

"Yeah," Ro said. "Weird. Anyway, in terms of timing, I wanted to know when Amrita got her watch back. So I kept asking Amit if she was wearing a watch when he saw her. He couldn't remember."

Ro paused. Fairuza sat, waiting.

"But later that night, I saw him looking at Catherine and Mahesh talking, and he got this weird look in his eye. I guess we'll never know for sure. But I think he'd noticed the difference in their kurta pajamas."

Ro lifted his arm.

"The guest sleeves end just below the elbow. The staff sleeves go down to the wrist. I think he'd realized the person he saw that night was wearing pajamas with long sleeves."

Fairuza looked down at her covered wrists. She pushed each of her sleeves up slightly.

"What did you use, by the way?"

"I'm not telling you," Fairuza replied, looking at him suspiciously. "I wouldn't want to give you any ideas."

"Fair enough," Ro said, chuckling.

He immediately turned somber again, remembering Amit.

"Did you have to kill him? I think he was in love with you."

There was a long pause.

"Maybe I was developing feelings for him too," Fairuza said. "To the extent possible, at least."

Ro remembered Mahesh's words again.

Bad blood.

"It doesn't matter," she continued. "He would have never understood."

Ro thought that Amit might well have understood the desire to kill Amrita, given their conversation in Rishikesh, but decided there was no point in telling Fairuza. Not at this stage, anyway. "He was a good man," he said simply.

"He was in a great deal of pain," Fairuza repeated, as if to herself. "His life wasn't easy. I think his next lifetime will be better. I hope so."

Ro was taken aback.

"I really don't think you should be telling yourself that to feel better," he reproached her. But then he smiled to himself ruefully. "I suppose it's true. Nobody thinks they're a bad person. Myself included."

Fairuza opened her mouth, then closed it abruptly.

She paused, thinking.

Then she reopened her mouth, about to speak.

"Don't," Ro said softly. "Please don't."

He began to pace.

"On to poor Sanjay. Onto whom the Universe clamped its jaws. Poor Sanjay, and his terrible digestive problems. Problems that meant he had no alibi at the moment of Amrita's death."

He realized something and turned to Fairuza.

"Maybe it was because of something in his sleep tea."

She remained immobile.

"So the official story is that Sanjay killed himself. After having confessed to absolutely everything. How very convenient."

Fairuza shrugged.

"Funny that he did it with cyanide," Ro mused. "Pretty brutal."

"Quick, though," Fairuza said, crossing her arms. "It's what Hitler did."

"You know, I think you're confusing Hitler with Goebbels," Ro said, forgetting Sanjay for the moment. "Or at least the Goebbels kids. I'm fairly sure Hitler shot himself."

He paused.

"But that's not the point. The point is that guns can make a mess."

"They can," Fairuza agreed, nodding. "With cyanide, his iPhone still recognized his dead face. Which is helpful when one tries to access someone's Notes app."

Ro processed that.

"Had you always planned for Sanjay to take the fall?"

"Yes," she replied. Her tone was matter-of-fact. "He was a truly foul person. You can take my word for it. Also, she's a nice lady. She deserves better."

"I wholeheartedly agree," Ro said. "Did you hear they found the evidence Amrita had on him? In a safe deposit box in Bombay?"

"No!" Fairuza replied, interested. "I hadn't."

"The same day he died. That's why it was all so open-and-shut."

"That's unbelievable." Fairuza whistled. "That was sheer luck." She smiled, shaking her head. "Amrita certainly loved her safe deposit boxes. Quite retro."

"Also surprisingly effective," Ro replied, mentally filing the strategy away. "Oh!" He remembered something else. "When you put Amrita's headband back on her body, did you notice her earrings were gone?"

"What do you mean?" Fairuza asked, her eyes opening wide.

"Never mind. Long story."

Ro turned away, thinking about how to proceed.

"Let's move forward now. Instead of backward. In fact, let's move to Switzerland."

He turned to her.

"You're leaving for Gstaad soon. In a few days." It wasn't a question.

"The day after tomorrow."

Ro began to pace again.

"There were a couple of things I was expecting the police to find in Amrita's room. But they weren't there."

He stopped.

"By the way, her room was a mess. And she wasn't a messy person. Someone was looking for something in a hurry. Something that wasn't in her safe."

He was enjoying the dramatic tension, he had to admit.

"In terms of ID, the police found Amrita's Belgian passport and OCI. Which reminds me. I almost forgot."

Ro reached into his other pocket, pulled something out, and tossed it to Fairuza.

She caught it.

"Your passport," Ro said. "It says you have green eyes. I guess turquoise wasn't an option."

Fairuza looked at him, then put it in her pocket without comment.

"But Amrita was also Swiss. By marriage. Widowed."

Suddenly remembering something else, he grinned and looked at Fairuza. "You know how he died, right?"

"It was some sort of skiing accident, wasn't it?"

"Yes. He fell out of a helicopter," Ro responded, his eyes twinkling. "Mrs. B. told us that he landed like a plastic bag full of soup."

They both giggled for a moment.

The air lightened.

"But anyhow," Ro continued, "if she was Swiss, where was her Swiss passport? Everyone I know travels with all their passports. You never know these days." He closed his eyes. "I just thought of something, so bear with me."

He reflected.

"Amrita's Belgian passport was in the name of Rita Dey," he continued. "That was her birth name. But everywhere else, her name was Amrita. You know, I forgot to ask what it said in her OCI. I bet it was Rita. But that doesn't matter either."

Ro opened his eyes, but still appeared to be lost in a dream.

"I'm just guessing, now, but maybe her Swiss passport was in the name of Amrita Leclerc. Her married name. Not Rita Dey. Two identities would be so useful. Taxes. Company ownerships. Bank accounts. Any number of things."

He looked at Fairuza. Fairuza nodded. Almost imperceptibly.

Ro nodded too. "It would probably take a good while for anyone to connect the death of Rita Dey of Belgium to an Amrita Leclerc of Switzerland. Particularly over Christmas and New Year's. I mean, I'm not even sure that Belgium has a government at present."

He looked down at his hands, realizing something else.

"And Amrita Leclerc's hypothetical Swiss passport would be for a woman with green eyes. Or blue eyes." He smiled. "I guess turquoise could go either way, couldn't it. Also," he continued, looking back up at Fairuza, "you took her keys."

Fairuza nodded slowly.

"OK, maybe rich people don't carry keys."

Ro registered Fairuza's look of mild surprise.

"Yeah," he informed her, shrugging. "Apparently, they don't. It's a thing. Maybe you don't have house keys if you live in a castle. But Amrita was going to London from here. To her flat in London. She must have had the keys to her flat with her."

He closed his eyes. An idea was about to arrive.

"And maybe she had other keys too," he said softly. "Like, I don't know, to a safe deposit box. Or several of them. You said she loved safe deposit boxes. I'm just spitballing here."

He opened his eyes. Fairuza's eyes were narrowed.

"At a Swiss bank."

There was a long pause. Ro sat back down.

"You said your brother's a banker in Switzerland."

"He is," Fairuza replied. "Such a coincidence."

"I bet he has brown eyes," Ro said.

"Good guess."

They sat, thinking.

"Do you think I should do it?"

Ro thought for a long second. "To be honest, I don't really see many obstacles. Nalini couldn't care less because Amrita didn't leave her anything."

He looked at her.

"It's just a question of speed. If you're going to do it, you should do it now. Right now."

Fairuza nodded. "I know."

"You have your visa. You can enter Switzerland on your own passport. You'd only need to use her passport at the bank. Nowhere else."

He paused.

"And, coincidentally, your brother's a banker in Switzerland. Perhaps at that very same bank."

"Perhaps," she replied.

They sat in silence for quite some time.

"So the police aren't on their way?"

"Why would the police come? Nobody's called them."

"Why didn't you?" She seemed genuinely curious.

Ro thought for a long moment before responding.

"It doesn't have anything to do with me. And, with whatever intuition I have, I do feel like the Universe is satisfied. With how this has turned out." He looked into Fairuza's dark, obscured eyes. "I don't think it's my place to judge you."

Fairuza looked at Ro for a long time, then nodded. He saw that she'd understood. "I don't think it's my place to judge you either."

"Thank you," Ro replied, gracious.

He looked at his father's watch on his wrist.

It was time to give it back, he decided spontaneously.

Not for any particular reason. It was just time.

"Our time's almost up," he said to her, standing up.

Fairuza remained seated.

"I would have liked to wish you luck, but somehow that doesn't seem entirely appropriate," he continued, fishing a small packet out of his pocket. "So I'll just say this."

Kneeling, Ro clasped one of Fairuza's hands between both of his, transferring the packet to her.

"I know that everything that happens will be what was supposed to happen."

Fairuza slowly opened the packet, revealing Amrita's earrings.

Magic Alhambras, made of pavé diamonds and turquoise.

Gorgeous.

Ro stood back up. "Goodbye."

He crossed the room, opened the door, and left. He did not look back.

* * *

Now in neck-to-ankle Vuori, Ro looked around his room. He was ready to leave.

He checked his watch. It was still New Year's Eve in San Diego.

Impulsively, he took out his phone and dialed.

"Hello?" a voice said, after a few rings.

"Hello, Mother," Ro said.

"Ro!" She sounded surprised and pleased. He could hear voices in the background.

"Just wanted to call and wish you a happy New Year. Where are you guys?"

"The beach club. You're still at Samsara?"

"Yep."

"How is everything? Are you OK? Your father said someone had been murdered?"

"Thought you'd never ask," Ro almost said, but he restrained himself. "Yes, Mother. There were a few murders, as it happens."

"A few murders?" she gasped. "Ro! Are you all right?"

"Yes, Mother, everything is fine," he replied, rolling his eyes. How had he immediately become a teenager again? "It was all quite fascinating, actually."

He thought for a moment and smiled to himself.

"Turns out you're not the only one who believes in population control."

His mother chuckled.

"Anyway, I'm leaving today," he continued. "It's over."

"I'm glad to hear that, at least. You're headed back to London?"

"Actually, no. I'm staying in India for a while."

"Oh!" his mother said, surprised. "I was just invited to a conference in Kerala in February. You should come."

Ro's turn to be surprised and pleased. "I'd love that," he replied after a moment. "Send the details."

"I will. In the meantime, please call us if you need anything."

Ro hesitated for a moment.

"Actually, Mother, can I ask you a question?"

"Of course."

"Why did you leave India? You had everything here."

There was a long silence.

"Why did you leave the US, Ro? You had everything here," his mother responded quietly.

Ro winced.

"Anyway," his mother continued after a moment. "Happy New Year. Sending love."

"Me too," Ro said. "Also to Father."

"Speak soon," his mother said.

They hung up.

* * *

Two men loaded Ro's suitcase and hand luggage onto a golf cart. Ro climbed on as well.

"Could you please drop me off at the Forresters' but take the bags up to the Palace?" He had one more goodbye to say.

The driver nodded briefly. He came to a stop a few moments later.

"Thank you," Ro said, clambering out. Once the golf cart had disappeared around the corner, he started climbing up the stairs.

* * *

Catherine was on the terrace with her glasses on, peering at a folded copy of the *New York Times*, holding a pen in her right hand. The table in front of her was cluttered with the remains of breakfast, magazines, newspapers, and an open laptop. Mango sat placidly on the floor next to her. "Hello there," she said, taking her glasses off.

"Hello." Ro flopped down opposite her. "The crossword? What day?"

"Last Friday's," Catherine responded. "'It's a blank.' Ten letters. Ends in SA."

Ro counted quickly on his fingers. "Try TABULA RASA."

She wrote it in. "Coffee?"

"No thanks," Ro replied politely. He had decided not to eat or drink anything else before he left Samsara.

"Civilian clothes." Catherine sat back in her chair, appraising him. "You're leaving?"

"Sure am."

"Where are you headed?" She scratched Mango's neck.

"First, Bombay for a few days." Ro paused. "You know, I always say Bombay but I have no idea whether I should be calling it Mumbai. I guess I'll take a poll when I get there."

"And then?"

"And then I'm not so sure." Ro shrugged. "I might go to the South for a while. Tamil Nadu."

"That sounds nice."

"My family's from there."

They sat quietly.

"Are you officially off duty now?"

"Yeah, pretty much." Catherine thought about it. "The Amrita situation is handled, anyway."

"Glad to hear it."

Ro paused.

"What's going on with the child pornographers?" he added, seemingly as an afterthought.

"Good grief." Catherine snorted. "It was the tip of the iceberg. Four-ring circus. But I handed everything over to Justice yesterday. Told them as of now it's a YP."

"What's a YP?"

"Your problem." Catherine paused, a smile playing at the corner of her lips. "You know, it really was tremendously lucky that the VB turned out to be a child pornographer. Funny how the world works."

Ro started to feel a little uneasy. "Lucky for whom?" he asked, casual.

"For the government of India, of course." Now she was smirking openly at him.

"Don't forget the Indian children who would've been exploited," Ro reminded her. "It was pretty lucky for them too."

He felt a little sick, he realized. He stood up and moved toward the railing. "Whoever killed the VB really deserves a medal."

"What do you mean?" Catherine replied, her tone mild. "You think someone should give Sanjay a medal?"

Ro froze. For a millisecond. But it was a millisecond too long.

"Yep," he continued, breezy. "At least he got one thing right."

Catherine smirked again.

Ro leaned onto the railing and gazed out over the trees. There was a light breeze. The trees swayed gently.

He couldn't see anything but trees. A few monkeys playing, here and there.

He had just made a very grave unforced error.

"Noncommittal committal. Thirteen letters," Catherine said behind him. "I think it might end with 'maybe.'"

"Try DEFINITE MAYBE," Ro suggested.

He heard her pen moving.

They were silent for a moment.

"So, Ro, I've been meaning to ask you this," Catherine said. "What are your plans for the future?"

"No idea," Ro replied truthfully, happy to talk about something else. "I don't feel remotely ready to think about it. Definitely need some time off first. A lot of it."

"For sure," Catherine agreed. "Must've been grueling, working on the Radetzky Center."

Ro stiffened. He turned back to face her. "Who told you I worked on the Radetzky Center?"

"I don't remember. Joss, maybe?" She shrugged. "Anyway, it's not a state secret."

Ro considered it, then nodded.

Catherine was right. It wasn't a state secret. It was public knowledge, even.

"How'd you go from being a corporate lawyer to being in charge of the Radetzky Center, anyway?" She looked at him, intent. "Seems like quite the career jump."

"Long story," Ro replied, neutral. "Unfortunately, I have a plane to catch." He turned back to the trees.

"Totally lost with this one," Catherine said behind him. "Kitchen gadget known as a Parisienne scoop. Eleven letters."

"Oh." Ro grimaced. "A cuillère Parisienne. Ugh. I don't know how to say that in English." He turned back to face her, making a gesture with his hand. "It's something you use to scoop a ball out of a melon."

"Oh!" Catherine said, pleased. "A melon baller."

She wrote it in.

"Why's your French so good, anyway?"

"Another long story," Ro replied. "For another time."

"Is it as good as your English?"

"More or less." Ro considered it. "It's pretty much the same to me. My English is better, though."

"Anyway." Catherine put down her pen. "Back to your future."

She looked up at Ro.

"Would you ever go back to your old job?"

"No." Now Ro was surprised. "Definitely not. Absolutely not. Why do you ask?"

"I don't know. Just curious, I guess," Catherine said conversationally. "Since that latrine of a manager you hated so much is out of the picture and all."

Ro froze again.

"What do you mean?"

"Oh, didn't you hear?" Catherine replied, offhanded. "She died."

There was a long silence.

"Oh."

There was another long silence.

"How?"

"Not when?"

"That too, I guess."

"Let me see."

Pulling the laptop closer, Catherine put her glasses back on. She typed a few words.

"Ah. Ah, yes. Here."

She peered at the screen.

"On the 23rd. In Prague. The morning after the grand opening of the Radetzky Center."

She looked back at Ro.

"How interesting," Ro said. "I was in the air that whole day."

"Oh?" Catherine said.

"Commercial," Ro specified, perhaps gratuitously. "Lots of people around. Full flight."

He looked back over the railing. Trees and more trees.

"It was a freak accident," Catherine continued from behind him. "She was leaving town the morning after the gala. And somehow her taxi to the airport just exploded. Burst into flames. Right in the middle of Prague."

He heard more typing behind him.

"So she burned alive."

"Oh," Ro said again. "Is the driver OK?"

"Yes," Catherine replied. "Curiously, yes. Somehow, he got out of the car. But she couldn't. The rear doors were jammed shut. Somehow."

She paused.

"So she burned alive."

"So you're fond of saying," Ro replied.

They were both silent.

"Sad," he added politely.

"Apparently," Catherine continued, still looking at her screen, "she screamed and screamed for help. For almost half an hour."

"Did she now? For that long?" Ro said, unable to contain his interest. "People heard her? Is there a link to any audio?"

He moved over to Catherine and peered over her shoulder at the screen.

"No." Catherine flicked her laptop shut.

"Ugh, that's annoying," Ro said. "They better have gotten some. They promised."

There was another long pause.

Catherine looked at Ro, appraising.

"It's true," she said. "You really do have great hair."

"Yes," he agreed. "Shame about my personality."

Ro decided that he had just about had enough. He sauntered across the room and picked up a bottle of water. He gently turned the cap back and forth. It hadn't been opened.

"May I?"

Catherine nodded.

"Thanks," Ro said. He opened the bottle and took a small sip. It tasted fine. He put the cap back on the bottle and placed the bottle on the table.

"So. We were discussing your future."

"Yep." Ro flopped into a chair, considering his future. "I feel like the only place I could work at this point is FIFA."

"Not necessarily." She looked at him. "I was wondering if you'd consider coming to work with us."

"Who's us?"

"Maybe you could think of us as the Nice Department. It's not Belarus, anyway. Promise."

Ro's eyes narrowed. "How do you know about the Nice Department? I've never talked to you about my sister."

"Actually, you have," she replied, smooth, "but I think Joss mentioned that to me. Anyway. It's cute."

Ro's phone buzzed. "One second. Sorry, I have to take this."

Catherine nodded.

He pressed a button and held the phone to his ear. He nodded vigorously. "Ja," he said. "Ja, genau. Danke. Tschüss." He hung up and looked back at Catherine.

"Sorry. What were we saying?"

"I was about to say that you're a talented guy."

"Thank you." Ro smiled at her. "Genuinely. It means a lot to me. How would you see us working together?"

"I think you'd be great in an executive role," Catherine replied.

"An executive role? What does that mean exactly?"

"Right." Catherine paused. "From what I've seen, I think you could have a real talent for execution."

What did she mean, from what she'd seen? Ro leaned forward, suspicious.

"For putting plans or actions into effect," she clarified. "Moving things along."

Ro decided not to react. He looked at his watch. "I have a plane to catch. Make me an offer. We can take it from there."

"Sure. In fact, I'll make you an offer right now. As long as you accept it first."

Ro laughed. Catherine didn't.

"I'm interested," Ro said. "Truly. But I need to know a little more."

"I think it would be in your best interest to say yes now," Catherine replied. "And I'm telling you that as your friend."

"Look, Catherine, I'm sorry, but I need a minute. I hope you understand. As my friend." Ro grinned at her. "I really do feel a little burned out after my last job."

"Ha ha," Catherine said.

"You know, I'm so burned out, maybe I'll go to Burning Man," Ro mused.

"I think that's enough for right now," Catherine replied.

"You're probably right. I should get going, anyway."

He placed his hands on his knees, then stood up.

"What about the VB?" Catherine continued, tranquil, as if Ro hadn't spoken.

Ro stiffened. "What about him?"

"Oh, nothing." Catherine smirked again.

What was she getting at?

Ro ambled to the railing and casually walked the perimeter of the balcony. Nothing but trees. You couldn't see the meadow where the VB had been killed. Not even close.

"Take the elevator," Catherine said from behind him. "It's quicker."

Then Ro knew.

His blood flash-froze, but he was already sufficiently on guard not to show it.

"Let's chat soon," he said. He stooped to scratch Mango, then looked back at Catherine. "You know, actually, I do have one last question."

Catherine looked at him. "Shoot."

"How on earth did you get a dog into India?"

"Oh!" Catherine said, surprised. She looked down at Mango and smiled lovingly. "PJ," she murmured.

"Goodbye." He walked past her into the villa and pushed the button for the elevator.

"I'll call a golf cart."

"Thank you," Ro said.

Catherine picked up the phone and said a few words that Ro couldn't quite catch.

The doors of the elevator opened, revealing a breathtaking view over Samsara.

The elevator was made entirely of glass.

Ro had already guessed that, though.

"Safe travels," Catherine said from behind him.

The elevator began to descend.

Ro nodded. Yes.

She'd actually watched him do it.

Catherine's glass elevator directly overlooked the meadow where Ro had ended the life of Mitchell Charney.

* * *

The golf cart moved sedately toward the Palace. The sun shone through the trees. Ro tried not to panic. He sure hadn't seen that one coming. In fact, he'd more or less managed to forget about that whole situation.

Then, glancing down, he glimpsed one of the rocks lining the path. The glimpse brought back what had happened that day. The day they went to Rishikesh. Right before they left.

The ceiling fan spinning in Room 5 was Pendy's sign. It was time.

Going to the sauna, more or less in a trance.

Standing in the sauna window.

Watching the VB take the path into the meadow.

Slipping out of the sauna via the terrace door.

Creeping around to the main path.

Picking up a rock.

Then—

Ro shuddered. He would stop there.

No need to relive the very ghastly parts. Unlike Amrita's death, the VB's death had not been immediate.

Then an unwanted flash—

His hand, tangled up in the prayer beads around the VB's neck, squeezing, frantically trying to—

Stop.

Right now.

No point in dwelling. Ro focused on his breathing.

He began to calm down.

You really had to hand it to Pendy, he thought. Ro had known when and not why, but had learned why later. Just like Pendy'd promised.

And it was a worthy why too.

But something else was gnawing at him. He didn't know what, but he sensed that it was unrelated to the VB. It would come to him if it was meant to.

Eventually, the golf cart swept up the gravel circular driveway and came to a smooth halt in front of the Palace. Ro's luggage waited for him patiently on the right side.

To his surprise, Sundar was waiting for him at the top of the stairs in full uniform.

"Hello, Mr. Krishna," he said, smiling warmly. He held out a silver tray with an envelope on it.

"Thank you," Ro said, smiling back. He already felt much better.

He opened the envelope to find a card from Mrs. B.

"Dear boy," the card said. "Please allow us to cover your stay this time, with gratitude. As well as any future stays with us. For the rest of your life. We won't take no for an answer. Can't wait to see you next week. Much love from Mrs. B."

Ro looked up. "This is so kind of her. She doesn't have to do this."

Sundar looked left and right to make sure no one could overhear, then leaned in. "I wouldn't argue with her."

"You're right," Ro laughed. "Thank you."

He bent over to take a couple of things out of his carry-on, then stood back up.

"I have a quick errand to run. I'll be right back."

* * *

Even though he was about to leave, Ro couldn't stop himself from scanning the shelves of the library. The collection was, as ever, arbitrary and transient, yet so many of the books called out to him. He would practically have lived in here if Dr. Menon hadn't ordered him to stop reading, he thought.

So it goes.

He hadn't even read the book in his hand, which he'd run up the stairs to return. He glanced down at it.

Le meurtre, est-il facile?

It was a good question. Good enough to deserve a moment of his time.

He debated it for a moment or two, then came up with his answer. "Oui et non," he replied, aloud.

He gently placed the book back onto the shelf. "Thank you," he said to it.

Then, sitting down, he carefully opened the pouch he had removed from his carry-on and took out Pendy.

Pendy dangled from his palm, neutral.

"Are you ready to talk?" Ro asked.

Pendy gave a swipe to the left. Yes.

Ro hesitated. Where to begin. He had so many questions. But he had to start somewhere.

"Did Catherine mean what I think she meant? When she was talking about executive roles?"

Pendy swirled slowly to the left. Yes.

Despite himself, Ro was impressed. Catherine really had put the B in subtle.

Pendy jerked briefly. He agreed.

Ro thought of something else. Something important.

He leaned forward. "Does Catherine have video? Of me and the VB?"

Pendy hesitated. Then he swung forward and tapped Ro right between the eyes, so that Ro would be able to understand him. He came back to center, then flicked to the right, dismissive.

Don't worry. It doesn't matter. If anything leaked, you'd be a national hero.

"It's not just about the police. I mean, if there's a video . . ." Ro shuddered, trying not to think about how horrid the contents of that video would be. "Do I have any reason to worry about this?"

No. You've got nothing to worry about. Promise. Three quick, decisive clockwise circles. Then a few counterclockwise ones. I'll take care of it.

Ro wasn't sure he believed that, but whatever. Nothing he could do about it now. He paused.

"Do you think I should do it? Work with her, I mean?"

No. Pendy described a strict clockwise circle. Absolutely not.

"Good." Ro nodded vigorously. "Because I don't either."

Ro sat for a moment, contemplative.

"I'm not sure how to express this," he said finally. "Maybe it means I'm a monster, but I have zero regrets. I'm pretty sure I've rid the world of two particularly vile pests." He hesitated. "But that doesn't mean I want to do it again. In fact, I don't want to do it again." He looked at Pendy. "I have to say, I'm relieved you agree."

Pendy paused. This wasn't going as planned.

He decided to keep things breezy.

Don't worry about any of that right now, he replied, reassuring. Relax for a while. Right now, you need a break. The Caribbean's a great idea. Keep things simple. Ad hoc. Go where the day takes you.

As he saw Ro's eyes narrow, Pendy realized he'd laid it on a bit too thick.

Ro held him up and looked him dead in the eye. "I'm not doing it for you either. By the way."

Baby steps, Pendy told himself.

Why not? he asked Ro, all nonchalant.

"I just don't want to. And that's it. That's all. That's enough of a reason."

Sure. I get it. But why don't you want to? Pendy continued, deliberately keeping his tone super light. Theoretically, of course.

Ro didn't say anything. Or think anything.

If you feel like answering, Pendy added. I'm just curious.

"It's complicated. Let me think."

Ro sighed, clearly chewing on the question.

"I guess the simplest answer is that I don't like how it makes me feel."

Pendy was unable to resist. Because it makes you feel good?

Oops. Ro was pissed now. "Shut your face," he snapped.

There was another long pause.

Pendy saw Ro turn his attention inward, then take a slow, deep inhale.

Then a slow exhale.

Then another inhale.

And another exhale.

Ro opened his eyes. There was something in them that Pendy'd never seen before.

"Find someone else."

Pendy hesitated. Then he shrugged.

Fine, he replied. If you say so.

"I do say so." Ro stood up. "And now we really have to get going."

It might not be entirely up to you, though, Pendy added silently, as Ro put him back into his pouch.

* * *

As Ro walked downstairs, he saw a commotion in the lobby. Three men in uniforms were struggling with a number of hot pink Goyard suitcases. Ro recognized them as Mrs. B.'s. He saw the suitcases were monogrammed "N.B." in sky blue and realized, with some amusement, that he didn't know Mrs. B.'s first name.

In fact, it was Nila, which means "blue" in Bengali . . . but that was probably just a coincidence.

He walked outside. Sundar was still standing at the top of the stairs.

"Is Mrs. B. leaving today?" Ro asked him, surprised. "She didn't tell me she was leaving."

"Yes, she decided last night," Sundar replied. "She's flying to Delhi, not Bombay. Otherwise she would have given you a lift."

The men began stacking the pink suitcases on one side of the portico. Ro's sole battered Rimowa trunk stood alone on the other side.

Idly, Ro wondered what on earth was in all those suitcases. Especially considering that, as far as he knew, Mrs. B. had worn nothing but kurta pajama during her stay.

"Ah," Sundar said. "Let me take your carry-on." He smoothly removed the bag from Ro's arm and, crossing the portico, put it down next to the trunk.

"Oh, thank you," Ro said. He looked down and saw that he was still holding Pendy's pouch. He stuffed it into his pocket.

Two Land Rovers, one cream, one green, drove up and parked in front of the Palace. The drivers got out of the cars and began to confer with the staff.

"Which car is mine?" Ro asked.

Sundar listened. "It seems they don't know."

"Is the other one for Mrs. B.?" Ro looked again at the pile of pink suitcases. "Where's her car?"

"She sent her driver ahead two days ago so that he could spend New Year's Eve with his family," Sundar replied with a smile.

Eventually, after much hemming and hawing, Ro's suitcase and laptop bag were loaded into the back of the cream Land Rover. Sundar carefully placed his carry-on duffel bag in the back seat next to him.

"Thank you so much, Sundar," Ro said, taking Sundar's hand in both of his.

"See you very soon, Sir."

As Ro got into the car, he felt eyes on the back of his neck. He looked up at the Palace.

Someone abruptly pulled a curtain across half a window, obscuring whoever had been there.

A chill came over him.

Fairuza?

Then, suddenly, he realized what had been gnawing at him earlier.

A bolt of ice went down his spine.

How did Catherine know that he had called his old manager a latrine?

His mind raced. He had definitely never told Joss that. In fact, he couldn't remember ever having said that to anyone.

Ever.

Except Alex and Bronya.

Then he realized something else.

He thought he'd told Joss and the Forresters about Samsara.

But Catherine had already planned to meet Amrita here.

And Alex had told him about Samsara.

Alex and Catherine.

Catherine and Alex.

How could he have been so stupid? And what could this possibly mean? Not right now. Too much happening. He'd have to process this later.

Shaking his head to get the thoughts out of his mind, Ro got into the car.

"Are you ready, Sir?" the driver asked, looking at Ro in the rearview mirror.

"Yes, thank you," Ro replied, already dreading the drive down. He began to rummage through his carry-on, searching for his over-ear, noise-canceling headphones. Finally, he found them and carefully put them on. Taking out his phone, he scrolled for the Spotify app, then opened it. He hesitated for a moment. Finally, as he often did, Ro selected a random playlist. Ro trusted the Algorithm.

Then God, in Their Infinite Wisdom, chose to play "Punkrocker" by Teddybears and Iggy Pop, because that was the mood They were in. They hoped Ro would enjoy it.

The driver started the engine and slowly rolled through Samsara's gates. The gates of Heaven, Ro thought idly to himself.

The driver paused to let traffic pass. Then he turned right and started to make his way down the mountain.

Right away, the Land Rover began to gather speed.

Ro was already feeling a little nauseated in the back seat of the car.	
The driver took the first two turns a little faster than Ro would have liked, but he forced himself to relax. The drivers knew what they were doing, after all.	*See me driving down the street* *I'm bored with looking good*
Suddenly, Ro was suspicious. Was this driver the maniac golf cart driver he'd had his first morning at Samsara? Ro peered at him but couldn't tell. He decided to close his eyes, discretion being the better part of valor.	*I got both hands off the wheel* *The cops are coming*

But then the car kept going faster
and faster, and Ro realized there was
a problem.

He opened his eyes again. Even from
behind, the driver looked terrified.

I'm listening to the music with no fear

You can hear it too if you're sincere

"What's wrong?" Ro said sharply.

"The brakes," the driver stammered.

"What about them?" Ro demanded,
leaning forward.

'Cause I'm a punk rocker, yes I am

"Not working." The driver was almost
in tears.

Well I'm a punk rocker, yes I am

"Steer the car into the side of the
mountain," Ro ordered. "Right now.
Before we go any faster." But the driver
was paralyzed with fear. Ro thought
about pulling up the emergency brake.

'Cause I'm a punk rocker, yes I am

But looking to his right, he realized the
car would go through the guardrail if
they went into a skid. The car kept going
faster and faster around the curves.

Well I'm a punk rocker, yes I am

Ro dived into the front seat, trying to
grab the steering wheel himself. The
driver, panicking, pushed him away.

I see you stagger in the street

Ro fell back onto his duffel bag, his mind
racing. Then, suddenly, he remembered
what Lala'd learned in kidnapping
training. Ro could roll out of the car.

And you can't stay on your feet

And you're faking in your sleep

The bag would cushion the impact.

But then he remembered Amit. Collateral damage. How wrong that had felt. How wrong it still felt.

He would not let this driver meet the same fate as Amit, he decided.

Looking down, Ro saw the sturdy metal umbrella. He picked up the umbrella and aimed for the middle of the driver's skull. Crack.

The driver slumped, unconscious.

Ro dived again into the front seat and kicked open the passenger door. Then he grabbed the driver by his belt and yanked him across the gearbox. The driver's head lolled. Ro tucked it under his own head and wrapped one arm around the driver's neck. Then, wrapping his other arm around the driver's waist, Ro rolled them out of the car as gently as possible.

He failed. The impact was brutal. The two of them bounced in a full circle twice before they slammed into the rock face of the mountain. Ro lay there for a moment, catching his breath, then stood up and crouched, hands on knees. Somehow, no broken bones. Except maybe a rib. He looked down. The driver lay there semiconscious, moaning,

You wish that you were deep

But you can't hear me laughing to myself

If you could, you would be someone else

'Cause I'm a punk rocker, yes I am

Well I'm a punk rocker, yes I am

'Cause I'm a punk rocker, yes I am

Well I'm a punk rocker, yes I am

See me die on Bleecker Street

clutching his arm. A dislocated shoulder, Ro thought. But they were both alive.

Ro's headphones were cracked but the song still played into his right ear. He was not listening, though, because he was watching the Land Rover gather speed down the straightaway.

When the next curve arrived, the Land Rover plowed straight through the guardrail.
A crash. Then reverberations, more and more faint.

Then an explosion.

Ro grimaced. He would almost certainly have to buy a new laptop, he realized.

Mechanically, he checked his pockets. He had his wallet, his pendulum, and his phone.

He nodded to himself.

He would be all right.

I'm bored with being God

See me sneering in my car

I'm driving to my star

I'm listening to the music with no fear
You can hear it too if you're sincere

'Cause I'm a punk rocker, yes I am

Well I'm a punk rocker, yes I am

'Cause I'm a punk rocker, yes I am
Well I'm a punk rocker, yes I am

'Cause I'm a punk rocker, yes I am

Well I'm a punk rocker, yes I am

0 1 2 3 4 5 6 7 8 9 10 11 12 15 19 20 25 27 39 43 50 78 A Aaron Aarthi Abby Abdellatif Abel Abhijit Abigail Abraham Actions Adalvalan Adam Adele Adeline Adex Adi Aditi Adria Adriano Adrien Aeacus Aethusa Agatha Agathe Aglae Agnar Agni Agraulos Ahirbudhyna Aimee Air Aisha Aishwarya Ajaikapada Akhila Akshay Akula Alan Alana Alanis Alastair Alba Albert Albus Alceste Alejandro Aleksei Alessandro Alesteir Alex Alexa Alexander Alexandra Alexandre Alexandria Alexey Alexis Algol Ali Alice Alicia Alison Alistair Alixe Aliénor All Allison Ally Alyson Amalia Amanda Amandine Amara Amelia Amelie Ami Amir Amirdham Amit Amphialus Amphitrite Amrita Amuka Amy Ana Anagha Anand Ananda Anantam Anastasia Anders Anderson Andrea Andreas Andrew Andromache Andy Angela Anjaneya Ankur Ann Anna Anne Annibale Anselm Anthony Antje Antoine Anton Antonin Antony Anumati Anuradha Anwar Anya Apah Apara Aphrodite Apollo Apostolos Appar April Aquamarine Aquarius Aranka Ardra Ares Areti Ari Ariane Arianna Ariel Arielle Aries Arlene Armen Arpana Artemis Aru Arun Aruna Arvand Aryaman Asana Ascanius Ashadha Asher Ashlesha Ashley Ashton Ashvini Ashvins Ashwani Ashwin Astraea Astraeus Astrid Astyanax Atalante Athena Atibha Atichandika Atlas Atropos Atticus Audrey August Augustus Aurelia Aurica Aurimas Austin Auxo Avashya Ayan B Badrinath Bailey Bala Baldr Balthazar Bambi Bamini Bandhanan Bank Baptiste Barbara Barbora Bardi Batia Beatrice Beatrix Beau Beck Becky Bede Bela Belcalis Ben Benjamin Benno Benoît Bernard Bernie Bert Berthe Beth Bethany Bettina Bhadrapadha Bhaga Bhairav Bhairava Bharani Bhargavi Bhudevi Bianca Bjorg Black Blake Blue Bob Boreas Brad Brahma Brangaine Brayden Brenna Brent Bret Brhaspati Brhmacharini Brian Brianna Brit Britt Brittany Brody Bronya Brook Brooke Brooks Brown Bruce

Brumaire Bryan Bryce Bud Buddy Budh Buenaventura Buffy Bunny Byron
C Caddy Cadmus Caitlin Cale Calhoun Calliope Calvin Camilla Camille
Cancer Candice Capricorn Cara Cardi Carey Carl Carla Carlo Carlos
Carmine Carolina Caroline Carolyn Cary Caspian Cassian Castara Cat Cate
Catherine Catrina Cecile Cecilie Celine Cerisa Chakra Chakrika Chanchala
Chandanayika Chandarupa Chandogra Chandra Chandraghanta Chandrika
Chantal Chantilly Chariot Charis Charles Charlie Charlotte Chase
Chelamma Chelsea Chera Cheryl Chiara Chicko Chips Chitra Chloe Chola
Chris Christian Christina Christine Christoph Christophe Christopher
Citrine Claire Clamantis Clara Clare Clarissa Clarisse Claude Clement
Cleopatra Clifford Clio Clotho Coeus Colette Colin Colm Colman Colombe
Con Connie Connor Constance Contessina Corazon Corey Corinne
Cornelia Cory Costas Courtenay Courtney Craig Crius Cronus Cup Cybele
Cynthia Cyril D Dagny Daisy Damian Dan Dana Danae Daniel Daniela
Daniele Daniella Danielle Danilo Danny Daphne Dara Daria Darrell Darren
Darryl Dave David Davide Dayna Dean Death Deborah December Declan
Deepa Dejanira Del Demeter Demian Denis Denny Deserto Desikan
Desmond Deva Devi Devil Devyani Dhanishta Dhanus Dharana Dhruv
Diamond Diana Dickory Diego Dimitra Diomedes Dionysius Dirk Disk
Domenico Dominica Don Donnie Dori Dorianne Doris Dorit Dorothee
Dorothy Doug Dougan Drew Drisana Dulce Durga Dutch Dylan Dynamene
E East Easton Eben Echo Ed Edda Eden Edgar Edie Edith Edouard Edward
Edwin Egeria Eileen Eleanor Elena Elinor Elisa Elisabeth Elisabetta Eliza
Elizabeth Ellen Ellie Elliot Elliott Ellis Elodie Elsa Emerald Emi Emil
Emiliano Emilie Emily Emma Emmeram Emperor Empress Enid Eniko
Enrico Eos Ephraim Erato Erebus Eric Erik Erika Erin Erinye Eris Eros Erse Est
Esther Esunertos Et Eugenie Eunomia Euphrosyne Eurus Eurydice Eurydike
Eurynome Euterpe Eva Evadne Evan Evangelia Even Ezra F Fabien Fairuza
Faith Fanny Farah Farai Fatima February Federica Felice Felipe Ferdinand
Fides Fiona Fionnuala Flavia Floreal Florent Floriane Flynn Fool Fortune
France Frances Francesca Francis Franco Frank Franny Frantisek François
Frederic Frederick Fredrik Freida Frey Freya Frieda Friedrich Frigg Frimaire

Fructidor G Gabriel Gabriela Gabriella Gabrielle Gaelle Gaia Gala Galatea
Ganesha Gareth Garnet Garrett Garson Gautama Geb Geirahöd Geiravör
Geirönul Gemini Genghis Genie Georg George Georgia Georgie Georgina
Gerard Gerhard Germinal Giacomo Giorgiana Giovanni Gita Giulio Giuseppe
Gladys Godric Golfito Gotham Govindachari Govindarajan Grace Graham
Gray Green Greer Gregoire Gregory Gretchen Gretel Grey Grimnir Gudr
Guillaume Gulden Gundelinde Gunter Guru Gypsy Göll H Hades Hagen
Hamsa Hand Hanged Hania Hanif Hannah Hans Haripriya Harley
Harmony Harry Harsh Hasta Hatem Hathor Heather Hector Hegemone
Helen Helena Helene Helenus Helga Helgi Heliane Helios Heloise Henny
Henri Henry Hephaestus Hera Hercule Hercules Herfjötra Herja Hermann
Hermes Hermit Herve Hesperia Hestia Hierophant High Hildr Himanshu
Hipparchus Hjörprimul Hlökk Homer Honor Honsa Hope Horace Horus
Howard Hrist Hubert Hugo Hyperion I Iapetus Ilias Ilonka Imogen In Ina
India Indigo Indira Indranee Indu Ines Inga Ingrid Irina Iris Isabel Isabelle
Isadora Isis Ismene Isolde Itay Iyengar Iyer J Jack Jackariah Jacobine Jacques
Jade Jaime Jakob Jalaja Jambhavati James Jamie Jamison Jan Janamodini Jane Janet
January Janus Janusz Jaren Jasmin Jasmine Jason Jasper Jay Jaya Jayalakshmi Jean
Jeanne Jen Jenica Jenna Jennifer Jeremie Jeremy Jeri Jerome Jerry Jesse Jessica
Jesus Jethro Jhanvi Jhumpa Jill Jimmy Jis Jnyanam Jo Joachim Joan Joanna Joanne
Jodie Jody Joel Joelle Joey Johan Johann Johanna Johannes John Johnny Joie Jon
Jonah Jonathan Jordana Jose Josefa Joseph Josephina Josephine Josh Josie
Josquin Joss Joy Joyce Juan Jubilatrix Jude Judgement Judith Jules Julia Julian
Julianne Julie Juliette July June Jung Junko Juno Jupiter Justice Jyeshtha
Jyostna Jyoti K Kaali Kaaran Kalaratri Kali Kalyani Kamala Kamalika Kandi
Kapalika Kara Karen Karessa Karina Karthikeya Kasia Kaspar Kat Kate
Katherine Kathleen Kathryn Kathy Katie Katja Katrina Katya Katyayani
Kaula Kaulika Kay Keith Kelli Kelly Kelsey Kenneth Kerry Ketki Ketu Kevin
Kimberlay King Kirk Kiska KKim Knight Konstantin Kris Krishna
Krishnaswami Kristen Kristin Kristina Kristy Krittika Kriya Kriyalakshmi
Kseniya Ksethra Kshirsa Kubjika Kubla Kuhu Kula Kulesvari Kundalini
Kushmanda Kyle L Lachesis Lakshmana Lakshmi Lala Laleh Lalima Lamech

Lance Lanka Lanna Lapo Lara Lars Laszlo Latona Laura Laurel Laureline
Lauren Lauryn Lazarus Lazzie Lea Leah Lech Leda Lee Leeor Lefteris Leigh
Lejo Len Lena Lennox Leo Leona Leonore Leslie Leto Leucadia Lexy Liam
Libra Lila Lilith Lilly Lily Linda Lindsey Link Linzee Lionel Lisa Liv Livia Liz
Lizzie Loki Lola Lorenz Lorenzo Lori Loro Lorraine Lothair Louis Louisa
Lovers Lucas Luciana Lucie Lucrezia Lucy Ludivine Ludo Ludwig Luigi Luis
Lukas Luke Lula Luna Lutecia Luthern Lydia Lynn Lynne M Maamritat
Maddalena Madeleine Madhavi Madhu Madonna Madras Maffeo Maggie
Magha Magician Magna Maha Mahadevi Mahagauri Mahalakshmi
Mahendravarman Mahesh Mahlke Mai Malko Malti Malu Man Manasi
Mangala Manikkavacokar Manisha Manjushri Manuel Manushri Mar Mara
Marc March Marco Margara Margherita Margia Margot Mari Maria Mariana
Marianne Marie Marina Marine Marion Marisa Marissa Mark Markus Mars
Marsha Marshall Martin Martine Martyn Mary Masa Masha Mateo Mathias
Mathieu Mathumai Matt Matteo Matthew Matthieu Maturin Maud
Maureen Mauricio Maurizio Max May Maya Mazarin Medea Medusa
Meenakshi Meg Megaera Meghan Melanie Melissa Melpomene Mercedes
Mercury Meredith Messidor Metis Michael Michel Michele Michelle Michiko
Midas Mikey Milan Mildred Milena Miller Milo Mimi Mimmi Mina Mindy
Minerva Minos Mir Mira Miranda Mist Mitchell Mitra Mlada Mnemosyne
Moana Moar Mohammed Mohan Moira Molossus Momus Mona Monica
Monika Monique Moon Mora Morgan Morgane Moros Mors Morvern
Mrigashirsha Mrityor Mukshiya Mula Murali Muriel Murugan Muthu
Mystelle N Nadine Nagas Nalini Namah Namo Namrata Nancy Nandika
Nandini Naomi Naryanaya Natalie Nataraja Nathalie Nathan Nazaire Ned
Neil Nemesis Nephthys Neptune Nereus Nessus Neville Ngowari Niccolo
Nicholas Nick Nicky Nico Nicola Nicolai Nicolas Nicole Nicolette Nikhil
Nikhila Nikki Nila Nilanjan Nils Nimeshika Nina Nipa Nirrti Nitsa Nivose
Njord Noah Noel Noelle Nora North Notus Nouska Novella November
Nuno Nut Nysa Nyx O Oceanus Octavia October Odin Odysseus Of Olivia
Olivier Olympia Om Omar Omer Onyx Oonagh Opal Opgalli Ophion
Opinion Orange Orpheus Oscar Osiris Oskar Ossian Oswald Otis Otto

Ouroboros Owen P Paddy Padma Padmanabhaswamy Page Palatia Pales Pallas Pallichal Pamela Pan Pandyan Parama Parameshvara Parthenope Parvati Pasithea Patience Patricia Patrick Paul Paula Pauline Pausanias Pavel Peaches Pedesi Peleus Pendy Pentacle Peppi Percy Pergamus Peridot Perrine Persephone Peter Petr Petra Petronius Phaethon Phalguni Phatiwe Pherusa Philip Philippe Phillip Phocaea Phoebe Photis Pielus Pier Piero Pierre Pietàs Pihor Pilar Pisces Pitchumani Pitha Pitrs Pluto Pluviose Polyhymnia Pontus Pooja Poseidon Prachanda Prachi Praevalet Prairial Prajapati Prakruti Prasanna Preethi Priestess Prince Princess Priscilla Priya Prometheus Prosper Prudence Prudr Psyche Punarvasu Purnima Purva Pushan Pushtivardhanam Pushya Pyrrhus Q Quaoar Queen R Ra Rabindranath Rachael Rachel Rachna Radgrid Radha Raeli Rafik Raghuram Rahu Rahul Rainulf Raissa Raj Rajagopalan Rajashree Rajathi Rama Ramaa Ramachandra Raman Ramaswami Ramona Rana Randgnio Randgrid Rangaswami Ranjan Raphael Raphaelle Ratan Ratisbon Ravi Rebecca Rebecka Rebekah Recompenses Red Reese Reginleif Regulus Reka Rena Renato Rene Renee Resa Revati Reza Rhadamanthus Rhea Rhiannon Ricardo Richard Richilde Risana Rita Ro Rob Robert Roberta Robin Robo Rochelle Roderick Roger Rohan Rohini Rohit Roland Rolands Rollo Roman Ron Roni Roopa Rory Rose Rosemary Rosie Rowan Rowena Ruby Rudra Rudrachanda Ruee Rukmini Ruth Ryan S Sabesari Sabeth Sabrina Sadhana Sadie Sagittarius Sahara Sakiko Salazar Salman Sam Sambandar Samruddhi Samsara Samuel Sancus Sandra Sandy Sanjana Sanjay Sapna Sapphire Sara Sarah Sarai Saranam Saraswati Sarita Saroja Saturn Satyabhama Satyam Savitri Schwarzschilde Scorpio Scott Sean Sebastian Sebastien Sedna Segolene Selene Selinur Semele Semo Senectum Senthil September Set Seymour Shaheen Shailaja Shailaputri Shakira Shakti Shanakara Shanda Shani Shannon Shari Sharir Sharon Shatabhisha Shayna Shazia Shilpa Shiva Shivaya Shonda Shravana Shreeya Shruti Shu Shukra Siddhartha Siddhidhatri Sidra Siegfried Sieglinde Sigismond Sigmund Sigune Silvain Silvia Simon Simona Simone Sirius Sisyphus Sita Skandamata Skeggjöld Skuld Skögul Smith Smriti Sol Soleil Soma Sonia Sonya Sophia Sophie Souls South Spes Spica Sridevi Srinivasan Sriram Stan Star Stefania

Stefanie Stella Stephane Stephanie Stephen Steven Stieg Strength Suchitra
Sugandhim Sujatha Sun Sundar Sundarar Sune Surya Susanna Susanne Susie
Suzanne Svati Svava Swarna Swati Sword Sybil Sydelle Sylvia Sylvie T Tadzio
Tamara Tanja Tara Tariq Taruni Tassilo Tatiana Taurus Taylor Ted Tejaswini
Telephus Temperance Tereza Terpsichore Tethys Thalia Thao The Thea Theia
Thekla Thembi Themis Theo Theodo Theodor Theodore Theresa Therese
Thermidor Theseus Thetis Thibault Thierry Thilo Thomas Thor Thora
Thyagaraja Tia Tica Tiffany Tigranes Tilottama Tim Timothee Tisiphone
Tobias Toji Tom Tommy Tonio Tony Topaz Tori Tory Tourmaline Tower
Tracey Tracy Travail Tressa Tricia Trini Tripurasundari Tristan Tryambakam
Tryshe Tulasi Tuppence Turandot Turquoise Turtle Tuuli Tyche U
Ugrachanda Urania Uranus Urhixidur Uruvarukamiva Usha Uttara V
Vaishali Valerie Valery Vanessa Varada Varuna Vasantha Vasuda Vasus Vayu
Veda Vedavalli Vedavati Veena Vendemiaire Venkateswaran Ventose Venus
Vera Veritas Verity Veronica Veronika Vertu Vesper Vicky Victor Victoria
Vidrir Vidya Vijay Vikash Vikram Vilgot Vimala Vincent Violet Vipedu
Vipera Virginia Virginie Virgo Viroopa Vishakha Vishnu Visra Visvedevas
Volodya Vox W Waker Wallace Wallis Wally Walt Waltraut Wand Wendy
Weng Werner Wes West Wheel White Wil Will William World X Xanthe
Xavier Y Yajamahe Yama Yann Yellow Yohan Yolanda Yulia Yullia Yuriko
Yves Yvette Yvonne Z Zach Zadie Zaira Zak Zaki Zelda Zephyrus Zeus Zita
Zooey Zoser Zsolt Zuzana

THANK YOU

About the Author

RAM MURALI was born in New York, NY.
This is his first novel.